THE 1001 NIGHTS OF DRUMMER MACLEOD

Born in 1913 in Lancashire, Harry Hopkins was educated at Oxford University and worked as a journalist and diplomatic correspondent for several English newspapers. He is the author of numerous highly acclaimed historical and political books such as *Egypt, the Crucible: The Unfinished Revolution of the Arab World* (1969); *The Strange Death of Private White: A Victorian Scandal that Made History* (1977) and *The Long Affray – The Poaching Wars in Britain 1760–1914* (1986). Hopkins spent the final years of his life in Spain and London. He died in 1998.

The 1001 Nights
of
Drummer Macleod

HARRY HOPKINS

CANONGATE

First published in Great Britain in 2000 by Canongate Books Ltd,
14 High Street, Edinburgh EH1 1TE

10 9 8 7 6 5 4 3 2 1

Copyright © the Estate of Harry Hopkins 2000

British Library Cataloguing-in-Publication Data
A catalogue record for this book is available on
request from the British Library

ISBN 0 86241 890 9

Phototypeset by Intype London Ltd
Printed and bound by WS Bookwell, Finland

Oh, cursèd, cursèd be the day that e'er the wars began,
For they've ta'en out of Scotland full many a pretty man:
They've ta'en from us our lifeguards, protectors of our isle,
And their bodies feed the worms on the banks o' the Nile

– 'The Banks o' the Nile', early nineteenth-century
ballad

In the *argot* of the Levant a *renegado* was a European
or an American who had, for one reason or another,
'taken the turban', embracing Islam, wearing Turkish
or Arab dress and assuming an Arab name. In 19th-century
Egypt this was a substantial and varied class, which included
the Swiss explorer J. L. Burckhardt (Sheikh Ibrahim), Colonel
Octave Josef Sèves, formerly of Bonaparte's *Grande Armée*
(Suleiman Pasha), the American Marine officer, George Bethune
English (Mohammed Effendi) – and Drummer Donald
Macleod, late of the Ross-shire Buffs, well known about Cairo
as 'Osman Effendi', Hadji Osman – or 'Osman the Scotsman'. I
have often asked Osman to tell me a little about himself, but
I remarked he always endeavoured to change the subject. I did
not press it. Possibly the recital of his tale would have occasioned
the recollection of many who were dear to him . . . who if they
survived, were beyond the deep blue sea and knew not even that
he lived . . . He must have seen a great deal and been in
possession of many facts that his country would value . . . It is
greatly to be regretted that Osman did not employ his leisure
hours in writing an account of the important changes and events
he witnessed during his long residence in the East . . .

– Dr William Yates, *The Modern History
and Condition of Egypt* (1843)

This autobiography,
like the life contained in it,
has been dedicated to the memory of
MRS JEANNIE MACDONALD
of Lochaber, North Carolina, and Egypt
well known to the fellahin of the latter country as
'Sitt Amerikani'

CONTENTS

Dawn to Midnight, 16 November 1869, Port Said

I reached the so-called Quai Eugénie soon after dawn. My heart sank. A Mediterranean storm had whipped up overnight; the three pavilions on the beach where the Grand Opening was to take place in the presence of the crowned heads of Europe were awash. The scarlet and green and yellow pennants and banners and drapes were ripped and sodden and dripping like sea-tangle newly forked out of Loch Bracadale.

As I mounted the steps to the main platforms, the red carpet squelched under my feet. I thought of the Empress ascending that salt-stained, sopping carpet. Oh yes, I tell you, my heart sank! But then has there ever been a week in my ten years working with Ferdinand when it hasn't? I know now why the 'Pharaoh hardened his heart', as it says in the Bible.

I hardened mine double-quick, and rousted out a mongrel crew of labourers from Arab Town and set them to shovelling away the wet sand that spilled over the long plank-walk from the landing stage. I sent my son Mohammed, Nura's boy, to el-Azhar to organise a new supply of green flags for the pavilion and kiosk facing Mecca. I put Greek and Coptic workmen to replacing the clustered flags of the Catholic nations, so that Orient and Occident could salute each other (as M. de Lesseps has it).

On Sunday Prince Henry of the Netherlands and his Princess dropped anchor in his steam yacht; on Monday the *Herta* with the Crown Prince of Prussia; followed by Emperor Franz Josef of Austria, in the *Greif*, and the pride of the P & O's fleet, the *Delta*, with the directors aboard, not to mention 'Crimea Simpson' of the *Illustrated London News*. After that, representing the Tsar of all the Russias, the Grand Prince Michael in his sloop; then the

Peluse, crack steamer of the Messageries Impériales. By the time the French imperial yacht, *L'Aigle*, appeared over the horizon, inner and outer harbours were packed, two hundred vessels – fifty warships among them – flying the flags of all the nations of Europe.

At 8 a.m., by which time the pavilions were beginning to look presentable again, *L'Aigle* weighed anchor, and – tricolore streaming from her raked mast – slipped between the two great breakwaters on course for the outer harbour.

I could make out the proud figure of the Empress Eugénie on the bridge, acknowledging the cheers. I wished her well: not many know that she is at least one quarter Scottish; her grandfather William Kirkpatrick, Jacobite turned Malaga wine-merchant, is one of us – of the great scattering of the clans. We are all sorts, as Tom Keith, used to say. The Butcher Cumberland blew, and we were scattered. How we were scattered! Blown off course. But defeated, no!

As *L'Aigle* slipped by, paddle-wheels churning, the gunners of the five ironclads of the British Mediterranean squadron delivered themselves of a 101-gun salute, ships dressed overall, Jack Tar manning the yards. The Italian man-of-war joined in with cannonades, then the Swiss, and the Austrians and the Prussians. National anthems rolled from their decks. The curtain of smoke was so dense that Captain Surville had to stop his engines, waiting for it to clear.

Through the grey curtain I spotted a squat figure advancing purposefully towards me, strangely clad in riding-breeches and a large pipe-clayed sun helmet, followed by a tail of Arab urchins yelling *bakshish*, and *Inglees*, and no doubt proffering their sisters, 'Very nice, very clean, all pink inside like Queen Victoria.' This was only Thomas Cook's second excursion to Egypt, but already the little devils knew a *kukucki* when they saw one.

I smoothed down my new *stambouli* – the frock-coat is *de rigueur* in Ismail's 'Paris-on-the-Nile' – and I waited.

'You, Thomas Cook's man, eh?'

I shook my stick and the urchins fled. He was consulting his Arabic phrase book.

'Koo-ook,' he grimaced. 'Comprendo? Dragoman? Taiyib! Shabash!'

It is mortifying. Once a dragoman, always a dragoman. Pandering gets into the blood, I suppose. Even Macleod blood.

I drew myself up to my full height. I took a dignified pull on my cigar, although to tell you the truth I would have found more comfort in my old *chibouk*.

I said gravely: 'I regret, no, Monsieur. It is Osman Effendi whom you address. I have the honour to be the personal assistant to Monsieur Ferdinand de Lesseps, President of the Compagnie Universelle du Canal Maritime de Suez.'

A puzzled look spread across the *kukucki*'s unctuous features. Was it my accent? Even now, I retain a douce note from the Gaelic. With typical English sang-froid (that's what *they* call it!), he recovered his composure.

'In that case, sir, you're the very man I'm looking for. Tomorrow, our ship, the *Amerika*, joins the Grand Procession through the Canal. There's an English engineer in our party tells us she'll never get through . . .'

He scanned my face closely. I took another puff on my cigar. I stared at him with all the well-known 'inscrutability of the Orient'.

'He says that a fortnight ago they found a thundering great rock-ridge across the canal bed.' He glared at me accusingly. 'A thundering rock-ridge – that's what he said.'

I did not flinch. From the very start, the English have done everything they could to wreck de Lesseps' great enterprise – the way their Post Office did with Tom Waghorn's. Dogs-in-the-manger – it's in their blood.

'The ridge has been demolished,' I said, with more conviction than I felt.

He persisted: 'They say the canal sides will fall in from the action of the paddle-wheels.'

I began to wonder who might have sent him.

'The English also said that the water would evaporate from the Bitter Lakes,' I said. 'I haven't noticed it.'

He would not leave it. 'There's a rumour that Ismailiya has been burned down by fire.'

'There is no fire.'

He brought out his trump card. 'I hear tell that de Lesseps has gone off his head. They're keeping it dark, naturally.'

Somehow I kept my temper. Does not Islam advise calm and dignity at all times?

'His Excellency,' I assured him, 'is in good health. At this moment he is aboard the imperial yacht, attending the Khedive Ismail as he welcomes the Empress.'

The smoke curtain lifted at last. The *kukucki* turned his attention towards Arab Town, straggling along the beach to the west.

I followed his glance, for at the nearer end of the line I had erected a screened marquee with an excellent view of the central platform. For my harem.

As the quickening throb of the drums and the sharp wail of the *nai* drifted across from the palm-and-bamboo shacks, I saw a certain look every dragoman knows steal across the *kukucki's* stolid features. I had observed it even on the gentlemanly visage of Mr Kinglake, asking to 'inspect' my harem when he lodged with me in Cairo.

How can I describe it? A glisten of prurience? The birth-pangs of a leer? I've often thought that if the truth were known, it is this prospect which draws so many of these inquiring Christians to 'the Orient'. Granted, that charlatan Captain Burton – and Louis and I penetrated Mecca forty years before he did – disguised his consuming lasciviousness in 'scholarly' footnotes about the lengths of Negroes' *zubb*s.

I knew exactly what this pilgrim to the Orient was about to say now. 'Ah, the gorgeous East, as Mr Wordsworth puts it ... the *Thousand and One Nights* ... Tell me, sir, is it true that the Khedive has five hundred concubines?'

I fished out my *sebbah* – which the English call worry-beads – and began to flick slowly through the thirty-three Perfections of Allah.

He pointed to a distant shack.

'Tell me now, sir, are those your famous dancing-girls? I am told I must not miss the danse du ventre ...'

At that very moment the muezzin of the new Port Said mosque ascended the minaret, and launched into the noon call to prayer. I removed my shoes, turned towards the Kaaba and, lifting my arms, palms forward to the level of my ears, launched into a *tekbir* ... 'Allahu Akbar!'

Out of the corner of my eye I saw the *kukucki* scurrying off towards Arab Town.

*

There are just too many 'ifs'. *If* I hadn't got down to the pavilions before dawn . . . *If* de Lesseps hadn't been there to bring up two thousand soldiers to deluge that fire in Ismailia with water . . . Imagine it! The fools had stored the fireworks for the celebrations in a timber-yard on top of a powder magazine!

No question about it: Ferdinand is a great man! He's driven the Great Ditch – this hinge of continents – a hundred miles from sea to sea, Europe to Asia, against every sort of obstacle and the endless mischief-making of the English. He's an optimist. He's like an American – like Jeannie. He thinks all things are possible. He just refuses to acknowledge that this is the land of doing things *bukra* – tomorrow. And not only *bukra*, but *bukra, inshallah* – and after that, *malish*.

It's a great honour, of course, that my son Sami is to be First Officer on the *Latif*, chosen to prove the Canal ahead of the Grand Procession of ships. The crown of the boy's naval career, a feather in Clan Osman's cap. But I had a dream last night . . . the crowned heads trapped in mid-desert . . . the ships piling up . . .

I am trapped myself. The crowd has been building up between the quay, the pavilions and the water's edge. A sea of top-hats, red tarbushes, turbans of many shapes and colours, ceremonial uniforms, brown burnouses, blue *galabiya*s . . .

The guns roar and the cheering begins, running towards us as if someone had lit a powder-train. The long snake of monarchs comes down the plank-walk, led by the heir apparent to Egypt's throne, Prince Tewfik, the Princess of Holland on his arm, the overture to the entrance of the Empress Eugénie herself, in lavender silk, on the arm of young Franz Josef, Emperor of Austria, in white tunic and white-and-scarlet pantaloons. She wears a kerchief of tumbling white lace which sets off to perfection her slender neck and proud bosom. As she pauses to ascend my newly carpeted steps, she turns, enabling me to catch a fleeting glimpse of her face through her lightly spotted veil.

Forty-three years old, sorely tried by all accounts – but still a beautiful woman. It is as if Cleopatra had returned to the Nile. They say she's brought with her a hundred new dresses from Worth, her Paris couturier. They say that after her visit to the Seraglio in Istanbul on the way here, Abdul Aziz, the Padishah, God's Shadow on Earth, was driven half mad by the demands of his wives and concubines.

I looked towards the marquee on the shore, and hoped that my own harem had a good, but not *too* good, view.

A bearded old man in a wide green turban – the Grand Sheikh of Egypt – mounted to his wooden pulpit, unrolled a scroll and embarked on a prayer. The crowned heads on the opposite platform shuffled to their feet and reverently removed their headgear, thereby offering to Islam the grave insult of an unclothed head. As they shuffled, hoping to conceal their confusion, I caught sight of Jeannie, Jeannie Macdonald, standing behind them. She was wearing a small Tyrolean black hat set off by an aigrette. Ridiculous at her age, of course. As the old Sheikh quavered on, it dawned on me that the aigrette was the decoration I had been awarded for service in Mohammed Ali's long war against the Wahabi in Arabia. That was when the Old Man was still building himself up, currying favour with the Sultan. Fighting his battles for him, the way we Highlanders did for the English, although all *we* got for it were torched roofs and a lot of peg-legs.

She couldn't see me down below, of course. She was in Draneht Bey's party. Draneht Bey, chief of the new Cairo Opera House, superintendent of the Alexandria-to-Suez railway, principal loanmonger to the Khedive. Draneht wore a smart new 'Imperial' on his chin now, but I remember him when his name was Pavlos Pavlides, and he was a ragged refugee boy escaping from the Turkish wars. Pavlos had come out on top through four reigns, even Abbas's. But then, come to think of it, so had I. So far . . .

On Jeannie's other side I spotted the son-in-law, George Jesus Girgis, a Coptic accountant who had imbibed compound interest with his mother's milk. For the last ten years George has been floating high on the cotton boom, with Jeannie at his elbow. Macdonald and Girgis, or Girgis and Macdonald, cotton-ginners to half of Egypt.

Sometimes I ask myself: is this *really* what it's all been about? Was it for this that Tom Waghorn sweated his heart out to create the Overland Transit, for this that Giovanni Belzoni fought day after day, month after month, against the encroaching sand? For this that the old Pasha sent his young men to Paris to learn from the West?

The Sheikh subsided. Enfolded in rich silks and brocades, the mitred Patriarch of Alexandria ascended the steps to the altar, and, in the flickering light of a thousand candles, the black-bearded, black-turbaned priests of the Coptic church wove about him an intricate tapestry of chant in the dead language of the Pharaohs.

Then, in purple cape and biretta, a bright-faced young Frenchman took over the pulpit, Monsignor Bauer, the Empress's personal confessor. The Monsignor saluted the Khedive's vision, extolled the Empress's 'noble sympathy', and called de Lesseps 'the Columbus of our time'. How did it go? 'On this wonderful shore, beneath this marvellous sky, an era is marked out in the history of mankind. The Glorious East, the Wondrous West . . . salute each other . . . A horizon more vast than any known before opens out before us . . .'

The Monsignor's rich baritone voice rolled on.

I wondered what new horizons might be opening up for my *kukucki* friend in Arab Town. I wondered how many Suez Canal 1868 Bonds, issued at 25 per cent Monsignor Bauer might hold. 'The new Columbus', I noticed, looked wan and worried.

The Empress rose, and escorted by the portly, red-sashed, red-bearded Ismail, a glittering scimitar at his side, began to descend the stairs to the plank-walk. The soldiers lining it crashed to the salute. And two young girls ran out in front of her, clutching bouquets of flowers.

Empress Eugénie smiled, bending forward to receive their offerings. The sun caught her Titian hair, with its simple parting, unadorned save for the flowers at the nape of the neck (the arrangement they call *à l'Impératrice*, Jeannie tells me).

I saw that one of the girls was my granddaughter, Leila Girgis. It gave me quite a pang, for with her jet-black hair and total self-possession she reminded me sharply of Jeannie Macdonald when I first set eyes upon her at my grandmother Beaton's waulking party at Skeabost on the island of Skye. Leila would be fourteen, just about the same age. Then I caught a glimpse of my daughter – *our* daughter, Flora – looking on with maternal concern. Jeannie was at the bottom of all this for sure.

The top-hats were disengaging themselves from the tarbushes, the tarbushes retreating from the turbans. 'East' and 'West', having met, were losing no time in drawing apart again.

Through the widening gap I spotted a familiar figure, small blue lunettes gleaming on his nose. My old friend Auguste – Mariette Bey, Director of Antiquities. My son Ibrahim, Elena's eldest, works for him now, saving the Pharaohs from the plunderers. A case of poacher turned gamekeeper, I fear.

'Sheikh Osman! Sheikh Osman!' he called, still some yards away.

Tall as I am, Auguste Mariette towers over me. A huge man – but then this is a land of giants, of men larger than life, of what my countryman, Mr Thomas Carlyle, calls 'Heroes'.

'Auguste,' I said, 'you know full well that I am no sheikh or even, like yourself, a bey. I am Osman Effendi, the renegado.'

My speech had its usual effect on Mariette. He threw back his great head and roared with laughter. 'Ah, mon cher Sheikh, today we are all renegados – one way or another – from the Khedive downwards. What is this miracle we celebrate here today but a miracle wrought by renegados? And talking of miracles, the Khedive thinks you can order a new opera the way you do a new odalisque. Now he's asking Verdi to name his own price.'

'And the Maestro?'

'I've sent telegram after telegram . . .' He shrugged.

The Khedive had set his heart on an opera celebrating Ancient Egypt for the Canal's Grand Opening. Auguste had supplied the story. The Khedive wanted Verdi, but the Maestro procrastinated and the new Opera House had to make do with *Rigoletto*. Ismail had not been amused. The situation could turn nasty.

'You must bring Verdi into line,' I told Mariette. 'My granddaughter, Leila, has her heart set on a place in the chorus.'

'I will inform the Maestro,' Auguste said. He turned to go, then stepped back, gripping my arm. 'Ah, mon Dieu! I forget. A young compatriot of mine is most anxious to meet you – an écrivain called Emile Zola. He questions me: is it really true that this fellow came to Egypt as a drummer-boy in a Scottish regiment at the age of seventeen and was sold into slavery?'

Mariette must have seen my face. He clapped me on the shoulder. 'Never fear, my friend! I did not betray you. But he scents a great story – a brilliant new novel. He aspires to strip the veil from the Orient.'

So it was starting again. I've lost count of the clients who have pressed me for 'my story': I've had to live the horrors of Rosetta and el-Hamed over and over again. I'd thought I was finished with that. I thought I could at last banish from my dreams Colonel Patrick Macleod's bloody head impaled on a pole.

'Emile has been making his own inquiries. He asks me is it really true that Osman and his *copains* were sold for seven Maria Theresa dollars a head?'

I had met this young French journalist with the Italian name. He was one of the Khedive's special *invités* at the Grand Opening – a rising man.

'He's inquiring about your harem, too.'

'Oh no! He's been reading Kinglake, has he?'

Mariette laid a sympathetic hand on my arm. 'Voyez, mon ami, yours is a great story. But if you want it told the way it was, you have no choice. You must write it yourself!'

I cut him short. 'Time enough for that.'

Inshallah!' he said.

I felt a tug at my coattails and, turning, saw my granddaughter.

'Grandma wants to see you at the Grand Café de Paris. Halan! Immédiatement!' She thrust out a small hand and began to haul. Her strength these days astonishes me.

Mariette shrugged. 'Clan Macdonald is sending round the fiery cross.' He is one of the few left now who know our story.

I surrendered to Leila's tug and, hand in hand, we made our way between the raw wooden chalets, past the Company's hospital, and the Company's Coptic church, and the Company's mosque, and the Company's Greek Orthodox church and the Company's Roman Catholic church – all inserted into the neat grid of streets between the Quai Eugénie and the vast mirror of Lake Menzaleh. Banana trees waved around the Chief Engineer's residence, but the sand still lay heavy on the new streets, spurting up under our feet.

Coloured lanterns dangled from the long poles lining the streets. Then we were engulfed in the babel that was the Grand Café de Paris, the machine-gun rattle of French, carried away in throaty surges of Arabic. Thin as bean-poles, Nubian waiters with red tarbushes perched rakishly on ebony foreheads dashed about with *fingan*s of coffee on silver trays, or brought up glowing charcoals for bubbling water-pipes. The handclaps of the *habitués* summoning them were counter-pointed by the palm-to-palm gunshot reports of Levantines sealing deals.

I spotted that little black Tyrolean hat at a table in the far corner. She was still wearing the dress she had worn on the platform, and I saw now that the silk trimming round the bottom of the cape had a tartan pattern. A gaggle of village sheikhs hung around, no doubt hoping to raise new loans on cotton not yet in the ground.

The paper tablecloth was covered with pencilled calculations. The fellahin call her 'Sitt Amerikani' – the American Lady – when they're after a good price; and at other times 'el-Koton', the press, on account of the way she squeezes the last para out of them.

I nodded towards the dark tartan trimmings. 'Is it proper that a Macdonald should flaunt the *breacan* of Clan Macleod?'

She waved the sheikhs away.

'Don't you know, Dhòmhnaill *Bhàin*, that tartan is de rigueur this year? The Empress herself has been wearing it at the Château de Compiègne.' (I happen to know Jeannie still gets old numbers of *Harper's Bazaar* from America.)

'Twenty fellahin families could live well for a year on what that dress cost,' I said. 'It's as grand as the Empress's.'

She was delighted. 'Donald, my dear, it *was* the Empress's!' She condescended to explain that at the French imperial court it would be considered a grave breach of etiquette for the Empress to wear the same dress twice. The ladies-in-waiting make a very nice thing out of selling off the daily discards.

'You must see, mo chridhe, that we American ladies *must* keep up. I could never have worn my Bismarck brown – or Metternich green. Definitely passé.'

'Mo chridhe', she'd called me. 'My heart.' It was something at least that the Gaelic still rose between us.

'Look, Dhòmhnaill *Bhàin*, I didn't send for you to discuss Second Empire fashions. I've just found out that Sami's ship, the *Latif*, is going to sail tonight.'

It was the moment I had been secretly dreading for weeks past. After half a century of extraordinary vicissitudes, the fortunes of Clan Osman were at their peak. *Renegado* I might be, but no one was better respected than I: de Lesseps' right-hand man, one son in the Khedival Navy, another a clever engineer, manning the great machines which devour the sand, and Theo, Elena's boy, catering for the crowned heads at the Ismailiya festivities. But as they say: 'the higher they rise, the harder they fall'. I had given too many hostages to fortune.

I turned to Jeannie. 'Mariette has just been telling me I should write my life story.'

'So you should. "The Life and Times of Osman the Scotsman". You'd make a fortune.'

'No one would believe me.'

'Try them,' she said.

'It would be your story, too . . .'

She fell silent.

'I have no notes – not even my Ross-shire Buffs paybook.'

'What does a Highlandman want with *notes*? We have our memories. They are *all* we have now.'

'But how can I write the beginning when I do not know the end?'

She snorted. 'Mektub!' she said, mocking what she likes to call my 'Mohammedan fatalism'.

'Yes,' I said. 'It *is* written – but how do I know *what*? Allah alone can know that.'

'Write it for Him,' she said, blasphemously. 'Your hero de Lesseps has, Tom Waghorn did . . . even Sam Shepheard . . . Unfurl your Bratach *Sìdh* that put paid to the Macdonalds – as you used to tell me – back home.'

She laughed, less mockingly now, for by 'home' she meant *our* home, the Highlands of Scotland, not North Carolina, not America. I was astonished – and touched – that she still remembered the Macleods' fairy flag, the miraculous all-conquering fairy flag of Dunvegan, that pale yellow, elf-spotted silken banner, brought back from the East by some Crusader Macleod, only to be unfurled in the most desperate straits, but, once unfurled, omnipotent.

At least I could use the four days of the transit – the hundred perilous miles between Port Said and Suez, Mediterranean and Red Sea – to cast my mind back, dredge my memory, ask myself why it all happened the way it did.

BOOK I

The Dance Called America

... we performed with much activity a dance which
I suppose the emigration from Skye has occasioned.
They call it 'America'. A brisk reel is played. The
first couple begin and each sets to one – then
each to another – then as they set to the next couple,
the second and third couples are setting; and so it
goes on, till all are set a-going and wheeling
round each other, while each is making a tour of all
in the dance. It shows how emigration catches till all
are afloat.

– James Boswell, *The Journal of a Tour of the Hebrides*
(1773)

1 The Waulking Party

My mother had high aspirations for me, her only son. She wished me to have Latin, so as to be worthy of her family, the Beatons, who had supplied a long line of learned physicians to the Macleods, the Mackenzies and the Lords of the Isles. But my father was only a poor *màlair* and Bracadale had only a small parish school under the Revd Macaskill, who got £28 a year from Macleod. So she was doomed to disappointment, poor woman.

Every morning, after a cold bath, even in winter, I would set off with my nephew, Murdo, who was two years older, barefoot and bare-headed, to trudge the four miles across the moor to school. Each of us clutched a peat for the school fire, Mr Macaskill unfailingly administering five strokes of the tawse if we failed to deliver.

A portrait of my namesake, kinsman and boyhood hero hung in a frame on the schoolhouse wall: a short, wiry man, far famed for his feats with the broadsword. Even now I can remember the inscription.

> SEARJEANT DONALD MACLEOD
> Born in the island of Skye, Aged 102
> Who served under Five Crowned Heads
> And is in Good Health and
> Has twelve sons in His Majesty's service
> And One Son Nine Years Old

Donald had served with Marlborough in the Royal Scots, fought under Argyll at Sheriffmuir in the '15, and distinguished himself with the Black Watch at Fontenoy. He had his shin-bone shattered with Wolfe at Quebec, and, at sixty-seven, made his way to New York to offer his services to Clinton fighting the American rebels.

At the age of 102, he published his *Memoirs of the Life and Gallant Exploits*. I doubt whether he would acknowledge a fellow Skyeman called Osman Effendi, a *renegado* – or, as he would say, a damned deserter. All the same, I shall follow his example: I shall start at the beginning, and go on to the end, *inshallah*.

Like my brothers and sisters, I was born in the old box-bed in our 'black house' near the shore of Loch Bracadale, to my mind the loveliest of the sea lochs of Skye. Our mouldering thatch was held down by roped stones against the storms that blew in off the Atlantic. *Half*-brothers and sisters I should say, because my father, Ruairidh Og, married twice, and I was his last born, the only child of Mairi Beaton, the Reverend's daughter. I remember the dull glow of the peat fire, a comforting presence, the blue fragrance wafting gently upwards, weaving wispy patterns, coating roof-trees and under-thatch a rich velvet black. The floor I crawled over was beaten earth and all the light there was came from one small window, stuffed with turfs in winter.

It was enough. This, my first world – of so many – was a warm, embracing world and I throve in it. In the winter a couple of black cattle kept us company. A dark wall of peats outside bore solid witness to our prudent labours.

In the long dark nights we sat around the peat fire, and my father told stories of the great days of the Clan and its Chieftains. For he was a *sgeulaiche*, a teller of tales, a custodian of clan legend and memory – what the Arabs call a *sher*. He told of the valorous deeds of Alasdair Crotach, the Hunchback, the seventh Chief, who built the great keep of the Dun, and of Rory Mor, the thirteenth and greatest Chief, he of Rory Mor's Horn, the hollowed ox-horn that held a bottle and a half of claret, which each new chief had to drain. My father's tales of clan treachery and feud were bloody; I suppose you could say I cut my milk-teeth on the Battle of Waternish, a haunting Macleod triumph over the ever-treacherous Macdonalds, on the beach at Trumpan on the west side of our island one Sunday morning in the year 1578.

When all the Macleods were at worship in the little church, the dirty Macdonalds came over in eight galleys from Uist, crept up, blocked the doors and fired the thatch. A single woman escaped to raise the alarm at Dunvegan. The Macleod war galleys put out, cutting off the Macdonalds' retreat. Backs against a drystone wall, the Macdonalds were gaining ground, when the Macleods unfurled the *Bratach Sìdh*. The Macdonalds were slain to a man, and the stone dyke thrown down on their bodies. When I was a boy the place was still known as Blàr Milleadh Gàrraidh, the Field of the Spoiled Dyke. After a storm I have picked up human bones there.

Such was my boyhood education. With hindsight, it was not perhaps such a bad preparation for the strange future that lay in wait.

When my father was home, the old Highland world still glowed for me. Members of the Clan were still the 'children' of the Chief and the Chief was the father of the Clan, and yet the Clan was greater than the Chief – or so my father said – and all Macleods, whether humble *màlair* in his black-house or 'tacksman' kin of the Macleod in his white house, could be proud.

But when my father was away, as he was for weeks, driving the black cattle from Skye and the islands over the roof of the world and down to the Falkirk Tryst, the skies darkened. The running of our holding fell to Rory, the eldest of my seven half-brothers, the children of my father's first wife, Kirsty Mac-Crimmon of the famous piping MacCrimmons, whose school used to lie just across the loch from Dunvegan. Rory was a short, wiry fellow in his mid-forties with five children of his own, whom I suppose I must call my nephews and nieces, though all were older than I, save poor Jamie who was carried off one terrible year when the oats mouldered and the potatoes rotted away.

Rory was like a father to me, but when he presided round the peat fire at night, the talk was very different – of how the shielings were being closed to us so that we lost the rich spring grass; of how the Great Sheep were pushing in, pushing in, so that we were down to six or seven boggy, stony acres near the shore; and how the moment a son could handle a plough and buy a cow he would marry and put up another black-house on the family holding, till the black-houses clustered like limpets along the rocky foreshore. The lairds liked it fine, said Rory, for to harvest the sea-ware, the golden tangle, they needed to have some fools to cut it, standing in the icy sea water, forking out the slimy stuff. It took twenty tons of it to burn down to one ton of kelp. The Chiefs held down the price for the 'tangle', while raising that of their kelp. And all the time the lairds' ground officers were watching like hawks to see that the *màlairean* didn't carry away a single strand of the stuff to manure their own poor plots.

Rory was a bitter man. 'They bleed us the way we bleed the black cattle in hard times to mix their blood with the oatmeal!' he used to say. He had been a lad at the time Norman – the 'Wicked Man' as folk called him – was wasting the Clan's substance on the gaming-tables of London.

Ships lined up in the western sea lochs, waiting to carry hungry Highland folk off to America where, it was said, land and food could be had in plenty. Rory wanted to go. But my father would not provide the three pounds for the passage. Desperate, Rory proposed to go as an indentured servant, working off the cost of his passage. My father forbade it. For him it was desertion.

'Macleod has not let in the Great Sheep,' my father said, loyal to the last.

'Not yet,' Rory said grimly.

My father stared out to sea towards Macleod's Tables, wreathed in cloud, saying nothing.

Like me, my father was flaxen-haired, freckled, long-nosed, long-faced, blue-eyed, and whenever I saw his face in my mind's eye, whether I was a prisoner in Mohammed Ali's Citadel in Cairo, or Osman the Scottish Mameluke in Ezbek Bey's camp in Minya, or was at Burckhardt's side before the Kaaba in Mecca, or as Osman Effendi shopping for a wife in the Cairo slave-market, I knew again who I was: Dòmhnall MacLeòid, son of Ruairidh the Younger, Sìol Tormoid – seed of Tormod, who was the elder son of whoever was begotten by Olaf the Black.

There are beginnings and beginnings. Trumpeted beginnings which turn out not to be beginnings at all. And small beginnings which open up new worlds, changing the course of a man's whole life.

Truly unremarkable, an event as inevitable as the annual trip to the moor to cut the peat, was the beginning which crept up on our house one spring morning in 1802: the descent on our island of a covey of unsmiling young men in dark suits and black nebbed caps, students from a theological college in Edinburgh, selling

Gaelic Bibles to reclaim the Highland savages, with a bit of cate-
chising thrown in and an eagle eye for Highland superstitions
such as the *bean-shìdh*, second sight, kelpies, the *Fèinn*, and what
their church called 'concubinage'.

They also brought news. The long war with the French, which
had lasted almost all my young life and filled our island with
cripples, was over. Bonaparte had called a halt with the Peace of
Amiens.

My father was indignant. 'You mean Addington has *signed*? A
treaty of *peace*?'

The young missionary nodded sombrely.

'But did not Abercromby turf the Frogs out of Egypt only last
year'?

Unable to meet Ruairidh Og's fierce eye, the student clutched
black cap and Gaelic Bible and looked at the ground.

'And did not Admiral Nelson send the French fleet to the
bottom of Aboukir Bay in '98? Peace with the Corsican! How
can the English be such fools? Don't they know a trap when they
see one?'

The student was desperately riffling through his Bible. He threw
out the text like a shield. 'Isaiah two, verse four!' It was the one
about turning swords into ploughshares.

There was a terrible silence. I watched my father, transfixed, as
he gazed witheringly at the student. 'Did not the Lord order Saul
to destroy the Amalekites *utterly*?' he demanded, and stalked out
of the house.

Visibly relieved, the young man felt in his pocket, and handed
my mother a letter from my grandmother, which had been
entrusted to him for delivery.

Long widowed, the old lady still lived with her two daughters,
my aunts, in the late Reverend Beaton's white house, up in the
Macdonald country of Skye. The elder aunt, Morag, was married
to Lieutenant Alistair Macdonald, who had come back from the
American war with only one arm, and now looked after the
Beaton farm. Around the younger aunt, Janet, there hung an air
of mystery, palpable even to a boy of thirteen. It was whispered
that as a young girl she'd gone off to work in the cotton-mills in
Glasgow, and had returned with a bairn, but no man.

Perhaps this accounted for the sly look on the young missionary's face as he handed over the letter. My mother thanked him,

and offered him a dram. She waited for him to refuse it and leave the house before she opened the letter.

A smile of pleasure spread across her face. 'Mother has a new plaid off the loom,' she announced. 'She's holding the luadh Wednesday week. She wishes me to lead the singing.'

I must explain, I suppose, that a *luadh* is a waulking, thickening and shrinking the new-woven cloth, a labour which like so many others in the island is made light by singing. My mother was far famed for the spirit and wit of her waulking songs.

'You'll be going,' we said.

'I'll not!' Her lips set in that determined line we knew so well. 'Last year she asked Meg Mackinnon as well.'

The leading singers at waulkings were as touchy as prima donnas.

I could see, though, that there was more in my mother's refusal than mere pique, for she went on to propose that her step-daughter, Mairi, should go in her place. Mairi had been a maid at the Dun since she was fifteen, and was now in her thirties and still unmarried, and, as everyone knows, when it comes to match-making a waulking party is without equal.

My mother decreed that our family piper, Angus, should accompany Mairi to the waulking and that I should go with them. That was the day I put on my first clansman's blue bonnet, my mother sewing the ribbons round the rim, bringing them through a slit in the back to form a bow. Mairi, who had got the day off from the castle, brought me a sprig of juniper, our clan emblem, to flaunt in it. I walked several inches taller that day.

Mairi wore her finest woollen snood and best linen gown, and Angus carried not only his pipes, but also a small keg to be replenished with *uisge-beatha* – the water of life – at my grand-mother's bothy, one of the most esteemed illicit stills in the entire island of Skye. Angus carried further whisky orders from my half-brother Peter, our boatman, who carried Grandmother Beaton's distillation down through the Western Isles to Glasgow. Peter knew every cave in every sea loch big enough to hide a boat from the Excise.

My grandmother's house at the head of the loch had always seemed like a palace to me. The stone walls were white and held together with cement, and my grandmother and aunts burned real tallow candles. Upright and imperious in her high oak-backed chair, the old lady herself was waiting to greet us. She wore a skittish mob cap with lace trimmings, and a fine plaid was draped over her shoulders. She made me stand in front of her chair and examined me steadily for what seemed an eternity, particularly since the left lens of her small steel-bound spectacles was a powerful magnifier, rendering her gaze cyclopian.

'Well, Donald Ban,' she said at last, 'I see you have your blue bonnet.'

She held out a curious silver-bound snuff-box, fashioned I believe from a sea-nut. 'You'll not take a pinch?'

While I struggled to play the man, Grandmother turned her formidable gaze upon Mairi, examining her from the *stìom* of fine, coloured woollen thread that confined her hair, betokening her unwedded state, to the fancy shoes. A great circular brass brooch, engraved with strange animals and patterns, held the plaid over her shoulders.

Grandmother reached out at last and fingered the brooch.

'It is a MacCrimmon heirloom,' blurted Mairi. 'Some say it came across from Ireland with Finlay, Finlay of the White Plaid.'

'Indeed,' said the old lady. 'And you are in good voice for waulking? Twelve there will be around the board and a young girl from the Braes of Lochaber, a Macdonald visiting kin.'

The old lady got up, and hobbled across to the sideboard. 'A charm from the MacCrimmons calls for a philtre from the Beatons.' She poured a large dram from a keg into a glass, broke an egg into it, then stirred in a spoonful of white powder (which I now know to have been sugar). She held the glass out to Mairi. 'Drink – and you'll have no cause to call on that fairy flag of yours at the waulking.'

Mairi shrank back. The old lady cackled wickedly. 'It's not a love-philtre, child. It's what the Beatons used for the wounded at Bannockburn. Some call it "Old Man's Milk". But I tell you, it's Maiden's Nectar too! It brings a fine bloom to the cheeks and the bosom, and there'll be a certain Murdo, a rich widower, a builder of boats . . .'

Fresh off my aunts' loom, the new web of plaid lay soaking in its tub of diluted *fual* in the smaller barn. There were those who found this indelicate, preferring ammonia from the bottle, but

Mary Macdonald – Grandmother Beaton – was not one of them. She held firmly to the belief that there was nothing like stale urine for imparting softness to a plaid.

I went to help my Uncle Alistair manoeuvre that *clèith luaidh* onto the piles of stones that served it for legs, marvelling at his dexterity despite the dangling sleeve where his arm had been blown off at Savannah. It was no easy job, for the waulking board was fifteen feet long and three wide, rough-ridged, and ordinarily served as the bridge across the burn.

As the women began to arrive for the waulking, my aunts Morag and Janet shooed us out of the barn. No males were allowed while the fulling was in progress. But I found a convenient knot-hole and took up my position.

Most of the waulkers were brawny, middle-aged women, with strong fists and fingers, and having been plied with a dram or two from my grandmother's bothy, they were already in boisterous mood. There were also a few young girls who – can this be the Arab in me speaking? – were putting their wares on show, like my sister Mairi. The island lads were drawn to a waulking like wasps to a jam-pot.

Elbow to elbow, facing each other, the women took their places round the board. They were in their best, but their sleeves were rolled up for the fray. Looking back – and I have gone over that scene in my mind a thousand times – I don't think I noticed Jeannie Macdonald's presence at first. I was worried for my sister, you understand.

Silent now, confronting each other across the waulking board, the women grew tense, awaiting the signal, as my Aunt Morag drew the heavy, sopping web from the vat and fed it onto the board.

Slowly at first, the women began to clutch at the unwinding plaid, grabbing, pounding, thrusting it first towards their partners, then on, so that it snaked darkly across the board.

The waulking songs began *sotto voce* at first, then the swelling chorus, solo line and refrain, pacing the cloth's undulations, empowering the flying, pounding fists:

> *Iomair o hò, clò nan gillean* . . .
> Waulk, o ho, the cloth of the lads . . .
> *Iomair o hò, clò nan gillean* . . .

I heard Mairi's voice taking up the solo line. 'From hand to hand, the cloth of the lads' – and then again the slow chorus, '*Iomair o hò, clò nan gillean*', punctuated by the steady thumps of twenty-four fists, keeping time, gaining speed.

> Let me waulk quickly the cloth of the lads,
> Let me waulk with joy the cloth of the lads . . .

Years later, I would see in my dreams (in my bed in the house by the canal in Cairo) the long band of plaid coming to life, quickening, swelling – for this was what they call a 'heating' song in the Gaelic, contrived to exhilarate the waulkers, get them into their swing.

Suddenly, a new mood – a song of love betrayed.

> *Fhir mhòir nan calpannan geala . . .*
> O tall man with white calves,
> You deceived me when I was foolish . . .

And cutting in, lest the women, overcome by the pathos of the story, should slow down, the lusty chorus, shaking the barn walls:

> *Hug o ro hò i a bhò . . .*
> I will not go alone to the moor . . .
> *Hug o ro nan hò i a bhò . . .*

I caught the tremor in my sister's voice as she again took up the story –

> But though you passed me by,
> My father would have counted young cattle for you . . .

The plaid was kneaded and grabbed and pushed and thumped as if the treacherous man of the white calves was under their hands.

A pause as the plaid was plunged back into the tub 'for another drink' – and now was the time for the 'tightening' songs, stepping up the beat, closing up the web, shrinking it to its proper proportions.

My Aunt Morag tested the plaid.

'Oran Arabhaig,' she ordered.

Now it was a 'flyting' song in which two soloists, from opposite ends of the board, tease and taunt each other.

> Daughter of the Macleods, with hair of golden hue,
> The year of your marriage seems long gone by . . .

The young voice, clear and crisp as a mountain burn, gave the jibe a stabbing immediacy, a dirk plunged into the heart.

I glanced anxiously towards my sister, but Mairi had withstood the blow, and she slashed back with the Macleod broadsword:

> Come, come! You fled away, you timid rabble!
> Remember the day of Glen Healtaine?
> You stood in the heather like hens;
> Into the loch you went like ducks
> And like the gulls went out to sea . . .

Drawn by the sounds of vocal battle carried on the wind along the shores of Loch Snizort, the menfolk of the surrounding settlements gathered around the door of the barn. Eye still glued to my private *camera lucida*, I saw Jeannie's head come up in that challenging way you can see to this day; her long, slender neck seemed to shine, and that liquid voice spilled out the ill-tempered, incongruous words of her flyting response:

> . . . the race of Macleods, the race of Macleods, crippled
>   and clumsy;
> Feeding on glass and coarse grass and black mill-dust;
> Greeted like horses with halters round their necks . . .

The red ribbon on her head broke and her raven hair spilled down her back. She paid no heed. Black eyes flashed: she was heart and soul in the part. Nourished as I had been on my father's stories, she appeared to me like some tribal goddess. I found myself trembling.

The combat had now become general. Between the thrusts of the flyting clan champions – the red-haired Macleod, the raven-haired Macdonald – the chorus dashed in with a crash and a wild shriek and a pounding and hammering of the plaid, as heart-stopping as the Highland charge that put the fear of Hell into Johnny Cope's men at Prestonpans.

The reek of the *fual* from the wetting of the plaid mingled with the fumes of the drams exhaled from brawny throats and the sweat of the pounding women. The board was lowered, thrusting legs brought into play. White thighs flashed.

At last Aunt Morag held up her hand. The plaid, erupting along the board like a wild thing, slowed, sagged, collapsed, and was still. My aunt, the midwife of the plaid, measured it at several points, turning the third finger of her right hand over and over to check whether the web had now shrunk to its proper width.

The waulking was over.

Now the men were permitted without forfeit into the barn. They shambled in sheepishly, a little awed, though putting a bold face on it.

My two aunts cleared a space for rolling up the new cloth, hitting it with the flat of the hand, straightening, smoothing as they rolled. This was the cue for the frisky 'clapping' songs, in which with much giggling, hoos and hahs, many a young girl's secret love was revealed, or the name of some widower became slyly attached to that of some unwed girl.

Whether Mairi's name figured I do not know, because as Morag and Janet clapped the plaid briskly, like midwives with a fresh-born baby, I found myself face to face with Jeannie Macdonald, her bare arms glistening from the pounding, her face still flushed from the fury of combating the race of the Macleod.

I gawped.

'And who are you?' she demanded.

I stared. I could not speak. 'Donald,' I gulped at last. 'Donald Ban.'

'Donald *who*?'

'Donald Macleod.'

'Macleod!'

Her dark eyes flashed; she was still in the flyting song. 'So where is the Red King's cross on your bonnet?'*

---

* I understand that this refers to the Battle of Culloden in 1746, when Macleod of Dunvegan not only failed to rally round the Young Pretender, Charles Stewart, but joined the repressive forces of the Duke of Cumberland, the man the Sasannachs called 'Sweet William' but the Highland men 'Stinking Billy' – with good reason. – F.M.

Having hurled this deadliest of insults, she turned away and vanished, leaving me stunned, cheeks burning.

Angus had already blown up his pipes, and as the celebratory drams of my grandmother's water of life began to circulate, he launched into a Highland fling which his august MacCrimmon forebears would certainly have considered a desecration of their high art. If you've ever seen the whirling dervishes performing at the *mulid* of Seyyid Ahmed el-Badawi you'll perhaps have some idea of a ceilidh after one of my aunts' waulking parties.

But that night the ecstasy of the ceilidh was not for me. I passed between the gyrating, leaping couples like a sleep-walker. In the midst of this overflowing joy I felt sombre and utterly alone. Ridiculous at that age, I know, but the extraordinary creature who had suddenly sprung up before me, with her black hair streaming down her back, and had spat her contempt at me, had taken possession of my being.

Then she was gone. I could find no sign of her.

In the strange way a Highland boy's imagination works, I found myself wondering vaguely whether she might indeed be one of the *mnathan-sìdh*, though she seemed too much of solid flesh and blood for that – or perhaps descended from one of those Spaniards (a favourite theme of the Revd Macaskill) washed up on our western shores from the battered Armada. That certainly would account for the dark eyes and hair – and the strangeness.

In the end, during a lull in the dancing, while Angus and the fiddler took a reviving dram, I plucked up courage to consult my Aunt Morag, who could give you a complete pedigree of every person on the island and their relationship back to Olaf the Black.

She looked at me curiously. To my annoyance, I felt myself blushing. 'Aaah, she! A fine cailin is Jeannie Macdonald, a spirited lass with a voice as pure and clear as a mountain stream. But she is not of Skeabost, nor even of our winged island at all. She visits her kin, the Macdonalds of Kingsburgh . . .'

'Then why is she not at the ceilidh?'

'She is clever also and attends the grammar school at Inverness, and a new trimester is about to begin, so she must return home at once to Tirnadris in the Braes of Lochaber, and the journey is long.'

Seeing my face fall, she added, 'She is one of the five daughters of Alasdair Mac Aonghais, a tacksman of Keppoch.'

My aunt's intended kindness merely plunged me further into confusion and despair. The daughter of a tacksman, boarding at a fine grammar school. She would speak the Sasannach tongue. She might even have Latin. She was far beyond my reach.

And yet she had insulted me. Worse, she had deliberately insulted all Macleods. I was my father's son. Clan honour had its imperatives and they were absolute.

As we dragged our weary way homeward it dawned on me that the Macleod drove, on its long journey through the glens and over the mountains to that great black-cattle market, the Falkirk Tryst, might pass through the Braes of Lochaber where Aunt Morag said *she* lived. I questioned Angus, who always went with the drove because my father held that the skirl of his pipes would keep the drovers in good heart through the worst downpours and keep the kyloes moving over the rock-strewn high passes.

It seemed that our drove halted for the night at 'Young Corrie's stance' near Spean Bridge. The Macdonald farm, Angus said, wasn't much more than a mile away, on the other side of the river.

I saw then what I had to do. I must become a drover. It wouldn't be easy. My mother would forbid it: droving was not what she hoped for for her only son. She'd never let me go. Well, she'd have to. The honour of the Macleods, I told myself, was at stake.

That was how it all started.

2 The Drove

I bided my time, living for the moment the departure of the drove for Falkirk Tryst would come round again. I told no one of my plan. How could I? My mother, who watched me carefully, thought I must be sickening for something, but when no rash or fever appeared, concluded it must just be that I was at an 'awkward age'.

If my brothers and sisters found me moody and silent, ours was a large family and we all had our own concerns. Besides, it had been a hard winter, and looked like being a worse spring. The oats had rotted in the rain and the potatoes were not ready. We have a saying in the Gaelic: 'Hard is the spring when the whelks are counted'; we lined our empty stomachs with them that year. The black cattle that shared our houses in the winter were so weak they could scarcely rise from their knees and gave but a thimbleful of milk.

My own hunger was of a different kind. Combing the shore with my brothers for shellfish, I would see her dark eyes staring out at me from the rock-pools, challenging me. As we sat round the peat fire in the evenings listening to my father's stories of the clan wars, the disgraced, thieving Macgregors and the treacherous Macdonalds would be eclipsed as a peat suddenly glowed red and in it I saw the final scenes of the waulking, her white thighs glistening as her feet pounded against the sodden plaid, thrusting it along the ribbed board.

I was in a sorry state. My father, hunting for every penny he could find, sought to instruct me in the art of making kelp from seaweed, for which the laird would pay a pittance, taking a huge profit on onward sale to Glasgow. I suppose you could say it was an art. First the sea-tangle had to be spread out on the beach to dry. Then a deep trench had to be dug and the sea-tangle piled into it and fired, stirred for several days with a ten-foot pole until rendered into fine ash for which the soap-makers would pay well. My father often complained of my wandering attention for, staring down into the incandescent mass, as the sea-tangle melted and bubbled, I would see the fierce dark eyes of my tormentress.

This girl had insulted me. I had to teach her a lesson. Brooding over it, I felt I could kill her. But was killing her what I really had in mind? Brought up in the close quarters in the black-houses, I was acquainted with what the Sasannachs call 'the facts of life'. I had viewed, without excitement, the antics of the kyloe bull covering our cows, and I had seen men and women kneeling on the penitent stool at the kirk. But none of this seemed to have anything to do with the strange world I had now entered.

I remember that day in the schoolhouse. The Revd Macaskill thumped on his desk for silence and, holding up his fresh copy of the *Edinburgh Advertiser*, proceeded to read out an item from the front page: 'The Corsican upstart whose style is Fraud and Insolence has seized Hanover and is forming the Army of England to "leap the Channel".'

So the truce which had so dismayed my father was broken. It was Bonaparte against the world again.

Once again the lairds and chiefs set out to demonstrate their loyalty by recruiting their clansmen to their Highland regiments, as they had done so many times before. There were few houses in the island that did not have their veteran, very likely crippled, who could tell his tales of far-flung battle-fields of the British Empire. But it was too late now. If the Chiefs could desert their 'children', the children could abandon the Chiefs. The emigration 'crimps', as my father called them, made better offers than the recruiting sergeants. The Highland Society offered an extra £2 bounty money to men who would take 'the King's shilling'. It was no good: five thousand Highlanders emigrated that year, 1803, from Fort William and the Western lochs, though many had to pay so much for the passage that they had no money left to tide them over the long, cruel winter in the new land.

For the island of Skye, and Highlanders in general, the resumption of the war had one powerful benefit. For centuries the wealth of the Highlands had lain in our black cattle, the shaggy little kyloes with their gentle pink eyes and fine curving horns; they could survive the northern winter, revive on the tender spring grass of the shielings and machair, before being driven over the roof of Scotland and down to the Lowlands to fatten on rich English meadows.

No one knows when the kyloes first came to the Highlands; what we do know is that they 'belong' as we belong, sharing our black-houses in the winter. They are our link with the outside world, our only 'cash crop', as the Sitt Amerikani would put it, and like us they are survivors, until some bloody English butcher puts the knife in.

As I learned to my cost later, the British Army is a prodigious consumer of beef, and, with the resumption of the war, prices at the Falkirk Tryst began to rise. Thoughts turned to forming up the drove early. It was the moment I had been waiting for.

To my astonishment, Rory, that disappointed man, supported my plea. If a Highland lad was to make his way in the world, he said, travelling with the drove, learning to do deals, to get to know people, was just the start he needed.

'Look at Young Corrie. When he started droving he had only four goats and his own strong legs. And look at him now, with a string of stances stretching half across the Highlands!'

My mother cut him short. 'My son will be no drover, nor cattle-dealer neither!' Fed on my father's gory tales of the *màll dubh*, the black rent, and cattle-reivers, she feared the wild Macgregors or Camerons might snatch her only son.

Rory laughed. 'Och, Mairi, Rob Macgregor's been in his grave at Balquhidder these seventy years!'

It was no good. My mother just switched from the physical to the moral perils of droving: she was not a daughter of the manse for nothing. She quoted one of the Revd Beaton's favourite texts, 1 Corinthians 15, verse 33: 'Evil communications corrupt good manners.' Was it right that a boy of my tender years should be exposed to all the temptations paraded at the Falkirk Tryst, the drink, the gambling, the scarlet women?

Then, one morning, quite unexpectedly, Nature – if Nature it was? – intervened. Macleod's Tables disappeared behind a thunderous black curtain, and a high wind came tearing out of the Cuillins, whipping up the sea to mountainous heights. Walls of spume poured over the rocks they call Macleod's Maidens, sitting there, mother and daughters, spinning and cutting the thread of destiny.

For two whole days the great storm raged, and when at last the sun came through it lit up great mounds of sea-ware heaped on the beach and scattered over the rocks.

Men were rushing from all directions, pushing out boats. The storm had harvested the sea-tangle for us. It only remained to get it in quickly.

Hooking up the slimy stuff, lodged in a crevasse of Sgeir Mhòr, my father slipped in the rocking boat and fell overboard. The dull red-brown of the floating mass was threaded by a bright scarlet ribbon. Roderick's leg was gashed long and deep on a razor-sharp rock. We got him onto the beach, staunched the bleeding as best we could and sent for some of Grandma Beaton's healing unguents for the wound.

I must confess that, while I was concerned for my father, the thought uppermost in my mind was that the drove, due to depart, would be one man short, not easy to replace at short notice.

Seeing that it was now inevitable, my mother put a good face on it. Until that moment like most Highland boys I had gone barefoot. But knowing that 250 miles of mountain tracks, rocky drove roads, moors, bogs and burns now lay ahead of me, she set about making me the finest pair of Highlanders' brogues ever seen north of the Great Glen. I watched her pounding away at the undressed cowhide with lime to render it pliable, piercing it to take thongs that wrap around the ankles, floating the whole thing in the stream until the hairs began to come off, cutting more holes in the sides so that the water would flow off . . . The English thought our brogues showed we were savages. They hadn't the sense to see that they suited our needs perfectly – we could always show them a clean pair of heels if it came down to it.

Then my mother gave me one of my aunt's stoutest plaids to keep out the cold and weather at night on the mountain-tops, and a jacket on which she sewed three big silver buttons which I could cut off and sell if in dire straits. Heirlooms, she said.

'The thieving Macdonalds of Keppoch will snatch him just for his buttons . . .' Angus teased her – and winked at me. I blushed scarlet, wondering how much he knew. Angus was in a bad mood. My father had just ruled that Dugald, our elder brother, should not only lead the drove but ride ahead as topsman to select the stance for the night. Angus had been doing the topsman's job for years while Dugald was away at the wars, fighting the American rebels. But he'd never risen higher than corporal, a fact Angus did not let him forget. Trouble was, our father had caught Angus sliding off to chase a girl in Falkirk, and Roderick the Younger was a man who never forgot.

The spring came at last and out on the new grass of the machair and up on such shielings as the lairds had left to us, the black cattle began to gain strength, and my half-brother Peter, the boatman, began to ferry them over the Minch from the old Macleod lands in Harris and North Uist. As Peter's boat beached, a young black collie dog leapt into the water, making a great splash, enthusiastically harrying the beasts out of the water and up the beach.

'A Dhòmhnaill! Mhic an Diabhail – nach ist thu!'

Startled, I at first thought Peter was cursing me – it wouldn't be the first time I'd been called 'son of the Devil'. Then I realised that Donald was the name of the dog, named after old Donald Macleod of Galtrigill, boatman and guide to the Prince in the '45, and one of Peter's heroes.

'He is foolish and stubborn – he will never learn,' complained Peter, shouting at the dog.

'He is young,' I said,

'So you can have him,' said Peter. 'I give him to you. Donald *Bàn* and Donald *Dubh* – you deserve each other!'

I still remember that misty June morning – a red-letter day in my young life – when I first moved off with the drove, with Angus at the head of the first column of thirty beasts. Besides the three dogs, including my new dog, Donald, there were two stocky, sure-footed garrons, one to carry Dugald ahead to scout out the land, the other for the leather bag of oatmeal, Angus's pipes, a few onions, several webs of my aunts' best plaid to sell along the drove ways, besides hiding the four kegs of my grandmother's choicest nectar from the prying eyes of the Excise. The smuggling tracks criss-crossed the drove roads like the veins of a hand, and our brother Patrick knew them all.

Kyloes and drovers flowed together until there were two hundred or more fanning out over the green hillside, stirks and stoys, old cows pausing to snatch a mouthful of succulent young grass, a slowly advancing russet carpet quietly kept on the move by our two sage dogs.

'Take it steady,' sang out Dugald. 'Let the beasts find their own pace.'

I felt a tug – and my young dog had broken loose, yapping furiously at the heels of a lagging stirk.

'He is a wild one! A broken man without a clan. We should get rid of him before he does us damage!' Dugald stormed.

'He is of Clan Macleod,' I said, staring Dugald in the eye. The ghost of a smile flickered on his lips as he turned away. I was filled with an exhilaration I recall even now.

As I brought up the rear of the drove, keeping Donald sternly in check, a solitary ray of the sun pierced the dark grey wall of mist that hung over the Cuillins, and Sgurr nan Gillean – the Peak of the Lads – sprang forth in all its majesty. Half an hour later the sun burst through in full splendour, bathing the green pyramid of Glamaig and the round breast of Marsco in unearthly light as the drove wound slowly down into Sligachan, and Dugald finally agreed that my dog might stay, on probation.

A few Yorkshire dealers were already nosing around at Sligachan, thick-set figures with strange corncrake voices. They had no Gaelic. But what they did have were money-belts bulging with golden sovereigns. Cash on the nail. All Dugald could offer was a promise to pay the stance rent on the way back from the Tryst.

I have never forgotten that first night with the drove in the stance at the head of Loch Sligachan, the gentle moaning of the gathered beasts punctuated by the steady slap of the small waves coming in from the Sound of Raasay. On moonlit nights the cattle are prone to wander, so Angus and I were told off to stay awake and keep watch. Come morning, he initiated me into the spartan routine of the drover: rousing the others rolled in their plaids, taking round the morning dram from the keg, and the wooden bowls for oatmeal and water, the *brochan*. The morning dram, handed round in our horn cup, is called in the Gaelic the *sgealp* – the slap.

Slapped into life at dawn we slowly worked the drove down towards Broadford Bay, where new streams of black cattle flowed in from Loch Eishort and the Mackinnon country of Strathaird, swelling the river of swaying horns, moving down to the old market stance of Skulamus where Yorkshire dealers were buzzing about like *meanbhchuileagan* on a warm evening in Skye.

A Mr Ramsbottom from Halifax – I recall his name because Dugald translated it for a laugh – had just slapped down two sovereigns, laboriously extracted from his money-belt to make them seem heavier, in front of an old woman who had a single heifer on a rope. She was, she explained, off to join her children in America, so *Obh, obh, obh, obh!* – there was nothing for it but to part with poor Morag. Enlarging with great eloquence on Morag's genealogy and unbounded promise, she pushed Ramsbottom's gold coins away with great dignity. In all creation, she declared, there had never been a more sweet-tempered animal. She was now in calf and without a doubt would give the sweetest milk this side of Paradise.

At this point, the Yorkshire philistine had the ill-grace to guffaw. The old woman glared at him as if he had been Butcher Cumberland himself and turned her back – which brought her face to face with Angus, whom she instantly recognised as the piper of my aunts' waulking party. Nothing would now do but that we take charge of Morag. Dugald explained that we had no golden sovereigns, but she waved this aside like a queen. The Macleod promissory notes had always been good enough for her man; they were good enough for her.

As the note was drawn up, Morag watched reproachfully from beneath her thick curtain of hair. She was indeed an unusual beast, dark red rather than black, with a good straight back and short, sturdy, shaggy legs, the mark of a good West Highland kyloe. But her outstanding feature was her horns. Long and elegant, curving into fine blue-tinted peaks, one pointed upwards, and the other down.

Rallied on this, the old *cailleach* cackled, 'Sure, one horn points to Heaven, the other to Hell! Keep your eyes on Morag, lad, and you have no need for the Minister!'

I reckon it must have been all of seven days before we reached the end of the world as I had hitherto known it.

It is a long, hard pull up the narrow old drove road that spirals over the lumpy heel of our island, especially when you have to make sure no beast misses its footing and plunges into the abyss below. But at last, rounding yet another bend, the blue of the kyle, Caol Reatha, which separates our 'winged island' from the Scottish mainland, lay below us. Beyond, over the strait, rose rank on rank, the wild mountains of Glenelg, Knoydart and Kintail.

As our drove plodded slowly down towards the strait and other droves followed, a green glen opened up below which was a moving carpet of shaggy Highland cattle, russet, brown and black. Peat smoke drifted up towards us from the stone and turf huts thrown up by the drovers, waiting their turn to 'swim' their beasts over the swift-running, icy waters.

I looked across to the white Ferry Inn on the other side and shivered. Like most Skyemen, I had never learned to swim. The water churned furiously offshore; two tides from the Atlantic meet and fight it out in this deep cleft between the mountains.

The ferrymen were waiting for slack water. Dugald went over and bought a coil of rope from one of them, expertly cutting it into lengths, measured between extended finger-tips. He showed me how to make a running noose at one end of each length and a slip-knot at the other.

'In Old Rory's time we twisted our ropes from the heather,' he said.

He wouldn't explain further. He liked his bit of mystery, did Dugald.

But all became clear at low tide next morning when, with much pushing and pulling and yelling, the waiting droves were moved out into shallow water. Attached by the ropes, muzzle to tail, tail to muzzle, the cattle were formed into convoys of six or eight behind the ferry-boats, and 'swum' across the kyle. With luck one boat could get a hundred beasts across in a day. We had three days' hard work ahead of us.

The first in from our drove was an old cow from North Uist, well used to salt water.

'Watch you get the jaw noose *under* her tongue,' snapped Dugald, 'otherwise you're going to have a drowned beast by the time we reach the other shore.'

Angus deftly drew another beast into the 'daisy chain'. Her bellowing stopped the moment she floated, and the curious flotilla was extended again, and attached behind the ferry-boat.

The less experienced beasts from Broadford market were left to the last. There was a wild look in Morag's eye, and her tongue was threshing wildly in the water as I struggled to get the rope noose around her jaw. Her nostrils flared in terror and I was flecked in froth. I looked into those frightened eyes, and, momentarily, took pity on her. Then it occurred to me that I was male and she was female, and I resolved to master her, hauling savagely on the rope. She submitted as I pushed her out into the water, her one upturned horn marking the end of that convoy.

The ferrymen bent to their oars, and we swung out into the churning stream. Angus and I followed in the rear boat, yelling and waving to keep the kyloes from trying to turn back. I was yelling with a strange exultancy, and I caught Angus looking at me curiously and found myself blushing. That was a long, long time ago, you'll understand, but some moments linger.

The strait was like a gigantic pin cushion, pink muzzles upturned, horns weaving, shaggy heads streaming, as the droves forged ahead. Then the tide started to turn. The steersman swung into a wide arc, taking advantage of the current. Morag was at the end of the line and, as the convoy swung round, a heavy strain was placed on the tow-rope I had attached to her jaw. Her muzzle was still out of the water, but I thought I saw a look of desperation in her eyes. As I watched, the rope began to slip from the tail of the animal ahead.

Morag was adrift in the middle of the kyle, legs threshing wildly. We turned our boat, pulling hard on the oars to catch up, yelling all the time, trying to turn her to safety.

The excitement communicated itself to Donald, who ran to the prow, barking and yelping. By now the tide was running too strongly for us.

There was a splash and the dog was in the water, struggling furiously to reach the stricken heifer. Miraculously, he did so, and managed to turn her in the direction of the convoy just in time. The effort had exhausted him. The last I saw of him he was being carried away, towards the point where the kyle widened out into the Sound of Sleat.

Beyond lay the immensity of the open sea.

3   The Shieling Hut

Angus took pity on me. 'He's a boatman's dog, remember. He'll be husbanding his strength. He'll bide his time until the current flows inshore, and then he'll make a push for it . . .'

I was grateful to Angus – he has a kind heart – but the moment our boat touched land I was off along the Glenelg shore, all the time dreading the moment when I would come upon a limp black-and-white body on the tide-line. Once, as I ran, I spotted a distant black-and-white shape coming towards me, and my heart leapt. But it was another drover's dog.

After a life like mine, with so much bloodshed, so much cruelty and loss, my readers may find it strange that I should make so much of a mere lost dog. But there it is. I tell it as it was. How long I ran miserably to and fro over the wet machair in front of the old military barracks at the mouth of Glen More I do not know. I remember questioning two crofting families, evicted by Glengarry, who had found shelter there. They shook their heads sadly. I appealed to some of the drovers who were already setting out over the mountain.

'Drowned, you say? What sort of a collie would that be that would get itself drowned, boy?'

I sank down, utterly exhausted, by the side of our drove and awoke almost at once to find Angus tugging at my tight-wound plaid. 'The cattle are well rested. Dugald wants to get an early start.' He was already handing round the drams from Peter's small keg; it was hardly light yet.

As the drove moved off on the track that rises steeply out of Glenelg Bay, my eye fell on Morag, moving along placidly, as if nothing had happened, one horn pointing heavenward, the other to the ground. That morning the drove felt different somehow. We had shaken down together, men and beasts.

We swung left into Glen Beag, and the kyloes spread out to forage. As we crept slowly forward, I became conscious of a faint yelping somewhere far behind us. It seemed to be coming towards us. I paid little heed, having suffered so many bitter disappointments the day before. And then the yelping became frenzied, and I made out a black-and-white collie leaping towards us. It was Donald, back from drowning.

That is another day I have never forgotten, nor ever shall. I was thirteen years of age, and in a single day my faith had been torn to shreds – and instantly made whole.

Sometimes the track was so steep, so covered in scree, that we had to literally push the beasts. Thus I learned the drovers' art.

'I want to get them to Falkirk fatter than when we started out,' said Dugald. 'Let them browse too much, and you'll miss the best of the market. Drive them too much and they'll come into Falkirk with their ribs showing and their hair falling out. "Look to the feet" was always Corrie's rule . . .'

Far below us the rock-bound Loch Hourn – 'the Lake of Hell' – shone leaden in the setting sun. Our route lay through the wild country known as the Rough Bounds, long the kingdom of the dreaded reivers. It was on their account that the next stance was enclosed by wall and timber; even so, Dugald refused to allow us to make up for lost sleep. 'This is the country of Coll Macdonald – the Cattle Protector,' he said.

That, it seems, was what he called himself – for he was a gentleman – but a better name would have been blackmailer. They say he had a silver plaque in his house engraved (in Latin, of course) with the words 'Overthrow the mighty and spare the humble'. But according to Old Rory, who had started our drove, if you were a drover and crossed his territory you paid the *màl dubh* or reivers came out of the forest and snatched your cattle.

I remember the day the drove at last came out of the wild mountains and we found ourselves following the smiling banks of the River Garry, fringed with silver birches and rowans, its meandering course threading a necklace of green islands.

Not Morag alone but several of the cows had now developed

tender hoofs. General Wade's 'English' roads, gravelled and unyielding, were cursed by every Highland drover.

'They'll have to be shod,' said Dugald. 'Murdo's our man.'

Murdo Macdonnell at the Tomdoun forge claimed to be able to get new cues on seventy beasts a day, and after I'd seen him at work I could believe it. Poor Morag found herself deftly up-ended by this giant of a man, legs roped, while the cues were swiftly nailed along the horn of her cloven hoofs.

It took all my strength to hold her head down on the smithy floor. I remember that soft, reproachful eye upon me and I was swept by a wave of compassion, loosening my hold for a moment; then, as Murdo hammered the last nails home, my grip hardened and I experienced a strange exultation.

Who are you? the girl had demanded. And I, Donald Macleod, had just stood there gawping. Even then, a year later, the thought of it brought the blush of shame to my cheeks. Well, now I'd show her who I was. I was a Macleod and a drover.

We awoke next morning to the unceasing bleating of sheep. The whole mountainside above Inchlaggan was covered with them. 'Glengarry's new clansmen,' said Angus, and spat – and we are not spitting men. 'Ah, well, he gave us a pretty wee bonnet.'

For the rest of the world 1792 was the year the French got rid of their king, but for us it was *Bliadhna nan Caorach* – the Year of the Sheep – the year the Lowland men pushed their great sheep up north of the Great Glen, nibbling, nibbling, nibbling, eating us up. We crofters tried to chase them back again, but a torch applied to thatch can be a powerful argument. The sheep spread the seeds of the accursed bracken everywhere. The Clearances began.

I was only a child at the time, but I can remember the bitterness, the sense of betrayal.

We took the drove across the shallows of Loch Garry at Inchlaggan, striking southwards, over the mountain and down into Cameron country, making for the Great Glen. And now we were overtaken, time and again, by Glengarry's evicted tenants, carrying all they possessed on their backs, making their way sorrowfully down to the emigrant ships at Fort William. Some were barefoot. I can see to this day one old woman who had her household goods, such as they were, on a sort of sledge, formed of two tree-trunks, dragged along by a pony.

One tall fellow was carrying his roof-trees on his shoulder, hoping to transfer some part of the old home to the New World. Dugald offered him a dram, asking where he might be bound.

'Glengarry.'

'Glengarry?'

'Glengarry in Ontario, in Canada. Five hundred of our kinsmen are there already – the laird burned *them* out twenty years ago.'

He swallowed the dram, picked up the smoke-blackened roof-trees and staggered on.

And so, at last, following the course of the River Spean, roaring along in its tree-covered ravine, we passed the ruined High Bridge where the first shots were fired in the '45 – when ten Macdonald pipers put the fear of Hell into two whole companies of Red soldiers – and we came to the country of Jeannie Macdonald. In desperation, I had taken Angus into my confidence: there could be no going back now.

Dugald planned to rest the drove on one of Young Corrie's lush grazings before tackling the long, hard pull over the eastern shoulder of Ben Nevis. Come to think of it, John Cameron – 'Young Corrie', the King of the Drovers – was perhaps the first 'self-made man' I ever encountered.

A wiry, hawk-nosed fellow, Corrie was rushing about sizing up the cattle gathered at this crossroads of droveways, striking bargains. He spotted me at Dugald's side, and fixed me with the most penetrating pair of eyes I had ever seen – that is, of course, before I encountered those of the old Pasha, Mohammed Ali. Corrie's appraisal seemed to last for ever. At last he nodded. 'A true son of Ruairidh Og,' he said. 'A true Macleod,' and he clapped hands with Dugald on the deal for the stance rent.

On the other side of the Spean I could already see the scattered buildings of Tirnadris, the home of the Macdonald family, which had so long figured in my dreams. The moment the drove was settled in, Angus, who had worked out some story for Dugald, gave me the nod, and I was away over the river to meet my destiny.

*

Tirnadris – 'the Land of the Briars' – lies on the lower slopes of Meall Luath, which means 'the Mountain of the Ashes', and rises steadily upwards from the northern bank of the River Spean. I marched towards it, my aunts' plaid over my shoulder, a sprig of juniper stuck in my bonnet, my mother's silver 'heirloom' buttons gleaming in the late afternoon sun. I swung my arms with a confidence I did not feel, particularly when I saw that the Macdonald family house was a 'white house' of neatly squared stones, with a well-fitting slate roof, as befitted a gentleman of Clan Keppoch.

The house seemed deserted. But the front door was open, and, just inside, a little table with a vase of fresh flowers extended a welcome. I accepted it, and was awed by the sight of a wooden dresser which bore many rows of plates. Through a doorway I could see a handsome birch-wood bedstead – and it was then I became aware of a woman about my mother's age, sitting at a table, writing intently.

Suddenly she dropped the pen, leaned back in her chair.

'Well,' she said, 'and who are you?'

I knew at once that she must be Jeannie's mother.

'I'm Donald,' I said, and then, recalling my father's dictum that any Macleod was worth three thieving Macdonalds, Lords of the Isles though they might be, I added: 'I am Donald Macleod, drover, on my way to Falkirk Tryst.'

A smile flitted. 'I see that you have a good conceit of yourself, Donald Macleod.'

It was almost as if she had been expecting me. She herself, I knew, hailed from Skye and was of the Kingsburgh Macdonalds. Like my mother, she was a second wife, and twenty years younger than her husband, Alasdair of the Keppoch Macdonalds. Jeannie was the youngest of her four daughters.

'They are away up the shieling,' she said. She laughed. 'Maybe you should unfurl the fairy flag of Dunvegan!'

She turned back to writing. 'This I must get off this night to my man's brother in America. Have you not heard of North Carolina?'

Who had not, ever since Flora, the Prince's saviour, and Alan Macdonald took themselves off there years after the '45. But Jeannie's mother wasn't expecting an answer. Her head was already bent over the letter again. I was dismissed, even as her daughter had dismissed me.

I took the path that led across the mountainside, climbing slowly up to the shieling. Here I suppose I should explain that a shieling means as much to a Highlander as an oasis to a Bedou. It is a life-giver, a high mountain meadow to which the black cattle are moved each spring when the snow melts and the early sun brings out succulent green grass. It wasn't only the cattle that migrated – half the family went too, most of the younger women, camping up there in the shieling huts, milking the cows, making butter and cheese, and savouring the new warmth and the freedom, the annual miracle.

As I climbed higher, leaping the streams that rushed down the mountainside to swell the Spean, my spirits rose the way they always do at shieling time: a joyous relief after the long, hard winter, a time of bursting out, as the buds burst out on the trees.

Above me as I climbed I could hear faint girlish laughter. I could see nothing. My excitement mounting, my ears were alert for the voice that had haunted me for so many months. I climbed on. Panting heavily, I came over the shoulder of the mountain. Skirts hitched up high, arms on each other's shoulders, two girls were standing upright in a wide wooden tub, their bare legs thrusting up and down so lustily that water and soap suds spilled over the sides of the tub, flecking the grass. Skirts, petticoats, blouses and aprons were spread out over the heather to dry.

Then one of them caught sight of me and stopped dead, almost causing her partner to fall out of the tub. They stared, open-mouthed. I couldn't take my eyes off those long, dripping thighs, halted in mid-flight.

Then a cow bellowed near at hand. The spell was broken, and I was able to steal a glance around the shieling.

Twenty or thirty kyloes were drifting about, grazing contentedly. Roofed with turfs, three or four low shieling huts were spread around the mountain meadow. There was a wooden churn and a cheese press in front of one of them and behind these a girl sat on a three-legged stool. I couldn't see her face, because her head was pressed against the cow's flank. But her hair was raven black and there was a red ribbon in it and there was something about the way she held her body.

Without a word I left the washer girls and went over. She was singing very softly, as Highland girls do to woo the cows to let down their milk. I recognised a well-loved Jacobite song which I will try to render into English.

> Morag dear! Thy lovely locks
> Are to me a constant snare,
> Though I would not seek to wed thee,
> I would ever be beside thee,
> And if good luck again should send thee,
> Only death, my love, will part us.

As I approached, the voice grew stronger. It was *she*, the scourge of the Macleods, angry no longer, totally absorbed in this old Jacobite song – 'Morag' being code for the Prince, of course.

Sensing an alien presence, the cow turned its head. She spun round then on the milking-stool and – astonishing creature – resumed our exchange at the point it had broken off at the waulking party.

'And where,' she demanded, 'were the Macleods when the Prince raised his standard at Glenfinnan?'

The masterful words I had prepared evaporated. No hiding the shame; the Macleod had abandoned the Prince – and worse. How could I deny it?

'You hanged my great-uncle at Carlisle,' she went on, mercilessly.

She was raking over the embers of Culloden as if it had all happened yesterday. Somehow I had to stop her heaping this monstrous burden of guilt upon me. But then I became aware that in the year or more that had passed since the waulking, Jeannie had developed. Her aggressive words were strangely at odds with the swelling softness beneath the plain milkmaid dress.

I pulled myself together. 'The Macleod tricked us,' I protested. 'He marched our men off from Dunvegan with white cockades in our bonnets. We thought we were away to fight for the Prince.'

Now I had my counter-attack ready. 'The Macdonalds ran at Culloden – they ran for their lives. They left old Keppoch to die from his wounds. They ran from the moor, my father told me.'

She whipped round furiously. 'Bi sàmhach! Shut up!' The cow complained as she pulled more violently on its teats. 'You don't know what you're talking about! We were on the wrong flank at

Culloden. Our place is on the right flank – where we fought with Bruce at Bannockburn. The fools put us on the left.'

In this curious historical courtship (which my English readers may find hard to credit) it was Bannockburn, 24 June 1314, that brought us together, for there I could claim that the Macleods had fought with Robert the Bruce too; and after that, thanks to my father's schooling, I threw in that seven hundred Macleods had died, far from home, fighting for Charles Stewart at Worcester against the Sasannach pretender, Oliver Cromwell.

The moment seemed full of promise, but, alas, was ruined by the arrival of Jeannie's two 'washer' sisters, demurely dressed now, come to inspect the only male on the shieling. They were soon followed by Isobel, the eldest sister, who eyed me with some suspicion.

'Who sent you up here?' she demanded. 'Has my mother seen you?'

Drawing myself up to my full height, which was even then considerable, I announced that I was a drover going down to the Falkirk Tryst and had business concerning their cattle. This seemed to amuse Isobel for some reason.

'Your mother was writing a long letter,' I added. 'A letter to North Carolina in America.'

This news seemed to excite them. Jeannie abandoned the cow. 'So she's done it at last. She's writing to Uncle Alan.'

Ignoring me, the sisters huddled around Jeannie in animated speculation. At last Jeannie took pity on me. 'It is a very, very important letter, you see, Donald' – the first time she had called me by my name! 'It is to my great-uncle in North Carolina, my Great-Uncle Alan. He has five hundred acres of wheat and peas and corn and four hundred black cattle. Oh, and six blackamoors.'

Isobel chipped in, 'He says it's the best poor man's country in the world.'

'He is seventy years old,' explained Jeannie, 'and he begs us to join him. He has been begging us for years.'

Like almost everyone on Skye, I had heard much of North Carolina. By this time it was almost a part of our landscape, a warm, luxuriant place, seen through a Skye mist, a sort of Tìr nan Og, that Land of Youth to which all good Gaels are transported when they die. Out there, I knew, even the black slaves who tapped the pine-trees to extract tar and turpentine spoke the Gaelic, although Campelltown on the Fear river had been renamed Fayetteville in honour of the French general who fought for the American rebels.

'But they are rebels!' I protested. Jeannie shot me a glance of total scorn. 'They have no king.' A country without a king, neither Stewart nor Hanoverian, I found incomprehensible.

'They have a president, elected by all the people. Have you not heard of a *republic*?'

It was a curious conversation, high up there in that mountain meadow, but this girl – my girl – had plainly discovered America and was eager to impart her intoxicating knowledge.

'Have you not read their Declaration of Independence?' She flung back her dark tresses, and began to recite: 'All men are created equal and are endowed by their Creator with certain unalienable rights.' I was pleased to note she stumbled a little over that long English word. The sisters, evidently knowing Jeannie in this mood, had faded away, leaving me her sole audience. A rapt audience, I confess.

'Have you not read the works of Thomas Paine – *The Rights of Man . . . Common Sense*?'

'I cannot read the Sasannach tongue.'

'I shall teach you,' she said, and plainly meant it. She was like that – still is.

It was a new world inside the shieling hut, warm and intimate, the rough stone walls roseate from the peat fire at the centre. Suddenly I found myself in the position of the honoured guest, sitting with the four sisters around the fire, eating a meal of *brochan*, barley bannocks, butter and fresh-made cheese. I imagine I made the best of my unaccustomed position, illustrating my prowess as a drover, boasting of my acquaintance with the great John Cameron, working up to an account of my epic rescue of Morag with the aid of my dog, Donald, during the swimming of the kyle.

Through the light veil of blue smoke ascending to the centre chimney, I could see that Jeannie's dark eyes were glistening. I had touched the springs of Jacobite aspiration, the lost, tragic dreams of our people, even now not wholly surrendered.

Then she poured out the extraordinary and moving story of

how her Great-Uncle Alan had come to leave the Highlands and
settle in North Carolina – and I began to understand why she so
hated Macleod, who had thrown in his lot with the English. After
Culloden Lord Saville, the Butcher's best butcher, first burned
down the dead Keppoch's house, and then took his troops through
the glens, hanging, raping the women before their menfolk's eyes,
taking off the cattle, laying waste the country. Men were flogged
to death and babies torn from their mothers' arms and skewered
on soldiers' bayonets. So Jeannie said.

Great-Uncle Alan Macdonald had taken to the hills with his
family, driving a few cows before them, skulking for weeks in the
woods, hiding in caves whenever the Red soldiers were sighted,
living on fish taken from the streams. A lad of ten, Alan had
somehow got separated from the family. He was picked up by
Red soldiers, wearing his plaid.

'Highland dress' had been forbidden: the English were set on
teaching the Highland savages a lesson they would never forget.
Alan was 'lotted' and drew the short straw. He was indentured
to a ship's captain, who hoped to make a profit selling his indentures to some settler in Virginia.

Then Alan's luck turned. When the ship reached Virginia he was
spotted by a Mr Macdonald, a tobacco merchant, who bought his
indentures and released him to join his Uncle Murdoch, who,
transported earlier, had found his way to Campelltown in North
Carolina. Murdoch and his nephew Alan built up their fortunes
together in the new land.

Highlanders are like Arabs – when the stories start, they flow
on like the Nile in flood. I capped the tale of Alan Macdonald
with that of my hero and namesake, Sergeant Donald Macleod,
of the 78th and the Black Watch, in whose blanket the dying
Wolfe had been wrapped at Quebec, and of brother Dugald, our
topsman, who had enlisted in the 71st, Fraser's Highlanders, as a
lad of seventeen, and had whipped the American rebels at
Savannah in Georgia.

'And ran up the white flag and got taken prisoner at Yorktown,'
snapped Jeannie, suddenly recovering her old waspishness.

I fought back. 'The Americans offered them land if they would
go over to their side,' I said, repeating one of Dugald's tales. 'Not
a single man in the regiment accepted.'

'More fools they,' she said.

By this time the fire had burned low and two of the girls were nodding off. But when I rose to take my leave, I was astonished to find that Jeannie would not hear of it. It was dangerous going down the mountain at night, she said. I must stay. Isobel frowned, then shrugged.

The girls set to raking out the embers of the peat fire at the centre of the hut, leaving a radiant warm circle of hard-trod earth. Upon this they heaped armfuls of heather, and on this cosy, fragrant and springy bed we five slept that night, or at least some of us did – the girls wrapped in their blankets, me in my plaid.

It was she herself who indicated my place, on the outer rim, but on her side of the circle. The hut was small, now illuminated only by the faintest glimmer from the fire, and, as the night wore on, and outside the cows pulled fitfully at the grass, my hand reached out, and came to rest on the slope of Jeannie's hip, and I found myself astonished by its sweet precipitousness, bodying forth in the darkness a whole secret world of excitement and wonder. In her sleep she must have moved nearer, and, as if self-willed, my hand continued its stealthy, inch by inch, exploration of the *meallan* and corries and straths and glens of Jeannie, gaining in boldness until I was deliciously terrified that she would awake, cry out, and shame me. But she just moved gently, sleeping on. (Today, of course, I am amused – touched – at my naïvety.)

A strange night it was, teetering between the sublime and the ridiculous, the ecstatic and the embarrassing, and yet how far-reaching in its effects on my life. I veritably believe it would require the author of *The Thousand and One Nights* to do it justice. Since Scheherazade is no longer with us, I can only do my poor best.

I slept at last, and shortly afterwards found myself being shaken awake by Jeannie, who had already washed in the burn. In deference to my drover status I was offered a brimming morning dram. The harridan of the waulking party had vanished. Promising to begin my English lessons on our return trip from Falkirk Tryst, she herself took me down the mountain on the first stage of my journey back to Corrie's stance on the other side of the Spean.

She lingered a moment on the way down to pick a small spray of *mòthan*, the tiny delicate white flowers called in English 'fairy flax'. As we came behind a great boulder, which concealed us from others, she seized me and kissed me fiercely, the tiny white flowers pressed between our lips.

Thus we parted.

It was only some days later I learned from my brother Angus, the piper, that *mòthan* flowers, gripped between lovers' lips, ensure eternal faithfulness.

4 The Tryst

By the time I got back, panting, to the stance, the drove had been waiting to move off for half an hour. I had never seen Dugald so mad. 'Never again!' he said. 'Never again will I take such a silly young puppy droving.' But Angus gave me a wink behind his back, and my self-esteem, already wildly inflated, soared. I made a point of keeping well out of Dugald's way, though.

The trouble was that prices at Falkirk looked like being the best for years, according to Corrie, and the toughest part of the journey was still ahead of us. As we were about to move off Angus spotted an old woman in a black shawl who had somehow got into the middle of the drove. She was plaiting a Mungo's knot on Morag's tail. Muttering to herself, she circled several cows and disappeared before anyone could reach her. I felt sure I'd seen her, fleetingly, up on the shieling. Mungo's knots are well thought of in the Highlands as protection against the Evil Eye. That morning, despite Dugald's filthy temper, the future seemed rosy.

The mood stayed with me through the first hours of our ascent through the turbulent sea of wild and desolate mountains that swirl around the cloud-veiled summit of Ben Nevis. Sombre grey walls of rock towered over us as the gorge grew narrower, penning us in, men and beasts alike. Now and again there would be a jagged break in the rock wall and, craning my neck, I could see the feet of the high mountains where Jeannie's Great-Uncle Alan, with his brothers and sisters, had skulked in those terrible months after Culloden. I began to see why she had rejected chiefs and kings and turned to the writings of that 'notorious sedition-monger and atheist', Tom Paine – I quote Mr Macaskill, the Bracadale schoolmaster.

'Keep them moving! Keep them moving!'

In my mind's eye I see Dugald running back. A young stirk at the end of my section has slipped on steep scree, almost pushing two other beasts over the edge plunging down to the River Leacach, tearing along far below. The animals bellow in panic. Soon we are in swirling cloud. We couldn't see more than three beasts ahead. The cattle's coats were sopping mops; the cold struck to the bone.

Then Angus took down his pipes and stepped out in front of the drove and gave us some of the tunes learned at his mother's knee: Macleod's Salute, then ''S Fhada Mar Seo a Tha Sinn' – 'We Are Too Long in This Condition' ... The cattle picked up their hoofs at the sharp, bright sound coming out of the mist and the drovers took new heart. I saw why the English generals had classified the pipes as a 'weapon of war' and forbidden them.

Then Angus abandoned the classics of the MacCrimmons and the notes that came drifting down the long column of labouring kyloes had a familiar sound and I recognised the song that had been sweeping the Highlands, 'Dol a Dh'iarraidh an Fhortain do North Carolina ...' – 'Going to Seek a Fortune in North Carolina ...'

It was up there, oddly, that for the first time, the reality of that distant dreamland across the sea took hold of me. I heard again the Macdonald sisters' excited talk of their Great-Uncle Alan's invitation: my world was expanding by leaps and bounds that day. I tried the tune out in my head: it went with a swing. The momentous thought struck me that I, too, Donald Ban, might actually go there – go with Jeannie. You could say, I suppose, that I was falling to the 'emigration fever' so despised by my father.

The Gaelic imagination flies as high as the eagles, and, as I know to my cost, may plunge to earth as swiftly. On the long descent to Kingshouse, pacing and encouraging the kyloes, covering ten or eleven miles between dusk and dawn each day, I had more than enough time to give it full rein. Even as we forded the Rath, the icy water biting the cattle's bellies, I saw myself lying with Jeannie on some palm-fringed beach, her young breasts only half covered by her black tresses as, book in hand, she taught me the Sasannach tongue. Day after day, as our drove crossed the tongue of land between lochs Eidle Mor and Eidle Beag, as we risked crossing the River Leven or slithered down the Devil's

Staircase by the old military road, I rejoiced in this bright burgeoning new world across the Atlantic and fiercely hugged my secret to myself.

Set down near the top of the old military road through Glencoe, the Kingshouse Inn is a welcome landmark for all droving men, offering food, shelter and a dram or two to fortify them against the abominations of Rannoch Moor. So desolate is the spot that the English government actually pays the landlord to keep the place open, and to keep an eye no doubt on the Highland 'savages'.

Here we met again my brother Peter; having disposed profitably of most of his kegs, he was now busy cementing a deal with the Government's landlord, who, being a Highlandman, did not see why the English Excise should benefit by the product of *our* fields, *our* peats, *our* sweat and cunning.

Dugald found, displayed on the parlour wall, a notice from that same Government ordering all reservists to report to the nearest recruiting office on account of the renewal of the war against Bonaparte.

At Kingshouse we were joined by the droves from Moidart and Ardnamurchan and Mull which had come through the pass of Glencoe. When we reached the other side of Rannoch we would be hailed by the drovers from Ross and Sutherland who had come by Wade's road over Corrieyarick, joining the dark stream that flowed down from Inverness through Strath Spey.

I reckon it was from the drovers in that old drovers' inn at Inveroran – a place famed for the number and lushness of its stances – that I had my first real lesson in the geography of my country, and the world beyond it. Crouching over the fire, resting their battered feet, drovers from all over Scotland spooned warm porridge from their wooden bowls, while all manner of news came drifting out of the fug of tobacco smoke and whisky fumes and peat smoke that hung about them: news of flooded rivers, and animals stricken by the murrain, stories of evictions and some new insolence of that French bullfrog, of the pigheaded Thomas Telford, the Lowland engineer, busy ruining the drove roads, laying down metalled surfaces.

I forget how the subject of America came up, but it did – as it always does. Some sang America's praises as the land of freedom and plenty. Others denounced it as a snare and delusion, as my father did. (Had not a recently returned Minister of the Church pronounced the people there to be 'two-footed beasts'?)

A drover from Moidart who knew that Dugald had served five years in America with Fraser's appealed to him to settle the matter.

Dugald did not hesitate. 'Scum!' he said. 'A rabble – you should have seen the way they ran from us at Savannah.'

This was too much for Angus. 'So why did you haul down the Union flag at Yorktown? You plied your arms for a rabble? Seven thousand of you – for a rabble?'

Dugald looked daggers. 'They wouldn't fight like men. They scrambled up trees and shot us in the back. *Sgùm!* Scum, I tell you, scum!'

'They licked you, brother. Knocked Cornwallis's wig flying, the pompous English bugger!'

'It wasn't them that beat us. It was the French – the French fleet that cut us off. We were down to seven bullets.'

Angus tossed off another dram. 'They licked you.' The old rivalry was never far below the surface.

Dugald played his usual last card. 'They offered every man of us free land out there. Not a man took it . . .'

All at once I heard my voice: 'Why didn't you go to North Carolina?'

Dugald spun round and stared at me. 'And how old is it you are now, Donald? And not a word of English in you! I knew the rebels before you were born, boy. The off-scourings of the world . . .'

Pandemonium broke out around the fire. Every drover, it seemed, had his tale of these people who had discarded both lairds and kings, just as every drover had his emigration story. I heard yet again of the *Fortune*, which had sailed from the Clyde with two hundred emigrants and only two cooking-pots between them – and of Peter Williamson, a fourteen-year-old from Aberdeen, sold in Virginia for £16 as a bond servant, working his way up to be proprietor of a great plantation.

'And where is he now?' yelled Dugald. 'Why, back in Aberdeen!'

He scrabbled around in his pack and brought out a faded screw of blue cloth. He flattened it on the ground, pressing out the creases, revealing several fragmentary red stripes, a phalanx of white stars.

'Their misbegotten bastard flag,' he yelled, well gone. 'Tore it down with my own two hands!' I was shocked. I had never seen my brother in that state before. And in a strange way that torn bit of blue cloth stirred me. As a flag, white stars, red stripes, it held for me – dare I say it? – a magic even greater than the fairy flag of Dunvegan. If all went well, I might even live my life under it.

A fiddler appeared from nowhere, and Angus joined him, and in minutes the mood had changed and the company was roaring out well-loved drover songs:

> 'Tis a fool I was that I ever did,
> 'Tis a fool I was that I ever did,
> 'Tis a fool I was that I ever did
> Go for a walk with a drover grey.

From this droving classic of love betrayed we progressed lustily through 'The Bold Drover' and 'The Drover Boy' and many others. Until, as the drams did their work, the moment came for the Lassie – 'The Lassie of Moidart':

> I lost a stirk on the shores of Loch Linnhe,
> Two stots at Salen Loch Sunart;
> O'er by Loch Shiel I lost my heart
> To Jean, a lassie of Moidart.

Jean ... Jeannie ... sung with feeling in those lusty voices, the lines echoed in my head, uncannily matching my mood in the aftermath of that night in the shieling. Boyhood innocence was sloughed; I trembled on the verge of a bottomless ocean.

> A-driving of cattle to tryst and to pasture
> Of her I'm dreaming a-wakin';
> Her vision is before me aye –
> It's sleep that has me forsaken ...

All of a sudden I was afraid that my face might betray me. I crept out to the place where the drove was cudding by the lake, wrapped my plaid around me, and gave myself up to 'dreaming a-wakin';

again my hand was over the swell of her hip and her black tresses were weaving wildly about her.

Dugald, I remember, jibbed at the two pennies a beast they wanted for crossing the Forth Bridge, so we took the drove across the river at Frew, where the Prince crossed, Stirling Castle rearing on its crag behind us.

Up in the Highlands the drove had grazed on the hoof where it listed, nosing out the fine herbs; but down here the ever-swelling river of bellowing beasts trod hard roads, pressed against fences, and every blade of grass was owned and held to account, the last penny extracted. I was shocked at this new view of the world. You could say that the Falkirk Tryst, too, bulked large in my early education. I can see it in my mind's eye still: the vast, broom-covered expanse of Stenhousemuir, a tossing sea of black cattle, dealers moving among them, prodding, sizing up, making bids, fierce arguments suddenly collapsing with the clap of palm against palm.

We cut ten good beasts out of our drove, putting Morag in the middle where the oddity of her horns might escape attention, and out of the throng stepped a stocky little Yorkshireman, an old customer of our father who owned many acres of fine grazing at Malham, down over the border. He agreed a price with Dugald in no time, and we went over to the tents to seal the bargain with a dram.

It seemed to me that for every drover who had earned his money by honest toil there were at least six people whose only object was to deprive him of it as quickly as possible. Cheek by jowl with the marquees of the Bank of Scotland and the Falkirk Bank and the British Linen Company were the tents of a thimbler, besieged by drovers eager to place their bets, a team of acrobats, and six young women dancing lewdly in dresses of which our Minister would certainly not have approved. One of them, I noticed, was making bold eyes at my brother Angus.

A spirited tune on the pipes, drifting on over the heads of the crowd set feet tapping. 'Cabar Fèidh!' muttered Angus. It was the marching tune of the Seaforths. The crowd round the tents broke apart, drawn across by the bright sound. Pennants streaming from their drones, a dozen regimental pipers paraded round a square. On a box in the middle, a scarlet-jacketed recruiting sergeant in the Mackenzie tartan was in full cry. He had the silver stag's antlers on his bonnet.

'Come on now, all ye young *spracks*, step up an tak a dram wi me!' He waved a whisky bottle. 'General Mackenzie Fraser himself invites every brave drover that's sound in wind and limb to join him in a dram.'

He looked around anxiously for some sign of encouragement, but received none. People had had enough. More than enough. Generation after generation of Highlandmen had given their blood for the British Empire – and what had they to show for it? Expulsion from their crofts. Clan lands turned over to sheep.

The sergeant squared his shoulders and tried again.

'Now my bold lads, ye'll know Bonaparty is mustering in Boulogne and says he's coming to get us. We'll let him have a Highland charge, boys. We'll drown the bastard, eh, lads?'

He looked around again for some response.

He waved his broadsword over his head, and nearly fell off the box. The crowd laughed. The poor fellow was getting desperate, 'Cabar Fèidh!' he yelled. 'See the world at His Majesty's expense! Join the heroes of Egypt and Hindustan! A twelve-guinea bounty, paid direct into your hand!' He gave a grotesque wink. 'And mark my words, this red coat fetches the girls!'

His voice hung in the air. Suddenly, from the back of the crowd, a voice: 'Mackenzie let the Sheep in. So let the Sheep fight for him!'

'Baa-baa baa-baa,' a raucous voice added.

'Baa baaaa-baaaa . . .' The drovers amused themselves with a storm of bleating, sharp, flat, long and staccato, in every key.

A few stepped up to take the proffered dram. But not one took the King's shilling.

On the moor new droves were shaping under new drovers, who would take them through the Lowland country and down over the border into England. By way of Solway Firth and Carlisle, by Selkirk and Hawick and over the end of the Cheviots, the lifeblood of the Highlands was coursing down into England, into Cumberland and Lancashire and rich, beef-hungry towns like Halifax and Leeds and Bradford, and onto the broad acres and lush grass of

Norfolk, a world beyond my ken which the Sasannach called civilisation.

But on that last day on Stenhousemuir it was a different sort of 'tryst' that was occupying my mind. On the return trip she had promised to give me my English lesson. Dugald was bidden to Stirling Castle to register as a reservist; Peter was off again on Grandma Beaton's business along the whisky roads. I would be making the return trip past the Macdonald farm alone with Angus and the dogs. I could not have hoped for a better ally. I could still feel the soft tickle of the *mòthan* flowers held between her lips when we parted.

5   The Handfasting

Unencumbered by the drove, we crossed the Forth again at Frew on the long trail home. Ahead of us two black-and-white collies marched side by side steadily northward.

'See those two dogs,' said Angus, 'you know where they're off to? They're on their way to Sutherland. The drovers – they take the boat from Leith to Dornoch. Their dogs *walk*. It's all of two hundred miles. The innkeepers know to feed them on the way.'

The sight of those purposeful dogs advancing confidently across Scotland caught hold of my imagination. Perhaps it was because, coming at that particular moment, they reflected a self-possession and capability I pretended to, but was far from feeling.

Had Jeannie's sudden change in attitude towards me been real? Or was it just one of those unaccountable, passing whims I had noticed in my sisters? Would she laugh in my face for taking a single, playful kiss so seriously? A girl like that must have had plenty of suitors.

I remember Angus yelling at me as we negotiated the bogs and lochans and peat-hags of Rannoch Moor. I had let my garron stray into a bog. Hope flickered as I extricated it. Was she really likely to have forgotten me – when she'd sent that old crone to tie a Mungo's knot on Morag's tail? But what *proof* did I have that it was she who had sent her?

So it went on, round and round. By the time we had got to the summit of the Leacach Pass and my promised land lay below me, the triumphant and delicious scenes I had so often played over in my head were in shreds.

The English have this saying: 'Fortune favours the brave.' Well, I wasn't particularly brave, but fortune favoured me that day –

outrageously. Just as Angus and I and our dogs trotted up to the inn at Spean Bridge, mid-afternoon, the Inverness coach pulled in. The ostler ran out to lower the steps, and the passengers, fussing with their parcels, began to descend. The last out was Jeannie Macdonald.

She was wearing her go-to-school coat and bonnet, a satchel of books dangling from her arm. As if in a dream, I watched her making her farewells to the passengers with whom she had travelled from Inverness. Then she set off briskly in the direction of her home.

I came out of my trance. Jumping off my pony, dragging it behind me, I ran after her.

'I . . . I . . . I've come for my English lesson,' I blurted.

She swung round, startled. Then her face lit up. 'Donald! So it's you . . . so you came.'

She hesitated, but only for a moment. 'We will go up to the shieling. It will be quiet up there – for the lesson.'

Clumsily, I helped her onto my garron, and we set off. Apparently there'd been an outbreak of smallpox at Inverness, and the school had been shut, the pupils sent home. Jeannie's parents were ignorant of this, but she did not seem in any hurry to go home to tell them.

'Where are your brothers?' she said suddenly.

'There's only Angus – and he's away to a meeting.'

Naïve as I was, and overawed as ever by her self-possession, I began to wonder whether an English lesson was all she had in mind. I was well aware – who wasn't? – that shielings were at this time of the year a frequent cause of scandal amongst the unco guid. Even as a small boy of eight or ten I had observed with keen curiosity the sniggering between older lads, conducted just outside my hearing; the gigglings and behind-the-hand whisperings among the girls that marked this time of the year, while the ministers in their pulpits fulminated against the sins of the flesh.

Most of the black cattle had by now gone back down the hill. Up on the shieling, only a couple of dairy-maids hung on. But blue smoke still curled from a shieling hut.

'It will be warm and quiet in there,' she said, tethering the garron. 'We can concentrate for the lesson.' She crept through the low doorway, motioning me to follow. I couldn't understand how she managed to stay so cool – she was only a year my senior

– even casual, as she embarked with deliberation on the promised lesson. I looked on, awed, in the dimness. She took off her school bonnet and placed it carefully on the ground, loosened her hair so that the black tresses rippled down her back, gleaming darkly in the faint light from door and chimney. Taking the books from her satchel, she selected a small, well-thumbed volume.

I took it, self-consciously, and stared at the faded gilt words that ran across the cover. They meant nothing to me. I was as a blind man and she was sighted. Leaning across, she ran a finger over the words. 'The – Rights – of – Man,' she read. The finger jumped on: 'by – Thomas – Paine.'

She translated for me: *Còraichean nan Daoine*, and then repeated the English.

Ignorant I might be, but I'd heard of him. Out of this strange schoolgirl's satchel came a notorious work, outlawed by the English government, denounced from the pulpits of the Kirk. And this was the book she had chosen to teach me the Sasannach tongue.

She was pointing to the dedication, reading the words slowly and clearly: 'To George Washington, President of the United States'.

George Washington, too, I had heard of from Mr Macaskill, our Bracadale schoolmaster. 'Preshident,' I parroted.

'Fear-riaghlaidh,' she explained, 'Man of government.'

I felt I was becoming entangled in a mass of waving sea-tangle and struck out to save myself. 'Mr Macaskill says Tom Paine is a Godless atheist, a Jacobin. He says his books should be burned.'

She was furious with me. 'Lies! All lies! The donkey's never read him.'

She snatched the book from my hand and riffled through it, found a page, and read. 'Every religion is good that teaches man to be good.' She translated it into the Gaelic. 'So how can he be an atheist?'

Her blood was up now, the way it was at the waulking. Few beginners in English can have received a stranger and more passionate introduction to the English language, ranging from the equality of men to the vanity of titles – dispensed with in America, it seemed.

For a while Jeannie's adolescent political passion and my bewilderment at the new worlds opening before me prevailed over our close propinquity, in the dimness of the hut, as she strove to imprint the English words on my fuddled brain. Then I became warmly aware of a breast thrusting against my ribs, and felt below a pulsing and a stiffening which would not be denied. I flushed scarlet and was thankful for the dimness, while Jeannie, purporting to notice nothing, continued to render the English word for 'aristocracy' into the Gaelic.

Then she rose and went out of the hut, leaving me in turmoil. (Later, it occurred to me that the reason she went out was to get rid of the two dairy-maids.) As it was, I waited in mounting apprehension.

She reappeared briskly, carrying an armful of fir-candles which she placed carefully about the hut on flat stones. The sun was slipping down behind the dark slab of the mountain, and in a few minutes it would be dark. Once again she ruled that it was too late for me to make the descent, and now there was no elder sister to gainsay her. There was a sort of routine now, a reassuring inevitability for which I was grateful. Once again we raked out the embers of the peat fire, leaving a circle of warm, much-trodden earth. Again we heaped this circle with armfuls of springy, sweet-scented heather. Again we lay together on this simple bed, and, as the lighted fir-candles smoked and flared and flickered and filled the hut with their resinous scent, my hand again climbed the hillock of her hip and – without the sisters' guardian presence – continued at leisure its explorations of this yet undiscovered continent, so rich in its protuberances and declivities, islets and secret oases, and her hand took mine with mounting urgency to guide me through the portals of delight with the same purposefulness that she had showed a little earlier, leading me through my first steps in English grammar.

The Highland plaid has many virtues, particularly as the nights grow colder. My grandmother's fine plaid was soon accommodating two tremulous and urgent bodies on that heather bed. Beneath it Jeannie's nipples seemed to bore into my chest as I clung to her like a drowning man, the thunder of the Minch in my ears. She cried out loud and her hand came down, and recharged my thrustings and all at once it was over and a great warm wave engulfed me, and the world, I knew, would never be the same again.

My readers will no doubt wonder how, sixty years and four

wives on, I recall this occasion – and with such clarity. But as my story unfolds, the more perceptive may understand that in those few hours in the shieling hut lay the beginning and the end, the alpha and the omega, of Donald Macleod, the key to his life, strange and eventful as that has been. And if my recollection appears preternaturally sharp, it is because I have been over all this hundreds of times, in many climes and situations: in the barrack room at Fort George, on sentry duty on the Rock, in the dungeons of Cairo's Citadel, in the Mameluke camp at Minya, opening Belzoni's Tomb on the West Bank, and – God help us – in the holy city of Mecca itself.

The last fir-candle flickered, then guttered out in a long curl of black smoke, and beneath the plaid, still now and at ease, we kissed with a lingering tenderness. Then, at last, she rose and kindled two more 'candles' and set them on two stones. They spluttered and flared, and then burned with a steady yellow light which gleamed on her tumbled black hair and picked out the curve of her naked back as she confided her dream of the new life of liberty and plenty awaiting her and her sisters under the Carolina sun.

Over there, she told me, the black cattle were twice the size of ours, and a few yards of land would produce more than a whole acre in Skye, and the Scottish merchants shipping goods up and down the Fear river grew more prosperous every year. According to Uncle Alan, there was a great call for teachers from the Old Country. Jeannie, it appeared, had already mapped out a brilliant career for herself as a teacher of English and Latin.

Perhaps she caught the look of dismay in my eyes, for she added, hurriedly, 'Of course you will come with us, Dhòmhnaill, mo chridhe' – as if all this were already arranged. In token reassurance, she lay down again beside me under the plaid. Already I could feel the warm Carolina sun on my back. Revitalised, we flew together again, I throwing back the plaid to devour with my eyes as well as my body.

Towards dawn, I finally dropped off to sleep – and saw myself and Jeannie kneeling on the penitent stool before the elders of the kirk while the charges – deception, lust, fornication, hochmagandy – were read out before the congregation.

'*No! no!*' I cried, as the flames of Hell began to lick around my feet.

I woke to find Jeannie looking down at me curiously. Still half in my nightmare, I spilled out my fears. Guilt lay crushingly upon me: I was a child of John Knox, remember, and for him even paradise is bleak, totally unprovided with the Koran's cool streams and voluptuous houris.

'Supposing the milk-maids tell ... your mother ... my father ...'

She listened to my ravings patiently. 'I know,' she said at last, 'we will be handfasted. It is as good as getting wed before the Minister.'

I found my bonnet and girt my plaid about me, and Jeannie put back on her go-to-school dress and hat. A pale moon still hung in the sky as we crept out of the hut. Two shaggy shapes came out of the morning mist, moving inquiringly towards us – a few kyloes remained on the shieling. Jeannie pointed to a solitary upright stone I hadn't noticed before, just visible on the far side of the shieling.

'That's it. That's the handfasting stone. That's where my Aunt Marion was married to John Mackay from Sutherland.'

As we drew nearer I saw that the monolith had a hole through the middle. A curiously smooth hole. Jeannie took command of the situation. Thrusting her arm through the hole, she motioned me to take up my position on the other side. She took my hand and gripped it.

'Now you from your side.' I gripped her slender fingers so firmly that she winced.

'Now you say: "I declare Donald Macleod and Jeannie Macdonald to be man and wife, as long as we both shall live." '

I mumbled sheepishly: 'I declare Donald and Jeannie to be man and wife.'

'As long as we both shall live,' she insisted.

'They shall be one flesh,' she went on, relentlessly.

'They shall be one flesh ...'

The first rays of the sun were coming up behind Meall Luath. We turned, and, hand in hand, led the pony slowly down the path, shrinking from the moment of parting we knew must soon come.

A light mist hung like lace over the mountainside. Dew-drops quivered on the purple bells of the heather; starry saxifrage twinkled beside the stream. Every detail stood out needle-sharp; it was as if I was seeing it all for the first time. A hare started up at our feet and bounced down the hillside. Normally, like any lad, I would have thrown a stone at it. But not this morning; this morning I overflowed with compassion for all God's creatures.

We became conscious that we had not eaten, that we were ravenous. From her satchel Jeannie rooted out a small wedge of cheese left over from the coach journey down from Inverness. I spied a patch of bilberries beside the stream, the bloom on them so delicate it seemed sacrilegious to pick and eat them. We did, though, gulping them down with the cheese, sitting together on a ledge of dark-brown rock, its felspar crystals glittering in the rising sun.

Now we had to face the practical world – at least, Jeannie had. Already she was scheming how best to break the news of our handfasting to her father, persuading him that I must go with them to their Uncle Alan's in North Carolina, even though I was one of the treacherous Macleods.

As we dawdled down to the point where house and road came into view, I was seized by a sudden panic. There was no ring. How could we be truly married when there was nothing to show for it? We must exchange pledges.

Then I thought of the silver American dollar which, wrapped in a bit of rag, had lain for years at the bottom of my pack ever since I got it when I was eight from Red Donald, Lieutenant Dòmhnall Ruadh MacCrimmon who had come back from Canada to pipe in Macleod of Macleod, Norman, the twenty-third of the line, coming back to us from India after conquering Tipu Sultan. I got it for lifting the speckled pipe for Red Donald as he piped the Chief in, his bags bulging with the spoils of the Maharajahs. From time to time I would take out my dollar and unwrap it and look at the words around the rim. E PLURIBUS UNUM. That much Latin I knew – 'Out of many, one'.

It seemed a fair enough pledge. We had hardly been many. But now we were one. I gave the silver dollar to her.

For once she was at a loss. 'Oh, Donald, my dear, I have nothing. No pledge to give you. You'll forget me...' She was near tears.

'Never!' I said.

Below I could hear the Spean roaring along in its ravine. Suddenly, she broke loose from my clasp, and reaching into her school satchel, brought out the much-thumbed volume of *The Rights of Man*. Her name was written inside the cover, and now she added mine. 'Tom will teach you English – with my love,' she said.

I had arranged to meet Angus at the inn at Spean Bridge, but I had a long wait. Angus was one of those drovers who, as they say of sailors, have a girl in every port. The sun was high before he showed up at last, leading his pony. He eyed me curiously, then slapped me on the back. That was all. There were thirty years between us. All the same, I felt that a barrier had gone.

That night, in our overnight camp above Kinloch Hourn, after a warming dram or two, Angus blew up his pipes, and what was the first thing he played but that popular ditty: '*Dol a Dh'iarraidh an Fhortain do North Carolina*' – 'Going to Seek a Fortune in North Carolina.'

6   I Take the King's Shilling

After my return from that dawn handfasting, the old family world of Skye lost its hold on me. I did my share of the work on the croft, getting in the peats when my mother agreed the time was ripe, as the moon was on the wane, cutting our straggly grain with a sickle whenever the rain let up, grubbing up the potatoes, cutting reeds for our roof thatch. But the clock had stopped for me: I existed for the moment the drove would move off south again and life – Jeannie's and mine – would start again in new and exciting forms as yet beyond my ken.

One evening in November, sister Mairi saw my grandmother, the Reverend's widow, walking down the path, her head enveloped in a grey mist. A terrible gloom fell upon our house then – for Mairi had the 'sight', and a head in a grey mist presaged death.

Sure enough, next morning a neighbour came over with the sad news: the old lady had died in her sleep in the night.

'A cuid de Phàrras dhi,' said my father. 'May she have her share of Paradise,' adding that having maintained so excellent a *poit-dhubh* safe from the Excise for so many years, she would undoubtedly be assured of Paradise.

We laid the old lady to rest in the little island burial ground that divides the River Snizort just before it falls into the loch. A black flag flying from his pipes, Angus led the long tail of mourners over the fast-flowing stream, while the bearers bore the coffin, *deiseil*,* around the tomb-heavy island.

But, fond as I was of my grandmother, the public lamentations

---

* *deiseil*: 'sun-wise'. My father pointed out to me that in thus following the direction of the sun, the Ancient Egyptians followed the Gaels. I recall his taking

of the mourning-woman had hardly died away before in my head I was back again with Jeannie in that other, warmer, promised land over the ocean.

Sometimes when I was alone and the coast was clear, I would retrieve Tom Paine's book from its hiding-place under the stones, and run my finger over the words, trying to wrest their meaning from them so that I might pass muster in this new land where no king was needed and all men were equals. I hoped Thomas Paine would throw some light on the matter, but his words stared up at me blankly, and I dared not ask Mr Macaskill lest he hurl the 'Godless book' on the schoolroom fire.

I got some small comfort from my elder brother Rory, who, noting my close attention whenever North Carolina was mentioned, dug out his old books on emigrating to America.

'Too late for me now, boy,' he said. 'But you . . . maybe, one of these days . . .' I smiled: little did he guess how close that day was.

There was one torn and stained booklet, printed in Gaelic in Glasgow, by a man who called himself 'Scotus Americanus'. I read that so many times I can recite it almost word for word even now. 'Of all the Colonies, the most propitious for Highlanders of all degrees if they wish to live in health, ease and independence is North Carolina. The cost of taking up 640 acres of land is £10. Slaves cost from £25 to £40 and are well treated. Poor men without passage money may go as "redemptionists" at the disposal of the ship's captain . . .'

I was relieved to read that the slaves were well treated.

Turning over a pile of yellowing leaflets advertising emigrant shipping, I learned that North Carolina had the best climate, possessed the greatest variety of soils, the richest mineral resources, in America. 'Fruits, both wild and cultivated, grow to a fine state of perfection, while gold, plumbago, iron and coal are found . . .'

I was sorry for Rory, who had lost his chance of all this. Jeannie Macdonald and I together would reap where he, poor fellow, had only dreamed. 'Scotus Americanus' – I liked that name, solid and

---

me down into Belzoni's Tomb to show me the pictures of the Pharaoh Seti in his sun-boat crossing the heavens, east to west, *deiseil*, navigating the perils of the Underworld. – F.M.

reliable; Latin, too, the language of gentlemen. In America, I decided, all men would be gentlemen, even those well-treated 'slaves'.

By the time the drove was again ready to journey south, my future seemed to be bursting with promise. So much so that I was terrified I might give myself away. I parted with my mother with scarcely a word: I told myself grandly that when we were established on our broad American acres I would send for them – all of them.

Etched on my mind with peculiar sharpness is that last sight of home – the curtains of cloud hanging over the steep green sides of Macleod's Tables; the Atlantic rolling in to erupt in spume and spray over the three tall rock-stacks we called Macleod's Maidens.

Reaching Loch Oich, I idly watched the movements of a small British naval vessel taking soundings for the great canal Mr Telford was to build across the Highlands.

I dismissed it: we had better fish to fry, she and I.

But as we progressed, all too slowly, from stance to stance, I felt my exhilaration seeping away. The country we were passing through filled me with foreboding. The streams of emigrants we had met on our earlier trip had vanished. There was no smoke now in the whole of Glengarry, nothing but the Lowland shepherds and the Great Sheep.

As we approached the Braes of Lochaber panic seized me. The moment the drove was settled on Corrie's stance, I was away over the Spean, running, running towards the white house at Tirnadris.

Rough planks were nailed across a window. Another window was already broken. Cobwebs were thick across the front-door frame. There were no beasts in the fields behind. The cheerful, welcoming house which had greeted me a year ago was desolate.

I snatched at straws. The shieling! She would be up there, waiting for me. With thumping heart I started off up the mountain. Desperation lent strength to my legs. Chest heaving, I surveyed the meadow. It was silent, empty.

I ran over to the stone hut where we had spent the night in each other's arms. The blackened stub of a fir-candle was still there on the stone where she had set it. I tried the other hut. Nothing but an old butter-keg, covered with a heavily studded round targe, pathetic relic of Culloden.

Bitterness and self-pity welled in me as I plunged wildly down the hill, stumbling, once falling flat on my face, cutting myself.

Gone – and not just gone, but gone without a word or sign. How could she have done this to me? Hot tears started in my eyes. Blinded by them, I ran into an old, black-clad woman. She glared at me as I picked her up. I recognised the crone who the year before had tied the Mungo's knot on Morag's tail as the drove moved off. She looked me over, and her eyes softened. She produced from somewhere about her person a small brown-paper parcel and thrust it into my hands. Before I could question her, she had vanished.

I slumped to the ground, tearing at the wrappings. The first thing that fell out was a silver quaich.* I turned it over in my hand and saw that it had a glass bottom. The glass was double, and imprisoned between the rounds was a curl of raven-dark hair.

The other thing in the parcel was a small, leather-bound book. I opened it at the title page and saw that it contained the Gaelic poems of Alexander Macdonald, the Jacobite poet they called the 'Mavis of Clanranald'. He was, I knew, a cousin of Jeannie's great heroine, Flora Macdonald, the Prince's saviour. I searched the fly-leaf and the covers for a word from her. Nothing! I began to turn the pages and I saw then that several lines of one of the poems were underlined:

> A Dhòmhnaill, a ghràidh mo chridhe . . .
> Oh, Donald, love of my heart,
> I am sorrowful, heavy and weary without you . . .

The poem told of Highlanders cruelly driven from their beloved native soil to America, far away across the sea. I read no more. My heart bursting, I ran back to the stance. The drove was waiting and the drove must be served.

All the way up the rocky defile of Làirig Leacach, urging the long column of shaggy beasts on towards the high pass, my mind raced, the questions came flooding in. Had our handfasting been prematurely discovered? Had one of the dairy-maids talked? Had Jeannie been carried off by her family by force?

---

* My father refers to the round, two-handled drinking-vessel used by Highland gentlemen on social occasions. – F.M.

What had the poem said? 'I am sorrowful, heavy and weary without you . . .'

In the end I had to face the question which had been forcing its way to the surface of my mind ever since I saw the boarded-up house. Suppose she had been merely amusing herself with a callow drover boy?

My mind swung wildly between resurgent hope and black despair.

As we rested among the clouds before beginning the long descent to Kingshouse, I took out the silver quaich, and covertly feasted my eyes on the thick curl of hair trapped between the glass. If she had taken the handfasting so lightly, why had she bothered to send this intimate token with the old woman? But then if she had been serious, why no hint of how and when I might follow her?

Where would I get the money? Since the new Passenger Shipping Act of 1803 had stopped the greedy ship-owners overcrowding, the fares to America had doubled. My mind dwelled on Mr Ramsbottom and his fat dealer's belt of golden sovereigns. When we'd sold the drove on Stenhousemuir we'd have money in plenty in our pockets. But it wasn't ours. It belonged to all those crofters – we'd given them our pledge. Could I not perhaps 'borrow' a little? I shrank from the notion.

So could I get away as a 'redemptionist', working off the fare over five years? But who would make a deal with a boy of fifteen, tall as I was, even then?

It was said that twenty thousand Highlanders would sail from western lochs and ports for America that year. Donald Macleod would not be among them. At the inn at Inveroran I sat silent, by myself, in a far corner, wrapped in my shroud of rejection and misery.

In the end I confided in Angus. He was kind – I see that now. He did not laugh in my face. 'Handfasted, a choin! – you rascal!' He put a brotherly hand on my shoulder. 'Well now, handfasting lasts for a year and a day. A Highland fling, you might say. But if the two stay together after that, well, then it's binding for life . . . I've known a few caught that way . . .'

I stared at him, aghast.

Angus winked. 'But then if there's a bairn on the way, it's as sound as a wedding before the Minister.'

A year and a day – it was already ten months since we'd parted. 'A bairn on the way . . .' Simpleton that I was, the thought had never occurred to me.

We have a saying in Gaelic: 'The sigh goes further than the shout.'

Not that there was any lack of shouting when the Macleod drove fetched up again on Stenhousemuir: gypsy tumblers performing to drum-rolls, fiddlers touting for a crowd, balladeers squeezing the box, tin-whistle virtuosos fighting valiantly against the bellowing of the kyloes and the yelling of the drovers and the barking of their dogs.

Flaunting the eagle-feather in their bonnets, the Seaforths' pipers were there again, marching and counter-marching; kilts swinging, pennants streaming as they belted out *Tulach Ard*, the gathering tune of the Mackenzies. I recognised the red-jacketed recruiting sergeant I had seen there the year before. Hoarse as ever, he was waving over his head a sheaf of Bank of Scotland five-pound notes.

'Twelve guineas a man bounty money, you'll never do better! See the world – King George pays! Kilt, plaid and Highland jacket thrown in for every man . . .'

A drover's head popped up in the crowd. 'Aye, a red jacket a'right – a *bloody* jacket, striped wi' cat o' nine tails . . .'

The sergeant stood his ground, nodding to two privates of the recruiting party who stepped out, carrying a replica of the colours of the new second battalion of the Seaforths – the Ross-shire Buffs. The sergeant pointed his broadsword at the Mackenzie motto, below the stag's antlers: 'Cuidich an Rìgh!' he roared. 'Help the King!'

'No King of ourn!' yelled the same Jacobite drover voice. There were jeers and cat-calls – and that mock baaa-ing of sheep again.

Just then the sergeant's roving eye fell on me. 'You, boy! You look a braw, brave lad! You'll not be feared of Boney, eh, lad?'

I tried to shrink back into the crowd, but by now he had me by the arm. 'Where you from, boy? I know you . . . what's your name, lad?'

All eyes were now turned on me. I was trapped, part of the show.

'Dòmhnall MacLeòid . . . I'm a drover.'

I pulled away, but he held me fast with his eyes, desperately searching his memory. Suddenly, he remembered, crashing fist on fist.

'Ye'll be kin of Old Donald, Sergeant of the Black Watch . . . of the 78th – him who wrote the book . . .'

I could not publicly deny my illustrious forebear. The sergeant hefted me in triumph onto his platform and turned me to the crowd. 'This here lad is kin of Macleod the Scotsman – there's an example for you. With Wolfe at Quebec! And when he was near seventy, the old fellow goes off to New York to join Clinton fighting the Yankees.'

I seized my chance, leapt from the platform, got away into the crowd. Despairing I might be, but I had no wish to sell out to Hanover! I had no wish to take the King's shilling.

I sought safety among the droves being looked over by dealers. There was reassurance in those down-to-earth men. A stocky dealer from Halifax sealed a deal with a drover I recognised from Sutherland with a mighty hand-clap, and I tailed after them into the dimly lit refreshment tent. A couple of fiddlers were hard at it in there, and a young girl was singing with them. Just then she moved into the light from the door and I saw that lustrous black hair tumbled down her back. My heart leapt. Then the singer turned towards me and I drank the bitter dregs of despair. It was then, I think, that I first began to fear for my sanity.

A wild notion struck me. Old Donald, my namesake, had got to America in the army; so had my brothers Dugald and Andrew. I took another dram. Could it be altogether a coincidence that the bounty the recruiting sergeant was offering was precisely the price of a ticket to North Carolina?

The fiddlers switched from a wild reel to a slow, melancholy air, and I recognised the strains of the drover's song which Angus had played in the parlour of the inn at Inveroran. The singer joined in:

> I lost a stirk on the shores of Loch Linnhe,
> Two stots at Salen Loch Sunart;

O'er by Loch Shiel I lost my heart
To Jean, a lassie of Moidart.

A-driving of cattle to tryst and to pasture
Of her I'm dreaming a-wakin';
Her vision is before me aye –
It's sleep that has me forsaken . . .

And now, as the fiddlers suited action to words –

A dram, another, and still yet another
Drowns sorrow most men are heir to;
To Spain, and bedenged to dramming –
Dramming, like love, is a snare too . . .

The Gaelic for 'snare' is *painntear*, and the young girl singer
lingered on it, drawing out the sound.

Dealers and drovers were oblivious, downing drams as they
capped each other's stories of bygone trysts. But the singer's words
were a sword through my heart. Brushing the tears from my eyes,
I ran blindly from the tent.

Swept up into the *siubhal* of the Seaforth pipers, I ran straight
into the arms of the red-jacketed sergeant. The impact of the
collision, the drink taken, knocked me out. The last thing I
remember was his hauling me into one of the recruiting party's
tents.

I don't know how long I lay there. Certainly long enough for
our drovers to have started for home. The first thing I recall was
the sergeant bending over me, shaking my arm. I was alone.

'Donald,' the recruiter said, his face close to mine, 'the officer
is after meeting you. An honour it is – for Captain Stewart,
Stewart of Garth, fought with Abercromby in Egypt; he was
wounded throwing the Frogs out of Alexandria – and now he is
after meeting you, Donald!'

A middle-aged officer sat at a rough trestle-table, piled with
regimental forms. That was the first time I ever saw Captain –
soon to be Major – Stewart, of Garth.

'How old are you, Donald?' he asked.

I was tall enough, so I put a couple of years on. 'Seventeen,' I
lied.

'Young – but two years older than I was when I got my first commission in the 77th Highlanders.'

'He's kin to Sergeant-Major Donald Macleod,' the recruiting sergeant put in. 'You know, sir, Macleod the Scotsman.'

'So you'll be a Skyeman, then,' the officer said. I had never met a man quite like this before, but instinctively I trusted him.* He seemed to give life again to my father's old dream of the Clan – the Chief and his Children: the Ross-shire Buffs was his clan, if you understand me.

'Now, Donald, being a Skyeman you'll not need me to tell you it was the 42nd – the Black Watch – that threw the Corsican neck and crop out of Egypt.' He handed me a cockade bearing a representation of the French imperial eagle.

'Alexandria, 1801,' he said. 'I took that off the body of one of Bonaparte's chasseurs. "Invincibles", he called them. But Abercromby and his Highlanders sent them packing!'

His face darkened. 'But, Donald, Bonaparte hasn't learned his lesson yet. He's gathering what he calls his Army of England just across the Channel; and he says he's coming over to finish us off for good and all!'

He reached out across the table. 'It's our island, too, Donald. England has sore need of her Highlandmen again.'

And that was how I came to do what I had sworn I would never do: I took the Hanoverian King's shilling. I became a *saighdear ruadh* – a Red soldier.

A renegade, she would say, from the very beginning – in short, a Macleod.

---

* My father never forgot this man who recruited him to the Ross-shire Buffs: Later, as Major-General Stewart, he wrote the classic work, *Sketches of the Character, Manners and Present State of the Highlanders of Scotland* (1822), which my father often commended to my attention; indeed, a footnote there refers to my father's curious story. – F.M.

Midnight to 2 a.m., 17 November 1869, Le Grand Bassin

I watched the *Latif* weigh anchor, manoeuvre slowly round into the Grand Bassin, then slip away quietly between the red-painted obelisks which mark the entrance to the Canal. In the light of the flares I could clearly see Sami on the bridge; a handsome figure in the gilt-buttoned frock-coat of a lieutenant-commander of the Khedival Navy. I thought how proud Zobeida would have been. He has her eyes. I used to say that I had followed the example of the Prophet Moses: I had married an Ethiopian.

What I saw, though, as the *Latif* came past, was not the grave senior officer of the Egyptian Navy entrusted with the proving of the Canal in front of the Grand Procession, but a spry, coffee-coloured five-year-old, leaping about our *dahabiya*, learning to haul in the great lateen sail as Giovanni Belzoni and I moved up and down the Nile, opening up to the light of day the secret world of the Pharaohs. By the time he was fifteen, Sami knew every trick of the Nile currents and how the sandbanks shifted. That was when Tom Waghorn used his influence to get him an apprenticeship at the Pasha's new dockyard at Alexandria.

I stood a long time on the dockside, watching the tall, raked masts of the *Latif* receding between the ruler-straight brown walls of the Canal. Then the noise bored into my thoughts, reverberating eerily between the Mediterranean and the lagoon, as that great rabble of nationalities and races moved feverishly between the night cafés and their dancing-girls, the open-air brothels and the casino where many lost on a single throw of the dice all they had made in months of back-breaking labour.

'Donald, have you talked to Giovanni?' Jeannie had discarded the Worth creation, and now stood at my side in a simple cloak.

'Giovanni has plenty to occupy him just now without being worried by his father.' Giovanni is my engineer son.

'His dredgers are working night and day down there between Lake Timsah and Suez and they're still not deep enough. He's frantic. He says that if the Procession doesn't get through, the Effendina will bury him alive.

'He'll bury quite a few of us alive. But de Lesseps swears the Canal's now twenty-two feet deep all the way from here to Ismailiya.'

'Lesseps!' she snapped. 'That man will swear anything. Why don't you listen to your own son? Giovanni says there's barely seventeen feet over the rock-ridge at Serapeum.'

'Seventeen feet will do.'

'The *Delta*, the P & O's paddle-steamer, draws nineteen feet – and all the directors are on board.'

I tried hard not to look worried. There is nothing the English would like more than a disaster in the 'French' Canal. I do believe they – some of them, anyway – would be willing to sacrifice a big ship to get it.

One of Mohammed Said's little 'jokes' when he became Pasha was to order his troops to walk through patches of hot gunpowder – to test their nerve. Tonight in Port Said, with only twelve hours or so to go before the official 'off', I understand just how those poor fellows must have felt.

7 A 'Battalion of Boys'

Chest pouter-pigeoned against his scarlet sergeant's sash, Baxter was waiting for us by the massive stone gateway of Fort George, under the Hanoverian arms. We had marched up from Perth and were footsore and hungry. As we straggled over the long wooden drawbridge he and his corporals set about us like badly trained drove-dogs, yapping and snapping, pushing and pulling us into parties and ranks.

We were 118 in all – Major Stewart had done the Ross-shire Buffs proud. But Sergeant Baxter did not seem to think so. 'Robbing the cradles again,' he muttered, marching up and down our ranks, prodding us like a dealer at the Falkirk Tryst. 'A battalion of boys – that's what they've given me.' He spat in disgust.

It was true, no denying it. Of the 900 men in the newly raised battalion, 600 were under age: I was in good company. King George was really scraping the bottom of the Highland barrel.

It was fortunate that few of us could understand the torrent of insults that little man poured upon us day after day. I would have been equally oblivious myself, had I not been standing in the ranks next to a Lowlander named Tom Keith, a gunsmith's apprentice from Leith. Keith, who had picked up a bit of Gaelic, took pleasure in translating for me Baxter's most offensive epithets. Keith just laughed – he found Baxter comic – which was as well. Fort George jutted out into the Moray Firth like some malevolent lizard, and with the great gates locked we were at Baxter's mercy in that cold English prison.

Fort William, Fort Augustus, Fort George: they had been set down along the Great Glen after Culloden to hold us savage

Highlanders down. The only mystery, it seemed to me on this morning, under the hail of Baxter's curses, was why we Highlanders, loyal as whipped spaniels, kept on coming back for more, spilling our blood all over the world for them.

Duncan Macgregor, a gentleman of eighteen, brought in enough of his clan to win himself a captaincy in this new battalion, the Ross-shire Buffs. From his remote seat at Bighouse in Sutherland, Colin Mackay brought down to Fort George a long tail of stout-limbed Mackays. Nor did General Mackenzie Fraser lack his Macrae 'coat of mail': eighteen Macraes followed Lieutenant Christopher Macrae into Fort George from Kintail, including that giant of a man, Sergeant John Macrae, a dab hand with the broadsword.

Not dab enough, though, as it turned out.

Then there were fifty Camerons and ten Donald Macdonalds and forty Macleods, many from the old Macleod lands on the island of Lewis – and of course, our commanding officer was a Macleod, Patrick Macleod of Genies, son of the Sheriff Donald Macleod who put down the sheep riots when I was three years old.

All the same, there were holes in the Highland plaid which had to be filled with Lowlanders like Tom Keith, and the flotsam and jetsam of Ireland and such odds and sods as the men from the Canadian Fencibles to whom our tormentor, Sergeant Baxter, had belonged.

Baxter was a disappointed man. He'd been promised land in Canada as his reward for his service in the Fencibles. Then they'd been disbanded. The authorities went back on their word. Baxter had been taking it out on recruits at Fort George ever since. I can still hear that bitter little man's strangulated screaming in my ear . . . 'As you stand, draw up your left foot to your right heel— LEFT FOOT, YOU IGNORANT FUCKER!'

Baxter could reel off whole pages of General Dundas's *Rules and Regulations for the Movement of His Majesty's Army*. It was just unfortunate that many of us Highland lads had trouble telling our left from our right in the Sasannach tongue. Baxter tied a bundle of straw to my left leg, drawing the string so tight it bit into the flesh and calling me hundreds of nasty names. We understood neither the commands nor the nasty names. Eventually one of the Macgregors went to Major Stewart to complain. Stewart laughed, and gave a corporal who spoke both English and Gaelic an extra sixpence a week to stand beside Baxter and translate the screams. After that things got a bit better, though we could never really understand the Redcoats' strange notions of fighting by numbers.

Each night, exhausted by the torments of the square, we would stagger back to our chill stone cells in the barrack block, each holding eight men, four beds, and one cauldron in which we had to cook our food – hunks of beef and potatoes, the gross way the English soldiers eat.

That was how I came to form an alliance with Tom Keith, the armourer. Tom was allotted a barrack room already crowded with three Macraes, three Macgregors and one Macleod. None had a word of English, nor wanted one, save me. With only a few words of Gaelic, picked up from his Jacobite grandfather, Tom was the odd man out, for to us Highland lads a Lowlander was little better than a Sasannach. So Tom, with his few words of the Gaelic, and I, with my few words of English, made a pair.

A wiry, bony-faced fellow, with a gleam in his dark eyes, Tom was two years older than I, with a vastly greater knowledge of the world. He hadn't taken the King's shilling out of hunger or desperation or force of clan habit, like so many of us. He'd had a row with his father, broken his gunsmith apprentice indentures and run away in search of adventure.

When Major Stewart found out he'd worked for a gunsmith, he was soon made up to armourer. As for myself, because of my age, I'd been enlisted as a drummer-boy, so my uniform set me apart: buff jacket with red cuffs and collar, and enough straps and buckles and hooks to drive you out of your mind. The particular bane of my life was the narrow strips which held the tight-rolled blanket high on the shoulders. Dundas's *Rules and Regulations* laid down that the strap-ends must terminate in a neat pipe-clayed spiral. My failure to achieve this made me a special target for Sergeant Baxter's venom.

I let it all wash over me, I was still like someone sleep-walking. Nothing Baxter would do or say could add to the hurt I already felt at Jeannie's betrayal – for that was how I now saw it. My hard-won pride at being a Macleod and a drover had gone. I floundered in the mud, almost welcoming Baxter's sadistic humiliations. It was Tom Keith who pulled me out of it.

*

Have you ever noticed how at the very nadir of one's fortunes some apparently chance happening sets the current of one's life pulsing again? 'Providential' is what the *giaours* call it, though meaning very little by the word. In my case the agent of Providence was, paradoxically, my tormentor himself, Sergeant Baxter.

It happened one morning on that bleak, windy square, during one of our everlasting musket drills: twenty-six clear-cut motions, as laid down in the *Regulations*. Day after day on the great square we banged those old Brown Besses about under the sergeant's unrelenting eye, biting off the ends of the paper cartridges till our own muzzles were black as dogs', pouring a little powder into the pan, the rest down the spout . . .

'Recover your rammers and shorten!' bawled Baxter.

'Return your rammers!'

'Cast about and cock!'

'PRESENT!'

It was not a Highlander's idea of fighting, not at all. We pined for the light carbines our fathers had used and for the Highland charge. With these cumbersome English muskets, at a hundred yards we hardly ever hit the cut-out body that was our target. Baxter worked himself into a frenzy.

'That man there!'

I had pulled the trigger on command, but my musket did not fire. Murder in his eyes, Baxter swept down upon me. He tore the musket from my grasp and at that moment the charge went off, enveloping him in a cloud of acrid smoke. Two or three men guffawed. Then there was a shocked silence.

Baxter crashed the butt down within a hair's breadth of my toes. He pushed his face into mine.

'You ignorant Highland scut! Do you know what yon gun cost His Majesty? Do you know how long *Regulations* say it's got to last? Twelve years! You'll be paying for that for the rest of your life – or until they hang you!'

I was ordered in disgrace to take the 'ruined' weapon round to the workshop on the east side of the fort. I was in luck. The armourer that day was Tom Keith. The reek of powder still hung about the muzzle. Tom examined it carefully. 'Thought as much,' he grunted, pointing to the lock-plate. The Tower of London inspector's mark was missing; the plate bore the initials UEIC, 1795: 'United East India Company'.

'More of the sepoy rubbish they're foisting on us. Ten to one the sear spring's gone again. It's a file and saw job.'

He saw my look of dismay, and laughed. 'Take no notice of that jumped-up clown Baxter. It'll nae cost you a penny, Donald, and when I'm through with it it'll be the best gun in Fort George.

Sure enough, I got the East India Company gun back next day, and, first shot on the range, scored a hit over the heart on the cut-out. Baxter was reduced to sullen silence. But that wasn't the end of the affair. Two nights later in our barrack room, as the Macraes and Macgregors were disputing in voluble Gaelic over the cooking cauldron, I noticed that Tom's index finger on his right hand was swollen and had been very clumsily bandaged.

'Just a scratch,' he said. I insisted on his taking the dirty bandage off. The rusty spring of my 'sepoy gun' had cut deep into his finger. Tom said: 'Duncan soused it with vinegar. It'll be all right.'

'It will not,' I said.

Duncan was Duncan Mackenzie, the hospital orderly. It was not my business. But was I not a Beaton on my mother's side? Heaven knows how many hours I'd passed as a boy watching my grandmother, the Reverend's widow, dispensing unguents and potions and infusions to an endless queue of sufferers. Hadn't I seen her boiling violets in whey for fevers, syrup of blueberries for fluxes, nettle-tops, chopped fine and mixed with white of an egg, to bring sleep, infusing wild garlic in boiling water for the stone?

I searched my memory to recall some Beaton specific for a festering cut in a finger. Seaweed! *Lìonaraich*, a thin, green sea-plant growing on beaches; I'd seen it work wonders in such cases. Grandma Beaton, I recalled, had used it on the gash in my father's leg.

That night I climbed down from one of the casements of Fort George. The sea was sweeping strongly in from the Moray Firth, but after a long cold search I found a few strands of *lìonaraich* creeping over the sand. I forget how I managed to get back into the fort. But I did.

Two days later I got an order to report to Mr Munro, the battalion surgeon, at the hospital. When I got there I found Tom Keith standing beside him.

'Drummer Macleod, did you bandage this man's finger?'

I noticed with relief that the swelling had gone. 'Yes, sir,' I said.

'With *seaweed*?' His dark eyebrows had risen high.

'Kind of,' I said nervously.

He examined Tom's finger closely. 'Extraordinary,' he said.

Surgeon Munro was a Highlander. We could speak freely in the Gaelic. 'Wherever did you learn that, boy?' I told him. His face cleared. 'Ah, yes, I should have known. A Beaton remedy! I once saw one of those old manuscripts of theirs. Translations from the great Arab physicans . . .'

He examined Tom's finger again.

'Donald, you seem to have inherited the Beatons' healing touch. You'll be wasted rapping the drums. I shall speak to Colonel Macleod in the morning.'

Surgeon Munro let me carry his case of instruments around the small barrack hospital, teaching me how to take the pulse properly, how to dose, bleed, blister, set fractures and apply cataplasms, administer mercury and jalop and apply tourniquets to stem the blood. I think I can fairly say I proved an apt pupil, and my hospital duties delivered me from Baxter's mind-numbing drills.

You might think that attending to the misfortunes of others would have taken my mind off my own. But no; as I bound up some injured limb or applied a hot poultice to a boil, I would find that desolate, boarded-up white farmhouse of the Macdonalds floating before my eyes, and be swept again by bitter feelings of betrayal. And then I would dig into my kit and bring out the small leather-bound volume of Alexander Macdonald's poems and turn the pages till I found the verse she had underlined:

> Oh, Donald, love of my heart,
> I am sorrowful, heavy and weary without you . . .

Was that really what she had felt for me? I should never know, now that the wastes of the Atlantic lay between us. I had really burned my boats by taking the Hanoverians' shilling. I could have deserted, of course. I still could, indenturing myself to some greedy ship's captain. But Tom persuaded me against it. Did I really want to bring shame upon my family, with my name posted on the kirk door?

And yet the more I tried to dismiss Jeannie Macdonald from my mind, the more she intruded. When down-to-earth Tom pointed out that I could not have been her first lover, that merely increased my obsession. Who was *he*? Then a truly terrible thought – suppose he had taken my place? Gone to North Carolina with her? Was that why there had been no letter? I continually worried the post corporal. I never stopped questioning lads who had relatives in America. I was making myself a laughing-stock.

Finally, Tom Keith took pity on me. On the pretext of a dying relative, we obtained a three-day pass to Inverness. From there we moved down the Great Glen, trying to pick up any news of Jeannie Macdonald and her family. It was a hopeless enterprise from the start. Old neighbours, bound for Nova Scotia or the Red River, no longer knew or cared about those pledged to Carolina or Georgia. All were swept up in the 'Dance Called America', whirling wider and ever faster now. They had no mind to stop and look back.

In despair I hunted everywhere for the old crone who had handed me the parcel containing the quaich and the book of poems. But she too had vanished.

Sick at heart, I was about to start back from the inn at Spean Bridge, when, all at once, she stood before us in that uncanny way she had. She gave no sign of recognition, though I detected a faint flicker in her strange, pale-blue eyes. We sat her down at a wooden table outside the inn and plied her with drams and questions. She grinned toothlessly as the *uisge-beatha* slid down, but said nothing.

Then, suddenly, her eyelids slid upwards, and her eyes seemed to mist over, and her head jerked back, and she began to speak in a strange, cracked voice.

'She waits beside a great river as wide as the ocean . . . I see a tall man wearing the *breacan* and a blue bonnet at her side . . . high trees lean in the wind, feathers hanging down . . . boats skim over brown water like butterflies . . .'

I hung on every word: had not Kenneth the Sallow seen the slaughter of Culloden years before it happened?

The old woman fell silent; then, with a curious rattle in her throat, she began again. 'I see a boy child, beside the great river. He is wrapped in a white shroud that drips water . . . I see a man's head, rolling across the moor . . . bleeding . . . more heads, rolling, raised on high poles . . .'

The old woman gave a sort of whimper, and, though we waited long, no more words came.

Fragmentary as the old woman's vision had been, it somehow gave me back my future; raised the curtain on life again. Night after night, back in the grim prison of Fort George I lay beside Tom Keith in that chilly stone cell and while he snored and the wind off the Firth howled, I went again over the stumbling words of the old *taibhsear*. Could that wide river have been the River Fear, of which Jeannie had told me so much? The tall man, wearing tartan? Could that be me? But why me? Why not the other, the one who had been before me? A chill fell across my heart. Tom Keith, the commonsensical Lowlander, begged me to forget the old woman's 'maunderings'. Nothing good could come of that sort of thing! I nodded, and kept my own counsel.

The twenty-fifth of February was my mother's birthday. It was also, by a cruel coincidence, the day in 1805 when I sailed away from Scotland for ever without a word to her. It has weighed on my conscience ever since.

They say – and say rightly – that a Highlander quitting his native soil does so with many a pang. And yet I cannot pretend that I was sorry to march out of King George's fort and along the stone quay in the slashing rain and onto the heaving deck of that small transport, bound for England.

What was its name? The *Neptune*? I can only tell you that, two weeks on, we left it with heartfelt relief at the port of Dover and marched on to Folkestone.

Some days, in our new barracks at Shorncliffe, we would hear the roar of the British navy's guns as they pounded away at the defences of Boulogne. We had orders to sleep with our guns at our sides. From our grandstand on the green plateau above Sandgate we looked out over an unfolding drama, a clash of empires which at last dwarfed, even for me, the fabled feudings of Macleods and Macdonalds.

I remember Sir John Moore passing his telescope around so that we could see the Emperor's pavilion on the French cliff-top. Bonaparte's 'Army of England', he said, was marshalled over there in four camps: 175,000 men with 2,000 or more flat-bottomed boats, only awaiting a naval escort to launch his invasion. The Corsican had 117 interpreters lined up, ready to give us our marching orders.

We'd left Baxter behind at Fort George, thank the Lord, and though there were two English regiments training with us at Shorncliffe, the CO of the 43rd was a Mackenzie, well versed in Moore's new 'light infantry system'.

General Moore was out on the square himself, often four times a day. He drilled the officers in the new movements first, and if they didn't pass in them, they had to go on drilling with us in the ranks till they did. I'd never seen an English officer like Moore before. I began to suspect he must have some Highland blood when he told us that every company should be like a family, with the captain as father; and for a court martial the captain was to be advised by two men from the ranks, presided over by a corporal. Every soldier had to nominate a mate, who'd fight alongside him and watch his back in a tight corner: his 'chosen man', the General called him. Naturally I chose Tom Keith.

But when I think now of those first few weeks in England, what comes to mind is neither the new drill nor Bonaparte, but boils, endless boils, big, angry boils, suppurating on men's necks, foreheads, faces, backsides. I attended the surgeon with his busy lance, cleaning out the mess, applying lead plasters, Goulard's extract, zinc ointment, hot cataplasms, *linseed oil cake one part, oatmeal two parts* . . .

The trouble was, though, as Surgeon Munro said, if that oatmeal had been applied *internally*, to our fellows' stomachs in the usual Highland fashion, we would never have had need for it on our backsides. We just couldn't stand this heavy Sasannach food – the daily pound of beef, the potatoes, the one and a half pounds of bread. Still, I opened a new chapter in my trade at Shorncliffe that summer. I even acquired a little dispensary Latin – *infusa* and *tinctura* and *spiritus rectificatus* and *unguentum* and *olea distillatus* – and I thought how proud my mother would have been of me, speaking Latin like a Beaton and a gentleman at last.

From our barracks high above Sandgate we watched the dark line of the Royal Military Canal creeping on towards Rye. But then a day came when, looking south across the Channel, we saw that something strange was going on.

Napoleon's great invasion army was fading away. Mr Pitt, they said, had brought Austria in on our side. Britain no longer stood alone.

At the end of September, the Ross-shire Buffs got orders to

march to Portsmouth. We reached the docks just a few hours too late to see Admiral Nelson set sail in the *Victory*. *Malish*! I can still boast, though, that I very nearly witnessed the Battle of Trafalgar.

Just south of Lisbon, the commodore of our naval escort signalled ENEMY IN SIGHT – PUT INTO PORT. When they let us out again, and we set course for Gibraltar, we found ourselves sailing past a long trail of blackened and scattered vessels. Some were dismasted, hardly able to sail, yet still proudly flying the Union flag. Behind them a sorry trail of shell-holed wrecks, Bonaparte's fleet, the tricolour in shreds, the red ensign floating above it.

Britain was delivered but – the news spread from ship to ship – Nelson was dead. Thus was I launched on my life as a soldier.

Three days later we landed at Gibraltar, and three days after that came the news that Bonaparte had crushed the Austrians at Ulm on the Danube. As we were settling into our new barracks at Windmill Hill, still worse befell: Bonaparte annihilated the combined forces of the Tsar of Russia and the Emperor of Austria at Austerlitz. King George, no king of mine, lost Hanover.

So there we were, on that rock, prisoners once again. We could look over into the Spanish towns of La Linea and San Roque. But Spain was under the Corsican's yoke – we couldn't go there. So we drilled, and counter-marched and formed column and line and stood guard and presented arms in twenty brisk movements as advised by General Dundas's *Regulations*.

And we hated it. There was but one way out, fleeting as it might be. Feeling responsible as he did for his 'battalion of boys', Colonel Macleod was ever warning the officers and sergeants to keep them out of the brothels of the Old Town. He might as well have tried to come between a Highlandman and his dram. Particularly since the girls did not stay back in the whorehouses, and had flashing eyes, red blouses and shining black tresses. So Donald the Leech received a thorough grounding in yet another branch of his medical craft, for often the lads would come to him, instead of reporting to the surgeon ... *submuriate of mercury in pill with opium*, night and morning, *potassium nitras gryii, pulveria trag. comp.* Nine months we were on that wretched rock, and by the time we sailed, you might say, I suppose, that I had become an experienced pox doctor, a qualification not to be despised in a medical orderly standing at the gateway of the mysterious East.

My readers might imagine that these somewhat sordid experiences would have cured me for ever of my adolescent romantic obsessions. Quite the contrary: the handfasting in the dawn took on an almost sacred quality. Some days I still hoped; others I despaired, yet the dream was renewed, more compelling than ever. Sometimes, taking my turn on sentry-go, I would do the turnabout – one, two, one, two – and come round to face the smooth limestone glacis of el Peñón in the moonlight, and I would see her face up there, raven hair cascading down her back, eyes challenging over the top of Tom Paine's book as we struggled with the Sasannach tongue and the meaning of the word 'president'.

BOOK II

The World Turned Upside Down

The constant petition at grace of the old
Highland chieftains was delivered with great
fervour in these terms: 'Lord! Turn the
world upside down, that Christians may
make bread of it.' The plain English of
this request was: That the world
might become, for their benefit,
a scene of rapine and confusion.

– Thomas Pennant, *Tour in Scotland and a Voyage
to the Hebrides* (1774)

8   The Nile Runs Red

You'll find Maida, 1806, on the battle honours of the Ross-shire Buffs – and I can say I was there – but I doubt you'll find Rosetta or el-Hamed, 1807, and I was there, too.

Looking back, of course, I see that the whole enterprise was doomed from the start.

Ten days out of Syracuse, sick as dogs in the stinking 'tween-decks of our troopers, we dropped anchor off Arab Town in a Mediterranean storm. A sparkling white coastline, sand and salt, flat and featureless; the land of Egypt lay before us.

We'd embarked in good enough order in Sicily: thirty-three transports, six thousand men, the Ross-shire Buffs, the 31st Foot, a battalion of the Sussex Regiment, and de Roll's, who were mainly Swiss and German, the usual odds and sods. But the storm had taken its toll and half the convoy had gone adrift. General Mackenzie Fraser didn't want to land without his full complement of Highlanders.

We saw a boat put out from the shore, making for HMS *Tigris* where the General had his HQ. We crowded the rails to watch a stout little man being hauled on board, crippled evidently, dragging himself on one leg. None of us had ever set eyes on him before, though we'd all seen more than enough of him before the end: Major Edward Missett, His Britannic Majesty's Agent in Alexandria.

Five years earlier, when Abercromby's army had turfed the French out of Egypt and sailed for home, they'd left Edward Missett behind – to look after the shop, so to speak. Unfortunately, Bonaparte had had the same idea, and had posted to Alexandria his old victualler of 1798, Matthieu de Lesseps. As I learned later from his son, Ferdinand – *le grand canaliste* – Matthieu had secret instructions 'to seek out some person, bold, intelligent, and trustworthy, to bring order' – French order, naturally – to the anarchy into which Egypt had fallen.

Now Matthieu de Lesseps was a shrewd picker of men; Edward Missett, aided by the British Foreign Office, a very poor one. By the time we landed in Egypt in March 1807, Matthieu's man was riding high in Salah el-Din's Citadel, an officer from the Albanian contingent of the Ottoman army, his name, Mohammed Ali. Missett had gone on backing Elfi Bey, a survivor of the Mameluke chiefs who had ruled and plundered Egypt for almost six hundred years until Bonaparte's artillery blew them and their 'splendid cavalry' to bits at the Battle of the Pyramids in 1798. Major Missett, it seems, hadn't noticed this.

(All this I learned later.)

But Major Missett was 'our man on the spot'. He insisted on Fraser's landing his troops at once, whatever the state of the sea. The Turkish garrison of Alexandria, he said, would open the gates and lay down its arms when they saw us.

By the time my turn came to go over the side the surf was mountainous. Flung out of the boat, I lay winded and half-drowned on the sand for some time. By nightfall we had 400 men ashore and another 600 by the next morning. A thousand men to capture a walled and heavily fortified city.

Our puny column pushed on along the strip of sand that lay between the sea and the lake – Mareotis – and on by Pompey's Pillar to the south-east corner of Alexandria's walls. According to Missett we would find the gates wide open to receive us. We found them firmly shut, musket fire raining down from the walls.

We dug water from under the palm-trees, and rested on the warm sand that night. Next day the missing transports dropped anchor in Aboukir Bay and the Turks sallied out to continue their 'welcome'.

Yet, the day after that, all the Turks had mysteriously melted away. The city of Alexander the Great was ours – a heap of mouldering ruins, Arab shacks, muddy alleys and drinking dens. Few of us were over twenty, though we were no longer a 'battalion of boys'. On our way here, at Maida, in Calabria, we'd faced

Bonaparte's crack troops, steel to steel, and they'd run before us. We wore our Mackenzie tartans with an air that day; the stag's antlers fairly seemed to leap from our cap badges.

Arabs swarmed around offering scrawny chickens, eggs at one penny a dozen, fly-blown sweetmeats, fresh-cut coconuts and their sisters. This, said an old soldier of the Sussex, was going to be a 'cushy billet'. That was the first time I heard the word '*bakshish*'.

Although it was only March the sea was warm and the sun shone, and some of us took to swimming on the shore at a point just outside the walls where an ancient obelisk called Cleopatra's Needle saluted the sun. Another obelisk lay prone beside it.

Floating on the gentle swell one day, I thought I was in a dream when I saw a gaggle of big black girls gathering around the kit we had left on the beach. Their eyes laughed, their ebony skins shone in the sun, their thighs were lustrous, and their breasts as bold and round as Glamaig and Marsco, the twin green *meallan* that the drove plodded round south of Sligachan. I watched, spellbound.

At that moment, I recall, Sergeant Macrae rose from the waves like Leviathan, and let fly a flood of Gaelic curses. The girls fled – for Macrae was a giant of a man, the biggest I had ever seen until the day I encountered Giovanni Battista Belzoni, the Paduan Hercules, blocking Mr Burckhardt's staircase in Cairo.

It was just as well the black beauties made themselves scarce, because a couple of minutes later Colonel Macleod came by on his inspection. Like Major Stewart, Patrick Macleod had served in the 42nd here with Abercromby, and liked to give us the benefit of his experience. He went over to the fallen obelisk, where Tom Keith and John Macrae were sitting wrapped in their plaids after the swim.

Macleod began to clear the sand away, motioning us to join him.

'What do they say Bonaparte said at the Pyramids? "Forty centuries look down"? Well, my boys, you've been sitting on at least thirty of them.'

He cleared off the last veil of dust to reveal a line of fat Egyptian geese, cut with magical precision, then an owl, then a horned serpent, a fierce-looking beetle . . . a teeming menagerie.

'Hieroglyphics,' said Patrick Macleod. 'The writing of the gods.' He shrugged. 'Some say the symbols come from China. Some say they stand for words, some for letters. You'd have to roll the clock back forty centuries to find out.'

It did not occur to me then that we should do just that in the end, Giovanni and I, and Mr Salt the Consul, and Mr Bankes, and Mr Burckhardt, better known as Sheikh Ibrahim – and Robert Hay, a mighty wielder of the *camera lucida*.

From time to time we would spot a Turkish horseman, scouting about in the desert. But the weather was summery, our duties were light, and there was the promise of the laughing black girls. I would say, in fact, that the only man not well content in our camp was Major Missett. He was demanding that we march on Rosetta, fifty miles to the east, near a mouth of the Nile. To secure our food supplies, he said. Scouts had reported Arnauts* around Rosetta, but Missett swept that aside. 'A mere rabble,' he sniffed; Elfi Bey's splendid Mameluke cavalry was even now riding to our aid.

So it was with easy hearts that we watched our comrades of the 31st Foot march off along the shore towards Rosetta, stars gleaming in their shakoes, fifes and drums flaunting their regimental march, 'a southerly wind and a cloudy sky', the *Chasseurs Britanniques* cantering on their flanks. In all, 1200 men, two six-pounders, two howitzers, *and* two generals, Meade and Wauhope, enough you would think to seize a small town, let alone banish a mere rabble.

We returned to our 'cushy billet' among the palm-trees, to await the black girls. The Colonel had given Sergeant Macrae strict orders to keep the women away; but the second Macrae's back was turned, they reappeared.

One, bolder than the rest, an enormous black woman with blinding white teeth and enveloping breasts, danced up to us, erupting with laughter.

'Couchez avec moi!' She rolled her eyes skywards. 'Faites jig-a-jig très bonne . . . ver' good! . . . shabash.'

Her gleaming belly churned like the rotation of the earth. She

---

* *Arnaut* is the French term for Albanian, referring here to the Albanian detachment from which came Mohammed Ali, founder of a new Egyptian dynasty – F.M.

got near enough to Tom to snatch at his kilt. The men roared, yelling lascivious encouragement in Gaelic.

'Look – see what she's got on her head,' Tom yelled. It was the bonnet of the Black Watch. Then another girl, a Nubian with a skin like burnished copper, opened her hand to reveal a tricolour cockade – and their whole strange story came out.

Bonaparte's army had spent three years in Egypt. When Abercromby threw them out in 1801, the soldiers had a big auction in Alexandria of all their possessions, including their bedmates. Some of these were bought by the victorious British soldiers before they, too, sailed for home. When the girls saw us in the sea that day, they imagined their 'husbands' had come back to them.

Poor girls! A soldier's life is full of the unexpected. They were doomed to be disappointed yet again. Less than a week had passed since we had watched the lads of the 31st march away. We had heard no word from Rosetta, but then we expected none.

I shall never forget the day the bloody remnant of that detachment staggered back into camp, dragging a terrible tail of wounded and half-dead, staining the sand. Being a medical orderly, I was kept furiously engaged from the start, improvising a field hospital in the sand dunes, while the surgeons set about their bloody work. I became hardened to dressing stumps, burying legs – and often the trunks after them, for shock and gangrene were swift assassins. I was with the lad who had told me that Alexandria looked like being a 'cushy billet' when he died, chest sliced by a Turkish sabre.

Moving round among the stretchers, lending a hand to the surgeons when I could, I was gradually able to piece together the appalling story of folly and disaster. Set in palm groves, inlaid with plantations of orange-trees, the white walls of Rosetta had seemed compact with promise. The gates stood open. A few fellahin were still about, working their fields. Otherwise the town seemed to have abandoned itself to the siesta.

Leaving a couple of field guns to command the Heights of Amandour above the town, General Wauhope gave the order to march into Rosetta, heading for the market square. High, windowless houses with projecting balconies gave shade to the narrow, deserted streets below. The only sound was our own men's marching feet.

The British column was deep into the town when, somewhere, a silent order was given. Suddenly, bullets were raining down from the roof-tops on the soldiers trapped in the narrow streets below.

Men fell in heaps, blocking escape for those behind. The sharpshooters Moore had so carefully trained at Shorncliffe were powerless. The enemy was out of sight on the roof-tops. General Wauhope was among the first to fall: General Meade was seen to be badly wounded in the head.

Then the Arnauts poured out of the houses, firing at pointblank range, hacking with their sabres. Nearly 200 of our men were slaughtered, 300 wounded. But what really upset our men most was what the enemy did to the wounded. Looking back, they would see some wiry little Arnaut hacking the head off a mate's body. It was the last thing one boy saw before he himself had been blinded by a blow from a sabre.

This time we needed no urging from Major Missett. We were crazy for vengeance – and now General Mackenzie Fraser turned to his Highlanders, to us, to the Ross-shire Buffs.

For some reason I made a note of the date in the back of Tom Paine (which I still carried everywhere at the bottom of my pack). I turn to it now. It reads: 'Started out 3 April, 1807 – Ross-shire Buffs, battalion of 35th, troop of 20th Dragoons, and de Roll's.' A string of camels padded alongside us, carrying the Engineers' equipment for laying siege to Rosetta. I recall vividly the nasty bite one of these vicious beasts gave me.

It was hard going through the loose sand, so we moved closer to the shore. Sun-bleached bones and a few skulls still lay along the tide-line at Aboukir, reminders of Nelson's victory. Then the palms gave out and we were half choked by stiflingly hot winds off the desert.

The first thing we saw as we approached Rosetta was the mutilated bodies of our comrades, scattered over the palm groves and sandhills like rag-dolls discarded by some petulant child. They lay everywhere, just where they been struck down in flight; a melancholy sight for a soldier. We set about the grim task of burial.

I remember our artillery scored a hit on the minaret of a mosque inside the walls and we cheered like maniacs. But though our guns pounded away day and night at the town's white walls, the only marks our balls could make were a few dark blotches. The mud swallowed them up. The town gates remained firmly shut.

Once Major Jamie Macdonnell, son of Glengarry, the sheep-lover, took a boat party of our lads across the Nile in the darkness to surprise the Arnaut gun-crew that had been firing into our positions. They turned its fire on Rosetta. I had that from Tom Keith, who had gone along as armourer.

But for most part it was a stalemate, as the Arnauts, seeing our small numbers, continually tried to break out then fell back inside the walls. Colonel Macleod told us that Elfi Bey and the Mameluke cavalry were on their way. Had Elfi not been taken by warship to London to meet King George, returning with a dozen bottles of finest milk punch? (How were *we* to know Elfi had been two months in his grave?)

Then a runner came staggering into our camp from el-Hamed, his head bloody from a sabre wound. A horde of Turkish horsemen had crossed the Nile. They had surrounded the outpost and cut up de Roll's. Only five had got away. The road from the south now lay open. General Fraser turned to our commanding officer, Patrick Macleod, dispatching him to el-Hamed with one company of the Ross-shire Buffs and a field gun.

By evening we had taken up three positions along the dyke and the canal which carries the flood waters off the Nile into Lake Edku. Tom Keith was in the westernmost post, I and most of the Buffs at the eastern end, our backs against the Nile bank.

A dog barked in the palm-fringed village on the opposite bank. Otherwise everything was quiet. As we settled down to keep watch a wonderful sense of tranquillity seemed to suffuse the countryside. The colour of amber in the clear moonlight, streaked with silver, the Nile poured steadily northward on its last few miles to the sea. It was a solemn, an unearthly, sight. It was as if the great river was possessed of some inexorable purpose. No one spoke. After the horrors of the last few days each of us was wrapped in his own thoughts. In the inconsequential way thoughts have, mine flew back to an earlier humiliation under Mr Macaskill's ferrule in school at Bracadale.

'Dhòmhnaill Bain, what is the longest river in the world?'

It was not a subject my father talked of round the fire.

'The Clyde,' I guessed.

The class sniggered. The ferrule hurt my knuckles.

'The Nile, boy. And how long is the River Nile, a Dhòmhnaill?'

The ferrule hovered. I guessed wildly. 'Four thousand miles?'

The ferrule was replaced on the desk.

'We do not know. Mr Bruce could not discover its source.' He picked up the ferrule again, tapping Africa. 'It rises in the middle of the Dark Continent . . .'

As the sky began to lighten and the palm groves on the opposite bank stippled the amber flow, I saw that the village fields were emerald-bright with Egyptian clover. Southwards (recalling Mr Macaskill) lay the Delta, the Nile's masterwork, built up over the centuries on the rich mud borne down from Africa.

And yet the Nile, I was about to find, possesses a power to destroy as well as build. The Nile is naked power.

As the first shafts of sun shot up from the east bank, throwing the village into relief, round the bend to our south, borne on its mighty current came a flotilla of broad flat-bottomed *djerms*, the sailing-barges of the Nile. Each boat was packed with Arnauts, armed to the teeth. Two boats mounted five guns. Racing on horseback between our three strung-out posts, Colonel Macleod yelled to us to abandon el-Hamed, and concentrate in the square on the sandhill near the centre.

It was the last order he ever gave. We had to leave his body where it lay. Then a howling Turk galloping by sabred Captain Mackay across the shoulders with such ferocity that I thought his head must be severed. His thick cape and neckcloth saved him, thank God, but the wound was terrible. That was when I got the blue scar on my forehead that I bear to this day. Sergeant Walters, an Englishman – and the only one of our party who came through unscathed that day – somehow managed to get poor Mackay under the shelter of our single gun.

The command now fell to Captain Vogelsang, of de Roll's, the next most senior officer. As the square grew smaller by the minute, I saw Vogelsang sticking a white cloth on the point of a bayonet. I heard Colin Mackay cry out from below the gun where he lay: 'No, no – not while we've one round left!'

Now that the Turkish horsemen were in among us, who could blame Vogelsang? He was a German, a mercenary. He had done what he was hired to do. But, then, come to think of it, this wasn't *our* fight either . . .

No sooner had the white flag been raised than the Arnauts were running madly about all over the place, each eager to secure his 'bag' of prisoners – or prisoners' heads: it seemed to matter little which. I saw two Arnaut soldiers almost tear one of the Macgregor boys limb from limb, disputing ownership. Other Turks and Arnauts were combing the sand dunes, hacking off the heads of the dead and dying. This was an army which was paid – *if* it was paid – 'by results'.

Thank God, Colin Mackay escaped their attentions, for soon afterwards the Turkish commander rode by, and exerted his authority. Astonishingly, he spoke some English:

'Where is the brave officer who would not surrender?'

We were afraid for Mackay then.

But the Turk took off his own sword and laid it at the Captain's side.

'I honour a brave soldier,' he said, and gave orders for him to be carried by four of his own men in a litter.

By this time the Turkish horsemen were riding around, whooping, with the heads of our comrades impaled on their lances.

I was grabbed and, with a man from the Sussex Regiment, forced to carry a bloody sack of heads towards the barges waiting by the Nile bank. Mercifully, there are limits to what the human mind can take in – and we had long passed them.

The Arnauts ran about like rabid dogs, yelling, pushing us into line, attaching ropes to men in tattered uniforms, men half naked, men whose faces were contorted with pain, men dragging hacked limbs. Thus we staggered southwards along the Nile bank towards the barges that had brought the Arnauts down from Cairo. I searched for Tom Keith, but did not find him. My 'chosen man' – yet I had not been there to watch his back. Moore had never foreseen anything like this at Shorncliffe. We had been over 800 at el-Hamed. We left behind us 280 men and twelve officers dead – and now probably headless – on the sand dunes.

Men were dropping all the time from loss of blood or sheer exhaustion. I hardly dared look behind me. We were not allowed to tend our wounded – save for Captain Mackay, borne along on his litter, unconscious and near death.

The cut on my head throbbed and white lights danced before my eyes and in my delirium I imagined I was back with the drove. But now the cattle had the faces of men, and mine was one of them, and I saw the big reproachful eyes of the old woman's heifer with the contrary horns and I knew I was in Hell. Dugald, I thought, would never have permitted the drove to be driven down to the Tryst in such a condition.

Beside each of the broad-bottomed *djerms* tied up at the Nile bank squatted a Turkish or Arnaut *yuzbashi* (captain), a money-bag in front of him. Each was surrounded by swarms of yelling soldiers, pushing forward their bedraggled human offerings.

There wasn't much we could do. Most of our officers were dead. All we had left were five lieutenants, an assistant surgeon, and the unconscious Captain Mackay. I saw that my captor had a gunshot wound in his right arm, but it did not seem to affect his left arm's vice-like grip. Using me as a battering ram, he burst through the mob, and thrust me in front of the *yuzbashi*, a fat little Arnaut with a hooked nose, sitting cross-legged on a fine carpet.

The *yuzbashi* took a long draw on his *chibouk* as he looked me over. 'Bene, bene,' he said at last, loosening the drawstrings of the leather money-bag and counting seven Maria Theresa dollars into the hands of my captor. It was clear enough that what had been a humiliating disaster for British arms had been a bonanza for the soldiery of the Ottoman Empire.

I was just about to be pushed into the waiting barge when a frantic row broke out somewhere in the middle of the swelling crowd of captors and prisoners. Shots were fired. The crowd swayed to and fro with yells and curses.

The *yuzbashi* rose slowly from his mat, striking about him with the long stem of his *chibouk*.

'Kalb! Kalb!' he shouted with each blow. 'Dogs and sons of dogs!'

The crowd fell back, and disgorged a battered and bloody Arnaut, fiercely gripping the rope which held his hard-won mer-chandise – my 'chosen man', Tom Keith.

9 'Sold into Egypt'

Tom Keith's drawn, grime-smeared face lit up when he saw me, but before we could exchange a word I was pitched from the bank into the barge. The hateful sack I had been forced to carry slipped from my grasp as I fell. I found myself beside the Macgregor boys and a lad from the Sussex whose foot had been crushed by a horse's hoof. A trickle of blood oozed from the sack, creeping towards me, a long, dark line in the sand that had blown into the bottom of the boat. I fell into an exhausted slumber.

I awoke, somewhere about Fuwi, to a cacophony of yelling voices. We were afloat on the Nile: the little Arnaut in front of me had just snatched Duncan Macgregor's feather bonnet, and, grimacing, was sticking it over his own red cap. Uproar in Gaelic, Arabic, English, Albanian and Turkish. I caught sight of Tom's craggy features a few yards down the boat. I knew then that, together, we would come through. Duncan, fettered at the ankles, was trying to head-butt the Arnaut. Under the weight of the Highlander bonnet the man's small round red cap fell off, revealing a shaven head with a little tuft of hair in the centre. Duncan grabbed his bonnet back. The Arnaut pulled a silver-plated pistol from his sash.

An Arnaut officer leapt to his feet, laying about him with a long hide whip. 'Ken e bir kenit! – Dog and son of a dog!' The blows rained alike on the just and the unjust. That was, I suppose, the first time I had seen the *courbash* – the principal instrument of government in Egypt since the time of the Pharaohs – and as effective now as then. The pistol returned to its holster, and the Arnauts settled down to gloating over their prisoners, canvass-ing the prices we would fetch on the Cairo slave-market, and indicating with their few words of French, Italian and English, mainly obscene, and accompanied by many lascivious gestures, what we had to look forward to.

'I'll shoot myself first,' burst out young Duncan, 'and take a dozen of these buggers with me.'

'Buggers is right,' said Tom. 'But what'll you use for a gun, lad?'

'You'll mak' me ane; Tom, will you no'?'

As, day after day, our barges slipped past endless mud villages, we arrived at a curious accommodation with these fierce, black-eyed Albanian freebooters, mountain men like ourselves, our tattered Mackenzie tartans alongside their stiff, filthy, white pleated skirts they call *fustan*s. Underneath their red and gold jackets they were all bone and sinew. Beaky noses and bulging foreheads set off by their little red caps, they were arrogant as Hell and trigger-happy. The Nile banks emptied as our barges approached. The fellahin were good at hiding – they'd had plenty of practice. Even the old women wrapped in black *melaya*s who trotted along the banks on donkeys knew that an Arnaut would use them for target practice as soon as look at them. Looking back with the perspective of fifty years, I can see that in fact we had a lot in common. We were both wild tribes, earning a living fighting other people's battles for them. But whereas we Gaels were as loyal as spaniels, these Arnauts were as treacherous as jackals. Mohammed Ali had used them to gain the Citadel, but no one knew better than he, who was one of them, that to stay there he would have to watch his back.

I remember the flies. Drawn by the smell of blood baking in the sun, caking on men's limbs, they formed a black, shining carpet, vibrating over the sacks of heads, peeling off to gather on the eyes of the wounded. At first the Arnauts would let us do nothing for our stricken and dying comrades. Then, Mr Leslie, our surgeon, sent for me to go over to the boat where Captain Mackay – for whom the Turk commander had ordered all honours – lay under a sail cloth on a bed of straw. The poor man was muttering deliriously in Gaelic. Mr Leslie took his pulse, frowned, and we moved on to others in that convoy of pain and shame. How many bullets we dug out of men's legs and arms and – once, I recall, jaw – that afternoon, how many times I tightened the old haversack strap that served as a tourniquet, I couldn't say. The trouble was our medical supplies had run out. We had to follow the Arnaut example, pouring raki on the wounds or using their salve of pine resin, green bark of elder, and white beeswax, mixed in olive oil.

We moved from boat to boat whenever the wind fell and the great lateen sails drooped. We were engaged in a desperate race with gangrene. 'Let me die! Shoot me!' one lad kept crying. I came up just in time to stop an Arnaut doing so. That one we saved. But others were lost, many others. No sooner had a man breathed his last than the Arnauts threw him over the side. Sometimes they didn't wait that long.

At home we called it *an fiabhras-critheach* – the shaking fever, *critheann* being an aspen-tree. But Mr Leslie called it *mal-aria*, on account of its being caused by the miasmas which nightly hung over the Nile. Whatever you called it, the effect of those convulsions on men already weakened by loss of blood was truly terrible to behold. (This was before the 'bark' had come into general use, you understand.)

Then I remembered one of my Grandma Beaton's more curious remedies. 'Take the gossamer threads of two spiders' webs, roll them into a pill...' As it happened, a great black spider was spinning away across the boat's ribs. What was there to lose?

I got the 'pill' down between the poor boy's chattering teeth, as the Arnauts watched, mocking. Half an hour later the terrible shaking had ceased; and an hour after that the man was sitting up, wiping the sweat from his face and asking for beer. The Arnauts were jabbering away excitedly amongst themselves.

It was just my bad luck that because of this 'miracle' I came to the notice of Ahmed Aga Bonaparte.

I lost count of time and distance as we sailed on, day after day, through the good black earth and rich crops of the Delta, a vivid patchwork, the bright emerald-green of alfalfa, the pale gold of *durra*, the dark green of beans, the orange of corn swelling on the cob. It would, I suppose, have been about the tenth day when the Libyan desert declared itself on our west, then closed in. That was the day the Arnauts threw overboard two Highland lads and an old sweat of the Sussex.

Sometimes the sand blew across the mighty river, making flurries on the surface of the water. That, I suppose, must have been the moment Drummer Donald Macleod got his first sight of the Pyramids, suspended, trembling, in the heat haze. I recall being surprised how puny they looked.

The Damietta branch of the Nile came in – no Barrage then, of course – and we approached Bulak, the port of Cairo. el-Bahr – 'the Sea' – as the fellahin call the Nile – was alive with craft of all sorts. The Arnauts started firing wildly into the air, fusillade after fusillade, and great clouds of duck and white ibis burst up from the river, filling the sky.

Nothing could have been more shameful than our landing in the port of Cairo. Still firing off their carbines, the swaggering Arnauts pushed and pulled us about, still roped as we were, forming some sort of column. A crowd gathered to stare and jeer.

I was lucky: I was carried off to attend Captain Colin Mackay, who was borne up onto the quay in a plaid in which four holes had been cut to take poles. Miraculously, he was conscious again, and looking about him.

My luck didn't last. I felt my right forearm gripped hard, and, swinging round, saw a young man in a magnificent orange turban. He was short, and his skin colouring put me in mind of what I'd seen when the Buffs were in Calabria. Paolo was my first Mameluke. I distrusted him on sight.

He was affable enough, certainly. 'Marhaba! Benvenuto! Willkommen! My Master el Excellente el Aga Bonaparte vous command!' Pointing to his eye, the way they do, he then gestured towards a large white house which stood a little back from the Nile quay.

He pulled me towards it, smiling ingratiatingly. The musk on his moustachios fought an uneven battle with the reek of the port. All kinds of workshops lined the mud quays: those of bullock-cart makers, potters and sailmakers next to stinking tanneries, slaughterhouses.

The clamorous ring of iron on iron came from a new building on our left. Paolo followed my glance. 'Fabbrica,' he announced. 'Fabbrica nuova for fucili – fusils . . . Bang, bang . . . Fabbrica of Pasha. Benissimo – no?'

A gaggle of Arnaut officers, hanging about outside the large white house, drew apart to let Paolo through.

We entered a room surrounded on three sides by low divans on which a score or more supplicants waited. Paolo swept past them and into an inner sanctum where the Aga 'Bonaparte' himself was enthroned. He sat on a mountain of cushions rising from the divan against the further wall, a five-foot-long jewelled *chibouk* to his puffy lips. He was as squat and thick-set as his namesake, but had the Arnauts' beetling brow, peaky chin and long, flat-backed head. Silver-mounted pistols gleamed in his scarlet cummerbund; the rubies set in the hilt of his *yatagan* glowed darkly.

He was, it seemed, much feared; he was not only Mohammed Ali's strong-arm man but a fabled drinker and braggart, and notoriously given to what my friend Sheikh Ibrahim – Jean-Louis Burckhardt – calls in his book 'lusts of the vilest kind'.

Not a man to cross. Bowing low to kiss the Aga's hand, Paolo tugged me forward, gesturing to me to do likewise. I remained as upright as I could.

The Aga stirred. His small, black eyes bored into me. 'Wallah! Wallah!' He savoured me slowly from head to toe. He seemed fascinated by my blond complexion, flaxen hair.

'Un ragazzo bello,' he said at last. 'Mameluke véritable! Mameluke écossais!'

He shot a malicious glance at Paolo who was now plainly sulking. 'Molto bello! Molto bello!' Bonaparte's lips parted in a smile that looked more like a leer. The gimlet eyes came to rest on the Mackenzie tartan of my tattered kilt. It seemed to fascinate him, for though the Arnaut soldiers wear a pleated short skirt called a *fustan*, they wear Turkish trews below.

'Komm herein!' he suddenly yelled; then, falsetto, 'Approches, mon brave écossais!'

The man was a clown. I edged towards the divan. Paolo, I noticed, had disappeared. Bonaparte beckoned me closer, holding me with his eyes. Suddenly, he reached out and grabbed my kilt, throwing it upwards. His jewelled hands lingered over my buttocks. He smiled ingratiatingly. 'Mameluke écossais! Molto bello!'

Repelled by the damp touch of those pudgy hands, I leapt back. His smile vanished. 'Giaour!' he yelled. 'Uncircumcised dog!'

He snatched a pistol from his sash. 'Death to Unbelievers!' His other hand flew to his yatagan. I stood transfixed. The Turks have a saying: '*Arnaut tutmak*' – 'to rage like an Arnaut'!

'Inglesi – pouf!' He threw his hands apart as if they were exploding. 'I shit on them! Yuzbashi Missett' – he rose to mimic Missett's dragging foot – 'woman... bint, imbécile... dummkopf! Mamelukes – FINISHED! Kallas! I, Ahmed Bonaparte, FINISH them.'

Back home in his native mountain village in Albania, they had called him Ahmed; it was the Egyptians – adept in these matters – who had christened him Bonaparte on account of his perpetual boasting. He had considered the name an honour, signing it floridly on all official letters and documents.

The Aga Bonaparte's mood changed yet again. He clapped his hands and summoned a servant bearing a bottle of raki. He was now proposing to drink me under the table. He leaned forward, handing me a glass while caressing my knee.

'I give you wise word, Mameluke écossais!' he croaked. 'Kiss the hand you cannot sever.'

It was fortunate that the commander of the prisoners came in to demand the immediate presence of the Scottish *hakim* at Captain Mackay's bedside. 'The brave Captain's life hangs by a thread.' Reluctantly, Ahmed Aga Bonaparte let me go. But I knew that he had set his mark upon me: the Scottish slave was his!

My heart sank when I got back to the Nile quay and saw that terrible parade of humiliation and shame, tartans torn and bloody, arms swathed in dirty bandages, the bonnets of the Highlanders looking like the comic hats of circus clowns. What would I not have given then for my brother Angus and his pipes: our own piper lay headless on the sand dunes of el-Hamed. Chivvied along by the Arnauts, kicking up dust, we emerged at last in an open space where the road turned south. Ahead, through the haze, I saw for the first time the crowding minarets and domes and towers of a great city, spreading out below bleak ochre cliffs.

Grand Cairo! Despite my weariness, excitement stirred in me. But a march of over a mile still lay ahead of us – if such a word as march could apply to that sorry straggle of the lame and the halt, the sick, the wounded and the dying. Glorious in their red and gold tunics, the Arnauts strutted around us, letting off their muskets in triumph. I walked alongside Captain Mackay's litter, trying to keep the flies off his mouth and eyes. Tom Keith was up front somewhere, I didn't know where.

To one side of our road now fields of corn and beans and bright green *bersim*; to the other, great mounds of ancient rubbish, layer on layer, the detritus of ages, of endless, long-forgotten lives. At home, in the Highlands, we bestrode our land, at least when it was still ours to bestride; these people seemed to sink into theirs.

Our fetters reduced all to the speed of the slowest. By the time we reached the Ezbekieh Gate into Cairo our sorry column – 500 officers and men of the Ross-shire Buffs, the Sussex, the 31st, de Roll's and the Dragoons – stretched back for half a mile.

Their kettle-drummers formed alongside us, and to that menacing *tap-tap, tap-tap* we passed into the square. Then the howls of the mob hit us – a tidal wave of hatred and execration. Ezbekieh Square in those days was a mile long, part cornfield, part military parade-ground, part swamp, lined on two sides by tall white houses, the 'palaces' of the rich, with groves of ancient sycamores and palms. As I became more inured to the dervish howling, I was able to look around a little.

I saw then that the 'square' was ringed by long poles, stuck into the ground, and that each pole was crowned by a round object. I tried not to look up, not to connive in any way, to give our captors the least satisfaction. But in the end, as we were driven past pole after pole, I had to look. And what I saw came out of a nightmare: the hacked-off head of Lieutenant Christopher Macrae. The fierce sun had baked the blood, giving a ghastly sheen to his features. The face looked old and wizened. He was twenty-one.

After that I kept my head down until our sorry procession was passing the late Elfi Bey's palace (once Bonaparte's headquarters) and a great roar of anger went up from the Highlanders ahead. I looked up then. Fully recognizable, his features set in a rictus which was a cruel caricature of a smile, the head of our commanding officer, Colonel Patrick Macleod, was before us, a trophy impaled on a high pole.

And yet – life is very strange – shortly afterwards, I experienced a lifting of the spirits. We have a saying in the Gaelic, '*Che robh bàs fir gun ghràs fir*' – 'Never a man dies but another is grateful'. All these men had perished, yet I, Donald Macleod, the drover-boy from the isle of Skye, was alive and intact, eighteen years old with his whole life before him.

Round and round the Ezbekieh they dragged us, kettle-drums beating their exultant tattoo, until at last the procession was turned east through the narrow streets of the Frankish quarter, where laden camels bore down upon us, donkey-boys abused us obscenely and the mob bayed for our blood.

I became aware of someone marching alongside me. It was Paolo, Ahmed Bonaparte's personal Mameluke. Instinctively, I shrank from the fawning creature, who took malicious pleasure in translating in his curious mish-mash of tongues the curses which the crowd was heaping upon us.

'Englishmen! why have you come in your ships to kill us and our children! Sons of dogs! Go home! – or we will tear your hearts out and eat them!'

Wounded men were now dropping in the road. When I tried to fall out to do what I could for them, I would get an Arnaut bayonet in my ribs. We couldn't go on much longer.

Then, as we were dragging ourselves past el-Azhar, some sort of miracle happened. An aged sheikh in a green turban came up with a donkey and ordered bystanders to hoist poor Duncan, with his horribly swollen leg, onto its back.

It was enough. The natural good nature of the Egyptian people reasserted itself. They came out of their houses offering food to us, flat Arab bread and soft white cheese and plates of *ful mudames.** (Christians will tell you the Muslims are cruel: don't believe it. The Holy Koran enjoins compassion.)

Then another small miracle occurred – a daily one. As the sun sank lower in the sky the great yellow cliffs of the Mokattam Hills which form Cairo's backdrop flushed scarlet, suffusing Salah el-Din's majestic Citadel, perched on its rock, in an unearthly light. It seemed to me some sort of symbol, for if the Ezbekieh, where our long ordeal had begun, was the social centre of Cairo, the Citadel, where Mohammed Ali now sat, was the seat of power.

It was also to be our prison.

Our sorry column straggled around the towering walls of the mosque of Sultan Hassan, crossed the Rumeila, passed through the massive open gates of the Bab el-Azab, and somehow dragged

---

* Broad beans long boiled slowly, in oil, a favourite Egyptian dish. – F.M.

itself up the steep stone-walled lane that mounts to el-Katal, the Citadel. They were ready for us, pushing us into the janissary barracks, the dank cavern which was to be our home for the next five months.

The big rusty key turned on us with an awful finality. The senior surviving officer, Captain Vogelsang, felt it his duty to keep up our morale; but neither his English nor his Gaelic was up to it.

'Soldaten! Der König Hilfe send . . . schnell . . . schnell!'

He was ignored.

It was Vogelsang of de Roll's who had raised the white flag at el-Hamed. Somebody said that the name meant 'chicken'.

'Mackenzie Fraser's not the man to let his Highlanders down!' said young Donald Macleod, my namesake from Lewis. 'He'll be coming after us, man.'

'With what?' It was Tom Keith, always the practical man. 'How many of our fellows do you think he's got left now after Rosetta?'

There was a voice from the back. 'Don't fash yourself, Tom Keith, yon wee Missett's after sending in his Mamelukes. The cavalry's coming!'

That got a rueful laugh; for a moment we felt better. But the mood did not last. We all knew of the great Cairo slave-market. The Arnauts had made sure of that. We had seen the *yuzbashis* paying out good money for us on the Nile bank and, thanks to our Arnaut captors, we had heard much of the curious tastes of rich Turks.

Ribald speculation was cut short by a thunderous stamping of feet on the flags outside. Keys grated in locks, and an Arnaut officer with an armed guard stepped into that great cavern, our prison.

'The Effendina – His Excellency – vous attend,' he said, curtly. 'Les officiers solamente . . . Subito! Halan!'

Captain Vogelsang stepped forward, but the Arnaut brushed him off and made for Captain Colin Mackay, whose deep neck wound I happened to be dressing. Mr Leslie protested that Mackay was in no condition to be moved. The Arnaut ignored him, shouting orders to his escort, and four soldiers came in carrying a camel litter, suspended from poles. The Captain was gently lifted in and the Arnaut indicated that I was to go along too.

In this way, at the very outset of my curious career in Egypt, I got a close look at the remarkable man who, in one way or another, was to dominate my life – and part of Jeannie's – for more than forty years.

He sat cross-legged on a divan at the head of his audience chamber, rubicund, bearded and moustachioed, an immense white Turkish turban overhanging bushy eyebrows: the Effendina, Mohammed Ali, Viceroy of Egypt, Pasha of Three Tails by the grace of the Sultan-Caliph in Constantinople, and the absolute master of our fates.

He took the long jewelled stem of his water-pipe from his lips as our few surviving officers ranged themselves before him, Colin Mackay in his litter at their head, I standing beside him. Mohammed Ali eyed us carefully for a full minute without speaking. I noticed then how small and delicate his hands were, almost like a woman's. But what really struck me – struck everybody who met him – was the extraordinary penetration of his luminous blue eyes.

When at last those eyes released us, he spoke quietly and courteously in Turkish; he was the very antithesis of his ranting henchman, Ahmed Aga Bonaparte.

A tall, long-faced European stood at the Pasha's side, translating his words for us. He wore a French-style military tunic over Turkish-style baggy trousers, and spoke English with an Italian accent.

'The Pasha greatly regrets that, for some reason he is unable to understand, the army of England has come to attack Egypt, her old friend and ally. He is much hurt in his heart by this. Néan-moins, he promises the English prisoners good usage. While they are his guests in Egypt they will remain under his particular protection.'

Those eyes swept us again, then a hand was raised in dismissal.

'The Effendina,' announced the interpreter, 'now wishes his English guests good fortune, and takes his leave of you.'

The promise faded the moment our prison doors clanged behind us.

'His *guests!*' burst out Mackay. 'The bastard knows that as long as he holds us here he can demand his own price from General Fraser!'

'The màl dubh?' I said.

'Blackmail, yes, but it's not money that fellow's after. It's power.'

It was in fact only two years since Mohammed Ali had seized the seat of power in the Citadel and sent the Ottoman pasha packing. He had come up from nowhere. Some say that at home in Albania he was a poor tobacco-trader who had married the rich mayor's daughter in the next village. He'd come to Egypt as second-in-command of a small Albanian unit in the Ottoman army, sent to expel the French. There's a story that the British Admiral Sidney Smith saved him from drowning by pulling him out of the sea and into his gig at the landing.

He was ambitious. One day the severed head of Taher, the Albanian commander, had come flying out of an upper window. No one ever discovered who did the deed. But as my friend Louis – Sheikh Ibrahim el-Sharmi – used to say, Mohammed Ali was not cruel, but he always knew which heads to sever. He played the surviving Mamelukes against the Sultan and the Sultan against the Mamelukes, and his Arnauts against both.

For years the English had been roaring out, 'Britons never, never, never shall be slaves.' And now this man, whose name was still scarcely known, held two hundred officers and men of proud British regiments in his power, sold into slavery like children of Israel before them.

But what I think enraged us most was our discovery that the man in the French tunic who interpreted for Mohammed Ali was, in fact, Bonaparte's man in Alexandria, Bernardino Drovetti.

He'd rushed off to Cairo to warn Mohammed Ali the moment our ships were sighted.

As I've said already: we'd never had a chance from the start.

I have to admit that after Mohammed Ali's little speech the lot of his 'guests' did begin to improve. For one thing – and this was probably Drovetti's doing – Dr Royer, who had been chief pharmacist to Bonaparte's Army of Egypt, turned up at our prison door with a much-needed supply of French drugs. I confess we looked at them askance at first, since Royer was reputed to have poisoned the French sick and wounded hampering Bonaparte's retreat from Acre. Soon afterwards, our officers were allowed out on parole into Cairo, disguised in Turkish costume.

But what really set all tongues wagging was the news that Mohammed Ali was planning to send Lieutenant Matheson to Alexandria with a Turkish escort to negotiate an exchange of prisoners with General Fraser.

Suddenly all our talk was of home. My dreams of the Promised Land in North Carolina began to glow again. My handfasted bride, I was confident, would be waiting on the quayside. At that very moment a letter making the arrangements, in that confident way of hers, might be on its way to me.

We watched Matheson leave with great hope in our hearts.

When weeks, then months, went by with no word or sight of him, we grew thoughtful. At first we brushed aside our doubts easily enough. Clearly, it was taking time to recover our own Ottoman prisoners, already sent to Sicily. Arranging transport over the Western desert would take time, too.

As week after week went by and still no news came, and we lay about in that dark and foetid cellar, gloomier thoughts took over. Matheson had been shot by some crazed Bedou or Arnaut, before he had even reached Alexandria. Drovetti was playing some deep game – he had, after all, been one of Bonaparte's gang, a treacherous Piedmontese.

I do not need to tell my readers how bitter we felt, abandoned to our fate in the hands of the infidels. Rich Turks and a few of the bolder Mameluke beys had taken to touring our prison again, offering pistachio nuts, cooked fowls and sweetmeats to the younger and prettier lads. There were one or two obvious slave-dealers among them.

One day when I was dressing Colin Mackay's neck some sixth sense made me swing round – and there, watching me intently, was Paolo. My skin crawled; I felt sure Ahmed Bonaparte must have sent him. The instant he saw I'd spotted him he put on that ingratiating smile, offering a basket of peaches he claimed to have brought for me.

I confided my fears about Paolo to Colin, who undertook to warn Drovetti, which did not lessen my apprehension. Colin was getting stronger now by the day and one evening, with Tom's help, I managed to get him up onto the great stone platform atop the Citadel. As the sun slid down in a fiery glow behind the Mokattam Hills, we watched the ancient land spring to life in the long shadows. Over to the north Colin pointed out the Wind-mill Hills, so called because Bonaparte's *savants* had erected there the first corn mills driven by wind power in this ancient land. Westwards, the Pyramids floated mysteriously over a desert extending as far as the eye could see. Glints of silver from the palm groves betrayed the presence of the mighty Nile coursing through the yellow-grey maze of the city with its countless min-arets, domes, palaces, gardens, a mighty metropolis, pivot of continents.

Colin had spent his long convalescence studying the subject and had much that was strange to impart. He led us to the south side where the towering walls of the Citadel met the Eastern desert, stretching out to what Cairenes call 'the City of the Dead' where countless simple graves of ordinary men and women mingle with the now crumbling domes and towers of the majestic mausoleums of the Mameluke beys.

My eye was caught by a particularly splendid dome – splendid with an austere beauty.

'The mosque-tomb of the great Beybars,' said Colin, following my glance. 'He threw the Crusaders out of Jerusalem, turned back the Mongols and took the rule of Egypt into the Sudan. Yet he started life as a slave in Damascus. They say his first master sent him back to the dealer because he had a cast in one eye.'

My mind was reeling, and my face must have showed it. Colin laughed. 'It seems this very word "mameluke" means "bought man" – white slave. Beybars made his "bought men" into an empire that lived off Egypt for six hundred years.'

By that time Matheson had been gone for months. All sorts of rumours were circulating. It was said that Mohammed Ali was now demanding not only that General Fraser leave Egypt at once, but also that he pledge that Britain would never return. Rumour had it that this had stuck in the General's craw. I felt sure now that Drovetti was at the bottom of all this.

We talked of making a break for it. But our Arnaut captors were watching us day and night. At night they chained us to our beds. Duncan Macrae was the first to vanish, a handsome lad of eighteen. Just gone vanished overnight, his bed hardly rumpled. A few days after that, Lieutenant Walker failed to return from the streets of Cairo, and he was not the man to break his parole. Despite Mohammed Ali's so-called protection, it was becoming obvious that unless Matheson showed up very soon we must give up all hope of ever seeing our homes again.

Two days after that Colin got back in his Turkish 'parole dress' from a stroll through the bazaars, having picked up a rumour from Alexandria that the *askari Inglees* had boarded their ships and were sailing away.

A few, of course, just could not believe it, the way my father wouldn't have: Mackenzie Fraser would never desert his Highlanders, they said.

But as the days drifted by and there was still no word of Matheson, and more and more familiar faces began to disappear from our prison by night – clearly with the complicity of our guards – we were forced to the bitter conclusion that we had indeed been abandoned. To judge by the number of rich pashas and beys looking us over, they too had concluded that the market was now open to all comers.

Paolo was around our prison barrack almost every day, trying to curry favour with Tom Keith now as well as with me. An armourer *and* a *hakim* – what a feather that would be in Ahmed Aga Bonaparte's cap! Tom and I made a pact. We would keep

watch, turn and turn about, day and night. If one of us was forced
to drink Paolo's coffee or accept a sweetmeat, the other would
refuse it. These people, we knew, were fiendishly clever at drugging
their victims.

The nights, with the fetters on, were the worst. Somewhere in
that vast stone cavern one would hear a strangled cry; next
morning there would be another empty palliasse. Tom now slept
with an old horse-pistol he'd found and repaired hidden in the
straw of his palliasse. I sewed a lancet into a seam of my shirt.

Alas, we never had a chance to use them.

I was lying on the bottom of my half-brother Peter's boat, pitching
about in the Minch, and my father was at the oars, singing. His
song was not a boat-song, but the chorus of Jeannie Macdonald's
flyting song at the waulking. 'Iomair o hò, clò nan gillean . . .'
Then my drove-dog, Donald, broke out, yapping furiously, and I
became conscious of the fetters biting into my leg.

Reluctantly I opened my eyes, then shut them at once. The sun
was blinding. I opened them again, more cautiously, and saw that
I was sprawled in the bottom of a *cangia* that was moving slowly
down the Nile. Two dogs were barking furiously in a mud village
on the bank. The boatmen were at the tow-ropes, singing, as
Egyptian boatmen will. A few yards away, across the bottom of
the boat, Tom Keith was snoring stertorously. I wondered,
drowsily, how they had done it. Had Royer, perhaps, supplied
some potent drug?

I guessed that we were somewhere south of Beni Suef, moving
through sandbanks. I let Tom be. Then the high sandstone cliffs
moved in on us on both sides. We were sailing past the white
minarets of palm-fringed villages, and sometimes, the dome of a
church topped by a Greek cross. It was very hot: when the
boatmen leapt into the river to manhandle the craft off a sandbank
their dripping *galabiya*s dried on their backs almost instantly.

Then I saw Paolo coming towards me with a bowl of *ful
mudames*. It looked like brown vomit. I tried to hurl it at him,
but hadn't the strength. He just smiled that ingratiating smile of
his, the malice seeping from the edges, and came back a few
minutes later with a brass coffee-pot.

I pointed to the chains biting into my ankle.

'Ekta!' – Cut!

He smiled again and poured out a *fingan* of coffee.

'Where are you taking us?'

He put a hand on my shoulder, but made no attempt to remove the leg-irons. 'Lontano,' he said, 'Molto lontano. Très loin.'

So Ahmed Bonaparte was playing his own game like a true Arnaut, sending us far up the Nile into Mameluke country where the writ of the Viceroy, Mohammed Ali, hardly ran.

Paolo groped for some English in his rag-bag of languages. 'Minya . . . Ezbek – Ezbek Bey. Good, good!' he said.

Revived by the hot and bitter coffee, I moved over to where Tom lay slumped in torn kilt and filthy red jacket, and hauled him into the shade. He opened his eyes, trying to focus. They focused on Paolo. He spat out a curse, and pulled himself up, staring blearily at the mud banks of the river floating by.

'Where the de'il are we?'

'On the way to some place called Minya.'

'Where's Colin?'

'In Cairo, far as I know. We're on our own, Tom.'

We were sailing past what has since become familiar as Jebel Tair, crowned by its Coptic convent. All of a sudden the water was full of naked Copts, swimming around our boat, inflated skins under their arms. 'Ana Christian, ya hawagi,' they yelled. 'Bakshish, bakshish!'

Our boatmen beat them off with astonishing venom.

Tom beckoned me down to his level.

'First chance we get, we'll clobber the bastards and make a run for it.'

I pointed to his leg-irons. 'What, with these on?' The Arnaut guards were watching us. 'We're two hundred miles from the battalion in Alexandria, assuming there's anybody there any more.'

'First chance we get we'll jump them – make a run for it,' insisted my 'chosen man'.

'Two hundred miles – with white skins, no money, and next to no Arabic . . . we'd be lucky to get five!'

Two days later, we tied up at Minya.

Another landing in my life. As we struggled up the muddy bank in our chains, the muezzins of the town's mosques ascended their minarets and began the noon call to prayer.

'Al-la-hu Akbar! Al-la-hu Akbar! La-i-la-i-l-l-lah!' The declaration of faith rolled out over the town and the scores of boats tied up in the river. All around me I saw men spreading their prayer-mats, turning towards Mecca, and beginning to move patiently through the cycle of the *rekah*s. Strange as it may seem, in my confused and weakened state I found this reassuring.

A fair-skinned man of about thirty on a richly caparisoned horse cantered down to meet us. He wore a yellow turban like Paolo's, but I was astonished to hear him address Paolo and the Arnaut escort in the French of a Frenchman. 'Vite! Suivez moi! Son Excellence veut voir les prisonniers tout de suite. Dépêchez-vous!'

The great copper stirrups of his magnificent saddle gleamed in the sun as he wheeled his mount around and headed across an expanse of growing cotton towards the Bey's 'palace', a building of whitewashed brick between the Nile and the ancient channel they call the Bahr Yussef.

We were conducted by Paolo and the Arnaut guard through a large courtyard, bright with orange-trees and pomegranates, and past a splendid fountain. One whole wall of the 'palace' was blank, save for a lattice-covered projection high up. From this drifted faint sounds of fluting voices, interspersed by giggling. The Bey's wives and concubines and their slaves were watching us. They could see without being seen.

We were hurried past to the *selamlik*, the men's quarters. Ezbek Bey, I must confess, was a disappointment. A stout little man with a swarthy skin, hooked nose and a predatory smile, he received us reclining on a pile of cushions. He stormed at Paolo for not having removed our leg-irons. Clearly he saw us as valuable properties. The glory of a Mameluke chief lay in the magnificence of his corps and Ezbek Bey's camp contained a splendid diversity of pink-cheeked acolytes purchased from poor families in the Caucasus or Georgia, taken prisoner in the Greek wars, or picked up in the slave-markets of Hungary, Stanboul or Cairo. But recruits from the Highlands of Scotland – now *that* was something! That would confer a rare distinction.

'Six feet three, blond and freckled,' growled Tom Keith, the Lowlander. 'The bugger just can't wait to set his mark upon you!'

Our investiture, it now became clear, was to be performed by the French Mameluke who had met us at the landing stage.

His was a story hardly less strange than our own. After four years enjoying the flesh-pots of Bonaparte's occupation of Egypt, some thousands of French soldiers had stayed behind when their defeated army had sailed for home. François was one of them. He had been a *chasseur* in Desaix's regiment, sent up the Nile into Upper Egypt to wipe out the Mamelukes fleeing from the Battle of the Pyramids. One day he'd chased the Mamelukes too far into the desert and had been captured. The *chasseur* from Marseille had become the Master of the Bey's Horse, a post of much honour in the curious, antique world which, by one of history's wilder jokes, he now inhabited.

I think our arrival appealed to François's sense of humour. He set about the process of inducting us into this inward-looking, epicene Mameluke corps with obvious relish.

'Premièrement,' announced the Master of the Bey's Horse, 'il faut faire venir le barbier.'

The barber turned out to be a wizened old Greek, evidently the spoil of some earlier Ottoman war. He carried brushes, a box of scissors, a lathering cup, and a stool.

'Sit!' ordered the Frenchman. The old Greek began to strop a razor.

I leapt from the stool. Suddenly the enormity of what was about to happen dawned on me.

The Master of the Horse motioned me back onto the stool, explaining with many puzzling gestures that unless my head was shaved clean, the orange *kauk* which is the Mameluke's crowning glory would not fit.

'Best play along,' said Tom. But as I watched my fair locks fall, one by one, onto the sand, I felt I was losing my identity. I saw that the old Greek was picking up every single hair I had shed. In my vanity I thought this was because of the rarity of my sort of blondness in Egypt. Only later did I discover that Islam regards it as sinful to throw away, disrespectfully, any part of the human body. Even the foreskins, abandoned on circumcision, must be accorded the burial due to God's creation.

I was next fitted with a red skull-cap. This was the foundation of the Mameluke's elaborate headgear. Then François summoned Paolo, who turned out to be Master of the Bey's Wardrobe and

Bedchamber, to instruct me in winding the long band of white muslin that goes around the *kauk*, pulling it together amidships with a golden cord.

This was only the beginning of a process designed to transform a brawny, scrape-faced Highland lad into a blooming flower of this bizarre corps of 'bought men' who had plundered the people of Egypt for centuries. Garment was laid on garment: a gown of flowered silk over a shirt of yellow cotton; a pelisse of ermine over a rose-hued caftan.

Young Mamelukes stood around, giggling and simpering as my bedraggled old kilt was borne away in favour of Turkish trousers so cumbersome I could almost have got my entire body into one leg. I did not feel ridiculous so much as unutterably lost. Then Paolo reappeared with a smirk on his face, carrying a long Indian shawl of flowered silk, which he proceeded to wind around my waist. His fingers lingered in its folds, groping downwards, as he gazed into my eyes, lips parted.

The young Mamelukes tittered knowingly. Some, I noticed, had dark flirtatious eyelashes, and some, blue eyes and peaches-and-cream complexions. The favourites bore titles such as the Bey's Chief Chibouk-Carrier, or the Bey's Principal Cup-Bearer, or that much coveted post which – for the moment – was Paolo's, Master of the Bey's Bedchamber.

The Mameluke corps was renewed not by the children of the beys, but by a constant influx of new blood from the slave-markets of Asia. Beys were often succeeded not by the sons of their wives, but by their Mameluke favourites. A Mameluke bey had, in reality, not one harem, but two; his wives and concubines were often lonely, needing to deploy all their arts to distract their master from his current catamite.

'Sodom and Gomorrah, that's where we've landed,' growled Tom. 'Sodom and Gomorrah!'

Beneath its ornate surface, the Bey's palace fairly seethed with fevered jealousies, labyrinthine feuds, murderous lusts.

Paolo soon became convinced that I could only have rejected his advances because of an infatuation with Tom Keith. Were not we two always whispering together in corners? He laid his plans accordingly. After hanging around the *hammam* for days, he discovered that neither Tom nor I was circumcised. By sly hints at first, Paolo let me know he *knew*. He had us where he wanted us. That insinuating, malicious little smile of his hardly ever left his face. Henceforth, every day was lived under a terrible threat. Although, as that fine Koranic scholar Jean-Louis Burckhardt – Sheikh Ibrahim el-Shami – later pointed out to me, circumcision is nowhere required (or so much as mentioned) in the Holy Koran, 'Circumcision or death' had long been the war cry of the advancing hosts of Islam. The foreskin was the shameful secret that betrayed the *giaour*, the infidel, the spy in the House of Islam. There were many stories of uncovering and instant death. Paolo had chosen his ground well.

I proposed the obvious solution. 'Never!' said Tom.

I could understand his horror. We had given up everything. We had watched our old Ross-shire Buffs uniforms carried away and we had been compelled to put on these ridiculously flamboyant outfits. In a strange way our foreskins, that inch or two of flesh, were all that was now left to us – our last claim to identity in this mad Mameluke world.

Furthermore, I had seen the dirty razor of the officiating barber who in Egypt normally performed the operation on boys five or six years of age.

Paolo watched the two of us all the time, playing off the fear he knew we must have. At table, he would pick up a banana and, eying us lasciviously, slowly slice round the tip.

At last, in desperation, I went to François, who I knew detested the Sicilian. But he just threw back his head and guffawed. I'd forgotten he hailed from Marseille. To him the whole thing was one great joke and he refused to take it seriously.

It was only a few days later that I received a call from the Havinder Bashi who ordered me to report to the Bey immediately. The Chief Treasurer looked very grave. I went in fear and trembling, expecting exposure.

What I found was somewhat different; a pathetic figure, squinting up at me through a bleary, half-closed eye oozing pus. A golden *banduke* dangled from the edge of the Bey's turban over the bloodshot eye, a charm against one of the great plagues of Egypt, ophthalmia. Evidently my reputation as a *hakim* had gone before me.

A Mameluke is taught never to betray pain. But Ezbek Bey, hero of a thousand sabre cuts, was whimpering like a child.

'I beg you . . . please! In the name of Allah . . .'

Sufferers from ophthalmia describe it as like having a thousand slivers of broken glass behind sightless eyes. Thank God I still had a small phial of copper sulphate, left over from Royer's supplies, at the bottom of my kit.

I took the Bey's pulse. It was racing. As I moved his head towards the light to examine the eye, he drew back in agony. I ordered the Greek Mameluke at his side to hold a shade over his head. A velvety pus seeped from below the upper lid.

Untreated, this plague has made Egypt a land of the blind and half-blind. Yet it is easily enough cured. I measured out seven grains of copper sulphate into an ounce of boiled water and poured this into a small bottle. I inclined the Bey's head gently backwards, and a single blue drop trembled on the bottle's rim and fell into his eye.

I said: 'Have patience, O Bey, and inshallah all will soon be well.'

The Ancient Egyptians believed that a single tear, falling from the eye of the goddess Isis, gave birth to the Nile's life-giving Flood. I believe that single drop of copper sulphate, falling on the cornea of Ezbek Bey's suppurating eye in Minya that afternoon, preserved my life.

Ten days later, a bright-eyed Ezbek presented me with the handsome fur hat of his Hakim Bashi. Proud in my new Chief Physician's cap of office, I felt that, 'white slave' or no, I was my own man again.

When I think of that now, I could weep.

11 Haram!

Basking in the Bey's gratitude for having restored his sight, cutting a dash in my fur hat, I found myself wondering – with many a pang – what my mother would think of her only son now. Tom, too, was much sought after, for the Mamelukes used an extraordinary array of antique weapons, often more dangerous to their owners than to the enemy. Their horsemen fired small cannon from the saddle as they charged, or brass-barrelled blunderbusses, flint-locked, bell-mouthed. Tom was in his element, combing the *suks* of Minya for bits of metal to effect repairs in time for the martial exercises the Bey had announced.

Apart from pillaging the fellahin (which passed as 'collecting taxes'), these martial contests seemed to be the be-and-end-all of the Mamelukes' existence. They had been engaged in them for three centuries, and had still failed to notice that Bonaparte's artillery, blasting their beys to hell at the Battle of the Pyramids, had rendered such contests a grotesque irrelevance.

Protected now by my post of Hakim Bashi, I watched with mounting astonishment as François paraded the corps in all the glory of its bright silks and jewelled breast-plates in the spacious courtyard between the *selamlik* side of the palace and the harem side for the 'Trial of the *Djerid*'.

A long, pointed, wooden javelin, hurled at the enemy from horseback with ferocious cries, the *djerid* could send a man flying. It was a point of honour that every Mameluke horseman should prove his daring with it.

After that came the 'Trial of the Felt', in which a heavy cloth is stretched between two poles, and the horseman, galloping past, is required to cleave the cloth with a single blow of the sabre, even as he might a man's head. François could perform this feat, but no one else could that day. The Bey intimated that the thing was child's play, and unworthy of his attention.

It was with the exercise called 'the Jar' that trouble flared. Paolo came up to me, dragging one foot, claiming to have sprained his ankle, and requesting me, as Hakim Bashi, to issue a paper declaring him unfit to continue in the contests. Clearly, he thought that the hold he had on me and Tom was as strong as ever. He wore an expression of agony on his face, strangely mixed with a gloating smirk. I got him to lie down on a bench, and bent over him to run my fingers over the ankle. As I did so, he smiled slyly up at me, fondling my thigh. I pronounced him perfectly fit to take his place in the contest of the Jar.

The Jar was the target. The Mamelukes ranged themselves in a half-circle with an earthenware jar near the centre, and, sighting along their antiquated carbines, were required to break the jar with one shot. It called for a good eye and a steady aim and the blessing of Allah. Paolo fired wildly, fired again and narrowly missed. Then Tom fired, and, by the merest chance, the bullet ricocheted off the rim of the jar and whined past Paolo's ear.

Seething with rage, insanely jealous of Tom and convinced he had contrived the accident, Paolo hurled his heavy gun at Tom's head. Tom ducked in time, thank God. In the shocked silence that followed, Paolo stood there, immobile, stabbing a forefinger at his 'enemy'. Then, letting fly a string of curses, he turned on his heel and left the parade-ground.

Tom said nothing; the contest resumed. But a vendetta had been proclaimed before the whole camp. From the latticework above my head I detected a susurration. The harem, too, knew that trouble was brewing. Blood was going to be spilled.

The day after the martial exercises in the courtyard, a gangling, hollow-eyed negro called on me after dark – the Khislar Aga,* the Chief Eunuch of the Bey's harem. In a husky, yet oddly authoritarian, voice he informed me that the Khadin Effendi** was *mala* and required the attendance of the Hakim Bashi on the following afternoon.

* Literally, the 'Chief of the Girls' ** The Principal Wife – F.M.

This placed me in a fearful dilemma. '*Haram*' was – after *bakshish* – one of the first Arabic words I had learned. It was pronounced with passion, especially where women were concerned. So many things were *forbidden*. It was *haram* for a man to look upon the face of a woman not of his immediate family. How much worse if the man who penetrated Ezbek's harem should turn out be an uncircumcised Christian dog whose touch, even through clothing, would irreparably defile. Suspicion, I knew, was a eunuch's stock-in-trade.

Could the summons be just another of Paolo's diabolical tricks?

On the other hand, if I did not obey, the Chief Wife would complain to the Bey, who would consider this an affront to his harem. I had forgotten that I was a slave, despite that fancy hat. I was a Mameluke – a 'bought man'.

'Destour!' I sang out as I approached the door – 'Permission.' It is supposed to be a warning to the women to lower their veils and withdraw, but in my experience the effect is precisely the opposite; it signals excitement, delicious opportunity, the time to move into that hip-swinging movement they call the *ghung*. There speaks an old harem *hakim*; but at the time of which I write, all this was still a closed book to me. Fear fought with curiosity as, scowling, the Khislar Aga parted the heavy red curtains and hurried me past a succession of curtained doorways.

I was enveloped in a bath of warm air, laced with the scent of musk and sandalwood, the acridity of burned coffee-beans and the varying exhalations of forty or fifty idle females.

Two big-breasted Negresses and a willowy Circassian covertly eyed me from one doorway as the Keeper of the Girls hurried me along. The place was a labyrinth, since each of Ezbek's three wives had her own apartments and her own retinue of black and white slaves, not to mention those of the Bey's bedridden, half-blind mother, who presided in name at least over that overheated, pullulating female world.

At last the Khislar Aga came to a halt before a pair of fine brocaded curtains. He cried, 'Hakim Bashi,' and thrust me unceremoniously through them into Adile Hanem's apartments.

I found myself gazing desperately at a pair of great kohl-outlined eyes, all the more unnerving in that they were the only part of the Bey's Chief Wife then visible. She reclined amidst a frothing sea of pink and cream silks festooned around the divan, where two lissom Nubian slave-girls plied fans.

Watching my every movement, like a cat with a mouse, the Khislar Aga was plainly loth to depart. When Adile sharply ordered him to leave, he stood his ground, remonstrating in a high, husky voice which seemed gratingly over-familiar – as if the Bey's wife were an errant child.

I don't know what she said to him, but in the end he withdrew.

Language did not prove the obstacle I had anticipated. The 'patient' simply pointed to her mouth, and gave an order to the Nubian girl on her right, whose name was Fatima. I judged that she was about sixteen, and when she smiled that whole oppressive room lit up. Fatima lifted up the Khadin Effendi's long veil – for she had hidden herself under a *burko*, apparently on the eunuch's orders – thus revealing, as in a frame, the bottom half of a moon face, and an expression both petulent and sensual. The carmined lips bore a few small blisters which she indicated with a low sob.

I was puzzled. A few small cold blisters did not seem an adequate reason for an urgent summons to the Chief Physician. I bent to examine them more closely and was startled to see those voluminous silks erupting, parting, to reveal billow after billow of musk-perfumed flesh. Could those be love-bites, more inflamed than the blisters? Fatima's eyes met mine, and we exchanged a glance of perfect comprehension, slave to slave. Fleeting as our complicit glance had been, I was afraid the Bey's wife had intercepted it. I hoped my carelessness would not hurt the girl.

It was fortunate that in my medical bag I had a box of all-purpose pills, compounded from breadcrumbs soaked in the juice of bitter aloes. They had a taste so revolting that my patients were quickly convinced of their efficacy. These I now prescribed, with many assurances of their potency. I handed them over to Fatima, with instructions as to how they were to be administered, and promised to compound a powerful ointment for the following day's visit.

Next day I found the gaunt figure of the Khislar Aga barring the entrance to the harem. His mistress had no further use for my services. Unfortunately for him, a furious message requiring the *hakim*'s immediate presence arrived at that very moment. The eunuch surrendered with ill grace.

My lady now invited me to lay my *hakim*ly ear to her heart. I

contented myself with the pulse at her wrist. It was very fast. By
now I had arrived at a diagnosis: boredom, deep, deadly and
corrosive. I had also determined it was not going to be relieved
by a tall, blond, freckle-faced Scots Mameluke lately arrived in
Minya in a skirt. Tom and I were in more than enough trouble
already.

I ignored those fluttering black lashes, the invitation of the
slipping pink sheets and that ripe papaya of a body, while putting
on a show of finding the temptation well-nigh irresistible. On
reflection, this may have lacked conviction, because Fatima had
lustrous black hair cut shoulder-length in the style you may see
in the Pharaohs' tomb paintings, and she wore a simple white
dress which made the finery of Ezbek Bey's wives and concubines
seem trumpery.

On my next summons to the harem, Fatima had vanished.
When I inquired, as casually as I could, where my erstwhile
'assistant' might be, I received nothing but a dismissive wave of
a hennaed and jewelled hand.

The Mamelukes kept themselves to themselves. It was both their
strength and their weakness. Imagine my surprise, therefore, when
Ezbek Bey provided his Chief Physician with a house to the east
of the town, well away from the compound. I consulted François.
He touched his nose, grinning. 'He's had a look at you, hasn't
he? Ezbek's no fool. He's got his harem to consider. He thinks
it'll be a lot safer if you're outside the camp.'

In truth I was much relieved to escape from that gilded cage
and to have the chance to use my medical knowledge, such as it
was, on the folk who really needed attention, the Egyptian fellahin, the despised soil-grubbers who had been downtrodden for
centuries. And sure enough, as soon as the news got around that
the Bey's Hakim Bashi was in their midst, a queue began to form
outside my door. It grew steadily. They came from miles around.
I quickly acquired colloquial Arabic and I learned many things. I
consoled women whom Allah, as they said, had 'punished' with
a succession of girl babies and, probably unsuccessfully, I warned
the barren that it was no cure to eat the mud of the Nile. I told
men weakened with the worm migrating through their veins to
cover their feet when in the water, though I knew full well that

they couldn't or wouldn't. Since love-philtres were much in demand, I fell back on one of my Grandmother Beaton's recipes and hoped for the best. But I drew heavily on local folk-wisdom, too, gathering it from my patients as I went along: camel's urine to clear a head of lice, aloes to tighten the female parts (ensuring a supply of chickens from grateful husbands) and, for syphilis – another of the Plagues of Egypt – burying the whole person up to the chin in the hot desert sand. My readers may consider the last excessive, but I have been assured by Dr Antoine Clôt – the celebrated Clôt Bey, engaged by Mohammed Ali to start Egypt's first medical school – that the treatment is *'sage et rationnel'*. (His very words!)

So my fame spread, and the fellahin conferred upon me the title of 'Lord of the Bowels', which pleased me much more than my Mameluke title of Hakim Bashi, even though it carried no fancy hat. In short, everything just then seemed to be shaping well for me. Now that I was dirtying my hands with the fellahin, Adile Hanem no longer sent the Khislar Aga with urgent summonses to her bedside; Paolo, too, seemed to have given up, for the moment at least, his threats to reveal our shameful secret. I still worried over the fate of the Khadin's Nubian slave, Fatima. But so closely did the eunuchs watch the harem that there was nothing I could do.

There was just one fly in the ointment. My fellahin patients were becoming seriously worried at my continuing solitary state. For without a wife, a concubine, or even so much as a single slave-girl, they were convinced that I must look with lustful eyes upon their wives and daughters.

To remove this grave impropriety, numerous well-to-do fellahin offered their daughters, enlarging at length on their beauty and spotless purity, often forgetting that as the family *hakim* I might know otherwise. Some of the proffered brides were scarcely over fourteen, which shocked me – until I recalled that Jeannie Macdonald had been only a year or so older when we were handfasted up there on the shieling. She would now, I calculated morosely, be twenty-two.

As ever, just when I seemed to be finding my feet, an unforeseen event threw my mind and my plans into turmoil again.

It was a day in September when the Flood was at its height, and the islands in the Nile opposite Minya had long since disappeared beneath the water. An old fellah I'd been treating for lungs raddled by a lifetime among the cotton-bolls came to me with the news that a party of the Pasha's men had come up the river from Cairo and were asking questions about the English *askari*s – 'soldiers in skirts'. They were offering rewards for sightings.

I thought we'd done with all that. We'd been shamefully let down. It had been every man for himself. But now, it seemed, Mohammed Ali was standing by his undertaking to recover the prisoners of Rosetta and el-Hamed sold into slavery. The 'rescue' party had last been seen heading for Ezbek Bey's camp.

Once again I found myself facing a terrible dilemma; here was a chance to get back to Scotland, to show my mother what I had achieved and make her proud of me. Not only that – I might at last learn the truth about Jeannie, and why she had walked out on me without a word. Then a chill thought hit me. By now she might be married, even have children of her own. And what would the honourable office of Hakim Bashi count for in the island of Skye? Could I face going back to being Donald, the poor drover-lad? It was all too late. As the English say, I had chosen my bed, and now must lie on it. (Except that I hadn't exactly *chosen* it, had I?)

In the end, as has so often happened in my life, the decision was made for me. Before I could get to Tom Keith to let him know what was afoot, a party of Mameluke horsemen swept past, pulled me off my feet and swung me over a saddle. Ezbek Bey – or was it Ahmed Bonaparte? – was plainly in no mood to sur-render Scottish Mamelukes to Mohammed Ali, or even to King George of England. As the party galloped into the courtyard of the palace, someone threw a black sheet over my head. I could be taken for a woman. Ezbek was being clever: he was going to hide his precious possession in the one place Mohammed Ali's agents would never dare to look for it – his harem.

The Khislar Aga was waiting, a grim smile on his face. Grabbing me savagely round the neck, he dragged me along a corridor I had never seen before. He possessed astonishing strength. The corridor ended in a massive iron door. Holding me by the throat, he turned a grating key, swung the iron door open, and pitched me forward.

When I got my wind back, I saw that I was in some sort of

cellar. It was very dim down there, the only light filtering in from a grating high up on one wall.

Then I heard a whimper. In the thin shaft of dust-spangled light, I thought I saw the figure of a young girl prone on the earthen floor, tethered to the wall by a rope. My first thought was that this must be the punishment chamber for the harem's errant slaves.

With a wild cry, the girl tried to stagger to her feet and throw herself upon me. She was brought up with a cruel jerk by the rope. I saw then that it was Fatima. Her lithe arms were around my legs, holding on desperately, kissing them, stroking them, uttering little cries.

I took hold of her hands and tried to raise her to her feet. I tore at the knots that dug into her ankles. I had not forgotten that strange, instant wave of understanding that had passed between us as we bent together over Adile Hanem's over-ripe body that day in her harem. I would kill whoever had done this to her.

I managed to get her fully to her feet at last. We clung together. It was as if in this dark, dank cellar Nature was seeking to fulfil the biblical injunction: 'And they shall be one flesh'. The hard beaten earth was thrusting up at us, its ridges biting into us, she discarding old fears, I assuaging old hungers. We had, I suppose, nothing in common, not even a language, and yet, in a sense, we had everything. We were both exiles, languishing far from home. She was what Egyptians here called a *gubli* – 'one from the other side' – from that arid land beyond the Nile's cataracts, where strange tongues were spoken. But then, come to think of it, so was I – in the eyes of the English. More than ever now I was of the Excluded.

Together, she and I wrought a vibrant *inclusion*. I lost count of the number of days the two of us spent behind the locked iron door in that dark cellar, but I know that they were warm days in which we found a new language all our own. Somehow, dim and dust-moted as it was, the light that filtered in from the iron grille became ours.

Yet something 'shamed' the girl, marring her pleasure, and therefore mine. I sought anxiously to find in what way I was falling short, but I was repeatedly reassured that all was well, and as a harem slave she was well versed in these matters. I concluded that the 'shame' must be because Adile Hanem had stripped her of her harem dress and she was reduced to the dirty white sheet she was wearing when the slavers snatched her. I strove to show her I was not concerned with dresses. But no, it was shame worse than that.

Following the women of Egypt, Fatima considered female body-hair to be the mark of a slut. Imprisonment had cut off the supply of *liban shami*, a form of resin which she sedulously employed to tweak out every 'dirty' hair. When I ran my fingers through the lustrous forest where her legs joined, she felt humiliated, shamed. With no language in common but the language of love, I sought to excise the shame with a rain of kisses on that sweet spot. But it was hard to convince her – as hard as it was to persuade the English army that Highland regiments thrive better on a dish of *brochan* than a pound of boiled British beef. But I persisted and I think I must have succeeded in the end, for after that she taught me that there is not one language of love, but many, and in her months as a harem slave Fatima had learned most of them.

In the hours of satiation, when the bruises declared themselves, I would think of that clumsy, gentle initiation with Jeannie Macdonald, up on the shieling, and I would wonder.

I would wonder, too, about the Pasha's ransoming party and how Tom had fared. They must surely have gone back downriver by this time. No mistake: I had burned my boats – or had had them burned for me.

A day came when we woke to find the iron door of our prison standing open. The corridor was empty. Swiftly, Fatima took me through a labyrinth of passages to the *bab sirr*, the secret door of the harem. Unhindered, we made our way together to my *hakim*'s house at the west of the town. I found Tom Keith waiting for me. At first sight of the Cairo search party he'd jumped on a horse and ridden off into the desert, living with the Bedouin until news came that the ransomers had left. According to what Tom had heard through the Minya bazaars, all but fifty of the Mackenzie Fraser 'slaves' had been ransomed, and were now, presumably, homeward bound. Whether those outstanding absentees, Drummer Donald Macleod and Armourer Tom Keith, were posted 'Dead' or 'Missing' or 'Deserted' I never did discover.

Shaken up by the arrival of the search party, Tom was looking ahead again, full of talk of the opportunities opening up for such likely lads as us in Mohammed Ali's New Egypt. An admirer of Napoleon Bonaparte, proud of sharing his hero's birthday, Mohammed Ali was sending dozens of young Egyptians to France for training, while bringing in foreigners to modernise the fusty, dusty old land of the Pharaohs. Tom had his sights set on a manager's post in the musket-making factory the Pasha was planning below the Citadel.

I lacked his ambition. I was happy to be back in the house the Bey had given me, with the patients who so badly needed me gathered round my door, reassured, now I had the black slave from the Bey's harem in my bed, that their wives and daughters would be safe with me.

One thing worried me, though. If Adile Hanem thought that Fatima was taking her Scotsman from her, why did she have both of us thrown into the same dungeon? I questioned Fatima, but she went dumb and numb whenever the Khadin Effendi or the Khislar Aga was mentioned. It made me anxious. I feared I had thoughtlessly put the girl's life in danger.

In the end I went to François, that past-master of the bizarre intrigues and unending feuds of the Mameluke court.

'Mon cher Osman, mon pauvre enfant,' he cried, clapping me on the shoulder. 'C'est très simple. Cherchez l'eunuque – comme toujours!

'When Adile Hanem told that black monster to get rid of Fatima, he feared you were going to displace him in Adile's bed. So he went to the Bey and told him to give you that house well away from the camp.'

I stared at him. 'The Khislar Aga *told* Ezbek Bey?'

François laughed. 'You have much to learn, my friend. It is the eunuchs who command this place, and they command it through the harem. They hold all the cards – and they know how to use them. When the Khislar Aga was asked to hide you from Mohammed Ali's search party, he seized his chance and threw you where he'd already thrown Fatima. Killing two birds with one stone, you might say.'

My head reeled. That mutilated, hollow-cheeked freak slipping into the bed of the Bey's Chief Wife? It must be some crude joke of the Frenchman. But no. François de la Rosière had never been more serious – more 'professional'. ' "Eunuch" is Greek,' he explained. 'It means "Watcher of the Bed". But believe me, what the lot of them are watching for is their chance to slip into it!'

It may seem strange that a medical man such as myself should be instructed on such a matter by a Master of the Bey's Horse. But then the learned works of the Beatons dwell little on castration. François explained matters to my satisfaction, but I will confess I am at a loss when it comes to conveying these matters. On such occasions my scholarly friend Mr Burckhardt – Captain Burton, too – would fall back on Latin. I have no Latin, so I shall avail myself of Gaelic. It appears that in parts of the Ottoman dominions not all castrati suffer what François called 'the clean cut'; for many the barber's razor takes only the *clachan beaga* or the *magairlean* and these eunuchs are much esteemed by the knowledgeable ladies of the harem for their phenomenal powers of endurance.

'Durs comme un djerid,' grinned François, the Mameluke from Marseille.

It was a strange world that, willy-nilly, I had entered.

The festival of the Night of the Observation – *Leilet el-Ruya* – immediately precedes the fasting month of Ramadan. People eagerly seize on this brief respite. It is one of the very few occasions when the 'noble' corps of Mamelukes deign to mingle with mere townsfolk. Richly decked-out horsemen from Ezbek Bey's stables ride alongside the sheikhs of the town's trade guilds and the dignitaries of Islam to the place in the desert where they can give notice of the first sighting of a slender silver crescent in the sky – the new moon which signals the long abstinence. That night the mosques in Minya were ablaze with light and the streets were alive with people and laughter and music as criers ran through the streets warning of the imminent arrival of the Fast.

Tom Keith had been pressed into service, but it was only at the end of the parade, when he started to lead away one of the Bey's finest horses, that I spotted him. It so happened that just then the crowd opened and I caught a glimpse of Paolo. To my horror, I saw that he was creeping up on Tom. Clearly, this was the moment he had been waiting for: the streets were packed, people were preoccupied greeting their friends at the outset of this great annual occasion, the stern renewal of the Faith.

I yelled a warning to Tom, but there was so much noise he did not hear me. Unable to get through the crowd, I watched the whole episode, powerless.

When Paolo, edging forward steathily, was within three yards of Tom, concealed by the horse's flank, I caught a glint of steel. I panicked and and yelled again. This time Tom recognised my voice, swung round, and took in the situation in a trice. The next thing I knew Paolo was on the ground, blood pouring out of him, and Tom had vanished.

By the time I got through, Paolo was beyond any aid I could give. I won't say I was sorry. His threats of 'exposure' had been removed at a stroke. It had been kill or be killed. Having served in a Highland regiment, Tom Keith carried his *sgian-dubh* strapped to his right leg and knew how to use it.

It was two years before I set eyes on Tom Keith again, and then only briefly, in very strange circumstances.

2 a.m., 17 November 1869, Le Grand Bassin

I knew it had to be something pretty serious to make the 'American Lady' leave the select company of notables and international journalists Nubar had gathered on the SS *Mohammed Ali* and come running like this to 'poor Osman'.

She reached me at last.

'The *Latif's* aground!' She looked at me accusingly. 'She's hit the bank at el-Kantara and swung across the fairway. She's stuck. Stuck fast.'

I didn't want to believe it. 'It's the English, spreading their rumours again,' I said.

'Don't be a fool, Donald. I had it from Nubar Pasha himself. He's having our baggage unloaded from the *Mohammed Ali*. She's too broad in the beam to get past now. The Canal's blocked, a Dhòmhnaill. BLOCKED!'

'How can it be? It's absolutely straight there. The channel's marked with flags.'

She laughed harshly. 'Panicked, I expect. You know how they panic. Sami's Zobeida's son as well as yours, remember.'

To tell the truth, I've been secretly dreading something like this for days past. A Royal Navy man, Captain Mckillop, is in command of the *Latif*, but I know very well that if anything goes wrong, it will be Sami who gets the blame. 'Son of that renegado Osman Effendi, you know – Hadji Osman, the natives call him.'

'Come *on*, Donald. There's no time to waste!'

She grabbed me by the arm and dragged me across to where the *Mohammed Ali* lay, ready for sailing. Nubar himself was on deck, shouting orders, manhandling bags over the side into a small steam launch, a vessel narrow enough to get past the trapped *Latif*, with luck.

'Wait there,' she ordered. She hailed a rowing-boat and was taken across to the *Mohammed Ali*. I saw her on the deck, arguing with Nubar. I never cease to marvel at this woman.

Five minutes later she was back at the quay. 'Nubar agrees we can go on the launch,' she shouted up. The anchor was coming up. She fairly pushed me onto the overcrowded deck. I was glad my harem was not present to see it.

At once we were moving, our wake scribing a ruler-straight line down the centre of the canal as it bisects the shining expanse of Lake Menzaleh. Nubar pushed past, looking through me – although I've known him ever since he started out as a young interpreter for Mohammed Ali. Abbas made him a bey when he fixed the Alexandria–Cairo railway contract with Robert Stephenson; under Said he took over the Overland Transit; and now he's the Khedive Ismail's confidential agent and money man – Nubar *Pasha*. Nubar's a survivor. He knows when to get out from under. And Nubar is avoiding me.

I took a leaf from Burckhardt's book, and seized the bull by the horns. I got Nubar into a corner, His heavy eyelids came down like a stone slab sealing the inner chamber of one of Belzoni's tombs.

'Probably just a scrape of the *Latif*'s keel,' I said.

The eyelids rose, and I received the full force of his basilisk stare. 'Such a scrape that the Khedive is hiding his head in shame in Ismailiya. He promises an impaling.'

12 The Trap

In the uproar and confusion that followed Tom's flight, I was able to get away unnoticed to my house outside the town and resume the duties of country doctor as if nothing had happened. For months afterwards I cross-examined every traveller who arrived in Minya, seeking some clue to Tom Keith's whereabouts. I offered liberal *bakshish* to any Nile boatman who could help me, and eventually one fellow came to me with a wild tale about a tall, half-naked, straggle-haired *santon* or holy man he had spotted, moving from village to village. It was just the sort of trick Tom might have hit on to get through to Cairo and then to Alexandria, where the Greek consul was empowered to collect any still unransomed British slave and ship him back home.

Why, I asked myself wretchedly, was it always I who was left behind, was always deserted?

The only one who had stood by me was Fatima. In the febrile, dissolute atmosphere of a Mameluke camp, she and I were both, I suppose, innocents in our different ways, both reluctant exiles from 'home', which still rang clear like tuning-forks in our heads. We comforted each other. In the great Cairo slave-market Nubian girls were recommended for the remarkable coolness of their burnished brown skins in the most torrid summers. And that was indeed a very hot summer.

Yet there were times, too, when Fatima's ever-ready laughter rang hollow, and when only the urgent needs of my trusting patients kept me going. For one thing at least I was profoundly grateful: Ezbek's Chief Wife no longer demanded my urgent attendance.

Alas! I congratulated myself too soon. The very next day a

scowling Head Eunuch appeared at my door. I was to attend the harem immediately: Adile, it seemed, was tortured by stomach cramps. I prepared a large dose of jalap, the malingerer's restorative.

Afterwards I regretted my impulsive action. Adile might interpret my treatment as rejection. Her cruelty was notorious; she was a famous dispenser of *le café mauvais*. I would need to watch Fatima's food and drink night and day.

I forget at what point I at last began to think of myself as 'Osman', the name the Mamelukes had bestowed upon me. I imagine it was some months after Tom Keith's disappearance. He had been named Ibrahim – some say 'the first Muslim', since it was Abraham (Ibrahim) who on Allah's orders had built the Kaaba at Mecca – though of course he had always been Tom Keith to me. Two Scots together amounted to a nation, a nation against the world. But one Scot, that was a different proposition. I have to admit that 'Donald' was fading, and Osman – father of the Ottomans, if not the fourth Caliph – was what men called me. I tried it out, but my tongue still jibbed.

Then out of the blue, a trusted boatman, fresh up from Cairo, brought me a letter, strangely signed 'Ibrahim Aga'. I knew at once it was from Tom. The 'Aga' was new, though; it means 'Chief', 'Commander'. Evidently Tom was rising in the world. As ever, he had fallen on his feet. Having got through to Cairo disguised as a holy man, he had conceived the bold idea of calling on Mohammed Ali's first wife, Amine Hanem, and throwing himself upon her mercy.

He could not have made a shrewder choice. Amine had borne Mohammed Ali three sons back home in Albania, but it was not until he was firmly established as Viceroy in the Citadel that he had brought her to Egypt. The story goes that he led her into the palace between two rows of Circassian beauties in fine silks and satins. She turned to him and said: 'Mohammed Ali, I have been your wife until this day. But from now on we are strangers.'

Quite a woman, Amine.

Stranger she may have been to his bed, but she was not stranger to his councils. Mohammed Ali had great plans for their son, Prince Tousson, but the boy was then only sixteen, and without experience of the world. Amine saw at once that this strong-minded Scots soldier and armourer would make an ideal companion and counsellor for the boy. She knew, too, that the Mamelukes were not beaten yet. Madly jealous and contemptuous of the 'donkey-boy' who had usurped their throne, they were plotting to return to Cairo and somehow wrench back the Citadel.

As a Mameluke himself, who better than Keith to keep an eye on them? It seems that Tom set about this new task with his usual zeal, hiring spiced-meat sellers to attend the halls where the plotters were meeting. They were to keep their ears open and report back.

In this way, Mohammed Ali learned just when the knife was to fall. It was, he now saw, a case of kill or be killed. He had no intention of being killed.

It was the spring of 1811, and up in Minya my surgery was full to overflowing with fellahin with broken and bleeding feet. Ezbek was collecting the 'land tax' with the help of the bastinado. There were other diversions. One afternoon one of the Pasha's boats came down the Nile with what looked like an extra mast, the long, craning, spotted yellow neck of a camelopard, which we call a giraffe, a gift from Mohammed Ali to sweeten his master, the Sultan-Caliph in Istanbul.

The Sultan now had more urgent requests of his Egyptian Viceroy. Under their great chief, Abdullah ibn Saud, the fanatical Wahabi tribes had erupted out of Arabia and were threatening Damascus, proclaiming a *jihad*. They had already occupied Mecca and Medina, disrupting the pilgrimage in the name of purifying Islam. Had not the Prophet, they demanded, forbidden the wearing of silks and silver, thrown the graven images from the Kaaba and said that it was vainglorious for mere men to erect domed monuments to themselves? Islam was in peril. The sinful domes must be broken.

I had another letter from Tom. Responding to the Sultan's appeal, Mohammed Ali was throwing the whole weight of the Egyptian army against the Wahabi heretics in Arabia. Prince Tousson was to head it. Tom, Ibrahim Aga, was appointed commander of the cavalry.

'Don't delay any longer, Donald,' Tom wrote. 'Get down here

at once. There is work for all. There are already a thousand Greeks working in the Suez shipyards. This could be your last chance.'

I read and re-read Tom's letter, but could come to no decision. Fatima was now four months gone, and I dreaded leaving her exposed to the vengeful devices of the Bey's Chief Wife.

In the end, as so often, the course of events took the matter out of my hands, A courier arrived in Minya, bearing a large gilt-edged envelope from His Excellency, Mohammed Ali, addressed to all the Mameluke beys of the town and their followers. It was an invitation to attend a great feast to be held in the Citadel to mark the investiture of Prince Ahmed Tousson with the pelisse of honour as a Pasha of Three Tails, prior to his departure at the head of his troops for the holy war in Arabia.

An invitation of this sort was clearly a command, so I was astonished when François, the Master of the Bey's Horse, turned up at my house a couple of days before the date set for our departure, with red and streaming eyes and a request for a medical certificate of exemption. François was the last man in the world to malinger, yet it was obvious to me that his eyes had been 'doctored'. My first thought was of some escapade in the harem.

He waved this impatiently away. 'Just write Ezbek a note saying that I can't see,' he said.

I was baffled, but I wrote the certificate and handed it to him.

He sighed, putting a hand on my shoulder. 'Osman, mon vieux, je ne peux plus dire.'

At the door, he turned back for a moment, hesitated. 'Don't go, Osman.'

As with much shouting and cursing our horses were brought ashore in Cairo, I sought leave of the Bey to go in search of my old comrade. Since Tom was now high up at Tousson's court, he could hardly refuse. The affair of Paolo had now receded into the Mamelukes' monotonously bloody history.

I looked in all the likely places, ears alert for that careful Lowland voice, but I drew a blank. I tramped miles that day through streets that were already filling up, inquiring all the time, getting nowhere.

'Ibrahim Aga? It is he you seek?' asked a Greek servant coming down from the Citadel. I nodded gratefully.

'Bukra, bukra,' he said, and walked away. My heart sank: as the English say, tomorrow never comes, particularly in Egypt.

This time, though, memorably, it did.

The crowds were out in force soon after dawn. A Cairo crowd is always on the lookout for a free spectacle, and this one promised well, with gorgeously costumed Mameluke beys, performing horses, drums, trumpets, dancing-girls, magicians wreathed in coriander smoke, and the occasional shower of piastres and sequins to be scrambled for in the streets.

Up betimes, too, were the eighty-five beys and *kashif*s and their 400 Mameluke attendants and retainers, marshalling their cohorts for the grand procession to the Citadel, grooms rubbing down the fine Arab horses, armourers putting a sheen on the many silver-plated and jewelled scimitars with handles of rhinoceros horn, sheaths gleaming with gold. Infinite care went into adjusting canary-coloured turbans, and burnishing fine-wrought chain-mail that went back to Salah el-Din and the Crusades.

Everywhere now drums were beating, summoning the 'knights' to their rallying points: the Turkish janissaries, the Arnaut sharp-shooters, the Kurdish detachments of the Army of Liberation which was to march with the Mameluke column to the Citadel.

I was still rushing about, staring into the face of every aga or *bimbashi* in case he might be Tom Keith. I drew a blank. Exhausted, deeply worried now, I ran back to our Mameluke column just as it was about to move off, Shahin Bey resplendent at its head.

As the procession swung round into the Rumeila, the great open space below the Citadel, the crowd gave vent to its full-throated acclamation of the greatness and oneness of God, 'Allah! Allah! Allah!'

But what I myself heard, I fear, was the vengeful howling of the street mob four years ago as the Ross-shire Buffs limped by in bedraggled and torn red jackets.

The massive wooden gates at the foot of the Citadel swung open and the many-coloured snake that was our procession began its slow ascent of the narrow lane that winds upwards to the platform on which the palace stands. At the top, the order to dismount was given. The favoured beys were escorted into the hall of the palace to be embraced and offered *chibouks* and coffee, sherbets and rich sweetmeats. They fairly swelled with pride at the thought that the Arnaut 'donkey-boy' had at last been compelled to recognise their power. So gratified were they that they failed to notice how quickly Mohammed Ali had withdrawn or to wonder why Prince Tousson, whose investiture they were honouring, was nowhere to be seen.

The drums began to beat again, the trumpets shrilled. More arrogant than ever, flattered by the Pasha's attentions, the beys began to leave the audience chamber. The procession re-formed to join the great *jihad* against the heretics across the Red Sea: first the Turkish janissaries, all with gleaming kettle-drums; then the white-kilted Arnauts in their crimson and gold tunics and small red caps; and then, outshining all, the Mameluke beys, on their Arab thoroughbreds, each bey flanked by his handsomely clad, blue-eyed, pink-cheeked, long-lashed retainers.

I caught a glimpse of the magnificent moustachios of Ahmed Bonaparte as he harangued and cursed his men, and ducked behind a pillar. As I lurked there, I heard my name being softly called in the Gaelic.

My heart turned over. 'Dhòmhnaill! Dhòmhnaill!'

I waited. The voice came again, more urgent now – unmistakable. 'Dhòmhnaill'. Cautiously, I looked around.

A hiss. 'Dhòmhnaill *Bhàin*!'

I saw the dark face of Tom Keith peering from behind another pillar. He was beckoning. 'Come *on*, man! Follow me.'

Ahmed Bonaparte was looking belligerently in my direction. My feet refused to budge.

'Cabar Fèidh!' *Sotto voce*, the Seaforth war cry shook me out of my trance. I followed Tom through a maze of passages leading down through the eastern side of the Citadel. I tried to question him.

'No time! Keep going!'

He did not look behind him as he ran. I had never seen Tom Keith so on edge, not even at el-Hamed.

We were running steeply downhill now, inside the great wall. At last we came to a concealed iron door.

'The bab sirr. Please God it opens.'

He drew a rusty key from a pocket and thrust it into the ancient lock. It grated, but it turned. He put a shoulder to the studded door. It gave a foot. He thrust again and pushed me through.

'For God's sake – get away from here, Donald. Away man! Right away!' I heard the key turn in the lock behind me.

I was alone on the edge of the Eastern desert, at the point where it lays siege to the city amid a wilderness of mouldering tombs. I could make no sense of it. Tom was not a man given to panic. Then I remembered François's strange behaviour before we left the Minya camp. Deeply troubled, I made my way back through those splendid domed sepulchres of past generations of Mameluke beys, and round to the massive Bab el-Azab, the main gate of the Citadel, which I had entered only a few hours earlier as a member of that glittering assembly.

The Rumeila was still jam-packed with people waiting to cheer the Pasha's army of liberation as it descended from the Citadel to march off to war. I pushed my way through to the front, just in time to see the leading column of janissaries swinging out into the great square. Behind them, the Arnauts, a torrent of stocky, red-capped bodies, surged down between the high stone walls. I watched the leading ranks swagger out.

A sort of gasp went up from the crowd. The great wooden doors of the Bab el-Azab had begun to close on the marching men. One Arnaut company and the entire Mameluke contingent were trapped inside.

The crowd began to buzz like a hundred swarms of angry bees.

I was now so tightly pressed on all sides I could hardly breathe. Suddenly, from behind the tight-shut doors, the rattle of musket fire. It was steady, continuing, purposeful. A deep shuddering sigh went up from the crowd.

Behind the high gates, screams, curses, terrified neighing and stamping of panic-stricken horses. I saw then that along the tops of the walls which enclose the winding lane descending from the Citadel, lines of Arnauts had taken up their positions and were steadily firing down into the writhing mass of men and horses in the trough below. From the sounds that came from behind the gates, I guessed that the leading Arnaut party had turned round, and, backs to the gates, were directing a steady stream of fire on the Mamelukes who had followed them.

It had all been planned in cold blood. It was as ruthless, as treacherous, as the Campbells' massacre of the Macdonalds at Glencoe. I wondered how much Tom – and François – had known.

A stream of bright-red blood was coursing beneath the massive wooden doors. The crowd shrank back in horror, but was unable to break loose. The stream widened, tracing a serpentine path through the dust. Then, as it watched the main stream form tributaries, the crowd exploded. The square was emptying fast.

Tearing off my tell-tale turban, I took to my heels with the terrified crowd. As I ran, I picked up a handful of dirt from the road and smeared it over my face and hands. The firing had started up again. The Arnauts were out in the town now, determined to hunt down and exterminate every surviving Mameluke.

That was how my old dragoman pal Giovanni Finati, who went by the *renegado* name of Mohammed, came by his wife – 'looted' her, you might say, from the house of a slaughtered Mameluke.*

I wondered for a moment whether I should make for the Frankish quarter and seek the Consulate's protection. But I could already see the supercilious expression on those English gentlemen's faces. The way they saw things, I would be just another 'dirty Arab', or, if they inquired further, a 'damned deserter'. I gave up the idea and tried to look as much like a dirty Arab as possible. All the same, as I plunged after that mindless crowd, I knew that I was in grave peril. My fair complexion and blue eyes, the mark of the Mameluke, would give me away. Not to mention the fact that I not only looked like a Mameluke, I *was* one.

I do believe Allah Himself guided my steps on that terrible day. Caught up in the mad rush of the crowd, I was swept through the narrow gateway of the Bab Zuweila, and, ahead, saw the dome and three minarets of el-Azhar, the great mosque-university of Cairo. I glimpsed a vast courtyard, its flagstones polished smooth by the feet of countless pilgrims down the centuries. Whether on impulse or from sheer exhaustion, I joined the stream of young men going in through the Gate of the Barbers, shedding their shoes as they entered.

I must confess that despite my new name of Osman I knew

---

* Signor Finati – 'Mohammed' – himself tells the story in his *Autobiography*, in the composition of which he was assisted by Mr William Bankes of Kingston Hall, Dorset, who was also a client of my father in his dragoman days. – *F.M.*

little of Islam at that time, so I resolved to survive within el-Azhar by sedulous imitation. I chose one bearded young man who entered at the same time, and did as he did. Holding his shoes, sole to sole, under his left arm, he went over to the water tank and went through the sequence of ablutions prescribed before prayer. I followed his movements: detail was clearly life-preserving now. Tucking up my sleeves to the elbow, I washed my hands three times, throwing water into my mouth with the right hand, rinsing three times. After each action, the young man, my mentor, murmured a prayer. Much of this I couldn't catch, so I just murmured in a low voice. What I was really praying for was that Allah, in His mercy, would allow this uncircumcised *giaour* to pass as a True Believer.

Ablutions meticulously concluded, I followed the young man into the courtyard. Placing his slippers, sole to sole, before him, to claim his place, he embarked on a two-*rekah* prayer. It was then that I saw that, like many of the students and sheikhs at el-Azhar, he was blind.

I could not have chosen a better place to hide until the fury in the streets died away. El-Azhar's doors stand open day and night. As Mr Murray remarks in his guide book: 'Idlers of all descriptions resort there to buy and sell, to read and sleep, and to enjoy the coolness of its shady and extensive colonnades.'

Though I may have entered as an 'idler', I did not remain one. For behind the colonnades around the great courtyard lie twenty-four 'apartments' for the accommodation of students from the many nations of Islam who make their way to this place from all over the world. Every second day bread is distributed to them free, with oil for their lamps – which was convenient. Each 'apartment', with its own library, is dedicated to students from a particular country. That might have been my undoing, but by using the Gaelic (which none knew) I succeeded in passing myself off as a seeker after Truth from a remote Himalayan tribe. I ate the bread of the Afghan apartment.

So what might so easily have been the end of me became, in a strange way, a new beginning. Until this time I had conformed to the more obvious rules of Islam to find acceptance with my powerful masters. But though they claimed, of course, to be the champions of Islam, the Mamelukes were in no way devout. At that time, like most *renegados*, I was a Muslim for convenience.

It was the days I spent hiding in el-Azhar that changed me. Sitting at the feet of one or other of the sheikhs in their dark-blue kaftans, each beneath his pillar, I slowly entered a new and ordered world, a world that strove for the Good with cool but enduring passion. In the world of the Kirk, it had been made clear to me that I was not of the Elect, nor ever would be . . . But here, sitting at the feet of the sheikh expounding the Koran or the *Hadith*, the Traditions of the Prophet, or at the elbow of the sheikh teaching algebra or logic, I became aware of the existence of a brotherhood of many races, in which all men were equal, and in which neither priest nor presbyter need come between man and God.

I forget how long I enjoyed the hospitality of this extraordinary place, but it must have been two or three weeks before the streets outside had been cleansed of blood and what passes for order in Cairo was restored. By this time Tom Keith was well on his way to Arabia, at the head of Tousson's cavalry and Ibrahim Pasha, Mohammed Ali's eldest son, was tearing up the Nile valley with orders to wipe out fleeing Mamelukes. I was deeply worried about Fatima, whom I had left at Minya, pregnant with my child. Had François, who clearly had wind of Mohammed Ali's cold-blooded plan, been able to save her? Had he fled with what was left of Ezbek Bey's camp further up the Nile and into Sudan? Was she perhaps by this time back in her Nubian homeland? Or had she fallen victim to the Chief Wife's venom?

They were questions to which I had to know the answers. Whatever the dangers, I had somehow to make my way up the Nile back to Minya.

13 I am Discovered: 'In Every Respect a Complete Mussulman'

Dressed as a student at el-Azhar I got through to Minya without too much trouble. But it was a grim homecoming. For the second time in my life I found the house in which all my hopes had been invested – which was my whole future – deserted, abandoned, with nothing to indicate who had lived there or what had become of them.

My eye fell on a scattering of blue glass beads, the simple Nubian beads which so delighted Fatima, spilled across the bedroom floor. I searched everywhere for the phial of antidote, the powerful emetic I had left with her in case Adile Hanem tried some deadly brew while I was away. I could find nothing. A grain of hope – or no?

I walked across to the Bey's harem. The curtains gaped. The Khislar Aga had vanished. I searched till I found Adile's apartments. The thick curtain was hung now with cobwebs. The cloying scent of sandalwood still clung to them. I sank down on the bed on which she had set out her wares for the handsome new *hakim*, but only the scuttering of mice relieved the heavy silence.

Outside, I questioned half a dozen fellahin working in the cotton fields. They had seen nothing. Nothing at all. I recognised one of my patients and appealed to him. No, he had seen nothing. They were terrified. Ibrahim Pasha's tortures were spectacular. But François had been forewarned. He would have got to Fatima in time; in any case, news of the Cairo bloodbath would have reached Minya before Ibrahim's butchers did. Fatima could have been a thousand miles south by then, in one of those villages that grow, limpet-like, on the rock that confines the Nile in Nubia, dazzling white houses, with painted plates set in their walls, remembrances of some long-past pilgrimage. She could be safe again, back amongst her own people.

Which was more than could be said for me. I was utterly alone now. Tom Keith, 'chosen man' of my Ross-shire Buff days, was far away in Arabia; François had vanished, and Fatima's ever-ready smile no longer lit up the day for me. The child would have been born by now. Would I ever set eyes on my first-born? I tried to imagine some combination of Nubia and the island of Skye and failed. Perhaps when things settled down I would go up there and try to find him. (I don't know why I assumed he would be a boy.)

For the present I had at least the house that Ezbek Bey had given me. A queue of insistent patients had gathered outside the door the moment the news spread of my return. So I bent to pick up Fatima's bright glass beads, dabbled my fingers in the bowl of coconut-oil with which Nubian women are accustomed to dress their hair, and opened my door again for business. At least these people needed me, though sometimes the almost childlike trust they placed in me as the holder of the secrets of the West made me feel like a charlatan.

Since those days of shelter in el-Azhar, another matter had begun to gnaw at me. My patients took it for granted that I was 'one of them', a full member of the House of Islam. But though I diligently answered the call to prayer which rang over the roof-tops five times a day, I had not yet made the formal commitment – and I knew that he who is not within the House of Islam is of the House of Darkness. As my grateful patients heaped gifts upon me, I could not help but feel I was betraying them. I was a *renegado* twice over, and that seemed at least once too many.

Thanks to the Prophet, praise be unto Him, the requirements, if arduous at some points, are simple at others. I took into my confidence one of my patients, who happened to be a village *imam*, and one morning when the mosque was little occupied, I appeared before him and recited the Fattah, the first seven short verses of the Koran, a declaration of faith known as the 'Opening'.

In the Name of God, the Merciful, the Compassionate
Praise belongs to God, the Lord of all Being
The All-merciful, the All-compassionate
The Master of the Day of Doom . . .
Thee only do we serve; to Thee alone we pray for succour
Guide us in the straight path . . .

I was word perfect. '*Ma-shaa-llah*!' beamed the *imam*. 'God's will cometh to pass.'

I *belonged* again. And yet I would be deceiving my readers if I let them believe I was now wholly at peace with myself. True, Paolo was now no more than a bad memory, but his nagging insinuations had left their mark. For there remained one absurd respect in which I differed glaringly from my patients: I possessed a foreskin. It is true that circumcision is nowhere mentioned, much less required, in the Holy Koran. But it *is* in the Bible. I recalled the verse which brought on the giggles at school: 'And Abraham was ninety-nine years of his age when he was circumcised in the flesh of his foreskin as a token of the covenant between God and his people'. And was not Abraham also a great prophet of Islam, the 'first Muslim'?

In my solitude, the thing became an obsession. As at my daily sick parades I examined the eruptions of one kind or another on the *zubb*s of my patients, I became uncomfortably conscious of the guilt concealed by my robes.

For weeks I wavered on the brink; in my dreams the loss began to appear as some sort of death – the clean cut of the eunuch-maker. On the other hand, accidental discovery must be an ever-present peril. From Mecca came endless tales of *giaour*s who had been found out and impaled.

Despite Abraham's example, at my age I could hardly go to the barber. It would amount to a declaration of guilt in itself. But I was a Beaton, wasn't I? In desperation I steeled myself to perform the operation. I rigged up mirrors. The knife was sharpened to a high degree, cleansed in the flame. I adapted the barber's split-bamboo forceps. I told no one. Though I used a balm compounded to my grandmother's recipe, the pain persisted for eight weeks.

Obeying the Prophet's injunction that any discarded part of the human body is entitled to full respect, I buried my lost foreskin one night under a very tall palm-tree.

One more landmark in my strange life.

Suddenly the Nile was alive with soldiers and war supplies, reinforcements for Yenbo across the Red Sea, by the Kosseir route. Tom Keith was somewhere out there with the Egyptian cavalry, although I hadn't heard a word from him since he pushed me out of the secret door on that terrible day at the Citadel. It was obvious, though, even at this distance, that Egypt's 'holy war' to recover Mecca and Medina wasn't going well. Eager for martyrdom, the black-robed Wahabi tribesmen raided right up to walls of Yenbo. Tousson's men were being driven mad by thirst: it was now midsummer. It was said that Mohammed Ali had sent a Cairo merchant over the Red Sea with bags of gold to win over the Bedouin. But they were reluctant, hanging back for a better offer.

Another bey had moved into Ezbek's palace, a Turk, sent I suspect by Ahmed Bonaparte, Mohammed Ali's strong-arm man. I lay low behind the cover of my patients, and prayed that he would forget me.

And then suddenly the Minya bazaars were full of rumours. The young Emir Tousson was on the move at last, crossing mountains, making for the holy city of Medina a hundred miles away. He had made a brave speech, telling his men of the Paradise that awaited them over the mountain.

The rest we put together several weeks later, as the ragged, maimed survivors straggled back towards Cairo. Ambushed in a mountain pass, waterless under the consuming sun, Egypt's great army of liberation had broken and run. For three days and three nights, Egyptian ships sailed up and down the eastern coast of the Red Sea, picking survivors out of the water.

I learned from one of them that, towards the end, Prince Tousson and two cavalry officers had ridden about desperately trying to stem the headlong flight. Most fearless of all was a tall, wiry man with dark eyes and craggy face – some sort of *Frangi*.

Was his name Ibrahim – Ibrahim Aga?

The poor fellow tried to say something, but could not. He was in agony; his leg was gangrenous and he died soon afterwards.

Robbed of their hopes of booty, unpaid for weeks, hordes of battered, hungry and mutinous men dragged themselves back to Cairo. Mohammed Ali, it was rumoured, had shut himself up in the Citadel.

When I got a summons from the Bey to attend upon him immediately, I naturally assumed it must relate to this catastrophe. Despite his Turkish hauteur, I could see how distraught he was and jumped to the conclusion that Ahmed Bonaparte must be behind all this. He had set his brand on me long ago at Bulak, and now he had come to claim me. My heart sank. But, thank God, it turned out that this summons had nothing whatsoever to do with the war in Arabia or Ahmed Bonaparte. Out of the blue, three young English milords had just come down the Nile in a boat, tied up at Minya, and announced that they proposed to remain there until the plague raging in Cairo had abated. They carried a *firman* from Mohammed Ali, requiring governors and *kashif*s to render all possible assistance.

The Bey was out of his depth, fearful of 'blotting his copybook'; I was his lifeline. I was to attend upon the English milords – the first, I may say, of many. As the Sasannach bard puts it, 'Some have greatness thrust upon them.'

Mektub – it is written.

In truth there was but one milord, Thomas Legh, twenty-one years old, Member of Parliament for Cheshire, student of Oxford University, scion of Lyme Park, Cheshire, a fresh-faced young fellow, with a feeble straggle of hair on his upper lip, and, when I met him, a many-coloured turban overhanging his brow.

The other two members of the party were the Revd Charles Smelt, the young man's guardian and tutor, a man forever making notes, and a grizzled old fellow who spoke English with a peculiar yapping sound, whom I later found to be American. The young lord was on what is called his Grand Tour, diverted from Italy and Greece by the French wars. The old fellow, Jacoub Barthouw, a Yankee trader in the Orient, had been hired as an interpreter and guide – dragoman, you might say. It was he who 'discovered me' – although you'll not find any mention of that in the young lord's book.

On the Bey's orders I had taken an Arnaut guard of honour

down to the Nile bank. But the moment Barthouw saw their red jackets and white *fustans*, he went wild.

'Imshi! Imshi!' he yelled. 'You, boy. Get them crazy sons of bitches outta here. Get 'em away from me, clear away. You hear me!'

He stopped in his tracks, glaring at me.

'You,' he said accusingly. 'You're no God-damned Turk, nor Arab neither. Don't try to kid me. Who the hell are you?'

The suddenness and directness of the attack, after years of Oriental deviousness, threw me off balance.

'Donald,' I stammered. 'Donald . . . Donald . . . from the island of Skye.'

And that, I believe, is how I came to appear as Donald Donald in young Legh's *Narrative of a Journey in Egypt and the Country Beyond the Cataracts* that came out the year after Waterloo. It seems that he had run into Missett in Alexandria and had heard all about the shambles of the Mackenzie Fraser expedition in 1807. He introduces me in his book as a 'Scotchman who had been taken prisoner at Rosetta and been sold into slavery'. Fair enough, so far.

That book of his was read around the world. It even reached North Carolina, and in due course transformed my life, though I myself didn't learn of it until the new British Consul, Mr Henry Salt, came out with a copy in 1817. He lent it to Mr Burckhardt, who naturally showed it to me.

I must say I was upset when I opened it. The impudence of the fellow! 'Circumcised and in every respect a complete Mussulman', Legh wrote, as if I were one of his prize mastiffs at Lyme Park (a walled deer-park, as he told me, nine miles round). 'Having been in the country seven years,' he tells the world, 'he had nearly forgotten his own language.' It didn't occur to the young fool, of course, that 'my own language' was not English, but the Gaelic.

Ah, well, if he was the first to 'tell poor Osman's story' he was by no means the last. There's the Osman in James Silk Buckingham's *Autobiography*, there's Squire Westcar's Osman, Dr Richardson's 'my friend Osman', and of course young Kinglake's. I was Osman Effendi by then, dragoman to the Quality, but still 'poor Osman' to him, though I guess I made his reputation for him. But my 'strange story' as he calls it is mine and that's why

I'm telling it myself, before young Emile starts using it to 'take the veil off the Orient'.

Having 'discovered Donald Donald', this scion of Lyme Park was eager to liberate the 'Mahometan slave' and carry him back in triumph. I could see he was already preparing his parliamentary address on 'the glories of English liberty'.

He and Jacob Barthouw went before the Bey to negotiate my ransom. Barthouw introduced young Legh as a great lord of England with a castle twenty leagues round, a leader of the English Majlis and a Vizier of the Sultan George of London. I suppose it was from this Yankee that I got my first tips on the dragoman's craft. I saw the Bey's eyes glint when a ransom of 2,000 piastres was mentioned, but, as ever in this world, he concluded that if the Englishman was willing to pay so much for a mere slave, I must in truth be worth five times that.

While the milord's party waited, I furnished them with Mameluke costumes, and diverted them with the Mameluke exercises I had witnessed. And in the evenings there were the dancing-girls who so preoccupy the minds of Western visitors to the mysterious East. The young lord fairly goggled, as if committing to memory every thrust of the hip, every gyration of the shining belly as the small drums throbbed, faster and faster, and the tambourines quivered and rattled as the dance exploded in its ultimate frenzy. I noticed that Mr Smelt had closed his ever-present journal, and, as the last drum-roll died away, two of the most flimsily clad dancers bestrode my charges' laps, extorting *bakshish* as the rows of golden coins swayed and tinkled in their shining hair.

Turning to young Legh's *Narrative* later, I found a long footnote, commenting on 'the fantastical dresses of these ministers of pleasure whose charms are scarcely concealed, though the voluptuous and not ungraceful attitudes with which they commence their dance degenerate into movements not strictly decorous'. It was not Rabbie Burns, but it had its English charm, its inimitable hypocrisy.

The plague had now abated in Cairo and young Legh was anxious to be away. Before the party left, he made one more effort at ransoming me. 'His master,' he writes in his book, 'had agreed at one time to give him his liberty . . . but after the question had been talked of, his master seemed jealous of his [my] interviews with us, and a few days previous to our departure we were informed that the Bey had married him to one of the women belonging to his harem and we heard no more of him.'

I fear 'Donald Donald' was a sore disappointment to Mr Thomas Legh, MP. 'He had never shown much anxiety about obtaining his liberty', he tells his readers, failing to appreciate that liberty in a baronial hall in Cheshire is not exactly the same as 'liberty' in a Highland 'black-house' after our chiefs had sold out. It's a mistake these milords often make.

All the same, I will admit that I watched them sail away with a pang. This was the second time I'd thrown away the chance to go home, and this time offered on a golden platter. That left me still the property of that monster, Ahmed Bonaparte and, too late, it occurred to me that perhaps the Bey had turned down young Legh's offers on his orders. Since I'd lost touch with Tom Keith, I was at the monster's mercy.

Perhaps the trouble was that my thoughts had strayed elsewhere – to North Carolina. I had asked the Yankee Barthouw about it. 'You can't call that America,' he spat out. 'They're just a bunch of slave-holding tarheels.'*

* In fact, Jacoub Barthouw had been an officer on a New England slaver and may have had a guilty conscience. 'Tarheel' refers to the production of turpentine and tar from the local pine-trees. – F.M.

This is the longest night I have ever passed.

Up on the top of this high wall of sand, in the light of a hundred flares, we can see all too clearly how deeply the *Latif's* prow has bitten into the canal bank. The corvette has slewed round, and lies athwart the channel. Now she is caught in a spider's web of ropes and hawsers. Nubar's steam launch can scrape by, but no proper ship could.

They say the admiral, Hassan Pasha, is on his way down from Port Said, towing three flats with more hawsers, lifting-gear and a thousand soldiers and sailors.

In the smoky light of the *mashal*s, stuck in the sand, we watch them at work, some manhandling huge wooden baulks, some hauling on ropes or digging furiously into the sand around the *Latif's* prow. I know all too well the extraordinary adhesive quality of the mud at the bottom of Lake Menzaleh.

This is a job for my friend Giovanni Belzoni, who shifted the Young Memnon's head. If only we had him here at this moment!

Jeannie broke into my thoughts. 'Where's Sami, Osman? Have you seen him anywhere?'

As First Officer of the *Latif*, my son would have been on the bridge when she struck. Has Captain McKillop clapped him in irons? They always blame the 'native officers'.

They say de Lesseps is on his way down. Rumours everywhere.

In less than four hours the French imperial yacht, *L'Aigle*, with the Empress aboard, will enter the Canal, followed by fifty ships at five-minute intervals. I see them, the crowned heads of Europe, piling up here in the middle of this watery wilderness.

The measured, penetrating tones of the Compagnie Universelle's muezzin came floating through the greyness, intoning the 'first light' call to prayer. I was grateful for it, and, turning towards the Kaaba, I raised both arms, palms outwards, aligned by the ears, and pledged to execute four *rekah*s.

I was sorry for Jeannie, shivering and fretting alongside me, who could not join in this hope-renewing exercise. No doubt she was praying in her own fashion. But a Moslem does not pray as a Christian does. He does not ask favours. He salutes the Oneness and Greatness of Allah and submits to His will. And in my life – as she doesn't seem to understand – there have been many occasions when this has been not only wise but necessary. Nevertheless, I must admit that on this occasion I succumbed to a little Christian weakness and humbly petitioned that Allah would look with graciousness on my son Sami and thus preserve the House of Osman from the ruin which seemed about to engulf it.

It may be blasphemous to note this, but my self-indulgent prayer was almost immediately answered. The *Latif* gave a sort of long sigh, and slowly slid out of the clutch of the bank, slewed into the fairway, and floated free.

'Allah! Allah! Allah!' rose from a thousand throats. The salutation was like a roll of thunder gathering pace along the Canal. The Bedouin women who had been waiting for hours for the el-Kantara ferry to be resumed broke into an ululation that went on so long that their vibrating tongues seemed to ripple the water.

And I, Osman Effendi – Donald Macleod – throwing dignity to the winds, flung my arms round Jeannie Macdonald and wept, and was astonished to see that she was weeping too.

It had been a close-run thing. I could not help reminding myself that this had been the easiest part of part of the trip. Seventy-five miles of hidden hazards lay ahead of us.

In the Minya bazaars the talk was that Ahmed Bonaparte Aga had been placed in command of Egypt's flagging, long-drawn-out war against the Wahabi heretics in Arabia. I had hoped that Paolo's death would have broken the link, but no. In September I had a visit from the Bey's Chamberlain, bearing an order that the slave Osman was to report to the Egyptian army of liberation in Jeddah. Thomas Legh and the Revd Smelt would be halfway back to Lyme Park and its deer-park by now. Tom Keith, I knew, was somewhere in Arabia, but I had no idea where. It looked as if what I had long dreaded was about to happen.

On such occasions a man cannot always choose his company. I travelled to Arabia with a party of Arnaut freebooters who called themselves Egyptian soldiers, and strange fellows they were. When we camped each night on the Nile bank, they would form little groups after supper, playing the *ud* and singing with deep feeling the songs of their native mountains. Was it homesickness, I wondered, that drove them to their savageries?

At Nag Hammadi the Nile swings east, forming a great question-mark in the desert. The town of Kena lies on its upper curve, the pivot of camel routes between the Nile and the Red Sea.

A caravan from el-Kosseir on the Red Sea had just got in and the bazaars were abuzz with the latest news. Ahmed Bonaparte Aga had dug a tunnel underneath the walls of Medina. There had been a mighty explosion.

'Wallah! Wallah!' cried a merchant of spices. 'The earth and stones were blown so high they brought down an eagle.'

'Allah be praised,' said another man, 'the wall was breached, and the first through was the black-eyed Frangi.'

A black-eyed Frank? Could that be Tom? What was certain was that the man who had dug the tunnel was Ahmed Bonaparte.

In the six days it took my military caravan to wind its way down through rock-strewn, waterless wastes to the Red Sea port. I searched my mind for answers to these questions. I knew that my whole future – life or death – depended on them.

Shrivelled in that heat, approaching the old harbour of el-Kosseir, we passed another caravan on its way back to Cairo. News flew between us in a flurry of shouts. The castle within Medina had fallen. There had been great slaughter of the black-robed fanatics. Seas of blood. The road to Mecca now lay open. Mohammed Ali himself was in Taif, offering six Maria Theresa dollars for every Wahabi head brought in to him. Already, one fellow said, there were five thousand heads piled outside his tent.

If the Red Sea in August is like the vestibule of Hell, Jeddah, with its blindingly white stone houses, oven streets and salt-encrusted shores, is Hell itself.

The first thing I did on arriving was to put as great a distance as possible between myself and the Arnaut soldiery with whom I had travelled. The next thing I did was dig out of the bottom of my pack the fine fur hat of the Hakim Bashi which the late Ezbek Bey had conferred upon me.

I tried it on. Given my height, it lent me, I thought, a look of rare distinction. Thus equipped, I approached an Indian merchant, inquiring the whereabouts of the *diwan* of my old friend, Ibrahim Aga.

He eyed me suspiciously. 'It is of the khasnadar of the Prince Tousson that you speak?'

I bowed gravely. So Tom had been raised to the post of Treasurer at Tousson's court. As I've said, he had a way of falling on his feet.

'Then you have a great man for a friend. He has performed many valorous deeds. He is the most powerful man in all Jeddah.'

'More powerful than Ahmed Bonaparte Aga?'

The Indian looked around nervously, but said nothing. He pointed me on my way and scurried off.

The palace doorkeeper rose to bar my entry, then caught sight of my fur hat, and thought better of it. 'His Excellency Ibrahim

Aga commands my presence,' I said, and he detailed a boy to conduct me through the corridors to the Treasurer's *diwan*.

Sitting there, cross-legged on a divan, surrounded by the usual obseqious officials and waiting supplicants, his angular features blackened by the sun, moustachioed and bearded, with a massive white turban, Tom looked every inch the Arab grandee. I wouldn't have known him had I met him in the street.

People were drifting in and out all the time, in the usual Arab way of doing business. Because of this Tom did not see me at first as he turned from one petitioner to another, periodically taking a judicious pull at the long stem of his *nargila*, 'drinking the smoke' as they say. But his mood changed swiftly when an Arnaut officer complained surlily that his men had not been paid, and hinted at mutiny. Tom's dark eyes flashed and he half rose from his seat in his anger.

I moved deeper into the circle of supplicants. A servant came and offered me coffee. But still Tom had not seen me.

I remembered the trick he had used at the Citadel when he saved my life. 'Alba gu bràth,' I said, in a loud whisper.

I saw Tom's head whip round and his face lit up. The Gaelic is a douce language, but penetrating to the attuned ear, and 'Scotland for ever!' cropping up in an Arab *majlis* in Jeddah . . . !

Nevertheless, preserving the dignity and calm enjoined by Islam, he continued his business with a village headman for several minutes more. Only then, after dismissing the assembly, did he make his way across to me. We embraced, Arab fashion, then drew apart, looked at each other – and laughed like schoolboys.

We had not met since the bloodbath at the Citadel.

'Believe me, Donald, I knew nothing until ten minutes before the shooting started! Nor did Tousson! Thank God I spotted you in time. Ahmed Bonaparte planned the whole bloody business and put it to Mohammed Ali, who played it close to his chest, as only he can.'

He looked around him quickly. 'We can't talk here, Donald. I have a house by the sea. We'll be safer there – there is much to tell. I shall look for you at the time of the Maghrib prayer.'

Tom lived in a tall stone house just near enough to the Red Sea shore to give him the illusion, some days, of being back in the old gunsmith's shop off Leith water. So he told me – and I think

I know what he meant, for beneath the Arab robes of 'Ibrahim Aga' is the soul of a proud Scot. I recalled the day at Fort George when he took me to Nairn to see the statue of his namesake, Marshal Keith. Exiled for fighting in the Jacobite cause, Keith became a colonel in the Spanish army, then went to Russia where he became Catherine the Great's favourite general, the one she said was worth all the others put together. After that, Tom said, Frederick the Great made him Field Marshal Keith for winning Prussia's battles. It seemed to me that Tom was well on the way to emulating his hero and namesake.

A great tray of rice and lamb had been placed before us, and beside this we two oddly dressed Scots of the Ross-shire Buffs squatted, eating with our right hands, Arab fashion. Naturally, I congratulated Tom Keith on delivering the second most holy city of Islam from the Wahabi tyranny, opening up again the road to Mecca.

His face darkened. 'And do you know *how* we won it, Donald?'

'They say you were the first through the breach in the wall . . .'

He shook his head. 'We won by treachery. The Wahabis had retreated into the castle inside the town with all their women and children – they were ready to hold out until Saud relieved them. Then Ahmed Bonaparte solemnly undertook to provide 500 camels for their baggage and womenfolk with safe conduct into the Nedj – if they would surrender the castle.

'They thought him a man of his word. He provided the camels, but one hundred only. A mile out of the town they were overtaken by Bonaparte's men and slaughtered like cattle.'

I shuddered. *Hakim* I might be, but I was still a slave. With no paper of emancipation, I would be at Ahmed Bonaparte's mercy. I thanked God I had found Tom: as Tousson's Treasurer he was a power in himself.

'Where is he now?'

'In Medina. But don't worry. I have my men there. I'm keeping an eye on the bugger.' He had noted my consternation.

'Donald, I have a plan. I shall appoint you Chief Medical Officer to the Jeddah garrison. Out of sight, out of mind.

'Pity we can't take a dram.' Instead he produced a bottle of raki. Time for a good scrack: the wreck of the French fleet off Cape Trafalgar . . . the plague of boils at Gibraltar . . . the rages of Sergeant Baxter and the day he almost got the full charge of my musket in his face . . . on the seashore at Alexandria by the fallen obelisk . . . the black girls . . .

There were, too, the things we shrank from still – the humiliating five-hour parade through the streets of Cairo with our officers' heads impaled on poles. We had no wish to revive that shame. But as Tom poured out more raki I was emboldened to tell him the 'Arabian Nights' tale of my encounters with Ezbek's chief wife, of the Khislar Aga and of Fatima's disappearance.

'Poor Donald,' he said, 'you are unlucky with your women. I shall never forget that Macdonald girl . . . handfasted, weren't you? You were going off to North Carolina with her. Remember that old crone we found at Spean Bridge who claimed to have the sicht? "A tall man and a shrouded child beside a great river." '

Did I remember? Those were memories I was only just managing to push to the back of my mind at last, and now Tom, unthinkingly, was opening up the agonies of doubt again. All the same, I was touched that, after all he – we – had been through, he had remembered.

'Osman! Ya Osman! Yal-la!' It was a woman's voice from somewhere behind the door.

I jumped to my feet. Then the door burst open and a toddler entered and scampered over to hold onto Tom's legs. The woman called again from behind the door. I caught a glimpse of a slender arm, a warm copper colour in the light of the oil-lamp. The child's resemblance to Tom was obvious. So he had named his first-born after me! I envied him his secure position and domesticity.

I saw no more of 'Osman's' mother, for 'Ibrahim Aga' was by this time a good enough Moslem not to parade his harem in the way of the West. But as another bottle of raki was opened and its level sank, I learned that in the pilgrimage season Jeddah was full of Ethiopian slave-girls, shipped across the Red Sea from Suakin to provide 'wives' for the merchants who flocked there, combining Koranic duty with commerce and often staying for months, setting up second households.

'When in Jeddah, do as the Jeddans do.' It appeared that Tom had.

It was now very late. The bottle was empty. But when I got up to go, Tom put out a detaining hand. He seemed to hesitate.

'There's one thing you could do for me in your new post,

Donald – besides keeping my men from dying from the pox.' He hesitated again.

'There's a strange fellow just in from Suakin. Calls himself Sheikh Ibrahim el-Shami, but I'll be damned if he's any sort of Syrian or Turk or Arab. He was in rags when he got here, and I heard he sold his slave in the Jeddah market to get money to buy clothes. Now he's lodging at the *wakala*. I hear he's always writing, writing, and they say he can recite the Koran by heart. He's worrying the Pasha. Mohammed Ali's got it into his head that this fellow is an English spy.'

Tom looked me in the eye at last. 'I hear he's sick now with a high fever. He needs a good doctor. So if you could take a look at him and let me know what you think . . .'

I must have bridled.

'I know, old man. You're a doctor, not a spy. But you'd be doing us a favour, and doing him a favour, and it would stand you in good stead if Bonaparte cuts up rough . . .'

We parted with that old Highland blessing I remembered my mother using:

> May the road rise to meet you
> May the wind be always at your back
> May the rain fall softly on the fields
> Until we meet again.

Alas, we never did.

I have to admit that Tom Keith's account of the mysterious Sheikh Ibrahim el-Shami had aroused my curiosity. Since, apparently, he needed my medical services, I lost no time in making my way round to the port's many-galleried caravanserai.

It was early afternoon. The air hung in wet curtains across the steaming streets. The pipe-boys slumbered beneath the coffee-house tables; in druggists' shops the baskets of rosebuds from the hills around Taif, much esteemed for harem ablutions, were wilting. All the fight had gone out of the beggars who in the name of Allah usually assaulted arrivals at the gates of the great *wakala*.

As I reached the gates, I became aware of a very faint scratching sound and, looking around, I saw a tall, dark-bearded fellow, dressed like an Egyptian effendi, stretched out on a stone bench in the shade of a solitary sycamore. An inkhorn at his side, he was scratching away, copying from bits of paper onto a larger sheet.

He must have felt my gaze upon him, for as his pen reached the end of a sentence he glanced up and I found myself looking into calm grey eyes.

'You must be Osman, Osman the Scotsman,' he said quietly.

Close up, I saw there were tell-tale yellow streaks in his eyes. But for the present at least the fever of which Tom had spoken seemed to have abated.

'The Scots Mameluke,' he said. 'I heard of you just beyond the Second Cataract from a Frenchman fleeing with the Mamelukes.'

'François!' I shouted and showered him with questions about Fatima, and, possibly, a child. He could tell me nothing, except that the pitiful remnant of the once-proud Mameluke corps was at that time still retreating southwards, pursued by Ibrahim's slaughtermen.

'Sheikh Ibrahim' made space for 'Osman' on the bench, and, as he did so, a drop of sweat ran down his nose, and a blurr spread across the letter he was writing.

'Oh, verdammt!' he said. 'Sir Joseph will not care for that.'

He was, I discovered, a Swiss, and Sir Joseph was Sir Joseph Banks, secretary of the London African Association which had engaged him to trace the still unknown course of the River Niger. He was not a man who did things by halves. He'd first spent nearly a year in Aleppo, perfecting his Arabic, studying the Koran, converting Jean-Louis Burckhardt into Ibrahim el-Shami.* But nothing goes that smoothly in the East. The Wahabi fanatics had disrupted the pilgrimage and Louis had been kicking his heels for two years, waiting for the appearance of the Fezzan caravan. Ever restless, he'd filled in the time exploring the Nile as far as Shendi.

Though 'accidental', my encounter with Jean Louis Burckhardt in Jeddah that afternoon turned out to be providential, and as my readers may now know, I do not use the word lightly (as many Christians do).

---

* Mr Burckhardt makes mention of my father, 'Osman', when passing Kosh-tamna on the Nubian Nile in the first volume of his *Travels in Arabia* (1829) – F.M.

The Swiss was only five years my senior, a young gentleman who came from a solid, rich and cultivated Basle family. Burckhardt became this drover-boy's guide, philosopher and friend and, finally, benefactor. He opened up a new life for me.

And he had appeared at exactly the right moment: for only a few days after our late-night supper, Tom Keith was ordered over the mountains to bring some order to Medina, newly delivered from the Wahabi zealots' clutches. Should Ahmed Bonaparte's glance fall upon me, God knows what might become of me.

Not only that, but with the onset of peace, my medical work was becoming increasingly depressing. The Turks would insist that the 'camel's disease' or the 'French grain' were merely the result of the cold nights or the bad water, and if I taxed them with their perversions they would tell me with a leer that 'from the back a man is just like a woman'.

I think I should have gone mad had I not been able to go round to the *wakala* in the cool of the evenings when 'Sheikh Ibrahim' would tell me of the astonishing world of the Pharaohs he had discovered under the drifting sand. In a cleft in the rock at a place called Abu Simbel, four gigantic stone figures on their thrones rose out of the imprisoning sand. The exposed arm of one was one yard and six inches across. Louis longed to liberate the Pharaoh and enter the temple he felt sure lay beneath. But the hot sand trickled back as fast as he dug it out and, at that time, the heavy veil of the hieroglyphics still lay across the Pharaonic world. That merely excited him further, strengthening his determination to go back and clear away the fine, dry, slithering sand of Egypt infiltrating everywhere, burying long lost worlds.

In particular, in the desert on the west bank opposite Luxor, he had seen the vast head of a young Pharaoh, shattered at the neck, which for centuries had lain there where it fell. Greek travellers, who could conceive of no history but their own, had christened it the 'Young Memnon'.

The Young Memnon smiled seraphically skyward, as if cherishing some private secret. Burckhardt had conceived a grand design: by hook or by crook, to rescue him and carry him down the Nile and on to England.

I listened to him, entranced.

It was the beginning of many things.

15 'Here I am . . .'

After twelve years during which it had been blocked by Wahabi fanatics, the road to Mecca was open again. It was rumoured that the Kadi, the chief judge of Mecca, eager to mend his fences with the Pasha of Egypt, had despatched the most beautiful of his concubines to Mohammed Ali's harem at Taif.

On my visits to the Jeddah *wakala* now I found Sheikh Ibrahim's mood changed. The expected remittance from the African Association in London had still not arrived. He hated inactivity. He announced his intention to make the pilgimage without delay.

I was horrified. So early in the day the roads had not been cleared and restored, and Burckhardt was already suspected of being an English spy. Mecca was absolutely forbidden to Christians. Those even suspected of being *giaour*s had been set on by mobs, torn limb from limb, impaled at the gates.

When I pleaded with Louis, he just laughed.

'As you well know, Osman, it is the duty of every True Believer to make the pilgrimage to the Kaaba at least once before he dies. The chance may never come again.'

I reminded him that the Mecca road went high over the mountains; the Wahabis had smashed all the shelters and water tanks.

'You're not strong enough after that long fever. Arnaut gangs are on the rampage. You'll never get through alone.'

'Osman, I shall not be alone. You will be with me.'

This alarmed me more than ever.

'Ahmed Bonaparte is in Mecca. If I leave the medical post Tom fixed up for me, I shall be playing right into his hands.'

Louis waved all this aside.

'You cannot be Bonaparte's slave, my friend, if you are already the slave of a devout Egyptian pilgrim named Sheikh Ibrahim. We shall make the hadj together, Osman, you and I.'

Louis was both determined and persuasive; after a time I began to see the force of his arguments. I should be striking out for myself in a new world. In any case, what real choice did I have, now that Tom was gone?

Over the following days Louis went ahead steadily with his preparations: buying two good horses, visiting the tent-makers, getting in provisions, decking himself out for his chosen role as an Egyptian gentleman fallen on hard times, and buying suitable clothes for me, his slave.

And then, a bombshell! A special messenger arrived from Taif with a letter addressed to Sheikh Ibrahim el-Shami. It came from Mohammed Ali himself and requested the most distinguished Sheikh to attend his *diwan* in Taif immediately. Since the Pasha had heard that Sheikh Ibrahim had been observed walking in rags, he enclosed a note to the Jeddah customs house ordering them to supply him with cloth for a new suit, together with three hundred piastres for travel expenses.

The real sting came in the tail. In travelling to Taif, the sheikh was on no account to take the road that ran through Mecca. He must stick to the northern route which swung clear of the holy city. Mohammed Ali still clung to his suspicion that Louis was an English spy. Again I urged Louis to give up this mad idea. But Mohammed Ali's letter had merely made him more determined to accomplish the *hadj*.

We slowly climbed up into the red granite mountains, our spirits rising as the thermometer fell. There were sheltered valleys up there where figs and apricots and peaches and apples grew, and there were clear streams and the turf sprang under our feet, reminding us both of our homelands. Mohammed Ali's insistence on our taking this route added several days to the pilgrimage. But how right they were to call Taif 'Mecca's Garden of Eden'; every bush and every tree had its own fragrance. Up there we began to feel that we might be able to shed our cares and breathe freely again.

We could not have been more wrong. On the very day of our

arrival, Sheikh Ibrahim el-Shami was summoned to attend upon His Excellency Mohammed Ali. To my horror, Louis proposed to ignore this. He planned to send me with a letter, stating that Sheikh Ibrahim had been deeply hurt by the Pasha's order that he should not travel near the holy city. It would be impossible for him to attend upon His Excellency unless he could be received as a true Muslim, which indeed he was.

I begged Louis to tear his letter up. Why put our heads into the lion's mouth? Ahmed Bonaparte, author of the blood-bath at the Citadel and the sickening treachery at Medina was, I felt sure, working against us, madly jealous of Tom Keith's rise to power.

Louis was an obstinate man.

'Nonsense, Osman,' he said. 'As I told you, Mohammed Ali is a man who knows which heads to sever, and yours and mine aren't among them. He needs us as we need him. Bonaparte? He's just a vicious clown. Forget him, Osman!'

In the end I did as I was told; I delivered Louis's letter to Mohammed Ali's castle in Taif. I expected to be arrested. But what I actually got was a message saying that 'Muslim or no Muslim, Sheikh Ibrahim el-Shami would be more than welcome at this court.'

Swathed in a deep crimson mantle, a jewelled dagger in his sash, the master of Egypt and liberator of the holy cities of Islam, Mohammed Ali sat in his audience chamber in the castle of Taif, gravely conferring with a group of Bedouin sheikhs.

As Louis made his salaams and was motioned to a seat on the long divan next to the Kadi of Mecca, the Bedouin fixed him with the unremitting stare they bestow upon strangers, then resumed their discussions with the Pasha, entwined in arabesques of compliment and liberally decorated with the sayings of the Prophet.

The usual point of impasse having been reached, Mohammed Ali turned to Louis. 'Now tell me, my honoured and distinguished Sheikh, in what way I may serve you?'

Louis seized his chance. 'As Your Excellency in his unsurpassed valour has now made possible, I wish to complete the last of the five duties enjoined upon a True Believer. I wish to undertake the pilgrimage, to kiss the black stone of the holy Kaaba and drink the waters of Zem-Zem before I die.'

Mohammed Ali nodded gravely, but said nothing. It was evident that religious duties were not the first thing on his mind. News had just reached Taif that the Allies had entered Paris, that Napoleon Bonaparte – long Mohammed Ali's hero and model – had surrendered. The Pasha felt betrayed.

'He should have sought death rather than be caged like an animal.' Drilling Burckhardt with those extraordinary eyes of his, he said, 'Now the English will come back to attack me!'

'I cannot answer for England, Your Excellency, but I sincerely believe she wishes only to be your friend. But then I have heard it said that where Egypt is concerned you are like a young man who has taken a beautiful bride. He loves her dearly but he is racked by jealousy and suspicion if any other man draws near.'

Mohammed Ali's face lit up.

'You speak truly, Sheikh Ibrahim. It is indeed so. Though born across the sea, I have embraced this land with the ardour of a young lover. There is nothing I would not do to serve her.'

Louis tried to seize the moment to secure from the Pasha a *firman* lending us his protection in Mecca. Unfortunately, at this point the Kadi intervened officiously to cast doubt on our credentials.

That old devil the Pasha nodded gravely.

'Yes, it is true that the beard alone does not ensure the True Believer. On such matters the Kadi is a better judge than I . . .'

He was playing with us now. He had not finished with Louis yet. He pressed him on the signs of gold discovered on his travels in Nubia. And the number of surviving Mamelukes he had seen up there. The man's questing intelligence was palpable.

It was evident that we were not going to get our safe-conduct. The old fox was going to keep us hanging on here for his own devious purposes.

Or Ahmed Bonaparte's.

I forget how long we hung around Taif. Louis made it his business to cultivate the Kadi, selecting the longest suras in the Koran to recite when praying beside him in the mosque. To no avail. It seemed obvious we had enemies at court. I was all for returning to Jeddah while we could, but Louis was adamant. As Moslems, Mecca was both our right and an obligation.

Looking back, I am glad that I let Louis make the decision for me, because the few weeks that followed gave me strength to live my strange life with its many disappointments and reversals of fortune. It is hard to explain to anyone who has not made the pilgrimage. But I must try.

A sickening stink. The rotting carcasses of hundreds of camels marked our road up through the bleak red and yellow sandstone hills, a reminder of the bitter war that would soon resume. The first landmark on the journey – and it was to be a landmark in my life – came with Wadi Mohren, which is *migat*, one of the frontiers of the Mecca world. No unbelievers may go beyond, on pain of death. Here we discarded our ordinary clothes, and after ablutions and headshaving put on the *ihram*, two seamless pieces of thin white cotton cloth, one to wind around the waist, the other to throw over the left shoulder – leaving the head, the instep, the right arm and shoulder bare. In a few moments, the wealthiest pilgrims were no different from the poorest.

Ihram means consecration. Having donned it, no pilgrim may use perfume, curl his or her hair, or look lustfully upon a man or woman. Indeed, wearing the *ihram* is a penance itself. Under the scorching sun on those barren plains the exposed skin broils; by night in the mountains the thin sheet is no protection: the pilgrims' teeth chatter. On the gruelling climb over Mount Kara torrents of rain came foaming down the mountainside, and as Louis's bare shoulder began to shake from the cold, and our soaking *ihram*s clung to the skin, I started wondering whether he was strong enough after his fever to survive the trip.

An endless succession of rocky defiles led out at last onto a sort of rock platform. Suddenly we found ourselves looking down on the Holy City, the Great Mosque and its immense courtyard cupped in the grim pit of the gaunt mountains.

Other pilgrims, wraiths in their white *ihram*s, surged about us, straining for that first sight of the Kaaba, the holy cube, the ancient House of Allah erected by Abraham on Allah's orders.

An old voice quavered out:

> Labbaik Allahumma, Labbaik!
> La Sharia laka, Labbaik!

A grizzled Negro came in, and then a score of other voices – in a dozen tongues – took up the resounding affirmation of the 'pilgrims' chant':

> Here I am, O Lord, here I am.
> No partner hast Thou, here I am!

The full-throated testament echoed from the black rock and, swelling, seemed to fill the steely sky.

We descended the long flights of steps from the street and emerged into the vast colonnaded courtyard of the great mosque, and saw the Kaaba rising in the distance before us. A broad white stream of pilgrims, foamed around it – night and day – for at whatever hour he reaches Mecca the pilgrim is instructed by bakshish-hungry guides that his first duty is to perform the *tawaf*, the circumambulation of the Kaaba seven times, three circuits at a half-run, moving the shoulders, the remaining four at a comfortable walking pace. And at each of these *shaut*s the Black Stone, set in the south-east corner, is to be kissed or touched or saluted.

Silent and mysterious, its dark, rough-hewn stone blocks visible below its black silk covering, the Kaaba is a potent mystery, a unique, compelling affirmation. Men were on their knees everywhere, in tears, in torrential prayer, in ecstasy.

'Here I am, O Lord, here I am.'

Above our heads the courtyard was aflutter with the beat of pigeons' wings, thousands of them, blue-grey, wheeling, swooping, strutting over foot-burnished flagstones. The Meccans called them 'Allah's persuaders' from their way of bowing their heads, left and right, as if in prayer. And they insist that although the pigeons fly right over the Kaaba, they never desecrate it with their droppings.

Meccan women were selling little boxes of grain so that pilgrims could feed the pigeons, thereby laying up a store of merit before embarking on the prescribed duties, whereby year by year was re-enacted the stark and powerful drama of the birth of Islam in this desolate place.

Urged on by our guides, Sheikh Ibrahim and his slave Osman counted off our prescribed circuits of the Kaaba, touching the Black Stone, reciting after our guide the prescribed prayers in each position, raising our arms before the high silver door to make our private requests to Allah. Louis, I know, prayed that the Fezzan caravan would at last arrive to carry him towards his goal; I did not confide my prayer, but hope was renewed here that I would one day see her again, in reality as well as in my dreams – whether beside the Nile, as in the old crone's vision, or in North Carolina.

After that, we drank the holy waters of the spring Zem-Zem, paying the guardians a few piastres to give free glasses to the poor. The water was bitter. Sheets soaked in it were hanging out to dry, so that the pilgrims could carry them home for their winding-sheets when the day came. Some indeed, already wrapped in them, were breathing their last in sight of the Kaaba, happy, not alone.

It was the next duty – the Running – that laid Louis low.

The 'track' runs between two hillocks, Safa and Marwal. It was here that Hagar, Abraham's slave-wife, ran through the desert, desperately seeking water for her infant son who was dying of thirst. She had all but given up hope when, on the seventh attempt, a well bubbled up from the sand at her feet. Whereupon Allah ordered Ibrahim – or Abraham – to build the first House of Allah on the spot.

For Louis, debilitated by his earlier fevers, roasting by day, freezing by night in the thin *ihram*, the Running proved the last straw. Limbs shaking, teeth chattering, he lay day after day in his bed in our Mecca lodgings. I did what I could, but without the bark it was not much. Allah be praised, the fever died away at last and he began to gain strength and even tried to write up his notes for the African Association. I was able to escape from our crowded lodgings for an hour or two to take a look at the holy city.

Strolling along the Mesaa, the long central street with its *suk*, I spotted a gang of Arnaut soldiers advancing towards me. Only then did it come home to me what fearful risks I was taking. They could be Ahmed Bonaparte's men. They might recognise their medico from Jeddah. I dived through the doorway of a café and took a seat at a table in the darkest corner. Thank God, they swaggered past without a glance. I ordered a glass of 'cinnamon water', a milky liquid which all the Meccans there seemed to be drinking. My mouth was dry. I took a long drink – and almost leapt from my chair. The cinnamon and sugar failed to disguise the fiery raki. And this in the Prophet's birthplace!

A Meccan at the next table choked on his drink in amusement.

I was indignant. 'Does not the Holy Koran declare strong drink to be Shaitan's handiwork?'

Now on his third glass of 'cinnamon water', the merchant gave me a sidelong look. 'True, my friend, true. But this holy city is forbidden to infidels, and as for those of the House of Islam, Allah allows that many are great sinners, and, accordingly, is charitable.' He chuckled, and ordered another glass.

Discussing my experience with Louis, I learned that there is a subtle accountancy in these matters. For every circling of the Kaaba 70,000 sins are forgiven and 70,000 virtues added, and since seven circlings are obligatory, a pilgrim lays up a considerable credit balance. Meccans seemed to me to be adept at providing the means of working off the credits – and not only with cinnamon water. As Louis points out in his *Travels in Arabia*, the grain-selling women all too visibly feed other appetites than the pigeons'. I thought of the curving horns of the old woman's heifer in Broadford market, one pointing to Heaven, the other to Hell. Both from the same head. There I must leave it.

Bareheaded and clad in the white *ihram* like the rest of us, Mohammed Ali himself had arrived in Mecca to celebrate the resumption of the great pilgrimage. Next day, Amine Hanem, his first wife – the mother of Tousson, Tom Keith's master – followed from Jeddah, with a train of camels conveying her women and baggage. All around us now on the grim plain of Arafat, a camp four miles long was close-packed with the tents of the great Cairo and Damascus pilgrim caravans, an extraordinary sight.

We had two remaining duties of the *hadj* to fulfil, the Standing and Stoning. In the chilly dawn Sheikh Ibrahim el-Shami and his slave Osman pushed their way through the great white sea of pilgrims, gathered there from all points of the compass, to a good spot facing the Mount of Mercy.

We pronounced the *niyyat*: 'O God, I purpose to abide here until the setting of the sun.' It is a test, this Standing, which echoes the testing of Abraham, ordered by Allah to sacrifice his son here on the Mount of Mercy. Islam means 'submission': Abraham's was the first – and ultimate – submission. For a price, the Meccan guides will show any pilgrim who can climb that high the very cleft in the rock made when, in His mercy, God deflected Abraham's sacrificial knife.

As noon approached, and the sun drilled into our bare heads, we saw the Kadi of Mecca slowly ascending the Mount of Mercy on a camel to the rock platform from which Mohammed himself – blessings be upon Him – delivered the Arafat sermon on his final pilgrimage in 10 AH (AD 662). On the stroke of noon, still mounted on his camel, the Kadi opened his Koran. In fact, few of the pilgrims gathered below under the burning sun could hear him.

During the Standing we were all supposed to confess our sins, and ask Allah's forgiveness. But the heat was scarcely bearable, and most pilgrims seemed to pass their time gossiping and getting their things together ready for the stampede at dusk to the valley of Muna.

Muna seemed to me the perfect setting for the final duty; the Stoning of Shaitan. The rules are exact. The stones are to be the size of horse-beans and each stone must be washed seven times. Forty-nine stones are to be hurled at each rock-devil with the shout: 'In the name of Allah – to save ourselves from the Devil and all his troops!'

Fortunately, earlier pilgrims had left little piles of stones along the track. I'm afraid I took it for granted that they had been washed seven times.

The 'Great Devil' was a rock buttress nine feet high. The trouble was that we could never get near enough to score a hit. There was no lack of lesser devils in that rocky defile, however, and there was nothing to stop you appointing a devil of your own. I got in the necessary forty-nine hits on Sergeant Baxter, the sadist of Fort George, a fusillade on Ahmed Bonaparte Aga, plus forty-nine stones for Glengarry who burned his tenants out to replace them with sheep, and, as an afterthought, a big stone for the Macleod who had betrayed the Prince and so exposed me to the withering scorn of Jeannie Macdonald, which was the beginning of it all. Conducted in consort with thousands of brother believers, it was an exhilarating and heartening exercise.

I cannot tell you how glad we were to get out of those chilly white sheets and back into our normal clothes. Yet in those extraordinary days I felt a new, unshakeable foundation had been built under my life. In the privacy of our lodgings, Louis had already begun to copy out the minute notes he had scribbled on his little squares of paper, concealed in the curve of his hand. This was shortly to become the first detailed, accurate account of the great pilgrimage that lies at the heart of Islam, renewed from generation, century to century, all the way back to the Prophet. I was proud to have been of some help to Louis in accomplishing this great work, thirty years before that braggart Burton.

'And now,' said Louis, 'you can dye your beard a nice shade of orange and call yourself Hadji Osman. Believe me, you will command respect.'

'I doubt I shall command the respect of Ahmed Bonaparte Aga,' I said.

With the sudden death of the great Wahabi leader Saud in his capital, Dariyah, deep in the interior of Arabia, Mohammed Ali was determined to move in for the kill. Already he had commandeered 12,000 camels from the Damascus pilgrim caravan to fetch military stores from Jeddah. Prudence demanded that I resume the post Tom had given me.

Sheikh Ibrahim was anxious to go on to Medina. I gave him a letter to Tom, who I heard had become Acting Governor of Medina, assuring him that the bearer was no English spy. I was proud of Tom Keith. Imagine it! A Scots lad from the Ross-shire Buffs as Acting Governor of the second holiest city of Islam. At the same time, this meant that my protector was now a long way off. Travelling alone, I could be taken up. Like Beybars, Tom had risen out of slavery, but the badge of the slave still weighed upon me.

'Never fear, Osman,' Louis said, 'your position is not so dark as you think.' He quoted from Sura 24, called 'The Light': ' "Such of your slaves as seek a certificate of emancipation, write it for them if you are aware of ought good in them, and bestow on them the wealth which Allah has bestowed upon you."

'As soon as I get back to Cairo I shall take up your case with Mr Henry Salt, the new British Consul. He is a good friend of the Pasha. Do not fail to visit, Osman, when you get back to Cairo.'

'If I get back.' I said.

'Inshallah!'

BOOK III

The Curtain Rises

Nile-land was, then as now, a field for plunder; fortunes were made by digging, not for gold, but antiquities; and the archaeological field became a battleplain for two armies of Dragomen and Fellah-navvies. One was headed by the redoubtable Salt; the other owned the command of Drovetti . . .

– Richard Burton, *The Cornhill Magazine*

His ready genius explored and elucidated
the Hieroglyphics and other Antiquities of
this Country.
– Tombstone in Alexandria of Henry Salt, British Consul
1815–1827

16 I Meet Giovanni, the Paduan Hercules

As the war resumed, the pile of heads outside Mohammed Ali's tent grew even higher. The black-robed Wahabis did not flinch from martyrdom, they welcomed it. But the currency of heads was proving cumbersome so it was now supplemented by ears at ten dollars a pair. Bagged, these were more convenient for presentation to the Grand Seigneur in Istanbul in witness of his Egyptian vassal's zeal. And as a lean Arnaut corporal explained one morning when attending sick parade in Jeddah, ears had this further advantage: they were relatively anonymous. A Wahabi ear did not differ greatly from any Bedou ear. At the time, he was woefully exhibiting an enfeebled and ulcerating *zubb* – the result no doubt of his new-found wealth – while offering me a large sum of money to restore its previous, he bragged, prodigious powers.

It was certainly not for that that I remember this man. He had just arrived from Medina with terrible news. Tom Keith was dead, struck down in a Wahabi ambush. From what I could gather, Tousson with a column of horsemen had been cut off and surrounded and had sent an appeal for reinforcements. Tom had ridden off on the instant, but had been ambushed in his turn. Ibrahim Aga, said the corporal, had fought like a lion, cutting down four Wahabi horsemen before he fell.

Prince Tousson had been saved. But to me that was no consolation. I felt absolutely bereft, totally let down. Had not Tom solemnly undertaken to protect me? What right did he have to go risking his life in this reckless fashion? True, I had seen little of him since the night he slipped away from Ezbek's camp after ridding us of Paolo. Yet in a curious way he had been ever-present:

in a tight corner I would always ask myself: what would Tom Keith have done? Through all those years since we sailed out from the Moray Firth, he had been my lifeline, rudder and anchor too. True, I had made the pilgrimage. Readers may ask why I did not now feel the new assurance I then avowed. But if Allah indeed knows all, why had he permitted the killing of such a man as Tom Keith?

For days I brooded on this, and on all we had been through together – the outwitting of Sergeant Baxter at Fort George, the tense wait for Bonaparte's invasion boats that never came, fighting shoulder to shoulder at Maida, the hell of el-Hamed, languishing in the dank cavern in the Citadel – only to be imprisoned once again in the gilded cage of Mamelukery.

Now the book had slammed shut on all that. And I was sure that I wouldn't be able to find Tom's son; his mother would have melted back into the slave-world from which she'd come – I didn't even know her name. It came to me then that my actions, my life, up to then had been largely dictated by others: my father, Jeannie Macdonald, Captain Stewart, the recruiting officer at the Falkirk Tryst . . . Tom Keith.

Now I would have to strike out for myself. This bloody war in Arabia was no place for me. Desertion in the Ottoman army was not so much a crime as a way of life. So desert I would, without delay. Had not Sheikh Ibrahim bade me visit when I reached Cairo?

I dyed my beard with the henna of the *hadji*, which in truth I now was, and cast about for a way of getting back to Cairo.

Allah favoured my plan. It happened that a Bombay ship was in Jeddah harbour, captained by a certain Captain Bloag, a Scot, a friend of mine ever since I had been called out to a sick passenger on his ship, a young English newspaperman called James Silk Buckingham.* When I'd got the sick man back on his feet, there

---

* In his *Autobiography* (1855), Mr Buckingham pays tribute to care taken of him by what he calls 'this young Scotsman, Othman'. He also writes that unlike his co-religionist, Mr Burckhardt, Othman would not take a single glass of wine 'for fear of disgracing his faith'. When he finally did so on being much pressed he was sick, which he attributed to 'divine displeasure'. This gives the lie to all who say Osman Effendi was not sincere in his adopted faith. – F.M.

had been a dinner-party in Captain Bloag's cabin, attended by Buckingham, Mr Burckhardt and myself. Having heard my story, Captain Bloag at once agreed to take me over the Red Sea to Bir Saga whence many caravans led to Kena on the Nile.

I was in luck again at Kena. I was hailed by the *reis* of a great raft of the water-jars made at this place. It turned out that I had once relieved him of the belly-ache with a memorable purge. Learning that I was making for Cairo, nothing would do but that I sail down with him.

Donning the simple blue striped *galabiya* of the fellah, living on onions, beans, goat cheese, and endless little glasses of long-stewed sweet tea, I melted effortlessly into the Egyptian landscape as I lay in the shade of the great red pyramid of fat-bellied water-jars.

It was not until we slid at last into Bulak that I realised that Louis had not given me the address of his house, nor any clear indication of how to find it in the immensity of Cairo. I made for the Frankish quarter, asking servants I encountered where I might find the house of Sheikh Ibrahim. Receiving not a glimmer of recognition, I began to grow alarmed. Trigger-happy Arnauts, tired of the war, and no respecters of *hadji*s and their beards, roamed the streets in gangs, alert for opportunity of plunder. As an unredeemed slave – worse, a former Mameluke – I was in grave danger. Taken before a local magistrate, I might be bastinadoed to extract the truth.

In desperation I approached an Englishman strolling in the Ezbekieh.

'Sir, could you kindly direct me to the residence of Mr Jean-Louis Burckhardt, of the African Association of London?'

He jumped as if he had been shot. I had forgotten that I was still dressed like an Egyptian fellah. He stared at me suspiciously. But the shock – and the English language – prevailed.

'Oh, you mean that Switzer fellow – the one that wears a turban, the renegado?'

He looked at me curiously. I was afraid he was going to call the police.

'You'll not find him round here, lad. Try the Turkish quarter, by that stinking canal.'

Recognising the minarets of el-Azhar where I had found shelter in the great slaughter of 1811, I worked my way northward

towards the Bab el-Sharia, pushed this way and that by laden donkeys and camels, and deafened by the hammers of the coppersmiths in the Suk el-Nahassin. When I inquired here for Sheikh Ibrahim el-Shami, sometimes I drew a gleam of warmth and recognition. But it wasn't until I reached the market for second-hand clothes, old brass and chickens around the Suk el-Zalat that I found myself at last among Louis's neighbours, more than ready to point out the old Turkish house, built on the side of el-Khalig.*
A fat little man who said he was the *suk's* baker seized my arm, and eagerly conducted me to a rickety old wooden house of three storeys that overhung the old canal of Cairo. The Englishman had been right. The canal stank.

A donkey-boy dozed on the doorstep. I had a problem getting rid of the baker: I wanted to surprise Louis. But in this I was balked. When I had climbed to the second floor I heard voices. They seemed to be speaking English. One voice quiet, measured, I recognised as Louis's. The other voice was deep, sonorous, charged with emotion.

I admit I eavesdropped.

'Wood they gave me . . . I struggle with it . . . I show the Pasha Giovanni Battista Belzoni's water-wheel is fine . . . one horse give as much as twenty horses using the old Egyptian *sakiya*. It clear to see. The *stupidos*, they do not *wish* to see. They mock. They plot. They wreck my beautiful wheel. [a sob] My money is gone, my poor wife Sarah, the boy James . . . we will starve . . .'

I caught Burckhardt's quiet, reassuring tones, although his words escaped me.

I climbed higher. Belzoni stood in the doorway, his great mass blocking it as he poured out his tale of woe. I am over six feet myself, and far from lean, but beside Giovanni Battista Belzoni I am a stripling. It was not for nothing that back in London Sadler's Wells had billed him as 'the Patagonian Samson' or, more accurately, 'the Paduan Hercules'.

Giovanni, I know, would resent my telling my readers of his famous 'Strong Man' feats on the London stage. He always

---

* El-Khalig, the old canal of Cairo, was dug many years ago from the east bank opposite the old Nilometer in order to carry the Flood waters of the Nile through the city, refreshing the air in summer, but – as my father suggests – polluting it at other seasons. – F.M.

wanted to be known as a professional hydraulic engineer, and later as an Egyptologist, a professional exhumer of the Pharaohs. He was both of those things, but to me he was always 'the Great Belzoni'.

His arm blocked the doorway into Burckhardt's room as his tale of treachery and betrayal flowed on. Then the arm dropped in a gesture of despair, and, turning sideways, I managed to slip inside. As I did, I saw the tears welling in his soft brown eyes. Never a man to conceal his emotions, my dear friend Giovanni. I suppose that was one of the things I most loved about him. And a wonderful man, a hero. Why else should I have named a son after him?

Louis was sitting at a paper-strewn desk by the window that looked down on the stagnant canal, working, I guessed, on yet another report to the African Association.

He greeted me as if we had parted only yesterday. 'My house is your house,' he said, and I knew that with him it was not just a pious expression. 'The Franks,' he used to say, 'can't understand why I go on living in this "filthy native quarter". They forget I'm a native too, these days. The people here are good to me. I belong here.'

I wanted to ask him whether he had managed to deliver my note to Tom Keith in Medina, but Belzoni was already looking disconsolate at having lost Sheikh Ibrahim's attention. Majestic in his robes, with a full beard and massive white turban, he filled the little room like some Old Testament prophet.

'Signor Belzoni,' Louis explained, having introduced us, 'has a problem. When passing through Malta he was engaged by the Pasha's agent, a certain Captain Ishmael Gibraltar, to enter his service to design a better water-wheel for Egypt. This he did. He demonstrated it before Mohammed Ali himself in the Shubra Gardens . . .'

The giant burst out: 'The sheikhs are jealous. They send men into the wheel when it is revolving . . . they wreck my beautiful machine. I am ruined!'

'With the result,' continued Louis, unperturbed, 'that Signor Belzoni now finds himself marooned, without employment in Egypt . . .'

'And my poor wife, Sarah, is with me,' Belzoni almost sobbed.

'All our money is gone. I ask you, Mr Osman – what's to become of us?'

Theatrical as the Italian made it sound, it was, I suppose, a question each of us in that room had asked himself often enough. We were, in our different ways, all victims of the great tornado, the French Revolution, that had torn through Europe, sweeping lives off their courses. When Giovanni Battista Belzoni's studies in hydraulics had been violently interrupted by Bonaparte's capture of Rome, he had fled to England, living on bread and cheese until his remarkable physique got him a job as a circus Strong Man. As Bonaparte closed in on Switzerland, Jean-Louis Burckhardt, a son of a wealthy merchant family of Basle, also took refuge in England, and after two years in penury found employment with the African Association. I will not dwell further on the accidents of fate that brought me to this place, but my readers will recall that Napoleon Bonaparte's threat to invade England was the occasion of the raising of the Ross-shire Buffs.

And now all three of us, Swiss, Italian and Highlander, had been washed up in this room in an old Turkish house on the Cairo canal, awaiting our destiny.

As it turned out, the arrival of Belzoni on Burckhardt's doorstep proved providential – once again I find myself driven to that word. Burckhardt had long been haunted by the Young Memnon, the vast Pharaoh head he had found lying where it fell in the desert opposite Karnak, staring at the sky. He had conceived the ambition of somehow transporting it down the Nile and on to London. He had gone so far as to confide his plan to Henry Salt, the new British Consul.

But the head was of granite. It weighed three tons. Though the ancient Egyptians had built the pyramids, their successors had no lifting equipment, not even a wheelbarrow. Reluctantly, Louis had had to give up his dream.

On the stage at Sadler's Wells, I happen to know, the 'Paduan Hercules' had carried seventeen men, ranged in a pyramid, on an iron triangle.

'The Pharaohs have slept too long,' said Burckhardt. 'Now Allah has sent us the man to awaken them.'

Looking back, it seems to me that that was a moment of

extraordinary foresight. For Giovanni not only brought the Young Memnon down the Nile to captivate the citizens of London on his high plinth in the British Museum, but went on to lay bare a whole lost Pharaonic world. It appealed to his sense of theatre. He was indeed the first 'Egyptologist'. Providential, as I said.

Burckhardt went off to consult his friend the consul. Henry Salt, himself a keen collector – and salesman – of Pharaonic antiquities, agreed to put up some money to transport the Young Memnon. A few weeks later, I had my Certificate of Emancipation from Mohammed Ali himself, and Belzoni had a *firman* allowing us to carry away the great head. I was twenty-seven and opportunity was opening up before me, *inshallah*.

'It won't be easy,' Burckhardt warned Giovanni. 'But Osman will go with you. He knows the language and the ways of the people.'

We took on board stout ropes and some heavy baulks of timber at Bulak; and picked up a Greek carpenter when our boat reached Asiut. We tied up under an old sycamore-tree on the west bank opposite Luxor.

I have lost count of the number of travellers I have conducted over the ruined courts of the Ramesseum since then, but nothing has ever dimmed my memory of that first time with Giovanni and Sarah, his young Irish wife, who shared the hardships with him. I remember, as if it were yesterday, the moment we stepped out of the boat, climbed up the Nile bank, and set eyes on the place. It was as if we pygmies had strayed into a land of giants, men sixty or seventy feet high looming over us, a world of monstrously rotund columns, towering pylons, mortuary temples, all set against a backdrop of those barren, sun-seared hills.

No wonder those old Greek travellers were put in mind of their own heroic myths of Memnon, slain by Achilles. I myself was reminded of the *Fèinn* of my boyhood, the giants who would cross the Kyle in one easy bound. But our *Fèinn* had been playful creatures. These were sombre, oppressive, cruel. Sarah Belzoni shuddered as she caught sight of the engraving on the surviving walls of the Memnonium – or Ramesseum – a soldier pulling the beard of a helpless prisoner, four others battering a pleading captive.

Arms crossed over their chests, four stone high priests graced the temple court. Two were headless. Pitched from his lofty throne, the Pharaoh had spilled across the ruined courtyard, his great limbs in fragments, his face pressed into the sand.

'È terribile! È molto triste!' cried Giovanni. 'He make himself tall in granite to live for ever – and now he lies in splinters!'

A little further across the devastated court of the mortuary temple we found what we were seeking, the Young Memnon head. His face, fine-honed in red granite, canted skyward. Though Louis had talked of his seraphic smile, I will confess that he put me in mind of the Revd Macaskill, features set in the firm assurance that he was unalterably of the Elect. I could understand Louis's infatuation: after all he *had* lain there, immobile, wearing that inscrutable smile for thirty centuries. And now he was to make a move. That was our task.

I saw at once that there was no time to waste. It was now the end of July: the Nile was rising by the day, very soon the waters would flow over the strip of low-lying land that lay between the head and the Nile bank.

There was another reason for haste. Examining the Young Memnon, we found a small hole drilled in his left shoulder, big enough for a rope to be passed through. I questioned some locals and learned that a Frenchman had done it.

On our way up the Nile we had passed Bernardino Drovetti on his way down with a boatload of *antikas*. The French Consul was as ardent a collector for the Louvre as Mr Salt was for the British Museum. Drovetti claimed that the boatload was his final collection, and as a gesture of good will, had offered Belzoni a fine sarcophagus he had had to leave behind.

That simple soul poured out his gratitude. But I knew Drovetti. I felt sure that if he was offering us a fine sarcophagus it was either because it would be dangerous to get out or because it would delay us long enough to make sure the flood would defeat us.

So the race was on. I estimated that we had three weeks to move three tons of awkwardly shaped granite over irregular ground – some of it soft – to the Nile bank. We had no wheels nor pulleys nor lifting-gear. There was labour to be had in Kurna, but the local Arabs laughed at us. 'Caphany', as they called the Young Memnon, had never been moved, and never would be moved.

Giovanni addressed them. 'We shall move Caphany the way the Pharaohs brought him down from the quarries at Aswan – Caphany and all the other giants. We shall move him mounted on a sledge and you, my friends, will have the honour of pulling him.'

They stood around, unbelieving, shaking their heads as the Greek carpenter set about fastening together the baulks of timber we had brought up from Cairo to form a stout platform, which Giovanni called the 'cart'. I engaged about a hundred of these bystanders at 50 paras a day, well over the regular rate.

The next thing was to mount the Young Memnon on his chariot, using the leverage of long poles. It was a titanic struggle, conducted by Belzoni with great verve, as if he was still directing his troupe at Sadler's Wells. The Arabs responded well to the splendid figure who had come amongst them, and, though there were many mishaps, the Young Memnon at last reclined, enigmatic as ever, upon his wooden throne.

Then Belzoni ordered four palm-trees to be cut down, and amid much heaving and *wallah*ing we pushed them beneath the 'cart'. The temperature was well over a hundred in the shade. Sarah Belzoni had retired to set up home in a cave in the rock wall.

Four lengths of palm-fibre rope – each accommodating fifty hauling men – were then attached to the Young Memnon's chariot and off he moved, if only a few feet. Other labourers cleared rocks from his path and, behind, yet others stood ready to take out the last palm-trunk roller to be carried round to the front for re-use.

That first day we advanced four yards, and Belzoni sent off a runner to Mr Salt in Cairo with the news that, after three millennia, the Young Memnon was at last on his way to London.

The very next day the sun god struck down our giant. Unable to rise to his feet or keep down even a few spoonfuls of food, the Strong Man was as helpless as a baby. I moved him onto our boat on the Nile, where sometimes a cooling breeze blew, and he lay there, crippled by heat stroke, fretting that he was betraying the trust of Mr Salt and Mr Burckhardt.

Next morning, a miracle. Belzoni was gone from the boat. I found him out in front of the cart not long after dawn, guiding the haulers on the ropes, cheering on the roller-changers. That was Giovanni's way, unlike the English travellers who are always telling me: 'All "they" understand is the stick.'

Next day we ran into a patch of soft sand. The 'cart' stuck. I was in despair: I watched the Nile water creeping forward, cutting us off. But Giovanni coolly changed direction, building a 300-foot 'bridge' over the shifting sands to firm ground.

Three more days' hard work and we were nearly over the low ground. The rest seemed plain sailing.

We returned to the cart next day in high spirits, expecting to clear the danger zone. But save for the Greek carpenter, not a single one of our labourers, so happy to be making good money the day before, was present. No message. No explanation. Just a mass desertion. Already I could see trickles of flood water creeping towards that critical neck of land. My first thought was that Drovetti had chosen his moment well.

Giovanni didn't believe me, of course. He rushed over to Kurna, where most of our workers lived, and found them idling. The sub-governor had ordered them not to work any more for that 'Christian dog'. I happened to know that this man was one of Drovetti's most ardent collectors. He had removed himself to the other side of the Nile, to Luxor, out of our reach.

We pursued him. I produced the Pasha's *firman* and thrust it under his nose. The fellow just laughed in our faces: obviously, he had been well paid. He laid hold of Belzoni's sleeve as if to push him away. That was foolish of him. The Paduan Hercules pushed him off with one easy thrust; I saw the fellow reaching for the silver-plated pistols in his belt, and yelled. But already Giovanni had reached out; he grabbed the pistols, handed them to me, and pinned the fellow against a wall, knocking the breath out of him.

We lost no time in taking our boat up river to complain to higher authority, the Kashif of Armant. We found him at a feast to celebrate the end of Ramadan, and were cordially invited to join the table. At a suitable moment Belzoni spoke eloquently of the outrageous behaviour of his subordinate. Without blinking an eyelid, the Kashif insisted that our labourers were needed for the harvest: he, too, it seemed, was one of Drovetti's creatures. He had been greatly admiring the silver-plated pistols now in my belt. So I presented them to him. It tickled my fancy, to make a gift to the chief that had been taken a few hours earlier from one of his subordinates.

Next day we found our Kurna labourers waiting for us around the Young Memnon head, eager to get on. By 9 August he was beyond the reach of the flood. Three days later he was ensconced on the Nile bank.

Unfortunately there was no boat big enough and strong enough to accommodate him. We had to send down to Cairo for one. Waiting, we gazed across the Nile at the tumbled ruins of Karnak and Luxor, the mighty pillars, gateways and obelisks, each morning silhouetted by the rising sun. Over there, across the river, Giovanni saw a brightly lit stage promising an unfolding drama more spectacular than any he had ever played in at Sadler's Wells or Astley's Amphitheatre. With every day that passed, he grew more impatient to get across the Nile. When I urged caution, he showed me Mr Salt's instructions authorising him to collect on his behalf 'whatever antiquities appeared valuable and portable'. It was comprehensive, I had to agree. But before we left I insisted on building a wall around the Young Memnon head and mounting a guard.

I don't think either of us was prepared for what happened across the river. Instead of the usual throng of excited *antika*-sellers we met total silence. As we moved off through the ruined avenue of monstrous pillars and ram-headed gods, we felt that we were being watched.

(Later I discovered that the fellahin had been warned that if they sold a single thing to the big Italian they would be taken before the Kashif and bastinadoed till their feet dropped off.)

Giovanni was about to demonstrate that uncanny instinct he had for knowing just where to dig. At the southern end of the avenue of small stone sphinxes at Karnak he set twenty fellahin to dig at a spot near the Sacred Lake. Within five days he had unearthed a cache of twenty black granite seated figures, each with the head of a lion and the breasts of a woman. I watched them being brought out. 'Her' whiskers bristled and her cheeks were hollow, her mouth set in a grim line. She carried the sun-disc on her head. We had no idea that this was Sekhmet, the goddess of war, who went into battle emitting withering blasts from her nostrils. Though the granite figures were extraordinarily heavy, Belzoni at once had them loaded onto a boat and moved over the Nile to join the Young Memnon.

The French protested that they were being robbed, of course. We had invaded 'their' territory. Although neither Giovanni nor I knew it then, a ferocious war of Pharaonic hide-and-seek had been going on here for years, and was now becoming more vicious by the hour.

That did not stop Belzoni pushing ahead in search of the four colossal heads Burckhardt had reported set in the cliff face at a place called Abu Simbel. At Esna, where the temple was dedicated to the ram-headed Khnum ('the creator of all things'), rubbish rose to the top of the great portico; at Edfu the temple of the falcon-headed Horus was half hidden under the huts of the fellahin, who fertilised their fields with the dust of ages which filled its ruins; at Kom Ombo, the Nile was carrying away the temple of Sobek, the crocodile god.

Reaching Abu Simbel, Giovanni threw himself with maniacal energy into the task of uncovering Burckhardt's seated colossi. He engaged a hundred villagers. But the fine sand trickled back as fast as it was cleared, despite the palm-trunk pallisade he'd improvised.

Then a soldier appeared with an order from the Governor. We were to stop digging at once and return to Cairo. Forged, I thought – and I believed I knew who had forged it. Sure enough, when we got back to our mooring under the old sycamore-tree on the west bank, we found another boat tied up there. Three Europeans were moving around inside the wall we had built around the Young Memnon.

Sheepishly, they introduced themselves: Frédéric Gailliaud, a jeweller from Nantes; Jean-Jacques Rifaud, who described himself as an artist, although to me he looked more like some Marseilles thug; and a so-called dragoman, Giuseppe Rosignano, a Piedmontese – like Drovetti. They claimed to be private collectors of antiquities, but they didn't deceive me. They were the French consul's men.

They complimented us extravagantly on our enterprise, although they were clearly seething with jealousy. Then they fell back on denigration.

'Voyez-vous – que vaut un tête de Pharaon avec une couronne

cassée?' Gailliaud demanded loudly of Rifaud, pointing to the jagged edge at the left of the Young Memnon's headcloth.

Rifaud shrugged. 'My poor Signor Belzoni. No museum will give you a sou for damaged goods like that.'

'And see this hole drilled through the left shoulder?' sneered Gailliaud.

I could see Giovanni was getting redder and redder in the face, clenching and unclenching his great fists. 'Take no notice,' I whispered. 'They're trying to provoke you. Ignore them.'

Thank God, with superhuman effort, he did.

They departed, scowling, and Giovanni was able to give all his attention to the bridge of palm-trunks over which the Young Memnon was to be lowered into the stout boat that had now arrived. It was an eighteen-foot drop from bank to river level. Gailliaud, Rifaud and Rosignano hung about to watch. I didn't let them out of my sight for an instant.

As the last of the Sekhmets disappeared safely into the boat, Rosignano, the so-called dragoman, sidled up to Belzoni and whispered in his ear. As we cast off for the trip downriver to Cairo, I asked Giovanni what he had said.

Giovanni's eyes clouded. 'He said: "I, Giuseppe Rosignano, am a man of peace, but there are others who are not. If you and your friend go on digging, digging in our territory . . ."' At this point he had drawn the edge of his bony hand across Belzoni's throat.

Giovanni felt deeply hurt by this.

It was almost Christmas before we reached Bulak with our weighty cargo of antiquities. Giovanni went to seek further instructions from Mr Salt. I went to report to Louis.

I found Sheikh Ibrahim much as I had left him, sitting at his desk overlooking the Cairo canal, working on a plan of Mecca and another of the plain of Arafat for his forthcoming book, *Travels in Arabia*.

There was so much to tell him, I hardly knew where to begin. I was just getting into my stride when I was interrupted by a piercing yell from the floor above. A moment later the door of Burckhardt's study burst open and a small boy in a blue *galabiya* catapulted into the room with Louis's slave-girl, Zeinab, after him. Before she could grab him he had a thin black arm hooked round my left leg. Louis nodded to Zeinab and she left.

I looked down on an oddly piebald poll, and, a moment later, found myself looking into a pair of dark, lustrous eyes turned on me like searchlights. Eyes that spoke of total trust, and yet had a sparkle of mischief. Fatima's eyes.

Louis had been watching me. He smiled, perhaps a little sadly. 'Yours, I think' was all he said, and, a moment later: 'There is an Arab saying: "It is a wise son that knows his own father." '

17 I Become Osman Effendi, Dragoman to the Quality

They had looked in the pocket of his blue *galabiya* and had found, stitched in there, a crumpled square of rough country paper inscribed in some professional letter-writer's hand: 'This is Omar bin Osman'. He had appeared out of nowhere. Louis's slave-girl, Zeinab, had gone to the *suk* to buy eggs, and when she came back, there he was in the kitchen,

When questioned he would babble about *el-Bahr* – the sea – which is what the fellahin in Egypt who live so far from it call the Nile.

Thus, mysteriously and abruptly, I acquired my first-born, ready-made so to speak, five years old, lithe and lively, and named for the second Caliph, who was converted to Islam by his sister, Fatima. Of Fatima herself, the boy's mother, there was no trace, nor did he mention her. I decided that she was probably dead. But how had Omar discovered his father with such unerring instinct? I wondered whether my old Mameluke friend François had had anything to do with it. I inquired around the community of Nubians who come to Cairo to seek their fortunes, much as Scotsmen take the road down to London. I drew a blank.

A sensible man doesn't question miracles. Omar was an undeniable and profound reality that changed my whole life. As Tom Keith's death had cut my last link with Scotland, Omar had joined me to Africa. Some I know might have simply denied him, cut him loose again. Fatima, after all, had been only a harem girl. But when Omar turned those dark eyes upon me I was helpless. From that day I date the beginning of what another British consul, a Scot, was to call 'Clan Osman'.

The Turks who dominated Egypt at this time subscribed to the

Hanifi school of Islamic law that specifies that for his first seven years a boy should remain under the care of his mother. It was fortunate therefore that Zeinab, though she was not much older than Omar himself, took to this unexpected visitor and eagerly assumed the maternal role, thus allowing me to rejoin Giovanni who, after depositing the Young Memnon in a warehouse in Alexandria, had gone straight back to Luxor. Drovetti's agents had several years' start on Mr Salt, and our giant – now employed by Salt – was desperate not to let the Piedmontese steal a march on him. As it says in the book of Arabic proverbs Louis was then working on: 'A vinegar-seller does not like another vinegar-seller.'

Between times I would return to Cairo, to the house on the canal, where Sheikh Ibrahim, ever occupied with his books and reports to London, was like a father to me – and a grandfather to Omar. There was a reassuring regularity about life in Cairo in those days; we lived our lives to the pulse and rhythm of the Nile, much I suppose as the Pharaohs had. In mid-June came the 'Night of the Drop' – *Leilet el-Nukta* – the mysterious globule which fell into the river, causing it to swell mightily and to be delivered of the Flood.

Following age-old custom, Zeinab made five small cakes of dough on that night, and each of us, Louis, myself, Omar, Zeinab, and Ahmed, the donkey-boy, made our personal mark on the base of a cake. After the sun had gone down, but when the stone was still like an oven, Zeinab placed the dough cakes on the terrace to remain overnight. If in the morning the cake was cracked, that person would live long; if it remained solid, death would come within a year.

Sheik Ibrahim upbraided the girl for indulging in such superstitions, fit only for the 'Days of Ignorance' before the message of the Prophet, peace be unto Him. But on such a June night, with the people laughing and dancing on the banks of the Nile, who could be severe? Louis made his mark on the soft dough like the rest of us.

The following morning I had almost forgotten all this nonsense. But Zeinab hadn't. She was out on the terrace at dawn, turning over her cake and uttering a squeal of delight as she saw that it was well and truly cracked through the middle. So were Omar's and the still slumbering donkey-boy's. It's astonishing the hold these silly old games can have. I confess that my heart was pounding when I turned over my cake. At first it looked unblemished, then I detected a hair-crack across the lower corner – and a great weight fell from my shoulders. That left only one 'baked' cake: Louis's.

Something made me hold back. In the end I forced myself to pick up the cake. It was solid. I could not find even a suggestion of a crack.

We shouldn't have let the silly girl Zeinab play God, I see that now.

Every day from the beginning of July the Crier of the Nile and his boy would stand outside our house on the canal to proclaim the day's rise in the height of the Nile.

> I extol the perfection of Him who spread out the earth
> And hath given running waters
> Through which the fields become green
> *Ay, please God, five digits today!*
> The Lord is bountiful!
> *Bless ye Mohammed . . .*

And so it went on, verse after verse, until Louis, unable to work, would send Omar – *my* Omar – down to bestow on the Crier the daily two piastres expected of such a notable as Sheikh Ibrahim.

By this time the ancient canal which ran behind our house was bone dry, the last stinking puddle gone. The scene was being set for the great annual drama of renewal. Near the canal's point of entry from the Nile, by Roda island, the grave-diggers of Cairo – whose perquisite this was – were building an earth dam some three yards high across its dry bed, tapering to the top. Twenty yards or so in front of this they had constructed the *arusa* – the 'bride' – a truncated cone of earth, rising not quite as high as the dam, and on the flat top they had sown maize and millet. People say that before General Amr conquered Cairo for Islam in AD 641 the Egyptians were accustomed to throw a young virgin into the Nile to propitiate Hapi, the god of the annual flood. In the name of Allah, the Merciful, General Amr forbade such cruelty – hence the symbolic earth bride.

How different it all was in those days! Before the great cotton

boom, before Mrs Macdonald, the Sitt Amerikani, and her consul
friend Edwin de Leon and George Jesus Girgis, Flora's husband,
started importing those new McCarthy cotton-gins from America,
and the Pasha became the Khedive and travelled to Paris and
lusted after Hortense Schneider and built an opera house in Cairo
for her before Maestro Verdi had got a single line of the music for
Aida down on paper.

Every day the Crier of the Nile and his boy would come to the
houses announcing new 'digits' of the river's bounty, and Omar
and I would watch the river lapping against the feet of the 'bride',
wooing her, growing ever bolder as the inrushing waters of the
Flood thrust against the earth dam across the parched canal.
Then, as I recall, around the middle of August, the Crier changed
his tune, recruiting a chorus of boys carrying coloured flags to
announce the Completion.

'And the married man has added to his wife eight others,' he
sang.

'God hath given Abundance!' yelled the boys, waving their
flags.

'And the bachelor hath married eighteen,' riposted the Crier.

Excitement mounted with each verse. People threw off their
lethargy, and the heavy curtains of humid air seemed to part –
for next day was *Yom Gebr el-Bahr*, the Day of the Breaking
Through of the Nile.

Before sunrise on the previous day, the labourers had begun to
slice away at the top of the earth dam. By the time night fell it
was no more than a foot thick: the 'bride' was ready to surrender.

All along the banks of Roda island, facing the dam, crowds
were picnicking or sitting in boats, awaiting the great moment.
Rockets burst high in the sky. Some parties hired musicians,
others, dancing-girls.

As ever in Egypt, it was a long wait. But at last a boat – *the*
boat – manned by a very old man, an officer of the Wali of Cairo,
was directed at the shallow top of the dam. It broke through at
the third attempt and disappeared, plunging down the cataract it
had loosed. Grinding against each other, sails kissing, oars
clashing, rowers screaming, scores of other boats followed as the
dam disintegrated and water filled 'our' canal once more.

As the leading boat swept through, the Governor of Cairo
tossed in the traditional bag of gold coins. It fell wide, its contents

spewing out into the torrent, spangling the water. Scores of small boys, naked and slippery as eels, dived down after the money, yelling with delight. And I saw to my horror that one of them was Omar, my son, Omar.

Before I could get near, he had vanished.

People were laughing and shouting and singing and trying to sort out their rocking craft. I spotted three boys climbing up the canal bank with gold coins in their teeth. But Omar wasn't one of them. It would have been all too easy for him to have received an accidental blow from an oar or got trapped between two boats. The torrent was still pouring in from the Nile. I plunged in, recklessly searching downwards under the boats. But the water was dark brown, heavy with silt brought down from Africa.

A boat party of young men took pity and searched with me. We found nothing: Omar could have been lying there on the bottom for all we knew. Into my mind, unsummoned, came the picture of my dog, Donald, fighting against the current in the Kyle, legs moving more slowly as he was swept out to sea. Yet hadn't Donald got ashore? The thought put new life into me. I don't know how long I ran up and down the side of the canal, between the house and the dam, shouting at pleasure-seeking boating parties now able to use the canal once again. I dare say they thought I was just another madman. No lack of them in Cairo! Near collapse, I staggered back to the house. As I approached the neglected garden on the canal bank, I heard pitiful sounds of retching. Somehow, even before I caught sight of that piebald head bent over in the bushes, I *knew*. My first thought was that he was getting the water out of his lungs. Then I saw that there were three of them. They had already spent the gold coins on tobacco, and had been 'eating smoke' in imitation of their elders, using the seed pod of a water-lily for the tobacco and the plant's hollow stem for the pipe of an improvised *nargila*.

I was too exhausted – and too grateful to God – to be angry. But I realised then that Omar was going to be what my mother would have called 'a handful'.

Henry Salt had heard that the 'Young Memnon' had reached London. That massive granite head was causing quite a stir at the British Museum. Every month now more English milords were coming to Egypt, eager to snap up a sarcophagus or two for their parks, a mummy case, a papyrus roll, or, less ambitiously, a few amulets. The more scholarly were hunting for fragments bearing hieroglyphics, hoping to secure immortality by solving the mystery of the Rosetta Stone.

I could see that there could be a profitable future for me in the profession of dragoman. A fellow *renegado*, Signor Giovanni Finati, a native of Ferrara and yet another victim of the French Revolution sweeping across Europe, was now professionally known as Mohammed and was at that moment engaged by Mr William Bankes of Kingston Hall, Dorsetshire, to help him uncover the four colossal Pharaoh figures buried in the sand at Abu Simbel.

The hottest season of the year was now upon us: it was if the lion goddess Sekhmet was withering us with her fiery blasts. Sheikh Ibrahim took to his bed with a fever. Nothing new there: I had seen him through many such attacks; they were the price of consorting with Africa. I blame myself now, of course. I should have realised how much his constitution had been undermined, young as he still was. The fever gave way swiftly to the bloody flux, which I was unable to stem even with Grandma Beaton's 'Old Man's Milk'. I thought then of those dough cakes Zeinab had put out on the flags on the Night of the Drop. I wondered whether Louis was thinking of that, too. His pallor was terrible; and he had the bitterness of knowing he might die with his life's great work unaccomplished. But he was calm and collected, as if assured of its fulfilment in the hereafter. I know there are some Englishmen who claim Sheikh Ibrahim's conversion to Islam was only a matter of convenience, a sham, but having been with him at his death-bed I cannot believe that.

As his strength ebbed, Louis asked me to send for Henry Salt. I sent Ahmed, the donkey-boy, with strict orders to return at once with the Consul. He was a long time getting back, and then empty-handed. The gate to the Frankish quarter had been closed for the night. In any case Mr Salt had gone over to the Pyramids in Giza, escorting the party of Lord Belmore, of Coole Castle, who had just arrived in his eighteen-gun yacht, the *Osprey*.

As soon as my message reached Mr Salt he rushed back, bringing with him the Earl's personal physician, Dr Robert Richardson. I cannot tell you how relieved I was to see another medical man, although all Dr Richardson did was to go over to Louis, take his pulse and look at his eyes. He came back shaking his head. 'Too late, I'm afraid.'

Louis beckoned the consul over to his bedside. 'Sit down, Henry.' His voice was faint, but clear. 'Osman, bring pen and paper for Mr Salt.'

His first anxiety was to settle his debt to Mr Salt for his share of the cost of recovering the Young Memnon and transporting it to London. Then, slowly and systematically, he began to dictate his Last Will and Testament.

'I bequeath my library to the University of Cambridge in England. My European books to Henry Salt and the British Consulate in Cairo . . . I wish to leave a thousand piastres to the poor people of Zurich in Switzerland . . .'

Outside, in the street, a gathering crowd was beginning softly to chant the *Ya Sin*, the thirty-sixth chapter of the Holy Koran, appointed to be read in the presence of the dying. The people of the quarter were claiming Sheikh Ibrahim, late of Basle and Zurich, for their own.

I was pulled back into the room by the sound of my name on Louis's lips:

'Give my remaining 2000 piastres to Osman and also my male and female slaves, together with the house and whatever I have in it – let all these go to Osman.'

I had to bite my tongue not to burst into tears.

Mr Salt's pen scraped on: 'Let Mr Hamilton of the African Association in London acquaint my mother of my death, and tell her that my last thoughts have been of her . . .'

I was with him when he died, at two minutes to midnight on 17 October in the year 1195 AH.* He was in full possession of his senses to the end. It was I who could scarcely control the emotions and thoughts that pressed upon me: of my own mother, of my father and brothers and sisters, of the island life lost to me, the thread stretched and snapped. Better for them to believe me dead than, having exchanged the plaid for the turban, worse than a heathen.

'No man,' he once told me, quoting the Koran as he so often

---

* 'After the Hegira' – the flight of Mohammed from Mecca to Medina in AD 622. My father is following the Mohammedan chronology. – F.M.

did, 'knows the place where his grave shall be digged.' Jean-Louis Burckhardt, Sheikh Ibrahim el-Shami, was laid to rest in the great Muslim cemetery just beyond Cairo's Bab el-Nasr on the desert's edge. His is a humble stone, but to me it is not dwarfed by grandiose vaulted and domed mausoleums of the Mamelukes that rise around it.

The sheikhs of el-Azhar, his old teacher, Mohammed, his neighbours of the Suk el-Zalat and his old pupil and former slave, Hadji Osman, accompanied Sheikh Ibrahim to the grave. But none came who spoke his native tongue, nor any Englishman, for he had committed the ultimate sin in their eyes: he had 'taken the turban', and with humility and sincerity had become one of Them, a *renegado*.

I have always made it my business to keep Louis's grave clean and tidy, and whenever I have thought a client of mine worthy of it, I took him there to show him the grave of this man I was proud to call my friend. When I look back, I am astonished to find that I only knew him for three or four years, but those years transformed my life. From being a slave, twice a deserter, ever looking nervously over my shoulder, I had become my own man again.

Thanks to Louis's bequest of house and money I became Osman Effendi, Hadji Osman, Osman the Scotsman, man about Cairo, well placed to progress in the dragoman's calling.

Mr Salt recommended my services to the Earl of Belmore, then about to proceed with his party up the Nile to view the Pharaonic ruins. The one thing that made me hesitate was the thought of leaving Omar, but the girl Zeinab was getting older, and I felt sure she could now be trusted to look after him. And after all few dragomen could boast, as I could, that they had actually worked with the great Signor Giovanni Battista Belzoni, who was just then opening up on the west bank the deepest, longest, and most magnificently painted Pharaoh's tomb ever to be exposed to the light of day.

Shall I ever forget my first expedition up the Nile as dragoman to the Belmore party, learning my new trade as I plied it? If need be I can always refresh my memory with a glance at Dr Richardson's two-volume work, *Travels in the Company of the Earl of Belmore in the Mediterranean and Parts Adjacent.**

The good doctor leads off with a grand dedication:

> To the Earl of Belmore, the Master of Castle Coole, the greatest house in Ireland, who was the first and only nobleman who ever conducted his lady and family to visit so many scenes of ancient fame formerly regarded as inaccessible to all but the most daring adventurer.

He forgets young Legh of Lyme Park, of course; he overlooks the Hon. William Bankes of Kingston Hall, a great man for the hieroglyphics, even though he did leave England, as they say, for his country's good. But certainly he is right about the sheer size of the Belmore party which, in addition to the Earl, included his Countess, his brother (a captain in the Royal Navy), his two young sons – Lord Corry and the Honourable Henry – the family's chaplain, Mr Bolt, Dr Richardson, their personal physician, and Miss Brooks, the Countess's maid – not to mention Rosa, a King Charles spaniel with a voracious appetite for fellahin's heels.

As our flotilla of six boats, with cooks and servants, progressed up the Nile, it was Rosa who first drew Miss Brooks forcibly to my attention. Not that I would have failed to notice her in any case, for she wore a tight-fitting pink spencer and was rarely seen without her green parasol to ward the sun's rays off her delicate complexion. Rosa was Miss Brooks's responsibility. She was under orders from Lady Juliana, the Countess, not to allow her to mix with rude village dogs and to keep her on a leash in the villages to restrain her 'playfulness'.

As the Belmores' boat moved slowly up the Nile, accumulating the collection that was going to astonish all Ireland, Miss Brooks stayed for the most part in the cabin, letting it be known that such rough conditions were unsuitable for a lady's companion. But she was obliged to go ashore to accompany the Countess – and Rosa – when the party visited the temples of Abydos.

The ground around the temple was ill-suited to strolling with a parasol in one hand and a small dog heaving on a lead in the

---

* The interested reader will find a reference to my father, Osman Effendi, in Volume I (p. 95) of Dr Richardson's work. – F.M.

other. A snake slipped out of a patch of weeds; Rosa emitted a yelp of terror, tugged on her lead and streaked away. With a wail, Miss Brooks set off in pursuit. After twenty yards she tripped on her parasol, and there was I, the resourceful dragoman, ready to catch her. She fainted away in my arms, the pink bodice rising and falling deliciously. Her eyelids flickered, and I found myself looking into soft blue-grey eyes. I confess I had hopes – there are times when thirty seconds can be a lifetime. Then those eyes moved upwards and lit on my turban. She screamed and fainted away again.

'Don't be a fool, Brooks,' said the Countess. The Earl, a rubicund fellow with auburn curls descending to his collar and sensuous lips, winked at me. Rosa yapped furiously.

Strange how after all these years one remembers these things so clearly. Brief as it was, I found this incident deeply unsettling. I had grown accustomed to the sensuous world of the harem, eyes hinting the unutterable from behind heavy veils. Now Miss Brooks had plunged me back into the world of Jane Austen.

It was fortunate, perhaps, that I was kept busy by my dragomanly duties. At each stop villagers would crowd around the party offering scarabs, Pharaonic necklaces, 'eye of Horus' amulets, fragments of mummy cases, probably just then snatched from the cooking fire, and I had to pronounce on their authenticity. Meanwhile the Honourable Henry, aged fourteen, demanded that I should find him a crocodile to shoot and the Earl's brother, Captain Corry, having determined our latitude and longitude with his instruments, was eager for a suitable flat rock on which to inscribe it for posterity.

Soon we reached Kena. In between keeping Lord Corry, aged sixteen, out of the clutches of the dancing-girls who abound there, I was eagerly looking forward to meeting Giovanni. 'Belzoni's Tomb' – as, to his delight, it came to be called – had been open for only a week or two. It looked as if the Belmores and their dragoman would be the first Europeans to view its wonders.

Between the Nile bank and that desolation of desolation, now called 'the Valley of the Kings', lies a mile-wide strip of cultivated land, a bright chequer-board of colour. Giovanni was there to welcome our party. His handsome, bearded face bent low over Lady Juliana's hand as he ushered us into his kingdom. Ponies were at hand for the journey to the tomb.

The moment they had cantered off Giovanni turned to me.

'But where is my friend Mr Burckhardt? Does he not wish to see my tomb?'

'Giovanni . . . Louis is dead.'

He stared at me in disbelief. 'Morto? Morto! Non è possibile! He is young man, how can he die?' His eyes filled with tears. 'When?' he said, finally.

'A month ago – the seventeenth.'

'The very day I told my men to dig on the spot where we found the tomb.'

The thought seemed to bowl him over. He wept unashamedly. His great body crumpled. It was not only Louis's kindness towards him when he was at his wits' end; it was that he felt that here was a man he could rely on to see that he received proper credit for his feats. He suspected Henry Salt of trying to pass him over as just an Italian workman so as to hog all the credit for himself. Now he was on his own; I knew the feeling.

Salt had gone ahead with the party. Belzoni chased after them. I caught up with them outside the narrow door of the tomb. The Great Belzoni, impresario of the Pharaohs, was in full spate.

'Milord, your ladyship, I present to you the Tomb of Psammis. We shall now descend a hundred and eighty feet into the rock. You will behold many wonders. The tomb has fifteen chambers . . .' He passed me a bundle of candles. 'Osman Effendi will light our way.'

Behind us the yellow Theban hills rose starkly to the rounded summit the Arabs call 'The Lady of the Peak', her nipple the colour of rusted iron. A few yards ahead, through the black oblong of the tomb door, were the plunging stone steps.

Belzoni bowed, extended a hand in invitation. Lord Belmore looked queasy.

'Oh, come along, Somerset!' In her fragile pink gown Lady Juliana advanced boldly towards the steps. She was years younger than the earl. I could see that the Belmores' visit to Belzoni's Tomb was going to prove a stern test of my fledgling dragomanship.

I rushed in after the Countess. I don't think she realised quite how dark it was going to be in there. I lit a candle and held it high above our heads. Great vultures spread their wings, scrawny necks stretched out to strike, talons extended. Juliana did not cry out, I'll give her that, just shuddered and clung to my arm.

The tomb grew darker with every faltering step downwards. The Pharaoh himself, in shining white, loomed out from the wall as he made offerings to the sun god. Hundreds of small bright figures leapt out at us in the candle-flicker: falcons, owls, goats, hares, quails, detached hands, arms, bread loaves, women dangling children, men kneeling, snakes pulling back their heads to strike. Row on row of little figures, red, green and yellow, many not more than two inches high, yet precise, vibrant.

'What can it all *mean*?' whispered Juliana, between exasperation and wonder.

Nowadays, of course, I would just reel off what some waggish client once called 'Osman's Guide to the Underworld'. But at that time I was as awed and mystified as everybody else. Remember, Dr Young had deciphered only a few hieroglyphs – and some of *them* were wrong. He worked out that the Pharaoh of Belzoni's tomb was 'Psammis' – which is why Zobeida's first boy, now an officer in the Khedival Navy, is called Sami. (Ten years later, they discovered the hieroglyphics actually read 'Seti'.)

The rest of the party was coming down behind us. I could hear the Revd Bolt's voice: 'Idolatry run wild, my lord, truly a heathen spectacle.' They were passing a procession of painted gods, plumed, horned, jackal-headed, sun-disced, cat-headed, ram-faced.

Juliana put on speed, as if to keep ahead, tripping down the rough stone steps so that I had difficulty in keeping up. (I write 'Juliana', which some of my readers may feel impertinent, but that, in truth, was how I found myself thinking of her.) Then my candle went out. Two steps ahead in her descent, she stopped dead with a shriek. Raising my new candle, I saw that we were on the brink of a deep pit. A thirty-foot drop opened at our feet.

'Mille perdoni! Mille perdoni, Contessa!' Giovanni pounded down behind us, shattering our intimacy. 'I am desolate – I forget. This is what I find three weeks ago when we open the tomb. I thought we had come to the end. That is what they want us to think! Then, up there, in the wall, I see a gap. It is not the end, it is the beginning! Come, my lady, I will show you.' Bowing in his best impresario manner, Giovanni handed her ladyship across a palm-trunk bridge.

So I lost Juliana. My idyll in the Pharaonic dark had lasted less than an hour. All the wind knocked out of my sails, I tagged after the master showman, conscious now of the stifling heat in the deep tomb.

'This,' he announced, 'is what I call the drawing-room. Osman, per favore, hold the candle higher.'

My candle revealed four great pillars supporting the vaulted roof. Each bore pictures of the Pharaoh embracing the gods, Hathor and Isis, and Horus, Nephthys and Ptah, and of course Anubis, the jackal-headed embalmer, kept so busy here, outfacing death.

'Idolatry!' intoned the Revd Mr Bolt, duty-bound, his voice now faltering a little. We had reached the room where the sun-boat embarks on its long journey through the Ninth Division of the Underworld. Souls reported underweight by Maat, in the Hall of Truth, received their come-uppance from writhing black-spotted serpents, or were being roasted upside down in the furnaces of Hell.

My candle brought the scene to vivid, fearful life.

'Look! look! the snakes are moving, *moving!*' A woman's voice.

'Brooks! don't be a fool,' snapped Juliana. But Miss Brooks had swooned away again. In such circumstances a dragoman's duty is clear: to catch.

The deeper we descended into the Pharaoh's tomb, the more cruel and sinister this world became, and Belzoni was determined we should miss nothing of it. The candle, which I had handed to a boy in order to give all my attention to Miss Brooks, suddenly threw into prominence a line of bound and *headless* prisoners on their knees, imploring mercy, while serpents stabbed at their bloody throats, and a jackal-headed executioner roped more for the knife.

It was this jolly little tableau that finally brought my English rose to the trembling edge of hysteria. I instinctively gave her a sharp slap across the cheek. She thought better of it then, clinging to me with peculiar passion. It was fortunate that by this time Juliana was wholly absorbed in Belzoni's theatricals: under a starred and zodiac-vaulted ceiling, a hundred and fifty feet below the ground, he showed off his pride and joy, the alabaster sarcophagus of the Pharaoh. Holding a candle within it, he threw into relief a frieze of tiny gods and goddesses who danced and shone. Within, inscribed along the bottom of the sarcophagus, the slim, bare-breasted goddess Neith waited to receive the Pharaoh's mummy. But of the mummy itself, there was no trace.

Giovanni shrugged his great shoulders, and seemed about to weep. 'Alas, my lady, Biban el-Mamluk is a nest of thieves. The jewels, the gold, the silver – all gone.'

So the ignorant fellahin had defeated the mighty Pharaoh, robbed him of the immortality he had taken such pains to secure. I wanted to cheer!

On the long climb back to the surface, Belzoni went first with the Countess – in case she needed to be carried on the last stages. I brought up the rear, with Miss Brooks still clinging desperately to my arm, stumbling over loose rocks in the long dank corridors. She had lost her air of self-contained rectitude. Strands of dishev-elled fair hair brushed across my face as we climbed and her left breast now thrust shamelessly against my ribs. The slender arms that gripped me still shook a little. Incongruously, a strong scent of lavender water suffused the musty corridor. I saw that the pink spencer was bedraggled and gaping where buttons had burst. I found myself thinking strange, un-Scottish thoughts of soft English beds and cottages with roses round the door. After years of the cloying sandalwood of the harems, lavender water began to seem exotic.

It was Brooks – she was always just 'Brooks' to the family – who made the decisive move. On the next flight of steps – we were now well behind – her knees buckled and she fell back against me. Then she rallied, and slowly pulled herself up, grap-pling my long body, knees digging into me. I let her take her time, putting a supporting hand in the curve of her back. I felt a shudder pass along it. She moaned, and we fell back together onto the steps, the candle knocked out in the fall. How the remaining buttons on the spencer became undone I don't know. I will only say that the stone steps were hard and often jagged, but neither of us was aware of the pain of the cuts and bruises they inflicted.

I carried Miss Brooks as far as the last stone flight towards the sunlight. I put her down carefully at the bottom of the steps so that she could make herself 'respectable', as she said. So did I. Then, supporting her by the arm, I led her up to the narrow doorway. As we stepped out into the blinding sunlight the jagged shadows of the Theban cliffs were lengthening fast; the nipple of the Lady of the Peak flushed crimson in the setting sun.

Fifty yards away the Belmore party, Belzoni and Mr Salt waited for transport to the Nile bank. Brooks drew apart from me, smoothed down her dress, groped for her purse, selected a coin, and placed it in my hand with a tight little smile.

'Thank you, dragoman,' she said, and tripped over to join the party. It was a saadiya, worth approximately four piastres – or nine English pennies.

All in all, it was fortunate that Mr Salt required me to return to Cairo with the boatload of antiquities from Belzoni's Tomb and elsewhere. Meanwhile, Bernardino Drovetti put in an appearance to congratulate his fellow Italian on his magnificent discovery. 'Giovanni,' he said, 'you are a veritable magician.' He was all smiles, but I knew that below he was seething. The war in Europe had ended at Waterloo but in Egypt, among the tombs of the Pharaohs, it raged on. It wasn't only Mohammed Ali who would need to watch his back.

I stood and watched the Earl's flotilla set sail for Abu Simbel, by this time the *sine qua non* of every proper milord's trip. It was not altogether clear whether the gracious flick of the handkerchief which Miss Brooks bestowed from the deck was intended to include the dragoman. Nevertheless Osman Effendi, offered a suitably low Oriental bow. It was only then that it occurred to me that I did not even know her first name.

I stowed the two mummies, a man and a girl, with particular care in the forequarter of the boat. Entire mummies were getting hard to come by, such was the call for mummy powder, a renowned aphrodisiac through Europe and the East. An arm, a leg, even a head and shoulders; but a complete unplundered mummy – that was difficult. Yet somehow Henry Salt had managed to lay his hands on two to fill an order from his patron, Lord Valentia.

All the way down to Cairo I watched those mummies as closely as if I had been Anubis, the jackal-headed embalmer god himself. The larger, the man, was topped by a richly painted cartonage face from which two big, almond-shaped eyes stared fixedly. Seventy days in natron pickle, brains teased out with a hook through the nose, heart, liver and guts stowed away in canopic jars – it does not make for an animated expression.

It was the smaller mummy though, the girl, tightly bound from head to foot in criss-crossing palm-bands, that worried me more. The narrow shoulders seemed to be seeking to emerge from the strappings; the long curving haunch was witness to the lissom creature she had once been. What had been the shade of her skin? The burnished ebony of Fatima? The old ivory of Adile Hanem in Ezbek Bey's harem? The rose blush of Miss Brooks? As Tom Keith had once said, 'Poor Donald, you are unlucky in your women.'

To rouse myself from the morbid reflections which I seemed to be drifting into as our boat with its load of Pharaonic treasure slipped Cairowards in the current, I turned to sorting and wrapping the hundreds of *ushabti* figures Belzoni had found in the room behind the sarcophagus chamber. Only an inch or two high, carved from wood or shaped in clay, baked and painted, the *ushabti* are the 'Answerers' – the token craftsmen, labourers, clerks, butchers, architects, who respond in the Afterlife to the Pharaoh's needs and, to do so, are equipped with a whole token world of chairs and tables and bowls and bronze mirrors and glass neck-rests and toys and dolls.

I started numbering and wrapping the dolls. Some were little more than stumpy sticks with rope strands for hair; others were brightly painted but still primitive. Yet others were lovingly carved in wood, or moulded in clay, with swelling thighs and curving bellies and hips thrust provocatively forward. My son Ibrahim, now assistant to my friend Auguste Mariette, Director of the Egyptian Museum, tells me that these 'dolls' were in fact *ushabti* concubines. I must admit I found them lingering long in my hands as I prepared to wrap them for the boxes. As we passed through the luxuriant scenes of the Nile Valley the fellahin sowing seed over the rich wet earth, I began to feel like the god Min himself, the woman-hunter under his long plumed cap, unsated, insatiable *zubb* ever alert, erect, as I had recently seen on the wall of the Karnak temple.

Not surprising, perhaps, that I had some strange dreams on the boat. One night I saw Jeannie Macdonald emerging from beneath the palm-frond encasings of the small mummy, her dark eyes outlined in kohl; then Miss Brooks came tittupping across the deck with her pink spencer torn open and a sun-disc on her head. I awoke, covered in sweat, to the yapping of small dogs.

The heat, the windlessness, the Flood waters seeping from the soil. Somewhere south of Asiut, the mist enveloped us. The white-bearded old *reis*, who had been complaining incessantly – the way they do – about our dangerous overload of heavy *antikas* was wailing that we would go aground. You couldn't see a boat fifty yards ahead of you.

But there are other ways of detecting the presence of neighbouring craft on the River Nile. Eagle-eyed in the prow, the boat's master lifted his head into the murk, and sniffed. There was a curious acrid smell, curious and unmistakable, rancid coconut-oil, stale sweat, women's bodies packed tight as dates rotting on the stem.

'Gellabs,' the old man announced. Slave-traders carrying human merchandise out of Africa, a commerce even more profitable than dead Pharaohs.

Then the river swung round, the mist began to lift – and there they were, not far ahead of us, two boats, one packed with black women, the other with boys, moving down from gathering points in Dongola and Shendi and Sennar to the markets of Cairo and Alexandria and Mecca and Istanbul. The black gold flowing down the Nile to complement the white gold of Monsieur Jumel's new species of cotton-tree.

Half an hour later we overtook the slave-boats, now moored on opposite banks of the Nile. On the east bank, black girls of all shapes and sizes, aged from five to perhaps twenty, were washing and being washed under the direction of two old Negresses, those they call 'the Consolers'. Our sailors knew them well, judging by the ribald remarks that flew between them.

Two other old Negresses were rubbing coconut-oil onto the girls' skins till they shone. They were mostly Negro, but there was a lank Sudanese and a little Nubian girl – a child – with a leather-thonged fringe across her hips, playing some private game with stones.

The three *gellab*s stood aloof from all this, tall dark fellows with greasy plaited hair hanging over their ears. From the set of their shoulders I guessed that they were discussing money – some deal in Asiut, perhaps, where the caravans from Darfur came in.

Then at some distance, yet near enough for the *gellab*s to keep an eye on her, I noticed a girl crouching on the sand, manacled, head bent low. A slight figure, different from the others, with light copper skin covered by a dirty white sheet.

The *reis* followed my glance. 'They are tender of heart, these Abyssinians. They take it hard. They will drown themselves – I have seen it with my own eyes, Effendi. In Cairo, they will mope, and sicken and die. That I have seen also.'

Almost as if she had heard him, the girl threw back her head, and I could have sworn her eyes flashed defiance.

The other boat had tied up half a mile downstream on the west bank. Half a dozen boys had been disembarked, and were being marched off across a field. They were roped together, and guards with stout sticks marched on either side.

The *reis* looked black. 'Zawiyet el-Deir,' he muttered, as if the name explained everything.

Quite suddenly, I remembered what Louis had told me of this place. A Coptic village, it grew cotton and *durra* like other villages, but it also had another and more profitable harvest: it supplied some of the best harems of Egypt and the Ottoman world with eunuchs.

The strongest and best-looking boys were selected by the *gellab*s, according to the *reis*. The razor was wielded by two Coptic monks, well known for their dexterity and speed. Strong men were kept to hold the boys down. Secret oils and ointments healed their wounds. While mutilating the poor boys, the monks claimed that they had the best of care, though many died.*

'Nazrani dogs!' growled the old man, and spat into the water.

I wondered whether the corrosive malice and cruelty of the Khislar Aga of Ezbek's camp – I now believed he had strangled Fatima – had been born here and, for a moment, I almost felt compassion for that monster.

'Travel broadens the mind,' Mr Macaskill used to tell us as, ferrule in hand, he catechised us on the great rivers of the world. These days, though, I am not so sure what travel does. I suppose those brutes say *inshallah*, too. But how *can* He be willing, month after month, year after year?

Fortunately, I had little time for such broodings. The responsibility for seeing Mr Salt's load of Pharaonic treasures delivered safely to the Consulate lay heavy on me. My ears were cocked for that frightful crack that betokens a mummy disintegrating under the strain of five thousand years of immortality. I've seen it happen: the girl so carefully stowed in the front of the boat could fall apart like shattered glass. Mr Salt would not be pleased, much less Lord Valentia. For safety's sake I did not tie up at any town, much to our sailors' annoyance. The only exception was a brief stop at Reamun to deliver a letter from Mr Salt to a Mr Brine, an Englishman the Pasha had engaged to run his multiplying sugar factories. I remember only two things about that. The cloying, sickly sweet miasma that hung like a curtain around the place, and the bales of blue paper-bags in Mr Brine's house, shipped out

---

* In case readers believe my father exaggerated for effect, I refer them to Mr Burckhardt's *Travels in Nubia* and the *Travels* of Captain Light. – F.M.

from England because, otherwise, Egyptians wouldn't trust their own sugar. That would change though, for Mohammed Ali and his brood had sniffed the sweet smell of money on the air and his eldest son, Ibrahim, was digging his Ibrahimiya canal to run the waters of the Nile through the Western desert, turning the Said into a vast, back-breaking sugar estate and the Pharaonic white crown of Upper Egypt into a great Albanian sugar-loaf.

We were now only a couple of days from Minya, the hub of that strange Mameluke chapter in my life (as I was beginning to think of it), and there was a certain dancing-girl there, a grateful patient of the Bey's Hakim Bashi. I dismissed the thought. Too risky; in any case, I couldn't wait to see my son, Omar, all I had now outside the prison of myself. I had left Zeinab plenty of money to care for his needs. But, unaccountably, as we slid down the river towards Cairo, I began to experience faint misgivings.

The sun was sinking below the Pyramids by the time we docked at Cairo's Old City quay. I sent a messenger to the Consulate for a janissary to guard our boat, and half a dozen donkeys to unload the smaller boxes. The two mummies, the heavy granite gods, the tall wooden *ka* figure* I intended to leave for the following day.

By now Mr Salt's house in the Frankish quarter was beginning to look more like a museum or antique-dealer's store than a consulate. As I pushed open the door, the shadows of six lion-faced Sekhmets fell across the hall floor – and now I was to add another. A massive granite arm lay across the reception-room floor, two mummies on the carpet, awaiting some ship's captain brave enough to take them on board. Amongst the litter of Christmas cards on Mr Salt's desk were untidy piles of papier-mâché 'squeezes', copies of hieroglyphic inscriptions from tomb and temple walls: Henry Salt was a dedicated pursuer of the mystery of the holy writing.

Suddenly, in the dimness, a voice out of a far corner of the room, a gentleman's voice, clear and used to giving orders.

---

* Now safely in the British Museum. The *ka* was Pharaoh's *alter ego*, who took over after his entombment and saw that he lacked for nothing. This one, my father used to tell me, was as tall as Mr Belzoni himself, though his wooden nose was broken and his staff missing. – *F.M.*

'You may wear a turban, my lad, but I'll be damned if you're any sort of Arab, or Turk either.'

Whoever he was, he had evidently been watching me.

Peering into the dimness, I made out a young man in British officer's uniform. He had been helping himself to Mr Salt's brandy. He introduced himself as Lieutenant-Colonel George Fitzclarence, returning home from service in India by the overland route. Having that afternoon ascended the Great Pyramid, he now wished to pay his respects to the British Consul.

I explained that Mr Salt was away up the Nile with Lord Belmore's party.

He looked at me curiously. 'You must be Osman – Osmond the Scotsman.' Once again my fair skin and those damned freckles had given me away. I had no choice but to tell 'my story', as they always call it. (Thank God when this is finished I shall just be able to refer them to my book and hope they'll buy, not borrow, it.)

When *A Journal of a Route across India through Egypt to England* came out I discovered that this young officer was a son of the Duke of Clarence, his mother the famous actress, Mrs Jordan.

I wish he hadn't called me 'Osmond' in that book of his. That was careless of him. The only reason I mention him here is that he kept me so long asking all the usual damn-fool questions that the gates of the Frankish quarter were closed before I could get there. I was trapped for the night.

I was off as soon as the gates opened next morning, advancing with buoyant stride through streets filling up with carts bringing vegetables in from the villages. My spirits rose: I was going *home*.

All seemed as ever. Ahmed, the donkey-boy, sat idly on the doorstep with two of his cronies, just as I had left him. The pile of books Louis had bequeathed to the Consulate still awaited transport on the wooden stairs. Louis's old desk was inches deep under the powdery dust that infiltrates from the desert. A stray manuscript page of his 'Arabic Proverbs' fluttered to the floor. Omar, I guessed, must be out somewhere playing with his pals.

I went down to the kitchen to inquire from Zeinab. Piles of dirty plates and pans lay about the kitchen floor, half-eaten platefuls of *ful mudames* – Omar's favourite dish – congealed on the table. I yelled for the girl. The house rang hollow. Panic gripped me. I ran outside and grabbed Ahmed.

'Where is he?' I shouted. 'Where's Omar? Where's Zeinab?'

He smiled feebly. I caught a whiff of his breath. Hashish! What a fool I had been to leave my son in charge of an illiterate slave-girl, head full of God knows what nonsensical notions. I inquired of Nur el-Din Ali, Louis's old friend, the baker of the *suk*, a good man. Neither Zeinab nor Omar, he said, had been seen for some days.

It began to seem that my son had vanished from my life as abruptly as he had entered it. I was at my wits' end.

The baker laid a hand on my shoulder. 'Sheikh Osman, you have made the pilgrimage. Allah will protect you, Omar will return. As for the girl . . .' He shrugged.

In his drug-addled dream the donkey-boy had seemed to gesture towards the other old Turkish houses that line the Cairo canal. Some had luxuriant gardens on their banks, notorious for secret assignations. They were just the sort of place to which a young girl like Zeinab, head full of romances, might be drawn. Their harems were large and luxurious; an additional slave would scarcely be noticed, and where Zeinab went, Omar was sure to follow. The thought chilled me: it was notorious that these rich Turks had a taste for young boys.

The baker and I talked the matter over for a long time. It would be dangerous: the harems would certainly be closely guarded. Even so, we agreed to watch the gardens and houses day and night, turn and turn about.

It was five days before I caught a glimpse of the foolish girl, decked out in new clothes, cutting roses from a bush in a garden. I ask myself now why I did not simply go to the master of the house and reclaim my property. Pride, I suppose, the peculiar pride of the *renegado*: I feared humiliation at the hands of some arrogant Turk. More important, I had seen no sign of Omar in the garden but I knew in the end the girl would lead me to him.

I waited until she got near the garden gate, threw a sheet over her head, and dragged her back home. I was lucky. I suppose: I got away with it.

'Tell me where Omar is, and you can go wherever you wish. I will free you.'

What a fool I was! She let out a piteous wail. Free, she would have to work for her living; slave, she would be fed and clothed and could spend hours lolling about the harem.

'Sell me, sell me!' she demanded, swearing again and again that she knew nothing about Omar. I lost my temper and shook her violently.

'Tell me where he is, or I'll take you before the Wali and have you beaten. He'll put you on the list of public women.'

Her mouth set in a sullen line. In the end, though she would not tell me she agreed to take me.

The distance from the house on the canal to the Khan el-Khalili isn't much over a mile, but the area is a great maze of *suks* – cloth-makers, coffee and tobacco dealers, retailers of a thousand perfumes.

Our progress was slow, as I was riding on Louis's white donkey, with Ahmed in front, trying to keep a firm grip on the girl in case this was just another of her tricks. The long Sharia el-Nahhasin – the street of the coppersmiths – was an inferno of noise. I examined the faces of the small boys beating their tattoos on the copper vessels taking shape on the pavements. Once I thought I saw Omar; then the boy turned and my heart sank. Zeinab led us on into the great Khan itself. It was Thursday, which is auction day, and the *dallal*s were pushing through the crowds, holding their offerings above their heads – an old sword, a silk dress, a gun, the amber mouthpiece of a *chibouk* – yelling out the bids that came from the crowd. The owners of the articles tagged hopefully after them.

I took a firm grip on the sniffling girl.

'Where now?'

Sullenly, she nodded towards the alley of the shoemakers, where hundreds of slippers of red and yellow morocco with long curling toes hung in line like exotic fruits. Ahead, a heavy chain halted our progress.

Beyond lay the bazaar of the carpetmakers. Piles of rich carpets rose from the floor; others descended like great flags from the roof; yet others framed the merchants' shops. The whole place was a sort of majestic tent, a tent of emperors.*

---

* Readers wishing to visualise the scene cannot do better than study the painting by Mr David Roberts, of Edinburgh, who was one of my father's most valued clients. Indeed, my father conducted him to the scene. – F.M.

Zeinab pointed a grubby finger at a dignified, white-haired old Turk, sitting cross-legged among his carpets. 'There!' she said. As I stooped to get under the heavy chain, I felt a violent tug at my wrist. She was away into the crowd. I let the silly child go.

I think Ahmed Muhtar – for that was his name – at first took me for a dragoman preparing the way for a visit from some hovering milord. I didn't disillusion him and we embarked on the obligatory round of courtesies. We were less than a quarter of the way through when the merchant clapped his hands for coffee – and there, in front of me, stood Omar, my son Omar, the coffee-boy. He rushed across, and, just as he had done on entering my life, flung his arms round my legs, holding on tightly.

Ahmed Muhtar stroked his beard.

'Mashallah,' he said at last. 'Does not the proverb tell us that a wise son maketh a glad father?'

When I told him the whole story, he agreed at once to allow Omar to return to me. As for Zeinab, I was well content that she should remain in his harem.

All this was a very long time ago. I can't tell you the number of clients I've taken round to Ahmed's shop in the carpet bazaar since then. It's proved an excellent arrangement for both of us.

Back at the house on the canal, with Omar once again lighting up the place with that smile of his, I sat down and took stock of my position. The house was an echoing cavern, growing dustier by the hour. Omar was without a mother, sister, or any civilising feminine influence. The Miss Brookses of this world would plainly shrink from a *renegado* such as myself and I did not fancy submitting myself to an Egyptian match-making woman.

On Fridays I would find support and solace in the neighbourhood mosque, standing shoulder to shoulder with my brothers, rich and poor alike, at the noon prayer. They filled the place and carpeted the street outside. But when I returned I would find Omar, hanging around the stalls of the Friday market in the *suk*, up to every kind of mischief.

My friend the baker reminded me that the Prophet states that a boy should be able to say his prayers by the time he is seven, and if he cannot do so by the age of ten he should be beaten.

Clearly I was failing the boy: he needed to learn his letters, and without delay.

The baker recommended a *kuttub*: the Koranic school above the fountain, the Sibil Abd el-Rahman in the street of coppersmiths. The sheikh was a customer of his, a fine Koranic scholar and a disciplinarian. He'd sent his own boys there. Half a piastre a week, paid every Thursday.

Like all *kuttub*s, at which Egyptians, high and low, learn their letters, it announced itself from yards away with a sound like the buzzing of several swarms of bees. I looked in through a window and saw a hundred small boys around Omar's age clad in skull-caps and blue *galabiya*s, swaying to and fro as they recited in unison verses from the Koran.

When the lesson was over, I talked to the sheikh. He seemed a good man. But what decided me was that he had known and been a great admirer of Sheikh Ibrahim, indeed had attended his funeral. He seemed fully the equal of Mr Macaskill – and Omar would not have to bring his own peat every day!

So I paid my first half-piastre, and next day took Omar to school, complete with skull-cap and one of those wooden tablets with handles on which countless generations of Egyptians have learned to inscribe the elegant curlicues of the Arabic alphabet, the hieroglyphs of Allah, you might say. It seemed to me then that the hardest lesson my son would have to learn would be to sit still, a valuable one, though, and well taught here.

To those of my readers inclined to be critical of all this, I would say that, just as in England it is important for a gentleman to be able to quote Latin tags, in Egypt an ability to select verses from the Holy Koran for all occasions can be no less critical. I was ambitious for Omar.

That was only the beginning of my problem. There is no doubt that a young boy needs a mother. Here I was fortunate. Indeed you might say that it was Omar himself who cracked the problem. It so happened that Omar's school room above the great fountain overlooked the street of the coppersmiths, which was on the direct route to the Okela el-Gellab, the great slave-market of Cairo, and a prime 'sight' for travellers, as any dragoman will tell you.

It happened that, one afternoon, just as the boys were released from school, half a dozen newly landed Negresses were being driven past on their way to the Okela. In the cruel, thoughtless way boys sometimes have, some of them ran after the black girls, jeering and pulling at the rags around their waists until, greasy locks flying, the *gellab*s beat them off. Omar neither jeered nor allowed himself to be chased away. He just went on following the girls all the way to the Okela.

It was there that I found him some hours later and hauled him back home. That set me thinking. Could the black girls have evoked in him some buried memory of his mother? Of the lost years?

In Egypt there is no shame in taking a slave to wife: rather, it may be regarded as a meritorious act. I had often wondered just where Dr Abbott – who came out as a sick-bay orderly on a Royal Navy vessel – got that Armenian wife of his. She doesn't speak a word of English, and precious few of Arabic. Or for that matter where old Sèves – now Suleiman Pasha and busy giving Mohammed Ali a modern army – came by that beautiful Circassian who graces his harem. The same place, probably, where my friend James Burton, a Cambridge man doing a mineral survey for the Pasha, found his 'Blackie'.

What Louis would have thought of my proposing to use his 2000 piastres to buy a wife I hardly dared to think. I know how long it took me, a fellow Calvinist by birth, to get used to the idea. But where, after all, could a man command a wider choice than in the Cairo slave-market, its stocks endlessly refreshed by wars? I decided I would take Omar with me; after all, it was the boy who put the idea into my head in the first place. I need tell no one; as Mr Kinglake could never understand, a man's harem is *haram*!

Like all the great *khans* of Cairo, the Okela el-Gellab was a ramshackle old building that ran around a great courtyard: open stalls for the merchandise below, a succession of closed rooms ranged around the gallery above. On this occasion the yard of the slavers' *khan* was divided into pens, within which five or six hundred girls and women sprawled on mats. Most of them were Negresses from Africa, but there were some Nubians, distinguishable at a glance by their slimmer figures. The choicer 'items' were to be found in the rooms off the gallery.

A few of the girls shivered in blankets, but most, save for the odd rag or two, were naked. Twenty or thirty seemed to constitute the stock of a *gellab*. I should explain here that this word *gellab* means 'driver' – or, I suppose, 'drover' – and I must confess that all these pens, with their restless black bodies, and the cries of the *gellab*s stirred in my mind eerie memories of Stenhousemuir on the first day of the Falkirk Tryst.

One brutal-looking fellow pushed forward a sample of giggling Negresses, urging me to feel for myself the firmness of their breasts, the strength of the arm muscles and the perfection of the teeth. This he demonstrated by seizing one and holding her jaws open. Far from being cowed and ashamed, as Mr Wilberforce would have us believe, the girls laughed and rolled their eyes knowingly. One, it is true, did turn her back, but only in order to execute a little jig to show the splendid curves of her rump. I remembered Louis, who had camped with slavers at Sennar, telling me that the *gellab*s took care to 'initiate' all their stock themselves – 'thoroughly debauched them' were his actual words. No girl over the age of twelve reached Cairo a virgin, he said.

'Your Excellency, these are fit only for the fellahin.'

I looked round and saw a swarthy fellow at my elbow. He drew me out of earshot of others. 'Your Highness,' he whispered huskily, 'I have *for your eyes alone*, just in from Constantinople, a Circassian of sixteen summers, a pearl . . .' He was dragging at my sleeve. I permitted myself to be conducted to a room opening off the gallery of the *khan*. He unlocked the door.

'Skin like satin! Eyes of a young gazelle!' The room seemed empty. Then a heap of white drapery in a far corner stirred. 'I regret, O Bey, that I am not allowed to reveal from which far-famed harem she came . . .'

The face that had emerged from the drapery was indeed as 'white as the full moon' but the body beneath was a quivering mountain of flesh, tribute no doubt to the profusion of sweetmeats in the Turkish seraglio.

'Jariya baiza – white slave,' announced the *gellab* triumphantly. 'Such a pearl I could sell tomorrow to the Pasha of Egypt himself for twenty thousand piastres – but for you, O Bey . . .'

I assured him that the pearl was far beyond my poor purse, and he cut the price to 5000 without blinking an eyelid. When I indicated that this was also out of my range, he shrugged, and offered me one of his 'best Abyssinians'.

He clapped his hands sharply together as he entered the next room. Two girls disentangled themselves from a mat in a corner. One of them couldn't have been much over twelve, but the other, perhaps her sister, was nearer sixteen. She rose, holding a dirty white dress to her shoulders. She had a burnished copper skin and a delicacy of figure that took my breath away.

My reaction did not escape the *gellab*, who put out his stick and edged up the girl's dress, revealing a darkly gleaming haunch.

'The cushions of paradise, O Bey,' he said. 'A garden of delights!' The girl put out a delicate hand to push the stick away. She moved with a God-given grace and dignity. Glossy dark hair rippled down to the small of her back.

'She's is beautiful,' I conceded.

'Allah!' exclaimed the *gellab*, matching the client's mood.

'Buy me!' the girl shouted. 'Buy me, O Bey!' It was she herself who now thrust down the top of the dress. She had learned at least these two or three pathetic words of English.

'The rosebuds of Taif,' smirked the dealer, 'and for this princess O Bey – for you alone – I ask but four thousand piastres.'

I have to admit it: I started bargaining with the fellow. Didn't everyone know, I said, the Abyssinians are a sickly race: they did not thrive in Egypt.

He just laughed. 'Know you not, Bey, why my Abyssinians bring three times the price of Negresses? It is because they are *kabbazh* – clincher-women without peer, incomparable riders who conjure from their men the sweet milks of the garden of Paradise. I speak truly, O Bey.'

'Buy me!' demanded the girl.

As I recall, that was the point at which the *gellab* dropped the price to 2500 piastres. It was still more money than I had in the world. I do not know how things would have gone had I not looked around at that moment and caught sight of Omar at the open door. His eyes were on me, not the girl. A wave of revulsion engulfed me. Grabbing the boy, I rushed from the room, pursued by the *gellab*, now desperate to clinch the deal.

The last thing I remember was the girl's voice, between a scream and a wail, trailing away miserably as we went down the stairs.

That would have been the end of it – had not Allah intervened.

I was already halfway across the great courtyard on my way out when I noticed that Omar was no longer with me. Drawn by I know not what, he had drifted away towards a handful of disconsolate girls in a pen set well apart.

The *gellab* caught up with me. I asked who these sad-looking girls were.

'They will not be of any interest to Your Excellency.'

'So why are they here?'

He shrugged. 'They are disobedient. They are sick. They are wilful.'

Sick they certainly looked, both in body and in mind. They were mostly Negresses, but there were a couple of Nubians, and a girl of the slighter figure and sharper features I recognised as Abyssinian. Her knees were drawn up in front of her, and her head rested wearily upon them. I was about to leave, dragging Omar after me, when she flung back her head – and I recognised the girl I had seen, sitting like this on the Nile bank, in chains, watched over by three *gellab*s as our boat passed on its way down from Luxor. She was staring fixedly at me as if she recognised me, too, although I did not see how this could be.

I knew that sick or sickening slaves went at knock-down prices. Dead or half-dead stock, you might say. I called back the *gellab* and, pointing to the girl, bid 500 piastres.

'You insult me, Effendi!' (My rank was falling fast.)

'The girl is sick. If she stays where she is, she will die.'

'She is not sick. She is wilful. I punish her many times.'

'Well, then, you will be rid of her – and five hundred piastres richer.'

He took me aside again, dropping his voice to a whisper. 'Believe me, Effendi, she is special. You could go far and not find such a one. She is *mukhaeyt*.' He raised an elegant hand and, clenching the fingers, made them into a narrow tunnel so that the light barely showed through. 'For one such I cannot take less than fifteen hundred piastres.'

I knew what the word meant in everyday Arabic, of course, but, innocent as I still was, it never occurred to me to make the connection. A fortunate circumstance, because otherwise I might have walked off in disgust – which as things turned out, would have been a great pity. In the end I bought my dear wife, Zobeida, for 950 piastres – and never struck a better bargain my whole life.

As I write this, I cannot help feeling that many English readers may find all this more like *The Arabian Nights* (which my old neighbour, Mr Edward Lane, recently rendered into English) than a sober account of a Scotsman's life and times.

I am sorry, but I cannot help it. Scheherazade drew on fantasy in her tales to amuse the king and keep herself alive. My object is very different. I must tell it as it was, set the record straight. I can only refer my readers to a couple of lines in Lord Byron's *Don Juan*: ' 'Tis strange but true – for truth is always strange; Stranger than fiction.' In my experience, no poet ever wrote a truer line.

4.30 p.m., 17 November 1869, 70th kilometre, aboard SS Mohammed Ali

They had the best of it, the hundreds of people perched shoulder to shoulder on the top of the fifty-foot-high sand walls of the el-Kisr cutting. Up there they could see the whole unfolding drama, the long tail of ships strung out behind the imperial yacht, *L'Aigle*, thin wisps of white smoke hanging about the funnels, the national flags tinting their masts.

But down here, with the distinguished guests on the small government steamship the *Mohammed Ali*, all we could see was the *L'Aigle* towering above us, the yellow beading of her black hull catching the sun, moving very slowly, because Captain Surville was still taking no chances. He was out on the starboard paddle-box himself, checking the slope of the banks, passing orders down a chain of sailors to the helmsman. Not counting her paddle-boxes *L'Aigle* was nineteen metres long. To ground at any point on the canal's opening day would besmirch the honour of imperial France. The Emperor Napoleon III had staked much on the Canal, 'France's Canal', as Palmerston called it.

On water level at kilometre 75 there was no sound but the soft, measured splash of the paddle-wheels: Surville had insisted on absolute silence on board. The effect was eerie. The sun was now below the top of the sand ramparts, so that the people up there were silhouetted, looking like a long line of perching jackdaws. By contrast, the full beam of the sun illuminated the Empress Eugénie as *L'Aigle* emerged from the cutting. A shining vision in white flounced silk, she stood beside de Lesseps on the bridge, the very picture of assurance. Yet she told Ferdinand that she felt as if she had a ring of fire burning round her head. The Emperor

was at bay in Paris. He had twirled those imperial moustachios
of his once too often.

Like most of the slave-dealers' so-called 'Abyssinians', Zobeida was a Galla from the mountains of the south-west, close to where the Blue Nile rises. She was, in short, a Highlander like myself, and just as the English judged us savages, fit only to fight their battles for them, so the ruling class of Abyssinia, the Amharas, called the Gallas *shackala*s, nigger-slaves, and felt free to raid their villages whenever it suited them, disposing of their girls to the *gellab*s.

How many months, or years, it had taken Zobeida to complete the sad, two-thousand-mile trail down from her home that had now ended in the house on the canal in Cairo I never was able to discover, nor how many dealers' hands she had passed through on the way; nor where that obscene needlework was performed upon her which made her an object of great price: a *mukhaeyt*, a sewn-up girl. Nor did I really wish to know – all that was behind us.

She collapsed the moment Omar and I got her over our threshold, and I saw then that all my arts as a *hakim* and a Beaton – and a man – were going to be needed. My first thought naturally was of that famed Beaton restorative, much used by my grandmother – 'Old Man's Milk' – which I had used to great effect on the wounded at el-Hamed. (Sura 2 of the Holy Koran does say that there are times when strong drink has some usefulness, and surely this was one of them!) After that I sent her off to the *hamman* down the street on ladies' day, guided there by Omar; then I prescribed a fine striped silk robe, which I got at a bargain price thanks to Ahmed Muhtar, my friend in the Khan el-Khalili, and several necklaces made of those coloured stones the Abyssinians love. Not to mention a tiny phial of attar of roses got from the Suk el-Attarin.

That last prescription seemed to work miracles. Her eyes regained their interest in the passing scene, and her head rose on its elegant stem like a flower turning to the sun, and to my great satisfaction she began to prepare the meals, after her fashion, and to take a motherly interest in Omar.

And, much sooner than I had any right or reason to expect, the time arrived when, regaining the vitality of her mountain home, she came to my bed, eager to show her gratitude in the way she best knew. But first, I decided, Zobeida must be made whole. The desecration that lay between us must be removed, exorcised.

But when I broached the delicate matter to her as well as I could, trying to explain my knowledge of such matters as a medical man, she dissolved into tears. 'Why do you want to send me away? What sin have I committed?' That was, more or less, the sense that I was at last to tease out of her distress. A *muhkaeyt*, I learned, is normally totally unstitched only at childbirth, so the poor girl, unable to understand why I proposed to deprive her of what she had been led to believe was her greatest asset, had concluded that I must wish to rid myself of her.

Unlike Burckhardt, I do not intend to protect my readers from such unpleasant matters by writing of them in Latin; in any case, I have no Latin. But I will admit that such things much disturbed and puzzled me. The Arabs are famed for the passion and elo-quence of their love poems. The land throbs with their transports:

> Ya lel! ya lel! Allah ya lel!
> That night! the night! O Lord, the night!
> That brings thee, Hassan, to my arms . . .

As they say, 'Travel broadens the mind.' Or shatters it! A stitch or two or three: was this what it was all about? A friction of membranes? Was that the source and inspiration of this pulsating Arab poetry? I am a simple man. The thought troubled me. But, thanks to Zobeida, not for long. Thank God, she soon healed and was her own self again and I was able to assure her in a more convincing manner that, I, Osman, was well content with what nature alone had bountifully provided. And I told her the story of the breaking of the dam. She was, I said, my 'Bride of the Nile'.

Sami, who was very dark, was born in March 1819, the year after Belzoni found the chamber in the Second Pyramid that everybody had said was solid.

There is a chapter in the Koran called 'The Women', wherein it is stated that 'whosoever cannot afford to marry a free believing woman, let him marry from the believing handmaidens which his right hand owns . . . for the one of you is as the other . . . so marry them and give them their portions in kindness, they being honest, not debauched and of loose conduct'.

So I took Zobeida quietly before the Kadi and made her my wife, and, by reason of that, she was no longer a slave. As 'Om Sami' – and by courtesy of the neighbours 'Om Omar' also* – she ordered the house on the canal in a manner generally admitted to be fitting for a respected *hadji* such as myself, so that at last it was no longer the house of Burckhardt, the distinguished explorer, but the residence of Sheikh Osman, well-known dragoman to the milords, known to some as 'Osman the Scotchman'.

At long last the war in Arabia which had overshadowed so much of my life – and Tom's too – was over. I stood in the Cairo street with the crowd and saw the handsome young Wahabi chief Abdullah ibn Saud, being paraded in chains. Handsome and *brave* – through all the jeering he held his head high. Mohammed Ali sent him under a Tartar guard to be thrown at the feet of Sultan Mahmud in Constantinople, his 'loyal' offering to the Grand Seigneur.

For days the *imam*s strove to get the young man to retract his Wahabi 'heresies'. But he stood unwavering on the words of the Koran and the precepts of the Prophet. Had not the wearing of gold and silver been forbidden? Did not the existence of domed shrines of saints fly in the face of the central article of Islam – the Oneness of God? Was it for nothing that the Prophet had cleansed the Kaaba of idols?

---

* 'The Mother of Omar' and 'the Mother of Sami' – such were the honorific titles by which Zobeida, following custom, would have been known in the neighbourhood. – F.M.

So they bound Abdullah and for three days they dragged him through the streets of Istanbul; then they cut off his head at the gates of the Seraglio, and they pounded out his brains in a mortar and they hung the headless body on the gates, a paper denouncing his so-called heresy pinned to it by a dagger thrust through his heart.

I wondered what Tom – Tom Keith from Leith, Deputy Governor of the holy city of Medina – would have made of all this had he lived. It hardly mattered – with Mohammed Ali now firmly in the saddle, Egypt was embarking on quite new courses which had nothing to do with the Koran. Urged on by Mr Samuel Briggs of Briggs and Co., an Alexandrian merchant banker, Mohammed Ali was linking that Mediterranean city to the Nile – and to Cairo – by canal. It is true this canal ran crooked, since each village sheikh was responsible for digging a one-mile stretch. They say 20,000 fellahin died under the lash. But it worked well enough when it opened in 1820. Soon the population of Alexandria had doubled, and a strong infusion of European – or at least Levantine – blood was coursing through the desiccated veins of the Pharaohs.

New men were coming up all the time, men like Alexis Jumel, a young French (or Swiss) textile engineer commissioned by the Pasha to set up cotton-spinning and -weaving mills at Bulak. He hadn't been there much more than five minutes before he discovered, growing in the garden of a Cairo house, a different sort of cotton-bush from that normally grown in Egypt, a bush whose bolls opened out into long, lustrous strands. Within a year he'd planted an acre or two on an estate just outside Cairo. 'Jumel' brought three times the price of old *baladi* cotton on the Liverpool exchange, and Mohammed Ali ordered it to be grown wherever the soil was good and the canals deep enough. He engaged instructors for the fellahin.

I am relating this story now because, in one way or another, Monsieur Jumel's find in the Cairo garden was to have tremendous – and terrible – repercussions on my life.

By this time, you should understand that Zobeida had become a well-respected housewife with two boys of her own, Sami and his younger brother, Giovanni – named after Belzoni – in addition to Omar, and she had recently given birth to a girl-child, whom we had named Aisha. She had her hands full, particularly when I was away conducting milords. I was becoming worried about Omar, who was ready to leave the Koranic school. He wrote a good Arabic hand but was at a loose end, liable to get into one sort of mischief or another. It was then that I had this idea of apprenticing him to the up-and-coming young cotton specialist Monsieur Jumel.

How I wish now I hadn't.

Hard to describe the sound of Jumel's spinning- and weaving-sheds at Bulak: an extraordinary mixture of clanging iron, plodding oxen and braying donkeys. I should explain that whereas English mills then worked by water power, later by steam, Mohammed Ali had to rely on animal power, erratic at the best of times.

Pushing Omar in front of me, I moved down between the looms towards Monsieur Jumel, who was berating a fellah, grinning foolishly before a loom that had stopped.

'L'huile, l'huile, l'huile!' he shouted, plainly at the end of his tether.

'Hader, ya Bey. Bukra!'

'Non! Non, pas Bukra. Immediatement! Tout de suite!'

My heart went out to him. 'Malish!' I cried instinctively. 'Never mind!' *Malish*, I longed to tell him, is the essential oil of Egypt; it keeps things going somehow, even if it is absolutely no use for textile machinery. *Malish* when the tax collector beats one's feet to a pulp, *Malish* when one of the Seven Plagues of Egypt strikes again.

Jumel eyed my turban suspiciously, but the moment he saw that I was not 'another of them' he almost wept on my shoulder.

'They are clowns! *Clowns!* I cannot make them see that machines need oil. What can I do with such people?'

'Why should they see? They haven't seen a wheelbarrow yet. Even the Pasha himself...' He stared at me in disbelief.

'My name is Osman – Osman Effendi – and this my son Omar.'

His face lightened. He gripped my hand like a drowning man.

'Osman the Scotsman – I've heard of you.'

I could see that we were going to get along well.

'Remember these are pressed men,' I said. 'They do not *want* to learn. Now my son Omar here is a volunteer...'

Omar had wandered away and was watching the movements of a clanging loom and its flying shuttle.

Jumel watched him thoughtfully. I pointed out to him that, if he took on Omar, he could at least train up one engineer in a way engineers should be trained . . .

He handed the boy a big yellow oil-can. 'Voyez, Omar, oil is to machinery as the water of the Nile to your fields . . .'

A bearing on a loom had begun to squeal. Omar went over and dripped oil onto it. The squealing ceased.

Jumel shook my hand again. It was as if a burden had fallen off his shoulders. 'Eh bien, I will make of your son, Omar, an engineer.'

You might say this was the birthday of the cotton branch of Clan Osman. But that is another – sadder – story.

If the war in Arabia was over, the consuls' war – the war waged over the Pharaohs' tombs – was about to flare up again. Mr Salt and Signor Drovetti had drawn frontier lines, dividing Upper Egypt between themselves the way the Pope divided the New World between Portugal and Spain. Of course, with such prizes at stake it would have been too much to expect them to respect the frontiers all the time. As a dragoman, I had a ringside seat, particularly since one of my clients was by way of being the *casus belli*: William Bankes, long nose, humorous mouth, big, inquiring eyes, twenty-five years old or thereabouts, and a friend of Lord Byron's at Cambridge, or so he said. I've heard that he had to get out of England in a hurry, but then he had a passion for hieroglyphics as well as boys, and apparently unlimited amounts of money to devote to it.

On his last trip up the Nile he'd found a pink granite obelisk lying on the ground near the temple on the island of Philae, above the First Cataract. Hieroglyphics ran up and down its sides. Near by, half buried by sand, stood the plinth on which the fallen obelisk once stood. Bankes was excited to discover that it bore an inscription in Greek. He thought he had found a new Rosetta Stone. Already, using this key, he had identified the hieroglyphics for 'Cleopatra'. He was impatient to float both obelisk and plinth down the Nile and to England.

Both were enormously cumbersome and heavy. For such a task

I knew there was but one man, my friend the Paduan Hercules. But when Belzoni and I and Mr Salt stepped ashore at Philae to start the obelisk on its journey to England, we were confronted by an old man holding out a paper.

M. Drovetti, chargé d'affaires, begs European travellers to respect the bearer who is guarding the obelisk in the island of Philae which is the property of Monsieur Drovetti.
signed: Antonio Lebolo

The sheer effrontery of it took my breath away. Obviously, we had not a moment to lose. Belzoni and I got together a party of Nubians to lift the obelisk onto palm-trunk rollers. Bankes himself put other labourers to work lifting out the half-buried plinth. Then the old Aga appeared again, flourishing a letter just received from Bernardino Drovetti himself. It ordered the Aga on no account to permit any person or persons to remove the obelisk from the island.

Mr Salt was furious. He already had a *firman* from Mohammed Ali permitting its removal. He tore Drovetti's letter in half and threw it to the ground.

'That,' he said, 'is my answer to Signor Drovetti.'

The brief truce was over; we were at war again. Giovanni had already set the Nubians to building a pier, rock on rock, out from the island shore. It was late in the year and the water was getting dangerously low for the First Cataract to be negotiated by so heavy and oddly shaped a load.

The Sheikh of the Cataract, a grizzled old Nubian, shook his head. Impossible! With a load like that any boat would be holed in five minutes. Hadn't he refused the French the year before, when the water was higher than now?

Giovanni was unbeatable at this game. We paid the sheikh in advance, presented the Aga with a gold watch from Mr Bankes, and I at last found a boat-owner desperate enough for cash to embark on the four-mile run through the treacherous waters of the Cataract.

Every hour now was vital. The stone pier was ready. Slowly the twenty-two-foot monolith was edged on its rollers out onto the improvised pier towards the waiting boat. It had almost reached embarkation point when a small crack appeared in the rough stone wall. Before my horrified eyes, the crack widened and the whole structure began to fall apart. The obelisk slewed round slowly, and slid into the Nile. The Nubian loaders on the pier plunged into the water to get clear. Their women, watching from the bank, set up that maddening ululation. Belzoni threw up his great bear arms in despair. Mr Salt's mouth fell open.

Only William Bankes seemed unmoved. Cutting short the giant's overflowing apologies and excuses he rapped out: 'Signor Belzoni, your countryman have a saying, have they not? "Chi si scusa, s'accusa." I and my party propose to continue our journey up the Nile. When we get back I expect you to have dealt with this matter.'

I saw then why Giovanni sometimes seemed to resent so bitterly his English paymasters. Louis was the only one who gave him the credit that was his due – and Louis was dead.

But what a lion-heart the fellow was; he didn't despair more than five minutes before setting to work on a plan to get that great hunk of granite off the Nile bed and into the boat, using a system of levers and wedges. I shall never forget the sight of the obelisk emerging from the water, and beginning the climb up the bank, pink granite glistening in the sun.

Two days later, still unbroken, our obelisk, erected by Ptolemy II and Queen Cleopatra in 150 BC in honour of the island's goddess, Isis, lay roped on the bottom of the boat, ready for the shooting of the cataract.

The main controlling rope for the descent of the Cataract was wrapped around a tree and attached to the stern. The boat hadn't descended twenty yards before the rope snagged, frayed and broke. The obelisk was off like a bullet, the boat scraping against sunken boulders, shipping gallons of water, the Nubians pulling frantically on other guiding ropes as they swam alongside the plunging boat. When the boat spun round like a matchstick, I thought it was the end. But by some miracle, we eventually came through to the quieter waters that thread the sand dunes and little palm-fringed islands that mark the end of the First Cataract.*

As we dropped down the Nile towards Karnak, Belzoni fell to

---

* Thanks to the efforts of Signor Belzoni and my father, this obelisk in honour of Isis was erected in Mr Bankes's park at Kingston Hall, being 'opened' by the Duke of Wellington in 1827. – F.M.

talking of the great exhibition he was planning, a replica of 'Belzoni's Tomb' to be constructed at the Egyptian Hall in Piccadilly. All the *ton* of London would flock there. At long last all the world would know where the credit should go for the uncovering of the world of the Pharaohs.

I was happy for him. He deserved no less. We were both in an excellent mood when we tied up at Karnak, where Giovanni wanted to take another look at a small enclave among the ruins which had been allotted to the British under the terms of the archaeological truce with the French. You may imagine our confusion, therefore, when on reaching the spot we found half a dozen of Drovetti's men digging there. Giovanni checked his map. There could be no doubt. Drovetti had invaded Mr Salt's territory. It amounted to an unspoken declaration of war. Already Belzoni's Greek servant had drawn his dagger. 'No! No! No!' cried Giovanni, trying to knock the dagger away.

But the Greek began to creep up on the diggers.

'They rob you, signor. They must be taught a lesson!'

Giovanni shot out a huge arm and pulled the man back. 'Leave them, I tell you.'

A few minutes later, near the first pylon of the Temple of Amun, we were hemmed in by a mob of yelling Arabs. I looked around and spotted the malevolent features of Antonio Lebolo, the Piedmontese ruffian who had threatened us at Philae. Two steps behind Lebolo, on the outskirts of the mob, I saw Belzoni's old enemy Giuseppe Rosignano, another of Drovetti's gang.

Lebolo ran forward and seized the bridle of Giovanni's donkey. Before I could get to him I found myself pinioned from behind. I felt my pistol slipping from my sash, my arms being roped behind me. Out of the corner of my eye I could see Rosignano levelling his gun at Giovanni's chest, his sallow face contorted with rage.

'Tu bastardo! You stole my obelisk. You are a thief. You have always been a thief! Your father and mother were thieves!'

He was trying to drag Belzoni off his donkey. But Giovanni sat tight, planting his long legs on the ground. Had they managed to get him under the feet of the mob, he wouldn't have had a chance. I was struggling to get free when I recognised Bernardino Drovetti himself approaching. The cat was out of the bag now. He was scowling. He marched up to Belzoni, who was still astride his donkey.

'Why have you stopped my men working?'

'I have not stopped them. Why should I?'

'You lie! Get off that donkey!'

Belzoni didn't move. Suddenly a shot rang out, whistling past Belzoni's ear.

The shot, fired by the ex-policeman Lebolo, seemed to bring Drovetti to his senses. He shrugged and sloped off. The Arab crowd, seeing that the paymaster had gone, began to fall apart. We lost no time getting back to our boat. Giovanni and I both knew that, though no blood had been shed, after such a shot things could never be the same among the tombs of the Pharaohs in the upper valley of the Nile.

The period of innocence was over. As Giovanni wrote in one of his books, we began to feel that we 'were facing malevolent and evil beings'. I know how he felt. Scores of Pharaohs in their tombs and temples still lay concealed in the Egyptian rock and sand. But someone else would have to uncover them now; Giovanni was resolved to shake the dust of Egypt off his feet.

I saw him off from Alexandria in September 1819. It was like a bereavement to me, like losing a big brother. Even now clients still ask me what he was like. 'A giant of a man,' I tell them – and I do not just mean in stature.

So another thread had snapped. Right from the moment I crossed the Kyle for the last time, my life seemed to have been full of loose ends: my handfasted bride and the sun-gilded prospect of North Carolina, that thread snapped with a terrible abruptness; my mentor and liberator, Burckhardt, snatched from me still in his early thirties; Tom Keith taken in a Wahabi ambush, cutting my last link with home; now Giovanni . . .

Yet were they all really loose ends? Or might some of the broken strands yet be spliced, just as Omar deftly twists together the broken threads on his loom to bring them back into the pattern? It proved a timely question. Unknown to me, the gaudy, bloody Mameluke thread in the wild pattern of my life was about to reappear.

As we travelled slowly down from Luxor, bearing Bankes's obelisk – 'loot', my friend Auguste Mariette would call it these days – we found ourselves continually passing small parties of tall, thin, black men, fettered, being driven northwards. Mohammed Ali had sent one of his sons, Ismail, deep into the Sudan to raise recruits. The Arabian war was over but the Greeks were in revolt and the Sultan was again pressing his Egyptian Viceroy to fly to his aid. It had not yet occurred to Mohammed Ali that the soil-grubbers, the fellahin, could fight, so he had resolved to train the Sudanese. There were, after all, plenty of them.

Plodding along the Nile bank towards their fate, those Sudanese captives looked the very picture of dejection. I felt sorry for Colonel Sèves – of the French Marine, made captain during Bonaparte's Hundred Days and now picked by Mohammed Ali to whip the poor fellows into shape. I felt sorry for them too.

From our mooring place near Asiut we found ourselves looking out over a dusty square where ragged columns of black men were marching and counter-marching, shouldering arms, taking up firing positions, and generally being pushed about, kicked, cursed, yelled at by some dozen French drill sergeants in an atrocious mixture of French and kitchen Arabic. The 'recruits' wore white tunics and white trousers, which made their faces under cock-red tarbushes look blacker than ever. They seemed bewildered.

As I watched this farcical scene, between laughter and tears, a figure decked in gold braid marched out briskly from the barracks and over to the drilling squads. He looked vaguely familiar. As he approached, the white sergeants ran around more frantically than ever, yelling orders, pushing men into line, issuing terrible threats in a language their men plainly did not understand. It took my mind back to a very different barrack square, swept by chill winds off the Moray Firth. As ever, when memory is deeply stirred, its gyrations continued – and suddenly I knew who the officer with the gold braid was. Behind the red tarbush of Egypt's New Army I saw the flaunting yellow Mameluke turban of François, Master of the Bey's Horse.

Forgetting all dignity, I leapt ashore and rushed across the square.

'François! François! François . . .!'

He stopped dead in his tracks, staring angrily at my dragoman outfit. He called two NCOs: he was going to have me arrested – then, suddenly: 'Mon Dieu! Mon Dieu! Vraiment, c'est vous! Osman, l'écossais. C'est possible?'

Ignoring the NCOs, he fell upon my shoulder. As we embraced, his tarbush fell off, revealing a white scar that parted his close-cropped hair.

'You have been in battle?'

That old Marseillais guffaw again. He shrugged. 'You might call it that: a near miss, as you see; from Octave Sèves down we all show the scars. I tell you, mon vieux, Waterloo was a picnic compared to being a drill sergeant in the Pasha's New Army.'

He took me back across the parade ground to the officers' mess.

'It will be empty now – we can talk.'

The room had the usual dusty, abandoned look, but there was a picture of Napoleon Bonaparte on the walls, another of Mohammed Ali, and a third of his latest Commander-in-Chief, Suleiman Bey, Octave Sèves.

'Osman, my dear fellow,' François said, as soon as we were inside, 'I never thought to see you alive again after you left that day with Ezbek's party for the Citadel. Some celebration, eh?'

'You knew?'

'No. But the French Mamelukes got a hint . . .'

'Did it come from Drovetti?'

'Don't know – we got it word of mouth. Whispers. I tried to warn you, Osman, but you wouldn't listen.'

An orderly came in with papers. François cast an eye over them, and shook his head.

'Reports of mortality – these blacks from the Sudan – they obey, they drill, and then they die. They wish no more to live. You understand?'

I understood all too well.

Raucous cries drifted in from the barrack square. An orderly brought in a bottle of absinthe and two glasses. I pressed my old friend for news of Fatima: all he could tell me was that she had joined the flight south after the bloodbath in Cairo. He himself had ridden into the desert. He knew nothing.

I told him then how Omar had turned up without explanation at my house in Cairo. He swore that he had no hand in it. Then I told him of Zobeida – although not of where I had found her – and of our two boys, Sami and Giovanni – named for my friend Belzoni – of the house I had been left on the Cairo canal, and my new trade of dragoman to the Quality.

François grew silent and thoughtful as he listened to my tale.

Just as I rose to go – for I could leave the boat with its precious cargo no longer – he reached out to put a detaining hand on my shoulder.

'Osman, there is something you could do for me when you get back to Cairo . . .'

'Anything,' I said, which was rash.

'Will you go and see my daughter? It was before you reached Egypt, when I was in Bonaparte's service. Her mother was a Greek – of good family. I was billeted in her house, you understand?'

I nodded, I understood.

'A beautiful woman – Elena takes after her. But she is seventeen now, and headstrong. I was posted up here – well, you will see, I could not bring her with me – among these savages . . .'

I nodded, fearing what was coming next.

'Well, it so happened that Mohammed Ali had just given my *patron*, Colonel Sèves, a big white house on the Ezbekieh, suitable for the commander-in-chief of his New Army. A house with many rooms, many guards, a valled garden. Octave is a good fellow. We've been through a lot together. So I asked him whether he'd give Elena house-room while I was away. Keep a fatherly eye on her, you understand. . . .'

'Fatherly?' My eyebrows must have risen.

He nodded. 'Yes – but now Octave has changed his name to Suleiman and soon he'll be Suleiman Pasha. He's "taken the turban". I hear he's got a harem. He's a renegado and it makes me uneasy. Look at Menou: in command in Alexandria, called himself Abdullah and married some bath-attendant's daughter.'

I laughed. 'François, *I* am a renegado too . . .'

'Non, non, you are Osman – Osman the Scotchman. When you get back to Cairo I want you to go to that big house on the Ezbekieh and get inside somehow. Say you're the dragoman of the British Consulate – which will be true enough, after a fashion – with an important message for Suleiman Bey. Octave is bound to be away on some parade ground or other, being shot at by these bastards' – he waved towards the square – 'so you'll have a free run. Cast your eyes around. See what's going on. If you see Elena, give her my love. Tell her I'll be down to see her soon. Get a squint into the harem.'

I didn't like the sound of this. 'I'm sure Colonel Sèves won't have a harem,' I temporised.

François guffawed. 'I see you are still the same innocent you always were, Osman.'

Just then there was a ragged burst of fire from the barrack square, followed by a terrified yell.

'Mon Dieu! Either the recruits are shooting the sergeants or the sergeants are shooting recruits!'

He clapped me on the back. 'You see how I live, Osman.' He gripped my hand. 'Au revoir, mon vieux. N'oubliez pas ma fille, je vous en prie.'

He was off 'at the double'.

As his hoarse curses flew across the square, his last words were scored into my mind like a line of hieroglyphics cut in Mr Bankes's obelisk.

Don't forget Elena!

There have been times, many times, since then when I have dearly wished that I could.

20   Elena

What with Mr Salt's proceedings against Drovetti and his murderous gang, Zobeida's nearing her time again, and getting the
obelisk – and Giovanni himself – off to England, it was several
weeks before I could fulfil the solemn promise I had given to my
old friend François. To tell the truth I wasn't looking forward to
fulfilling it. The whole thing looked tricky to me, tricky and
dangerous.

There was no problem at all in locating Sèves's big house on
the Ezbekieh. The usual Nubian *bawwab* drowsed at the door
in the high garden wall. Flourishing my dragoman's silver-headed
cane, I told him, imperiously, that on the British Consul's behalf
I bore an important message from the King of England to deliver
to his master. Reluctantly, he roused himself sufficiently to
hammer on the door. After a while I heard the bolts being drawn
from the inside. A tarbushed Circassian in the uniform of the
Nizam Jedid opened the door a crack. I repeated my speech. He
eyed me with true Mameluke disdain. But behind him I caught
sight of a tall, slim girl in a black dress, black with European
style.

'You may go, Faruk,' she said, 'I will deal with the message for
the Emir.' He scowled, hesitated, and then turned on his heel.

The door opened wider, and I found myself swimming in a pair
of dark Grecian eyes. Accustomed as I had become to the veil and
the downcast look, I floundered. The dark hair, parted in the
middle, was braided around a high brow in the style I had seen
in Ptolemaic tomb paintings.

'I am Elena de la Tour,' she said loftily. 'I am gouvernante of

His Excellency.' Her voice challenged me to contradict her. 'You may entrust your message to me, dragoman.'

Could this really be François's daughter? Where on earth had she got that name? Could she already be something more than Sèves's 'housekeeper'? Or had she simply inherited from François the appetite for a *histoire marseillaise*? With her long, tapering face, her finely drawn but athletic body, and high-bridged nose, she certainly resembled him in no other way.

A dragoman needs his dignity. I seemed to be in danger of losing mine. 'The truth is,' I managed to say at last, 'that I am here because your father, an old comrade of mine, asked me to call upon you. He wished me to tell you how sorry he is that his duties keep him in Asiut. He wishes to know whether all is well with you. If there is anything I can do . . .'

It sounded a lame enough story. My voice tailed off for, as I spoke, her whole manner changed from *grande dame* to anxious child on the edge of tears . . .

She looked around warily, then led me round the edge of the garden into what seemed to be Colonel Sèves's billiard room, where the curtains were drawn.

'My father has sent you for my *anniversaire*? He has sent me a *cadeau*?' I must have looked at a loss because she collapsed onto a divan in a flood of tears.

I couldn't stand it.

'What a fool!' I said. 'I completely forgot. Will François ever forgive me? I left his present behind at my house. Forgive me, mademoiselle, I will go at once and retrieve it.'

I rushed over to el-Sagha, the *suk* of the gold- and silver-smiths. I confess I had little enough idea what such a child of Alexandria, half French, half Greek, would appreciate. But I ferreted around the stalls, and in the end picked a necklace of gold ornaments, interspersed with green faience beads which bore a discreet 'eye of Horus' on either side. Hinting that I had many rich clients I might steer his way, I knocked the merchant down to three Maria Theresa dollars.

'Take it for nothing!' he exclaimed in disgust.

She was waiting for me. She had recovered her poise.

'This way,' she said, and led me back into the darkened billiard room. 'In here the harem women will never see us. They are wicked gossips.' *Bavardeuses* was the word she used. We were speaking a strange mixture of French, Italian, Arabic and Greek. But those great eloquent eyes, focused upon me, said more than any words. I was more than ever conscious that in answering François's appeal I had embarked on a dangerous enterprise.

Faint twitterings, reminding me of finches in the trees at dusk, drifted up from the harem quarters. Octave-Joseph-Anthelme Sèves was in his early thirties, and had lost no time in embracing the style of his new paymaster. There were stories that the Pasha had already rewarded his services with a beautiful concubine or two. I began to understand François's misgivings.

'Close the door.' She motioned me to a place beside her on the shabby divan. 'We can talk here . . .'

The goldsmith had placed the necklace in a handsome case, and wrapped it impressively. 'From François, your father,' I lied. 'I hope you can forgive me for forgetting it.' She removed the paper slowly, layer by layer, extracted the case, opened the lid, and gave a child's squeal of delight. Her dark eyes shone. She reached across, seized my head, and kissed me enthusiastically on both cheeks like some overgrown child.

With what gravity I could muster, I drew her attention to the *udjat* symbols, explaining that these were the 'good luck' charms of the Ancient Egyptians. 'Count them and you'll find there are forty in all – that shows how determined François is to protect you.'

She burst into a flood of tears, burying her head in my lap. I wondered whether she had guessed that it was I, not her father, who had bought the necklace. She was, after all, not a child but a handsome young woman, who looked older than her seventeen years. As she sobbed convulsively, I found my feelings becoming rapidly less than avuncular.

Before the flesh betrayed me, I raised up her head, and, holding out the necklace, encircled her neck. Perhaps in doing so I disturbed some pin or other, because her dark hair found release from its braided splendour, and cascaded down her back, illuminated in a shaft of sunlight from a chink in the curtains. A wave of emotion engulfed me: I was transported on the instant to a heather-bed in a shieling hut in the Braes of Lochaber.

Could it really have been fifteen years ago?

She bent her head to ease my struggle with the clasp of the necklace. I could not forbear a fleeting stroke on the sweet curve of her neck. In an instant she swivelled, and fell into my arms. I don't know – perhaps the forty 'eyes of Horus' on the necklace were already exerting their protective power. Perhaps it was that sudden recurrence of the vision of Jeannie just when I had at last almost banished her from my mind. In any case, François had practically made me the girl's guardian. How could I betray his trust? I told my 'ward' to be good and with a playful slap on her bottom, which I fear both parties relished, I made my escape with my dragoman's dignity not totally destroyed.

When I promised to look in again shortly to ensure that all was well, Elena pointed out an overgrown summerhouse in the garden which she said was her private retreat. There, she said, we could talk undisturbed. The *bab sirr* – the secret door – in the exterior wall was close by.

My clients often tell me that 'these Arabs are terrible liars', and from their sidelong glances I am never quite sure whether or not they are including me. They don't understand, of course, how in the Orient fantasy and reality overlap and change places with bewildering rapidity. That year my sober and esteemed patron, Mr Henry Salt, the Consul, suddenly married a sixteen-year-old Italian beauty, a third of his age, snatched her from her parents on a brief visit to Alexandria. I personally superintended the unloading of the piano he imported from England for her. The story was that he rushed her to the altar because she so closely resembled a girl who had jilted him back home in England.

Well, I could understand that. And very nice the signorina looked when she sat at the piano, singing excerpts from Italian operas, surrounded by the applauding *ton* of Alexandria. Unsettling, though, my readers may agree.

Mr Salt's girl-wife was not the only occasion for celebration that year. Ibrahim Pasha, back at last from his victories in Arabia, declared seven days *en fête*. The Ezbekieh was crammed with revellers from early morning to late night. Great gusts of belly laughter exploded around the *kara-gyuz* a kind of Turkish Punch-and-Judy show, very earthy. Mouths agape, a score of blue-*gala-biya*-clad fellahin, up from the country, watched a *hawi* winding a cobra round his boy's head. A couple of Saidi, down from Upper Egypt, built like Pharaohs, tried to crack each other's heads in a stick fight. Stalls laden with sweetmeats, soaked lupin beans, sticks of sugar-cane, nuts in screws of paper were everywhere.

'My supper will be thy gift, O Bey,' announced a beggar, boldly.

'Allah yerzuk,' I retorted in standard form. 'God will sustain you.'

A few yards away a grave sheikh sat at a small table, busily inscribing *hegab*s – charms from the Koran – on strips of paper, potent verses, mystic numbers, the ninety-nine names of God. I was enveloped in a great cloud of acrid smoke, crackling, pricking my nose. A magician had thrown a handful of coriander seeds, a *hegab* and a nub of *liban*, or frankincense, onto his tray of glowing charcoals and now, emerging from his self-made reek, proposed to read my fortune.

I screwed up my eyes, for the smoke made them smart, kept them screwed up, and thus rid myself of the importunate sooth-sayer. When I opened them again I found myself facing a tall female figure enveloped in a gown of finest-quality silk, a white muslin *burko* falling from the bridge of her nose to her yellow morocco slippers. Her eyes met mine and, briefly, held them. They were Elena's eyes. She was with two other women, identically veiled, who were listening, spellbound, to the interminable romantic recital of an *Abu Zeidi*.*

The storyteller reached some crisis in his never-ending narrative, his musician stepped in with a few phrases on his *ud* to build up the tension, and Elena reappeared, beckoning me with her eyes. I looked around for spying eunuchs, but saw none. I followed Elena. She paused and pressed into my palm a large key.

'Tonight,' she whispered. 'During the fireworks. I shall wait in the summerhouse.'

Before I could make answer, she was back with her companions.

Again I had the deepest misgivings. But I had given my word to François. What could I do?

I waited till well after the sunset call to prayer. As I crossed the Ezbekieh, functionaries were checking on the positions of the

---

* An *Abu Zeidi* was a reciter of the well-loved romances of one Abu Zeid, an Arab of the Beni Hilal tribe, who according to one of his tales, had married ten wives, but could achieve only two children, both daughters. This was considered hilarious, according to my father. – F.M.

rockets, priming the Roman candles for the great fireworks display. The first swoosh of rockets spangled the night sky just as I arrived in front of the secret door in the high garden wall.

The key turned in the lock with surprising ease. Pausing a few moments to get my bearings in the garden, I crept up the rotting steps of the summerhouse.

'So Allah willed it' – a mocking whisper from somewhere at the back of the mildewed structure. She showed herself then, coming forward into the faint moonlight.

'I am glad. I am glad you did not desert me. I think I should have . . . I should have killed myself.'

'Killed yourself?' The reality of the situation in which I had placed myself – or allowed myself to *be* placed – was only now coming home to me. Suddenly she was reaching up – I am six feet seven inches tall. She had her hands linked tight round my neck, and was hanging on desperately, half laughing, half weeping, seeking my lips with hers. My turban fell off, revealing to my dismay my close-cropped hair; I have lived long enough now in the Orient to feel naked without a head-covering. I got my hands on her shoulders, trying to calm her, holding her off, but at that moment a shaft of moonlight penetrated the shutters, I looked into her eyes, those great, dark, tear-washed, pleading eyes, and I was lost.

My avuncular role as the young lady's guardian fell down with the turban and was sloughed with my robes, and the god Min, 'great of love', as it says on the Karnak temple, came into his kingdom. We fell together onto the dusty old divan that ran down one side of the mouldering summerhouse, which had no doubt seen many such assignations. Its ancient springs were no match for our urgencies, spilling us, unnoticed, onto the rotting floor-boards. Then Elena cried out with such abandon that I clapped my hand over her mouth, fearful that she would bring the eunuchs running from the harem.

I listened hard and long, but there was no sound but the deep breathing of the creature by my side. Educated in the harem, Arab women are trained in artifice, in pleasuring their men. This Levantine girl might have her own devices, yet she had an independence of spirit that gave zest to her possession.

Elena disturbed me. European after a fashion, relatively artless, she made me achingly aware again of the void that had followed the abrupt desertion of my first instructress. True, the pain had been assuaged by Zobeida and my Arab family but a haunting sense of hollowness remained. This young girl seemed to represent a way back, a new beginning, refreshing as the cool air that with sunset wafts along the Nile.

Did I write 'artless'. Ah, well, that was *then*. My life, I find, is full of *thens*. I have often wondered in the year since why she threw herself at me, a 'dirty Arab', the way she did, a Greek girl of good family, as François had said. Desperation, no doubt. Deserted by her father, shut up in that great house, spied on by a malicious harem – I represented, I suppose, the last chance of escape.

Signor Belzoni was now, I heard, the lion of London society as he paraded 'his' Pharaohs in the Egyptian Hall, Piccadilly. In ever great numbers, the milords flocked to Egypt, and, naturally, sought out Osman Effendi, who had been with the Great Belzoni when he made his astonishing discoveries. You could say, I suppose, that the years 1820 to 1830 were my great dragoman years. We had the Quality then, not ignorant *kuckuki* like that fellow who had accosted me at the Grand Opening. And there was never a man to match Belzoni: I was grieved when I heard of his death in 1823, at Benin on the Guinea coast, where he'd taken on his broad shoulders Burkhardt's unfulfilled mission to trace the course of the River Niger.

Fortunately for me, the very week after that assignation in the crumbling summerhouse in Suleiman Bey's garden I was engaged by Robert Hay, a Scots nobleman gripped by an ambition to furnish his mansion, Dunraw House, in the Border country, with the finest Pharaonic antiquities. He was twenty-five years old when I first worked for him, as rich as Croesus and quite determined to out-Belzoni Belzoni – and to crack the riddle of the hieroglyphs into the bargain. To this end he engaged a group of artists to make sketches of inscriptions and temples for him, Fred Catherwood and James Burton from London, Joseph Bonomi, my Cairo friend and neighbour, Edward Lane and John Wilkinson, not yet 'Sir John, the *Egyptologist*', word now fast coming into vogue.

Even with all these artists working for him, he was obsessed with that damned box of tricks, the *camera lucida*. You set it up at the mouth of a tomb or somewhere, then all you had to do was to trace around the reflections on the paper, and hey presto! you had a 'Panorama of the Nile Valley'. My job was to round up a few 'picturesque Bedouin' to stand about to give perspective.

I remember because I had to pay them bakshish out of my own pocket. Despite his wealth, Robert Hay was a man who counted the pennies. A hard man to please. I remember he once asked me to get him a new silk tassel for his tarbush, not an easy article to come by on the Upper Nile. I went to endless trouble to get him that tassel – and then he flung it back at me, saying it wasn't good enough for even a corporal to wear! He didn't say the same about Kalitza, the twelve-year-old Greek girl I bought him in the Alexandria slave-market. In fact he married her, and took her home to Scotland. And if any reader thinks that's just another Scheherazade-style Oriental tale, let him (or her) go up to Dunraw House and ask its mistress. I tell it as it was. But I'm getting ahead of myself. The war against the Greek rebels was not in full swing yet. Chronology must be observed.

That takes me back to Elena.

Getting back to Cairo after these trips with milord Hay and his artistic circus, I now had two welcoming visions before my mind's eye; my growing family and the secret door in Suleiman's high garden wall. I can claim that I attended to paternal duties first, pronouncing the call to prayer in my baby daughter Aisha's right ear, testing Sami on his arithmetic, hearing Omar's tales of the fight against the cotton-boll weevil. Yet all the time, I have to admit, I looked forward to escaping from young Hay's exactions to the sweeter, more sustaining tyranny in the summerhouse.

Until one day, back in Cairo to purchase more bags of plaster of Paris for Hay's endless casts, I found Elena waiting for me in the road, in a strange mood. How could I think of *that*, she burst out, when the Greeks, *her* people, were being massacred, tortured, castrated, eyes gouged out by those dirty fellahin, decked out now in Egyptian army uniforms. It had never occurred to me that she would take the Greek revolt in so personal a manner. After all, it was the Greeks who had started it, massacring their Turkish masters in the Morea. As ever, the Sultan had turned to

Mohammed Ali to save him. So in Elena's eyes, it was the Egyptians who were the villains of the piece. In short, it was entirely *my* fault. Did I not know that the noble Lord Byron had just given his life fighting for her poor tortured people, yet all I could think of . . .

I saw what had happened, of course. Seething with jealousy, the harem was taking its vicious revenge. They made sure that every bloody tale of atrocity against the Greeks found its way to her. The day Mohammed Ali sent a bag of Greek ears from the Morea to be nailed to the great gate of the Sultan's Seraglio, she would not speak to me at all. Her misery was heightened by the knowledge that François, her own father, was training the 'assassins of her people'.

After that, on my trips to Cairo I made it my business to bring myself up to date on the latest turn in this long bitter war of the Cross and the Cresent before presenting myself at the secret door. When the Turks and Egyptians seized the island of Ipsara, taking many prisoners, I found it prudent to stay at home with Zobeida and our new girl-child. But when the Greek 'freedom fighters' all but wiped out the Turks at Mitylene, I received in the summer-house a reception I remember to this day.

Unfortunately for me, there were few Mitylenes.

A trained and disciplined force 18,000 strong, the Egyptian New Army, recruited now from fellahin, had become a steamroller which could flatten the inconstant Greeks.

Alexandria was full of Greek women and children prisoners of war, spared when their men had been put to the sword. They filled the slave-market. When I landed at Bulak one afternoon, returning from the decaying tombs and temples of Upper Egypt, I was accosted by an agitated Elena who had been hunting far and wide for me, making no secret of our relationship.

She brushed my protestations aside. 'Don't you know my countrywomen are being exposed for sale in the slave-market? Girls of good family are being pawed over by dirty Arabs!'

Her voice rose higher and higher. Had not the English abolished the slave trade? I must go at once to demand action from my Consul . . .

Mr Salt, I told her, had troubles of his own. His young wife had died in childbirth. He was beside himself with grief.

Passing from anger to tears, she implored me to rescue the girls.

'You are an Englishman, are you not?' I was offended, as ever, but did not contradict her.

To live in the Orient and remain sane it is necessary to keep a firm grip on one's compassion. I knew that a fair-skinned Greek virgin would be well beyond my pocket.* Then I thought of young Robert Hay. Tight-fisted he might be, but the thought of rescuing a Christian Greek child from Mohammedan 'lusts' might open his purse: he was an earnest young man. I sent an urgent message upriver by a fast runner.

I had expected Hay alone, and was a bit put out when half a dozen of his friends and hangers-on turned up with him, all disguised as Turks. The *gellabs* saw through this in an instant, of course, and, scenting good business, were all over us the moment we entered the *okela*.

'Yunanni! Yunanni!' they cried. 'Greek, Greek girls! Bella! Bella!' kissing their fingertips.

Of all ages and conditions, dresses stained and torn, eyes swollen with tears, the wretched females stood around bewildered and disconsolate. Elena, who had insisted on accompanying me, enveloped in a silk *habbarah*, said a few words in Greek. They brightened and started chattering excitedly.

Young Hay, the new silk tassel of his tarbush gleaming in the sun – he had, it seemed, obtained one to his satisfaction – stopped opposite a delicate-looking young girl who held her head high, although her hair was matted and her dress ripped down to the navel.

'She is twelve years old, perhaps thirteen,' reported Elena. 'She says they seized her in Crete. Her name is Kalitza, and she says her father is the Mayor of Apodhule . . .'

The girl began to sob quietly.

Hay signed to me. 'Pay the brute his price!'

It was outrageous; I began to knock the dealer down.

'Don't bargain,' he snapped.

I knew just how he felt. Hay meant what he said when he talked of 'rescue'. I doubt whether many of the other young men

---

* Readers may check by consulting Mr Murray's *Handbook to Egypt* of 1844, in which the prices of slaves will be found after those of saddles, sea-salt, servants and sheep. – F.M.

who made purchases that day did, though – not in Robert Hay's sense, anyhow.

Henceforth Kalitza was to travel with Robert Hay in his boat, up and down the Nile, puzzling over two sorts of hieroglyphs, the Pharaohs' and those of her 'master's' language. At that stage he treated her like a daughter, teaching her to use the *camera lucida*, and attending to her education as far as he could. Osman Effendi now had many commissions for the purchase of English dictionaries, Greek testaments and books of grammar. Later, Hay went off with her to Crete to find her parents. When she was sixteen, they were married in Malta on the way home to Scotland.

Kalitza was one of the lucky ones. I happen to know that Hay wrote to the other young men who had bought Greek girls that day, urging them to follow his example. I doubt they did. I know James Burton considered Hay's letter a liberty and more or less told him to mind his own bloody business.

I sometimes wonder whether the mistress of Dunraw, Robert Hay's great house in East Lothian, ever remembers a certain Osman Effendi who had so much trouble getting her first English books.

Probably not.

Looking back, I see the year 1827 as a key year in my life. As ever, it was History – or the great History-maker above – that turned the key. In that year Henry Salt died, having never resigned himself to the loss of his pretty young wife. And I had to break to Elena the news of the death of her father, François, fighting – on the 'wrong' side – in the Ottoman–Greek war.

At this time the combined fleets of the Christian powers lay in Navarino Bay together with the fleets of Turkey and Egypt. The war was in the doldrums. Then a trigger-happy Turk fired on the ship's boat carrying a British naval officer under flag of truce. Admiral Codrington opened fire and sent the entire Turkish and Egyptian fleets to the bottom.

Overnight, in Elena's eyes, I changed from treacherous *renegado* to her shining hero, saviour of the Greek people, fit to stand alongside Lord Byron. I think it was on that night our first son, Ibrahim, was conceived. She wanted to name him Theophilus, explaining that in Greek this means 'beloved of God'. But Islam gives the father the right to name a boy-child, and I'm afraid I insisted on 'Ibrahim' in honour of my friend, mentor, benefactor and fellow pilgrim, Jean-Louis Burckhardt, whose spirit still moves in this old house. 'Theo', I promised, could – and did – come later.

As a Greek patriot, living in the house of the commander of the Egyptian army waging war on the Greek 'rebels', Elena's position was now, to say the least, precarious, and her pregnancy exposed her to the taunts of Octave Sèves's harem. Such was her lack of discretion, I feared her life could be in danger. It was then I recalled that a True Believer may take four wives, 'provided', as the Holy Koran says, 'he treats them equally'. To make sure I fulfilled this important proviso – and many, I fear, do not – I bought a second house on the Cairo canal,* married François's daughter, and thus became that thing which sends delicious shivers down the spines of English visitors to Egypt, a *polygamist*.

I was then called away by Mr James Augustus St John, a London journalist, who wished me to conduct him over the crocodile mummy pits at Manfalut, and was astonished on my return to find that my Greek *grande dame* had left the new house I had bought for her and moved in with Zobeida and her children in the old house. To my surprise, Zobeida showed no jealousy, but busied herself in preparation for the birth of my second wife's child. Perhaps, as first wife, she considered this her appointed role – I don't know. Elena, on the other hand, may have felt that at last she had secured a slave appropriate to her status. However it was, it worked out well enough at the time.

---

* Mr Murray's *Handbook to Egypt* of 1844 notes that Osman Effendi has *four* houses for rent to travellers in the Suk el-Zalat. – F.M.

BOOK IV

'All by Steam!'

Pasha: I know it – I know all – the particulars have been
faithfully related to me, and my mind comprehends
locomotives. The armies of the English ride upon the vapours of
burning cauldrons, and their horses are flaming coals! Whirr!
Whirr! All by wheels! Whizz! Whizz! All by steam!

– A.W. Kinglake, *Eothen, or Traces of Travel Brought Home
from the East* (1844)

I suppose I must have been in Egypt about fifteen years when Jean-François Champollion first cracked the mystery of the Rosetta Stone and Time rolled back three or four millennia. They called him 'the Egyptian', although whether this was on account of the sallowness of his skin or because he'd been poring over the mysterious hieroglyphics of the Ancient Egyptians since the age of sixteen I never did discover. He was thirty-eight by the time he came out to Egypt in 1828 and I ran into him.

Joseph Bonomi and I were up on the west bank on Hay's business when we noticed that the door of Belzoni's Tomb – as people still called it – was standing wide open. We went over to take a look, and what did we find within but a clutch of Frenchmen superintending an Arab mason brazenly cutting a relief from the wall.

We were struck dumb at the effrontery of it. Bonomi recovered his voice first. 'This tomb belongs to the English. You have no right . . .'

Champollion stepped forward. 'It does not. It belongs to Mohammed Ali and to Egypt. In any event, you can understand nothing here properly until I have published my Dictionary.'

The arrogance of the man! I happen to know that Henry Salt, and Dr Young and William Bankes helped him for years with squeezes, theories, endless suggestions in letters and never got a shred of credit from him for it.

What a decade that was, though. It was not only that with the piercing of the heavy veil of the hieroglyphics perspectives shot backwards, but they opened up in front of us, too. 'Timeless' Egypt, the land of *bukra* – of the tomorrow that never comes –

began to be pushed forward, paced, challenged, by the insistent moving finger of Lieutenant Thomas Waghorn's Patent Greenwich Chronometer.

I got back to Hill's Hotel in Cairo one day at the end of 1827 to find the proprietor standing in the middle of his front hall, holding a large business card in his hand, shifting uneasily from one foot to the other, and being harangued by a young fellow in a reefer jacket whom I'd never set eyes on before. Hill spotted me with evident relief and beckoned urgently.

The young man could be heard from three yards away.

'Sir Francis will tell you His Majesty's Mails must go round the Cape. He'll tell you the Red Sea is not navigable all the year round. Nonsense, sir! He forgets the power of steam. He forgets the steamship. But, believe me, sir, it's coming. It's going to change the world. You can't stop progress, sir . . .'

Hill put out a hand to grab my arm. 'Ah, Osman Effendi, just the man I was looking for. As I understand it, Lieutenant Waghorn here, of the Bengal River Pilot Service, is charged with carrying the mails of the East India Company's Court of Directors to the Governor of Bengal in the Shortest time possible. He needs camels.'

Hill handed the card to me and made himself scarce.

The card read:

Mr Thomas Waghorn
General Agent in India for Steam
Intercourse via the Red Sea between
England, India, Ceylon and China etc.

I studied the card carefully. I rather liked the 'China etc.'.

'We have no time to waste, Mr Osman.' He had pulled out his 'Greenwich chronometer' and was watching the march of seconds.

'I left Gracechurch Street in London by the Eagle coach at 7.30 p.m. for Dover. It is now 1.15 p.m. Greenwich Mean Time – 3.15 Egyptian time on 3 December. In five days the steamship *Enterprise*, my friend Captain Johnston commanding, will drop anchor in Suez roads to carry me and the Directors' mails on to Bombay. I need fast camels across the desert, Cairo to Suez.'

'Dromedaries,' I said. 'A good dromedary will cover the distance in half the time of a camel.'

'Dromedaries it is, Mr Osman – for myself, yourself, and for a Bedou guard and the baggage and the mails. I rely on you implicitly. You and I, Mr Osman, are going to show up Sir Francis as the dunderhead he is!'

'Sir Francis?'

'Sir Francis Freeling, the Postmaster-General. He says my notion of an Overland Transit through Egypt is a "wild scheme". He insists on sail round the Cape for the mails. Mr Osman, that pompous ass is the reason our people in India have to wait a year for a reply when they write home. A *year* mind you! A year!'

I confess I didn't know what to make of him at first, except that here was clearly a man who knew his own mind. Equally clearly, the poor fellow did not know what he was up against. He would need all the help he could get.

I sought out my friend Sheikh Ayd of the Towra Bedouin, and hired four of his best dromedaries and a Turi guard.

We pitched our tents that first night about six miles outside Cairo. 'Fine sand for the first five miles ...' Waghorn recorded in the book he called his Log. The next day we logged thirty-five miles – 'hard gravel, sandhills to our east and west'.

Waghorn was a great note-taker. One night in the camp he let me flick back through the Log, and my wonder at the man grew.

... Avalanche closes Simplon pass ... take Mount Cenis, adding 130 miles ... reach Trieste, hand copy London *Times* to British Consul ... TIME TAKEN EX-LONDON: through five kingdoms – 9½ days. Post Office TAKES FOURTEEN DAYS ...

Looking over my shoulder, Waghorn indicated a column marked DELAYS ON THE ROAD.

missed an Austrian brig bound for Alexandria by three hours. Hired postchaise and pursued down the coast to Pesano. As reached the wind filled her sails and she slipped away.

Having reached Alexandria, Waghorn noted:

Mahmudia Canal silted up owing to late war. Switched to donkey for Rosetta and Nile mouth. Sandflies! Made it my business to attend personally to the navigation of my Nile boat, my object being to sound the river.

There followed notes and records of depth, currents, shifting sandbanks. Then – 'Grounded off Shallakan. Hired fast donkey. Arrived Cairo two days later.'

During the day the temperature was well over a hundred degrees. The desert sand burned our feet. It did not stop this extraordinary fellow making notes all the time of the condition of the track. Already he was talking of building a grand road from Cairo to Suez.

The dromedaries were all that Sheikh Ayd had promised and we made good progress, Waghorn eagerly anticipating finding the SS *Enterprise* waiting for us at Suez under his mate of the Burma war, Captain Johnston. She was a steam paddler, with auxiliary sail, 120 horse-power, 475 tons, Deptford-built. Lieutenant Waghorn had, it seemed, commanded a flotilla of gunboats in the Burma war: the feats of the *Enterprise* had convinced him that the future lay with steam.

'That idiot Freeling will tell you Waghorn's Overland Transit can never pay because coal is £20 a ton at Suez. That's just because it has had to come round the Cape. You can get it for a tenth of that in Alexandria. The answer's simple. Coal by canal and the Nile to Cairo, then by pack camels over the desert to Suez. Osman, warn your friend Sheikh Ayd we'll need hundreds of pack camels. Horses, too, for the coaches.'

Coach and horses over a hundred miles of waterless desert? No wonder the old-timers in the snug of Hill's Hotel were calling him 'Mad Tom'.

'Vans – built for the job – with way-stations every ten miles for refreshments and changing the horse teams,' Tom rattled on.

I began to wonder then just what I was letting myself in for.

'The Bedouin will rob your passengers blind,' I warned him.

'The Bedouin will be our camel-drivers and guides.'

I shook my head. 'There isn't a drop of good water along the entire track.'

'I shall bring it from the Nile, build underground tanks. Camels again!'

In the distance we could now see a single tree – the only tree encountered on our whole journey. As we drew nearer I saw that it was a-flutter with strips of cloth and rags, offerings to some holy man. I had forgotten that our road was on the route to Mecca. Another problem there.

A few miles outside the crumbling little port of Suez we reached the so-called wells of Suez. I bent to drink – and spat out in disgust. But we had made good time. As we came down into the port, Waghorn pulled out his chronometer and his Log to record our triumphal entry:

8 a.m. December – reach Suez. *Distance: 72 miles Conveyance:* dromedary . . . Time en route: 2 days 18 hours. Distance travelled from London: 2967 miles.

It was here that the final link in Waghorn's grand design for speeding up the world was to be completed. However, because of a sandbar at the head of the Gulf of Suez ships were obliged to drop anchor three miles out. Waghorn and I swept the azure waters from the highest point we could find, but no *Enterprise* lay at anchor. Nary a puff of smoke could we find.

Waghorn's confidence in his old pal Johnston remained unshaken.

'It'll be this nor'wester slowing him down, considering the load of coal he'll have to carry.'

We paid off the camel-men and moved into a hovel called the George Hotel, after its Coptic proprietor, only to pass three more days vainly sweeping the waters for a sight of the *Enterprise's* smoke-stack: it looked as if the East India Company mails had finally come to stop in this God-forsaken hole.

Tom could stand it no longer. 'I'm going after him, Osman. If I take a small boat down the middle of the Red Sea I'm bound to meet him.'

I was aghast. 'In an open boat – with the storms you get here!'

'Osman, I am an experienced pilot of the Bengal River Service.'

'The Red Sea is not the Hugli River.'

'I know Johnston won't let me down.'

All I could do was to fix up the best boat deal I could with the greedy Copt who was the Company's agent. It was for a forty-ton *zaruk*, with a high-raking prow, and a villainous-looking crew of seven, a pearl-fisher's boat, though it stank of fish and rancid dates. Two hundred dollars if the *Enterprise* showed up before el-Kosseir, 350 dollars if Waghorn had to go on to Jeddah.

Speaking little but Bengali, Waghorn was keen for me to join him, offering me a post with the 'Overland Transit' as if this mirage of his were already a reality. But I had already been too long away from home; and I had to make sure that all was well with my new harem, that Elena and Zobeida were still at peace.

'Join me and we shall make history together,' said Waghorn. I contented myself with quoting a remark of the Prophet from the *Hadith*: 'He who embarks *twice* upon the sea is truly an Infidel'; I had already exceeded my quota. Waghorn looked at me curiously. But it finished the argument.

I do not deny I had fear in my heart as I watched the iron box containing the Directors' mail go aboard that stinking boat with its cut-throat crew. Sadly I watched the *zaruk* streak off before a strong sou'wester, Waghorn at the tiller.

I stood there a long time as the arid peaks of Jebel Ataka flushed pink in the rising sun, and the boat's mast grew smaller and smaller, until at length it disappeared.

Tom's last words to me were: 'I'll be back for you. Hire those camels. You know what Bonaparte called this place: the most important country in the world. It will be, my dear fellow. Steam power will make it so. You'll see!'

Well, of course, I have.

On the way back to Cairo, away from Waghorn, I began to have second thoughts. Mirages are after all common in the desert. Bright, utterly convincing, they vanish as quickly and as completely as they appear. And for all Waghorn's confidence, the *Enterprise* had failed to show up.

News eventually filtered through: four months and twenty-one days after leaving London, the mails had reached Bombay. Not good enough to win the prizes on offer, but impressive – especially since it turned out that the *Enterprise* had blown her boilers and had never left India. The old hands in the Hill's Hotel were in their element, of course: 'What did I tell you! The fellow's as mad as a hatter!' They made *me* mad.

Steering by the sun by day and the stars by night, Tom had taken that stinking *zaruk* with its cut-throat crew all the way to Jeddah, where he'd picked up one of the Company's sailing-barges. On arrival in Bombay, he at once sat down to write to the Colonial Office in London, drawing their attention to his 'rapid and extraordinary' journey to Suez, which had convinced him that 'for every purpose of interest, politically and commercially, the Overland Route through Egypt was the one to follow and would *halve* the time the mails took between London and India'.

I knew then, just as I had known with Tom Keith and Giovanni Belzoni and Sheikh Ibrahim el-Shami, that Tom Waghorn was a man to follow. As my readers may have noticed, I am rather a man for Heroes; and incidentally, Mr Thomas Carlyle includes the Prophet amongst his.

Returning from Overland business one day, I found Omar waiting for me at the old house on the canal. The black urchin with the piebald poll who had mysteriously turned up here was now nearly twenty and an inch taller than I was, though with a suppleness he owed to his mother, and a confidence all his own. He brought good news: he had just been appointed government instructor in the cultivation of 'Jumel' long-staple cotton. He had been lucky. Alexis Jumel had died still a young man (no doubt of frustration), within four years of reaching Egypt, and Omar, you might say, had been one of his heirs. A rising man. I was proud of him.

After congratulations had been exchanged, and his new striped silk and cotton caftan admired, and all the sweet cakes and dates and *shureik*s he had brought from his village had been consumed, it became evident that his appointment was not the only thing he had to announce.

It was Zobeida, with her woman's instinct, who got it out of him. In his round of the villages the young dog had spotted a certain Samira at the well – 'fair as the moon', as they say, and what was more to the point, daughter of the village headman, the owner of many *feddan*s of well-watered Jumel. Omar had enterprisingly engaged the services of the local matchmaker to visit the Omda's harem, and, in short, I might shortly expect a visit from a certain Sheikh Abdel Aziz Hassuna to discuss the marriage contract.

The new decade seemed to be opening with prospects set fair for the House of Osman. Mohammed Ali was engaging former

French and English naval officers to captain his new warships. It was clear to me that the time was coming when he would need Egyptians, and I resolved to make sure that when it came, Sami, who was shaping well as my boat-boy, would be ready. As for Zobeida's second boy, Giovanni, I was getting good reports of him from the sheikh of the *kuttub* and – you may laugh – I was already planning a place for him at the new College of Kasserlyne which had French and Italian teachers and a library of 12,000 volumes.

The English Prime Minister, Lord Palmerston, might call Mohammed Ali 'a coffee-house waiter' if he liked, but the fact remained that if my sons had been born to some poor Highland crofter back home, what chances would they have had?

Elena's two boys, Ibrahim and Theo, were still toddlers of course, recipients of much affectionate attention from their half-sister, Aisha. It was Aisha's future that was really worrying me. She was a lively little girl, with something of her mother's delicacy of feature. But she could neither sew nor embroider, nor read and write, and never would by the looks of things.

I couldn't bear to think of that lively intelligence withering behind the curtains of the harem – *my* harem.

It was then I remembered that since Mohammed Ali had enforced the toleration of Christians, an American Mission had arrived in Cairo. It had recently started a class for Egyptian girls, to 'rescue them', you understand, from 'Mohammedan backward-ness and superstitions'. If Aisha had been a boy I would never have dared. But as she was a girl, and thus of little account, I thought there was a good chance that my eccentricity might be overlooked. I was after all a *hadji*, and did not the Prophet – peace be upon Him – say: 'The ink of the scholar is more holy than the blood of the martyr'? You see, I followed Louis's example: I kept my chapter and verse ever ready.

Unfortunately, I had forgotten one person in my calculations: Aisha's mother. It was not that Zobeida had religious objections to the American Mission, for the Abyssinians trace their church's origins back to St Mark's arrival in Egypt, and you can't get more Christian than that. No, what was terrifying Zobeida was that in crossing the streets on her way to the Mission class some envious woman might cast the Evil Eye upon her pretty little girl, causing her to wither and die. Tearfully, she quoted cases well known to the neighbours.

Some of my readers may wonder why I did not educate my wife out of such 'ignorant superstitions', but the truth is that, as a Highlander, I understood her fears all too well. I could recall a certain cow at home that was alleged to have dried up just because some old crone had eyed her.

So I could not find it in my heart to mock. Instead I got together with Zobeida to put together an impressive armoury of repellents, amulets, charms, talismans. A necklace of small cowrie shells to go around Aisha's neck; a piece of alum to be attached to her tasselled snood right in the face of the enemy so to speak, and, lastly, my old Seaforth collar badge which Zobeida had dug out of some drawer. The stag's antlers and the Mackenzie motto in its scroll appealed to her as of particular potency. I was sent to the *suk* to buy one of the small triangular lockets in which such defensive charms are carried on the bonnet.

At the last moment, when all was ready, the sheer horror of the thing overcame her, and I was obliged to move into Elena's bed for a week before she consented to take her daughter not only to school, but to a *foreign* school. However, after a few weeks, when it was clear that Aisha had not only come to no harm, but was actually blooming, Zobeida came to accept the arrangement and I was able to resume my trade as Osman Effendi, Dragoman to the Milords.

22   Runs in the Plaid

I remember that as a boy I used to stand by my aunt's loom at Skeabost, watching, fascinated, as the orderly pattern steadily built. Then, unnoticed, a thread might break, and I would look on in consternation as the regular, determined pattern ran amok.

That has happened in my own life more than most. And yet often enough I have been able to feel in my bones that, sooner or later, the pattern would be resumed, renewed.

As always, the reappearance was unannounced.

Even as I walked home through the Suk el-Zalat I was conscious of curious glances. As soon as I crossed my own threshold, I saw that something was badly amiss. Zobeida pulled a black *melaya* over her head and face and left for the *suk* to buy provisions. Elena, with Theo at her breast, looked up, unsmiling, reproach in her big eloquent eyes. 'Elle est en haut,' she said coldly, in her 'great lady' style, and looked down again.

Elle? *Elle*!

Suddenly I knew. I bounded up the stairs and sure enough, there she was, as large as life, Aisha prattling at her feet. At such moments one takes in details in a flash, and I saw that there was a gap on the top shelf of my library – my 'Edinburgh Cabinet Library', as Mr Alexander William Kinglake calls it. She had taken down her schoolgirl copy of Tom Paine's *Rights of Man* and was turning the pages, scanning the underlined passages from which she had started out to teach her drover-boy the Sasannach tongue.

Aisha leapt to her feet, and pulled me towards where Jeannie Macdonald was sitting, as if nothing had ever happened between us, in my chair.

'Ya abo!' she cried. 'Sitt Amerikani, my teach-er,' holding on proudly to the two English words.

The 'American Lady' patted her head. 'Al bravo alek. Well done!'

I saw that she had lost none of the extraordinary self-possession that had held me prisoner as a boy.

Aisha, I saw, basked in her approval.

'Your daughter, my dear Dhòmhnaill,' said the Sitt, 'is a very clever little girl. She could go far. She deserves better.'

Her hair was still jet black, as I remembered it, but was now done up in a teacherly bun. She spoke in the Gaelic, as if to challenge me, but there was a hard edge on those soft sibilants, an American edge I remembered from the speech of Jacoub Barthouw, young Legh's dragoman.

I struggled to summon the Gaelic, but it would not come. My eyes filled with tears. 'Ahlan – Ahlan wa Sahlen,' I mouthed, stupidly, to fill the void 'Zai sahetkum – welcome – and how is your health?'

'Allah be praised!' she retorted on the instant, and I did not know whether she was mocking me or not. That old confusion, echoing from another time, another place, still unresolved.

All at once my Gaelic came surging back, and with it the resentment at my 'betrayal', building up over the years like the Nile waters rising against our earth dam.

'So our handfasting up there on the shieling meant nothing to you? You were just amusing yourself with a simple-minded boy?'

The moment I said it, I knew it wasn't true.

She lowered her eyes and was silent. Those twenty-five years in America, I realised, must have changed her, perhaps in ways I would not understand. She was still a handsome woman. I would have recognised her at once from those dark, flashing eyes – the eyes that had bored into me beside the waulking table at my grandmother's house at Skeabost – and the same firm lips, turning up at the corners, that had held the *mòthan* flower for our farewell kiss just before I ran down to join the drove.

For how many years had I dreamt of this moment of reunion and renewal? I had seen her free-flowing hair and eyes looking down on me from the blank face of the Rock of Gibraltar. She had haunted my prisoner's dreams in the vast, damp cavern in the Citadel. And now, when at long last the nagging pain of that rejection was beginning to be lost in the commodious bosom of my Egyptian family, when the memories that meant 'home' had all but been eclipsed in the deep shadows of the Egyptian sun, she had come back to me.

The self-pity welled up in my throat. 'Gone without a word. Oh, yes – you left a book of Alexander Macdonald's poems in the Gaelic. Do you know how many days, weeks, months, I spent turning those pages, brooding over your underlinings until they seemed to rise up and mock me?'

Her head flew up. 'No, no!' and I saw her eyes fill with tears.

'What choice did I have? I was only a schoolgirl, Donald, however you may have seen me. Our passage money – all we had – was paid, the animals sold. The ship was waiting. My father gave me no choice. My sisters were watching me. Believe me Dhòmhnaill, mo chridhe.'

I had never seen her like this before. She faltered, and suddenly quoted that underlined verse in the poems of Alexander Macdonald she had left for me,

'A Dhòmhnaill, a ghràidh mo chridhe . . .
Oh, Donald, love of my heart,
I am sorrowful, heavy and weary
without you . . .

'Those words were true, Donald.'

In the Gaelic, as she spoke them, I could not deny it; they carried a ring of truth all their own.

Then she dug into her handbag and brought out a big silver coin, handing it to me.

Our fingers touched fleetingly. I turned the coin over in my palm. E PLURIBUS UNUM, 'Out of many, one' – as Donald MacCrimmon, Macleod's piper had explained when he gave it to me for carrying his pipes that day with my father at the Dun. I had given it to her on parting, as a pledge to our future in that Promised Land across the ocean where we were to build our lives together.

'All those years in America . . . I did not spend that dollar.'

I could not speak. I was overwhelmed – we both were – by the ache of life unlived.

'So what brings you back now?' I asked, realising even as I said it how false the question must sound.

She laughed – bitterly, it seemed to me. 'Oh Donald, it's a long, sad story, and I'm telling it too late.'

'Tell it all the same,' I insisted.

She was silent for a while, then sighed.

'They call the place Lafayetteville now, but it used to be Campelltown. You'll still hear the Gaelic in the streets – we're mostly Highlanders, even now. Some of our neighbours had sons and brothers in the Ross-shire Buffs, so I'd heard you'd enlisted. Then one day we got the terrible news – the massacre at Rosetta – the prisoners sold into slavery. It was terrible. We were thousands of miles away . . . Eventually we got the Scots newspapers with lists of killed, wounded and missing. I searched those lists so often that people thought I'd taken leave of my senses. I couldn't find your name. Our neighbour's son had been killed at el-Hamed, but *your* name wasn't in that long list.

'Then I heard some of the Scots "slaves" had been ransomed. I grabbed every Scots paper I could lay my hands on. I searched every line. By then I was teaching Latin at the Academy, and a master, Duncan Campbell, wanted to marry me. I felt sure by that time you must be dead. Duncan was a good man, so I did. I married him.'

I felt a sharp twist of jealousy: that some other man should have had what was by rights mine. I said nothing.

She sighed again. 'A few weeks after the wedding Duncan was killed, fighting alongside the Cherokee regiment and Andrew Jackson's men against the British – the war of 1812. The British burned the White House. They still thought they owned us.

'After that, I went over the mountains to teach John Ross's children at Ross's Landing in Tennessee . . .'

'John Ross?' I said, trying to keep the jealousy out of my voice.

'Chief of the Cherokee Indians. His grandfather was old John Macdonald, from Inverness.'

I was out of my depth. I recalled the stories my brother Dugald – the one captured at Yorktown – used to tell around the family peat fire of those American redskins and their devilish tricks.

What I did gather was that while staying in the house of this John Ross, teaching his children, Jeannie had come across a copy of young Legh's *Travels*, telling of his encountering a young Scots soldier, one of those taken prisoner at Rosetta in 1807, wearing Mameluke robes and serving in the camp of a Mameluke bey in Minya.

'I didn't know what a Mameluke was, but I looked it up in the Academy library.'

She shifted in her chair, replaced Tom Paine on the shelf, and looked at me earnestly.

'The author said the Mameluke soldier's name was Donald Donald and that he came from Inverness. I did not see how it could be you, but somehow I felt it was. I read that passage again and again, a Dhòmhnaill.'

Just how much her decision to come to Egypt had been due to this, how much to the death of her husband, and how much to the advertisement of a post for a teacher in the American Mission in Cairo, I could not then make out. But the fact was that she had been in Cairo for several months, inquiring for a former soldier of the Ross-shire Buffs and failing to find any trace of me. And now that she had found me it had been through the merest accident – if indeed it could be considered an accident.

Jeannie Macdonald reached out and beckoned Aisha to her. She opened the small amulet case still fixed to her hair and drew out my Seaforth collar badge. Holding it in her hand, she read the inscription below the antlers: *Cuidich an Rìgh* in the Gaelic.

'I hadn't forgotten the Mackenzie motto.'

'To ward off the Evil Eye,' I explained, embarrassed. I didn't tell her it was Aisha's mother's price for allowing her to attend the Mission class.

'I know,' she said, 'just the sort of superstition we are trying to root out in my class. All this time I have been looking for Donald Macleod, an upstanding Highlandman – and now what do I find? A superstitious Mohammedan with a turban, a harem and a bright daughter, hidden away under the veil of ignorance. How *could* you, a Dhòmhnaill?'

She was the same old Jeannie, spoiling for a fight.

'The Koran allows four wives – provided they are treated equally,' I parroted, realising immediately how foolish it must sound to her.

'Talak, talak, talak,' she retorted. 'Three times, and you've divorced the poor creatures. Don't talk to me, Donald, I've seen it. I've seen it a hundred times.'

No use arguing – I've found that over the years as a dragoman. They're still fighting the Crusades. The Prophet got rid of our Days of Ignorance, but they cherish theirs. So no use my pointing out to her that the Koran makes wives' property their own, whereas in England their husbands take all, even now. No, we're all benighted 'fatalists', 'dirty Arabs', even though we wash five times a day before prayers, and they bathe once a week, if that.

I did try, though. I told her how the great brotherhood of Islam, with its obligatory tax for the poor, had sustained me through the years of servitude; how they'd accepted me without question; how rich and poor stood shoulder to shoulder at prayer in the mosques; how there were no Revd Macaskills, no sniffy Elders, since *all* who entered the house of Islam were of the Elect under Allah, the One and Only.

That at least was what I tried to tell her. I think I even said that in Islam I had found the sort of equality foreshadowed by Tom Paine in the book from which, all those years ago, she had begun to teach me English.

She laughed bitterly. 'How naïve I was then!'

'So you didn't find the Equality of Man you told me we were going to find in America?'

She snorted. 'You should ask John Ross – if he's still alive. John Ross, "White Bird", Chief of the Cherokees, one of the Five Civilised Tribes – the original Americans.'

Clearly there was much more to tell if we were ever to close the gulf the years had opened up between us. But how – and where – could we? For if Allah had at last brought us together again it was, it seemed, only to separate us again. Already there was turmoil in my once peaceful harem. Zobeida would by now have convinced herself that her worst fears had come to pass: the foreign woman had put the Eye on her beautiful daughter. Elena would be insanely jealous of the Sitt Amerikani's unveiled freedom. The *suk*, I knew, would buzz with scandalised whispers about the shameless and half-naked, unveiled foreign woman seen in Hadji Osman's *selamlik*.

When I hinted at some of these problems, Jeannie got up, decisive as ever. 'Poor Donald,' she said. 'You have made your bed, now you must lie on it.'

Head high, defiantly unveiled, the 'American lady' descended the rickety stairs and made her way back to the Mission.

I began to wonder whether I could have dreamed the whole thing; it would not be the first of such visitations. But the sulks of the harem and the stares in the *suk* told me otherwise. In my room, which had once been Burckhardt's, the chair where she had sat seemed conspicuously, achingly empty. There wasn't a day when I was not acutely aware of her presence not more than two miles away, at the Mission's refectory table or lying at night in her narrow bed. Aisha no longer formed a link between us since Zobeida absolutely refused to allow her to attend the class any more.

Looking back now, a few weeks after the Grand Opening, I recall the remarks of Monsignor Bauer, the Empress's confessor, who spoke of the imminent 'consummation of the marriage of East and West'. I cannot repress a wry smile.

With Aisha pining for her teacher, Elena still sulking, and Zobeida possessed by her ridiculous fears about the Evil Eye cast on her daughter, my position in the house on the canal was not an enviable one. The Mission, with little or no chance of making converts from Islam, fastened on the Copts and increasingly saw the surrounding Moslem masses as agents of the Devil. Ludicrous when you know how much Bible and Koran have in common. You might say that Jeannie and I were the victims of this situation, for I felt certain that once over the first shock, poor girl, she was as eager as I was to recover what had once lain between us. Yet I knew that, of all people, a *renegado* like myself, flaunting the cloven hoof, so to speak, would be the least welcome of visitors to the Mission.

It was Jeannie who at last found the way out of this wilderness. It was brilliant, yet laughably simple. Osman Effendi was a much-respected dragoman, was he not, possessor of shining testimonials from the aristocracy of England? What could be more natural than that an American lady, recently arrived in Egypt, should engage his services?

And so it came about that between the Virgin's Tree at Matariya and the Step Pyramid at Sakkara, the long and curious colloquy of Donald Macleod, the drover-boy from Skye and Jeannie Macdonald, the tacksman's daughter, was, after an interval of twenty-five years, resumed.

At the foot of the Virgin's Tree, where I told my usual tale – though she briskly pronounced this 'relic' a fake – I had from her own lips the true story of what, in my calf-love passion, I had seen as her betrayal. Alasdair Macdonald and his family had sailed from Fort William with three hundred other Highland emigrants, crammed for three weeks in the stinking hold of the *Carolina Packet*, her rigging rotten and the water blue from the indigo which had once filled the casks.

'All we had between us was two small sacks of potatoes and five bolls of oatmeal. My mother was sick half the time; twelve people died and were thrown overboard.'

After that, how could I complain of my sufferings under Baxter at Fort George?

Certainly, once the Macdonalds had staggered ashore at Wilmington, near the mouth of the Fear river, things had looked up.

'My Uncle Alan was embracing my father, whom he had not seen for fifty years. Alan was ten when he was taken at Culloden and "lotted" for transportation to Virginia. There he heard of two cousins at a place called Cross Creek in North Carolina and managed to join them. He said, "I found myself at home again. There were settlements of Highlanders for mile after mile up and down the Fear river, and their numbers grew as the Clearances started up . . ."

'Uncle Alan kept adding to his land as Cross Creek grew into Campelltown and then became Fayetteville. He kept writing home, begging my father to come out and join him. And now, at last, there he was, with his wife and four strapping girls.'

My hopes rose. The Highland plaid that had lain beneath us up on the shieling was tattered and worn thin. But perhaps enough of the pattern was discernible. I hired the finest lady's donkey I could find, and with a boy to hold the bridle, I conducted the Sitt Amerikani over Cairo's historic Citadel. I showed her the barrack dungeon where the Ross-shire Buffs had lain in chains, and the audience chamber in the palace where I had first set eyes on Mohammed Ali. I showed her the massive gates of the Bab el-Azab which had been shut on the Mamelukes that day. And, from force of habit – for this is an item in the dragoman's repertoire that always goes down well – I added that only one man escaped, and I pointed to the place where Emin Bey had leapt the wall on his horse.

Then I told her that in truth two men had escaped, and the second one was named Osman, but that this was for her ears alone, because why spoil so good a story? Then I showed her the dark blood-stains from that day on the great stones, set in the wall, they say, by Salah el-Din's Christian prisoners after the Third Crusade.

'All this killing! All this blood!' she said. 'Culloden . . . Trumpan Church . . . Moore's Creek . . .' her voice faltered, 'Horseshoe Bend . . .'

'Horseshoe Bend?' It meant nothing to me.

'Duncan was killed at Horseshoe Bend. Duncan Campbell, my husband. We had been married for two weeks.'

Her eyes had filled with tears.

'You see, Donald, Duncan was a true American. When the British Navy started stopping and searching our ships in 1812 he couldn't stomach it. Then Andrew Jackson issued his call to arms.' She still had it by heart: ' "Who are we? Are we the slaves of George III? No, we are the freeborn sons of America, the only people who possess rights, liberties, property they can call their own . . ." '

'Duncan threw in his teaching post to join Jackson's Volunteers – Andrew Jackson was a North Carolina man, you understand.'

All this was news to me, a long way from the idyllic scenes painted in the emigrant prospectuses we had pored over together up on the shieling.

It would have been a year or more after the blood-bath in the Citadel that Duncan Campbell died on the Tallapoosa River, an Indian arrow through his heart.

'An *Indian* arrow?'

'It was an Upper Creek arrow. Duncan was fighting alongside the Cherokees under their Chief, John Ross. The North Carolina Cherokees took the side of the Americans. Waterford's Upper Creek took the British bribes and fought *for* them.'

'Waterford?'

'The son of old Lachlan McGillvray who married a Creek

beauty. But the *Lower* Creeks under William Macintosh sided with the Americans.'

My mind reeled. So the American Indian clans had Scots chiefs and, as at home, the British played their old game of 'divide and rule'.

'And this John Ross?' Suspicion in my voice again.

'His grandfather was old John Macdonald, who emigrated from Inverness and started up as an Indian trader. The Americans called the boy "Little John" and the Cherokees "White Bird".'

The scattering of the clans seemed to have gone further than even I had imagined. I thought of Tom Keith, late Deputy Governor of the holy city of Medina, and of his namesake and hero, who had been Catherine the Great's favourite general – and now here were Red Indian chiefs named Mackintosh and Ross.

I needed space. I took her up to the wide platform atop the Citadel with its magnificent views of Cairo, threaded and nourished by the Nile.

My horizons widened that day. I no longer resented Duncan Campbell, the man who had taken the place which should have been mine, and who now lay deep in the swirling waters of the Tallapoosa river, a stone on his chest to stop the Upper Creeks taking his scalp.

Next day was to be devoted to the tombs of the Mameluke beys, but neither of us just then could pretend much interest in those 'masterpieces of Saracenic art'. The visit was postponed. She was desperate now to pour out the whole story of how she had become committed to John Ross and the Cherokee cause, and all the grief their betrayal had brought her. She knew, I guess, that she had found an understanding audience at last.

'There were many notables at my Uncle Alan's funeral. I remarked a stocky young man in his best dark suit standing outside the circle of mourners, watching me. Just as I was leaving the church with my sister Isobel [yes, I remembered Isobel], who had married a planter down near the mouth of the Fear river, he hurried over.

' "Mrs Campbell," he said, "I knew your husband. I fought beside him at Horseshoe Bend. Duncan was a brave man, a true American . . ." Then he introduced himself: John Ross, Chief of the Cherokees, the biggest of the Five Civilised Tribes.

'I knew something of his story, of course. His father, Daniel Ross, from Sutherland, had brought him up in the old Scots way, engaging tutors for the boy. But his mother, Quatie, was half Cherokee. "Little John" could have gone either way. But when his mother's tribe invited him to be their Chief, he did not hesitate. He cherished great ambitions for the Cherokee Nation. He wanted to give them a Constitution like America's, their own law courts, newspapers, schools . . .'

I was guiding her up the steps of Beybars's mosque-tomb. She stopped suddenly.

'Do you know what John Ross said to me, Donald? He said: "Mrs Campbell: you are a clever woman, a teacher, and, what is more, a Scottish teacher. The Cherokee Nation needs you. My children need you. I beg you to come and teach us. Remember, Macdonald blood runs in my veins. My maternal grandfather was from Inverness." '

We were attracting attention as we stood stock-still on the steps of the great mosque-tomb, so I guided her into the polished marble interior. It was cool in there.

'How could I refuse him, Donald?' There was a tremor in her voice. She was back in Campelltown, North Carolina.

Over her mother's protestations, she had thrown up her post at the Academy, loaded her books and clothes onto a six-horse waggon that lumbered west over the mountain ridges, and travelled to Ross's Landing in the Tennessee River valley.

'That was a wonderful time,' she said. 'The winters were mild and the springs were a blaze of flowers and there were blue hills all around us and great trees and clear rushing streams. A new school was built on old Macdonald's land and the Moravian mission joined us, and the Cherokee children were lively and keen to learn, and John Ross's house was always full of books and an old man, a cripple, devised an alphabet for the Cherokee language so that the people could send each other letters – "talking leaves" they called them – and I was able to teach the children to write out the Declaration of Independence in their own language.'

Inside, the white marble of the majestic tomb with its medallions and exquisitely incised Koranic texts reflected a merciless perfection. She was trying to suppress her sobs.

'Oh, what a fool I was! Teaching them about all men being equal and their "inalienable rights". I should have warned Little

John that all those treaties guaranteeing the Cherokee Nation its ancestral lands "as long as the grass grows and the water flows" were not worth the paper they were written on. What a fool I was! I didn't realise how evil men can be, Donald . . .'

I put my hand over hers on the marble.

'No, you weren't. Not a fool.'

'I should have known. We'd seen it all before – at home, I mean. I was so proud when Little John – White Bird – published his Constitution for the Nation. Any white American who married into the tribe could enjoy full rights . . .'

I was beginning to get some inkling of the depth and bitterness of her personal tragedy in this Promised Land.

The same Andrew Jackson who had welcomed John Ross and his Cherokee regiment to fight alongside him at Horseshoe Bend, becoming President of the United States, found them to be 'savages' – just as back home the English found the Highlanders who had won their battles for them to be 'savages' and their bagpipes intruments of war. The state of Georgia declared the Cherokee Constitution to be 'presumptuous and illegal'. Henceforth, in Georgia courts no Indian could bear witness against an 'American', which meant that the Cherokees could be stripped of their farms with impunity. Then, in 1828, President Jackson hurried through the Indian Removal Bill.*

She said: 'Little John could not believe it. Had he not christened his eldest son George Washington Ross? He got up a petition, put on his top hat, and left for Washington. Do you know what Jackson told him, Donald? "You're too damned late, Mr Ross." '

---

* I learned from my mother that the Cherokees resisted longer than other Indians, but were finally expelled beyond the Mississippi in 1838, John Ross marching with them. A quarter perished on the long trail west, Ross's wife among them. – *F.M.*

23   The Horns of Hathor

After the revelations at Beybars's tomb, I lost the resentments I had built up over my years of captivity. The betrayal she had suffered had been more bitter, more extensive, than my own. She had fled to Egypt, seeking hope and renewal, only to find that the drover-boy of fond memory had changed into a robed and bearded 'Mahometan' with, horror of horrors, a 'harem'.

History had left its cruel imprint on both our lives. Could we ever defy it, draw a line under the past, start again?

It was the 27th day of Ramadan, just before the Great Festival, the 'Night of Power' when the Holy Koran had been passed down to the Prophet – peace be upon him – and it is said that on that night the gates of Heaven stand open and all prayers are sure of success.

You may be certain that I took full advantage of such an opportunity. The mosques were ablaze with light that night, and as I threaded my way through the thronged worshippers I paused to add two supplementary prayers: that peace return to my harem and that Thomas Waghorn reappear at last, complete with his Greenwich chronometer, bringing with him hope for the future of Osman Effendi and the land of the Pharaohs.

But when, despite my fervent prayer, Jeannie Macdonald did not seek me out, I must confess I fell into a pitiful state of confusion, reminiscent, I'm afraid, of my calf-love turmoil back home at the age of fourteen. Now, as then, I desperately needed someone to confide in. But who would believe so bizarre a tale?

Then I thought of that wise old Turk in the carpet bazaar of the Khan el-Khalili who had kept my runaway son Omar safe for me. His discretion was absolute, his experience unbounded. I visited him on the pretext of seeking his advice on buying new dresses for Elena and Zobeida for the Great Festival.

Then I broached the subject of the American Lady, my 'hand-fasted bride' back in the Highlands of Scotland. I realised that to Ahmed Muhtar it must sound like a tale from the *Thousand and One Nights*, but he listened intently, nodding his head from time to time.

He mused for a while, asked some tactful questions, and finally proposed that I resume my dragoman role, no longer in the odiferous clamour of Cairo, but in a well-chosen *dahabiya* on the Upper Nile.

The *dahabiya* had red plush cushions, its cabin windows were newly curtained and I made sure it had been sunk in the river for three days to get rid of any insects or mice or rats. But as we skimmed before the north wind, past the Pyramids and that bright narrow patchwork of cultivated fields between the river and the desert, all she could talk of was the Cherokees' well-tended villages, their log cabins and gardens, and fine crops of Indian corn and tobacco, squashes and beans and cotton. We sailed past a line of young Egyptian women, water-jars poised on their heads – but all she could see was the 'disgusting', tumbledown mud villages, their roofs disappearing under piles of maize-stalks and full-bellied bean storage jars. She was, after all, a tacksman's daughter, so I did not remind her that an English army officer once described our 'black-houses' at home as 'smoking dunghills'. I let her talk, and waited for the Nile and the Pharaohs to do their work. There is an impressive inevitability about this land and this great river. The prevailing north wind carries the boats upriver, filling their sails. The Nile current, the sheer weight of water pouring out of the Ethiopian mountains, carries the boats downstream: the Ancient Egyptians' hieroglyph for 'going south' is a boat *with* a sail, the hieroglyph for 'going north' is the same boat *without* the sail.

There are times, though, when the wind drops and the boat is becalmed, and the *reis* has to tack for hours or the sailors sweat at the poles or take the tow-rope over their shoulders, jump in and pull. On such occasions they fall back on the national motto – *Malish*: Nevermind.

For what is the use of minding? *Malish! Malish! Malish!* A most serviceable word in this – and indeed any – land. (If only she could learn it!)

When we tied up for the night, the Sitt, drawing the curtains, slept on the narrow berth in the cabin. Osman Effendi, the well-known dragoman, slept on the deck, on an old plaid that had somehow survived from his days with the Ross-shire Buffs.

An extraordinary charade, the bitter-sweet dregs. Who would have believed two honest Highlanders could come to such a pass? As I look back now I have to laugh – to laugh, as somebody said, for fear of weeping.

Near the village of Hau, where the Nile swings eastwards towards Kena, an almighty clamour from another boat brought the Sitt from her cabin. My boy Sami, whom I had taken along as chaperone for appearances' sake, joined in the shouting: 'Sheikh Selim! Sheikh Selim!'

Jeannie pointed to the ragged figure squatting on the bank, a bundle of skin and bone. 'Who is he?'

'A *santon* – a famous holy man.'

The sailors were pitching coins into a long-handled net pushed out from the bank.

'What does he do?'

'Nothing.'

Another example of 'Mohammedan superstition' – of course! I could have told her that, on the contrary, holy men were rank heresy. I could have quoted Sura 4: 'Allah pardoneth not that partners be ascribed to him.'

But I didn't. I was relying now on the Pharaohs, that entering that bright, hard-edged, sidelong world would work its usual magic.

We tied up at Dendera. I hired donkeys and we rode across a bright carpet of growing crops to the Temple of Hathor. A villager, a giant with the broad shoulders of the tomb paintings, strode by, pacing himself with the inevitable *nabbut*, the long, stout staff of the Southland.

He greeted us with grave courtesy. 'Naharak said!'

'What did he say?'

'May your day be happy.'

She smiled. Her mood had changed.

And then the immensity and solitary splendour of the great temple rose before us, set against the bleak mountain wall that edges the Libyan desert.

We left our donkeys with the donkey-boy and walked together across the great temple courtyard. I took her arm and steered her through the loose rocks towards the great hypostyle entrance hall with its forest of massive stone columns.

And up the steps.

It takes a minute or two for the eyes to adjust. In the dimness she gripped my arm hard. She was staring up at the heads of the great columns. On its four sides each bore in relief the face of a woman with great oval black-lined eyes, and a wig, curled down on each side.

She whispered, awestruck, half to herself. 'But the ears – they are cow's ears. She has cow's ears, Donald!'

'She is Hathor, goddess of love, and also of music, dancing and joy, the daughter of Ra, the sun god, and mother of the Pharaoh. This is her temple. At Deir el-Bahari I will show you Hathor in the body of a cow, suckling the infant Pharaoh. The gods and goddesses of Ancient Egypt take many forms.'

I watched her startled eyes running from one to other of the twenty-four columns. From the capital of each, soft cow's eyes gazed through the stone forest to the green sunlit plain beyond.

I had spent weeks here with the milord Hay and his artists copying the hieroglyphs and reliefs and paintings that covered every inch of the walls, as they detailed the sacred rites attending the New Year birthday of Hathor when she ascends in procession to the roof of her temple to receive the first rays of the rising sun. I was well qualified to impress this very special client.

I led her now to the third column in the north-east corner of the temple's first hall, which carried a full-length portrait of Hathor, upright, in human form, left breast protruding, *ankh* gripped in her right hand, and, rising from her head, a pair of long, outward-curving horns, holding the sun-disc between them.

What I saw, as always here, was a great mass of black cattle stirring the dust, those long, curving horns swaying from side to side as the beasts flowed down through the glens and over the mountains to the Falkirk Tryst.

I hoped the magic would work for her, too, vaulting the years. But she was silent. Then, a thin shaft of light, full of dust motes, shot through the gloom, and fell on the horns of Hathor, which seemed to sway. She sighed – and I knew she had the same thought.

'You remember a kyloe heifer with a Mungo's knot for good luck on her tail?'

'Donald, my dear, it is Egypt we are in, not the Braes of Lochaber.'

It had the finality of the sea-gate clanging shut at the Dun.

I stuck grimly to my dragoman routine. I conducted the American lady through the Hall of Appearances and the Hall of Offerings and on to the double-doored Sanctuary where, once a year, on her festival day, the Pharaoh was permitted to knock and, after declaring his purity, to be admitted as Hathor was readied to salute her father, the sun god, on the roof.

Like the Pharaoh, *I* too had knocked on the double-doors, but I had not been admitted: *I* could not declare my purity.

'Look up,' I said. Across the ceiling, and extending down three walls of the chamber, the sky goddess, Nut, arched her slender, naked body, stretching her long arms, bracing her long legs against the floor – between the east and the west horizons – supporting the firmament.

As ever, a sharp intake of breath.

'You will see,' I intoned in my best dragoman voice, 'that the goddess Nut swallows the sun's disc through her mouth at sunset, and that it passes slowly through her body during the night to emerge from her womb at dawn to shine on the head of Hathor.'

I took her arm and guided her along the route of the great procession of priests and gods that would begin here in the dead of night, slowly ascending the long stone staircase, bearing the goddess in her shrine to her rendezvous.

She was silent.

I persisted with my routine. Pointing out the small kiosk on the north-west corner of the roof where the statue of Hathor, the Goddess of Love, was placed to receive the benediction of Ra, her father, as his first rays touched her at dawn.

We lingered a long time on the temple roof, standing together yet apart, not touching, staring out over that many-coloured carpet of luxuriant crops, magically touched by the sun god's dying rays, quickened by mirror-glass gleams from the many irrigation channels. A renewal of the spirit was what I, too, stood in need of – and this woman from America had the power to offer it if she chose. Boy and girl were now man and woman, with much bitter experience behind them. For me, at least, the memory of that night up there on the shieling with Tom Paine and Jeannie Macdonald was as sharp, as consuming, as ever.

'We were handfasted,' I heard myself muttering.

She was startled. 'Oh, Dhòmhnaill,' she said softly, 'you are the same innocent now as you were at fourteen. Did you not know that handfasting is for a year and a day?'

'Unless there is a child,' I said.

'Donald, there was no child . . . I was a schoolgirl.'

'There could have been – there could be.'

She turned away quickly. 'Donald, my dear, you have two wives already.'

I felt her slipping away from me. I panicked. 'The Koran permits four wives,' I said, stupidly, ' "provided they are treated equally".'

She laughed out loud. 'So you would have me equal with Aisha's mother who believes in the Evil Eye and won't let the girl go to school?'

She started off down the temple staircase to the ground floor. 'Donald, my dear Donald,' she called over her shoulder, 'you are a hadji, a much-respected family man. I am the Sitt Amerikani. Don't you see there is no place for us to stand together?'

I caught up with her on the bottom step. 'So we must *make* a place. We must make a child, a Highlandman – *he* will be our place. A Highland boy, no half-and-half, no renegado like his father.'

We had reached the place where the donkeys were waiting for us. She laid a gentle hand on my arm. 'Dhòmhnaill, mo chridhe – whether you are Osman or Donald – Donald the Scotsman – you are no renegade.'

Across the fields a *sakiya* squealed agonisingly as the ox plodded out its circles, turning the great cogged water-wheel the way its kind had turned since the days of the Pharaohs.

'On the contrary,' I said. 'It was you, Jeannie Macdonald, who made me a renegade the first time I set eyes on you at my aunts' waulking party, when you accused the Macleods of betraying the Prince.'

Ridiculous, of course, but this time she did not laugh.

*

A grin splitting his dark face from ear to ear, my son Sami clambered up the Nile bank to help the Sitt back on board the boat.

Arab boys of his age are all too knowing, so despite the turmoil in my head, I was at pains to hold my dignified dragoman pose, bowing the lady into her cabin. I sternly refused the *reis*'s plea to provision at Kena: there are far too many dancing-girls at that place, and who knows, one of them might imagine she recognised a certain patron. Also, despite everything, I had an uncanny feeling that somehow, between Kena and Luxor, our handfasting might be reborn. In the meantime I drew the Lady's attention to the domes and crosses and towers of the Coptic churches and convents on either side of the Nile. Out of force of habit, as we sailed past a palm-fringed village, I indicated a half-naked fellah working a *shaduf*, dipping and swivelling the long bucket and pole, the labour of eternity, to lift a little water from the stream onto his sun-baked earth. The sight of this primitive device generally produces exclamations of wonder from my clients. But Jeannie's attention seemed to have wandered to the old Mackenzie plaid from my Ross-shire Buffs days, which I had folded neatly and laid on one of the berths in the cabin.

When she saw that I had observed her, she lowered her head like the virgin bride at Omar's wedding.

My pulse was pounding. I reached out to her. She leapt back, raising a warning finger, nodding towards the sailors. The sails had lost their swelling glory and were suddenly flaccid. We had reached the point, seven miles below Luxor, where the Nile goes into a deep swing westward, and our sailors had unhooked the oars to pull us round into whatever wind or current there was to catch. She was right, of course: they passed the cabin window.

Pulling hard together to bring the boat round, they broke into an Arab boat-song, matching their strokes to its rhythm, the *reis* at the tiller singing the first line, the rowers roaring the refrain:

> My sons you are men, row away swiftly . . .
> *God and Mohammed!*
> The wind is against us, but God is for us
> *God and Mohammed!*
> The smooth river runs swiftly
> *God and Mohammed!*

Row on my sons, the supper is cooking
God and Mohammed!

In the course of my dragoman's duties I had heard such songs times without number, but with Jeannie Macdonald beside me, the boat-song opened the flood-gates of memory: I was Dhòmhnaill Ban again, youngest son of Ruairidh Og by his second wife, Mary Beaton, grandson of Rory Macleod, the Dunvegan ferryman, kinsman of Donald Macleod, the Prince's steersman, who had spurned the £30,000 offered by Cumberland's officers if he would betray Charles Stewart's hiding-place.

The sailors' song had worked the same magic for Jeannie, for slowly, *sotto voce*, she began to recite, then to hum, then sing 'Gàir na Mara' – 'The Roar of the Sea' – a boat-song of Skye.

Even now her voice had not lost its crystal clarity, that uncanny poignancy:

For the Isles my heart is weary . . . E – o – ro!
Dear loved island sounds I'm hearing . . . ho – ro!
Would I might see your ee – o – ho!

(I apologise for the translation but Gaelic, like Arabic a language of poets, resists the clodhopper tongue.)

As she sang on softly – for my ears alone – sometimes with a faint hesitation over a word, the Gaelic ascending mysteriously into the cloudless Egyptian sky seemed to form over our heads a sort of canopy, enclosing us in the old Highland world, although to the outside eye we were still two yards apart, Osman Effendi, the well-known dragoman, and Sitt Amerikani, the missionary lady.

The sailors' song had finished. They had brought the boat round, and the great white wings swelled again and we glided off on the familiar course for Luxor.

The constraint between us had lifted. We were at home on the Nile under the sun god's fiery sway, and at home with each other.

By the time we moored under the old sycamore-tree on the West bank, the sun god Ra was sliding down into the mouth of Nut, the sky goddess. My plan to show my 'client' the wonders of 'Belzoni's Tomb' would have to be postponed. Over on the east bank, across the golden river, the setting sun illuminated the

tumbled towers of Karnak; to the west it silhouetted the implac-
able cliffs in which the Pharaohs sought immortality deep in their
secret tombs.

Across the fields from Kurna – the village of the tomb-robbers
– drifted the faint, compulsive throb of a *darabukka*, broken by
the thin wavering shrill of a *nai*. Those genial rascals – who
had worked for Giovanni Belzoni when we moved the Young
Memnon's head – were evidently having a party, a circumcision
or perhaps a betrothal. Our sailors heard the sounds, and begged
to go. I let them plead for a while, then threw up my hands in
resignation. Our cook petitioned to visit his wife in a village near
Luxor, and, hearing this, our *reis* developed an urgent need to go
over to buy provisions. I let them all go, and sent Sami along to
help the *reis*.

Our boat moved gently in the deepening shade of the sycamore.
It was eerie: we were alone at last, Macleod and Macdonald, in
the land of Pharaohs. She had told me much, but there was still
much to tell.

With its usual curtain-dropping swiftness, the sun sank below
the dark western rock cliff sending many-hued shafts of light
fanning out over the rim of the earth. Words failing, I fell back
on my old dragoman formula: 'Hathor, the goddess of love, is
also known as "The Lady of the Sycamore", and sometimes wears
a sycamore leaf on her forehead below the horns.'

She laughed out loud. 'Oh Dhòmhnaill, Dhòmhnaill Macleod
you have not changed, despite your harem!' She reached up and
before I could hinder her was unwinding my turban. I leapt back
in dismay. In the world in which I now live, a man's turban is his
dignity; very nearly him. A Turk swears by his turban and when
he retires at night enthrones it on a special chair.

And now my turban, my dignity, lay in a shapeless heap on the
floor.

She was staring at my cropped flaxen hair.

'Now I know you, Donald Ban,' she said, reaching out, touching
my face where under the sun's burnish a boyhood freckle or two
was faintly discernible.

Her joy was my confusion: over the years Arab custom had
rooted deeply. I do not know what I might have done had she
not at that moment put a hand to her head, letting loose all that
lustrous raven-black hair. It came rippling down her back and

once again I found myself tremulous on the same brink where I had lain on the warm mud floor of the shieling hut on a Scottish mountain meadow. Only one thing was absent: the aura of Sin. In the Nile's luxuriant garden, it was the serpent who slunk away.

It was she, practical as ever, who resolved my remaining confusions, picking up my folded plaid, spreading it on the larger berth, calmly smoothing the dark green Mackenzie tartan – with the gash near a corner where the Turkish horseman's scimitar had caught me on that terrible day at el-Hamed.

'Come, Dhòmhnaill!'

Naked together, man and woman, woman and man, lovers reunited, on the old Ross-shire Buffs soldier's plaid we invoked the god Min's gift and the goddess Hathor's blessing and received them both in abundance.

Afterwards, bodies sated, memories released, the ugliness of the past washed away as the Nile moved gently beneath us, we talked long and freely, drawing together the threads of the gashed plaid until, as the night wore on and, more tenderly, our lovemaking resumed, it seemed that Macleod and Macdonald had opened up a whole new continent, neither of West or East, but their own.

The moon was caressing our narrow cabin with its soft clear light when we rose at last and dressed and climbed out onto the bank. For a while we stood there, side by side, saying nothing, rejoicing in the confident brush-strokes the Egyptian moon applied to the fields of ripening *durra*, the bright emerald *bersim*, the dark green beans, the earth awaiting the seed.

'Ban-rìgh na h-Oidhche,' whispered Jeannie, 'the Queen of the Night.' The old Gaelic phrase stirred memories of my mother, unwilling to start our cutting of the peat until the moon was on the wane.

The dawn can be chilly. I ran back to the boat for the old plaid and threw it over her shoulders, then led her by the path across the fields, between the irrigation ditches, towards the spot on the desert's edge where the twin 'Colossi of Memnon' – Tama and Shama, as the fellahin call them – sit on their stone thrones, straight-backed, side by side, great forearms ruler-straight along their thighs.

They were as majestically oblivious of us as they were of each other. The jackals howled, as ever, in the denuded mountains behind. On the other side of the Nile the first faint rays of the sun, having passed through her slim body, emerged from the vulva of the goddess Nut, awakening the non-monstrous ruins of Karnak.

I took her over to the northernmost colossus and showed her the many Greek and Latin names and 'messages' which countless generations of Roman and Greek travellers had carved on those great feet and legs, aping schoolboys or aping the Pharaohs in their quest for immortality.

'They came to hear him speak. They say he gives tongue at dawn when the first rays of the rising sun touches his lips.'

Fifty feet above our heads, craning our necks, we saw the sun tap lightly on that twenty-four-feet-wide shoulder. Jeannie leaned over to put her ear against the fissure in the gigantic foot from which the voice was said to issue.

We waited, watching the sun's pointer moving slowly up the battered chin before gliding over the lips. We waited long. But no sound came.

A phrase from the Revd Macaskill's Bible class, then vaguely exciting, came spinning up out of the deep well of memory. 'And Adam *knew* Eve, his wife.' Genesis, chapter one. I saw now that the translator's word was exact. 'And Donald *knew* Jeannie, his wife.'

This would be a different order of things, a firm foundation, not built on the shifting sands of Egypt.

Yet of course she was *not* my wife. Again I implored her to marry me, her fellow Highlander. Why otherwise had she come here, seeking me out? Why had Allah directed my daughter to reveal me to her?

She refused. She always refused. 'I'm not harem, Donald. I am Jeannie Macdonald, daughter of Alasdair Macdonald and Jean Macrae. I am who I am.'

There were three more words in that sentence from Genesis that had not failed to register on my memory: 'And Adam knew Eve, his wife, and she conceived.'

A short time after Osman Effendi, the well-known dragoman, had delivered his American client back to her post in Cairo, he was engaged again by milord Hay and his group of artists. It was a long engagement. Hay was thorough; he spent nine years scrutinising dead Pharaohs.

I got back to Cairo to find Jeannie Macdonald about to be expelled in disgrace from her Mission lodgings. Her pregnancy had become visible to a few and would soon be visible to all, and, worse, she had refused to admit her guilt and take her place on the penitent seat. There was a mighty clishmaclaver in Christian circles, with much dwelling on the moral damage her sin had inflicted on the unfortunate girls she had been engaged to 'rescue'.

I recalled my second house on the canal, which had lain empty since Elena, unaccountably, had refused to occupy it. Allah's intention in causing me to buy it was now crystal clear, and I offered it to Jeannie Macdonald. I knew she would deplore the 'sordid' surroundings, but she gritted her teeth and moved in. It would only be temporary, I promised her.

Then a thought struck her, and she laughed out loud. 'I will be your concubine – your American concubine. They tell me Mohammed Ali has eight hundred. You shall have one.'

10 a.m., 18 November 1869, at the Miriam Station aboard SS Mohammed Ali

We have left the *Latif* clear behind us at last – in fact, if not in mind. Shipshape again and dressed overall, she lies securely moored in the Ferdane siding, ready to salute the yachts of the crowned heads as they steam southwards along the Canal from sea to sea. But will Sami be there on deck to take part in that salute? Or will he be held below decks, in disgrace, a disgrace more public than an officer of the Khedival Navy has ever suffered before? Not knowing is agony.

Back again with Nubar and his distinguished guests on the well-scrubbed decks of the *Mohammed Ali*, I could not shake off the nightmare of that night. My mind kept going over the catastrophe so nearly averted – the monarchs of Europe and Russia marooned for days in that vast waste of water and sand . . . I found myself shivering uncontrollably. I gripped Jeannie's arm tightly, and she looked at me with real concern.

As we approach the Kisr Cutting new worries drive out the old. Here the banks rise seventy feet from the Canal bed. The sand of which they are constructed is very fine; it can blow. How it can blow! Some say these banks are unstable and may come trickling down into the Canal. I examine them carefully as we steam past, but can detect no movement. No tell-tale sand in the water. I cannot help feeling, though, that only I, through whose veins the Canal has coursed for the last ten years, am fully alive to the danger.

Nubar has ordered our vessel moored at the Miriam station, where we must wait for the approach of *L'Aigle*, the Empress Eugénie aboard, heading the procession. 'Miriam' had been de

Lesseps' idea, commemorating the passing this way of the Holy Family on its way into the Land of Egypt. Ferdinand has a flair for such things. There's a chapel on the site, and now the Company is adding a mosque. Perhaps I should pray in both for Sami. All my inquiries have met with embarrassed silence. Sometimes not even embarrassed.

A yell from the lookout. The distinguished guests, news-papermen and all, crowd to the bow. Nubar flourishes a pair of long naval binoculars and raises them to his eyes, focusing down the long line of the Canal.

'It's her! It's *L'Aigle* – she's coming through.'

As *L'Aigle* draws nearer we weigh anchor and lead the way slowly southward towards Lake Timsah and the Khedive's new desert capital, Ismailiya, where my son Theo, Sam Shepheard's apprentice, is preparing the banquet for the crowned heads. At last Elena will have something to stop the conversation in the salons of Alexandria she inhabits in her fertile imagination.

24   Rory

Since she remained adamant in refusing marriage, it had been agreed between us that if the child was a boy his surname would be Macleod and, if a girl, Macdonald. Either way, it seemed to me, the House of Osman would acquire its Scottish branch. To my delight, it was a boy and I gave him the first name of Rory after my grandfather, the Dunvegan ferry man who had begun our droving – and also after Rory Mor, the sixteenth Chief of the Dun, he of Rory Mor's drinking horn.

I still see him as I did during those first four months, not as a swaddled babe, but as a bonny Highland lad, with Jeannie's dark hair and eyes, yet every inch a Macleod, striding towards me over the desert, Rory bin Osman, a fine figure of a man, a contradiction in terms some might say, but not for me.

I sometimes wonder how things would have gone between us if Rory had lived.

Naturally, she blamed me, but no more than I blamed myself. What was I doing, far away in the Sinai desert, fixing up a camel deal for Tom Waghorn at such a time? And why had I insisted on calling in old Abbot? Granted, he had delivered my other children, but the truth was I didn't want to see her crawling to the nurse at the Mission: all the sidelong glances of the unco guid would have been more than I could stand.

I knew she didn't take to Dr Henry Abbot, as he called himself – though I happen to know he'd come out as a sick-bay orderly on a Royal Navy warship. A cheerful, roly-poly man, he smoked a water-pipe and wore Turkish clothes including enormously baggy black trousers. Sam – Sam Shepheard – used to say the 'Doctor' was the 'dearest' guest he ever had, since he never paid his bills at the *table d'hôte* and the bar. His fingernails were often black from unwrapping mummies, searching for papyrus scrolls. His heart was in his collection.

Yet the birth went well enough; and we followed the Highland custom of washing the new-born child in a bowl of cold water in which a silver coin had been placed, making use of my silver American dollar with E PLURIBUS UNUM round the rim.

Zobeida cooed over the new baby, seeing it as a natural addition to the Hadji's harem, though Elena hardly troubled now to disguise her jealousy. As for me, I was already scheming a great future for Rory as Chief of the Overland Transit which, according to Tom Waghorn, by the time Rory had reached his teens would have transformed not only Egypt but the world.

It was not only Waghorn who was determined to 'put Egypt on the map'. Mohammed Ali's warrior eldest son, Ibrahim Pasha, had just captured Acre, and was sweeping through Syria. By the end of 1832 Colonel Sèves's new fellahin army, had reached Konya in Turkey, and the road to Istanbul lay open. Sick and fearful, Sultan Mahmud, God's Shadow on Earth, lost no time in conferring the four pashaliks of Syria on his 'humble (but not unambitious) vassal'. Egypt now stretched from the borders of Ethiopia to the Taurus.

Down in the Delta, Omar and his partner and father-in-law, Sheikh Hassuna, were steadily adding to their cotton acres; in Middle Egypt, Ibrahim Pasha's sugar factories were spreading their miasmas along the Nile, and M. Linant de Bellefonds was reported to be planning a great barrage to hold back the Nile as it enters the Delta, raising the water level in the canals which run out like arteries and veins, thereby making Omar and his father-in-law and their progeny richer than ever.

Stirring times! And then, out of the blue, in the middle of the hot season, I got back to find Rory scarlet-faced and shivering in his cradle. Jeannie had slipped out for a moment or two to see a Greek merchant who was looking for a teacher for his children, leaving Elena to keep an eye on the baby. I sent the donkey-boy off at the double to bring old Abbot. Abbot was slow reaching the house, in a state of great excitement about a papyrus roll he'd just managed to pick up. It was, he said a part of a rare *Book of the Dead*. He barely glanced at Rory.

'Nothing to worry about, old man. Only to be expected at this time of the year.'

He scribbled a prescription for Godfrey's Cordial and was off to gloat over his new papyrus roll.

I have to confess I was far from easy in my mind. But I had this rendezvous with Tom Waghorn I'd been looking forward to for months, and since Jeannie had now got back, I passed on Dr Abbot's prescription and rushed off.

There's not been a day since when I haven't regretted that moment.

Lieutenant Thomas Waghorn greeted me like a long-lost brother.

'Osman, old fellow,' he said, wringing my hand, 'you are the only man in this country who doesn't think I'm raving mad. You – and the Pasha. The old boy has promised me all the help he can give. I told him that the Overland Transit is going to make history, change the world . . .'

'He's doing quite a bit of that already,' I said. 'Too much for some. I hear the *Enterprise*'s boilers blew up . . .'

He swept that trifle aside. 'Good heavens, man, haven't you heard of the *Hugh Lindsay* – four hundred and eleven tons, eighty-horse-power engines. Coal bunkerage for *eleven* days . . .'

As it happened, I *had* heard of the SS *Hugh Lindsay*. Who hadn't? The old-timers in the snug of Hill's Hotel called her the SS *Water Lily*, because she had to carry so much coal to fire those early boilers that on the Bombay–Suez run her decks were always awash. The saloon and the cabin were piled high with the stuff. It was said that the single passenger she could carry looked like a chimney-sweep when he stepped ashore at Suez.

But little things like that never deterred Tom; the mails were the thing.

'Have you heard what Freeling said, Donald?' He put on a high-falutin' voice: ' "Her Majesty's Post Office can have nothing to do with these wild schemes of Mr Waghorn." '

He just took it for granted I'd throw in my lot with him. 'Tomorrow,' he said, 'we go to Alexandria to fix up a deal with Mr Harris, the coal merchant. Might have a word with Samuel Briggs – a shrewd fellow I hear, often acts for the Pasha.'

The man's confidence was awe-inspiring.

'So you're going to move tons and tons of coal across a water-less desert, full of thieving Bedouin. You know what the temperature is there? Over a hundred degrees in the *shade!*'

'Camels,' he said. 'Camels to carry water from the Nile, camels to fill our bunkers at Suez, camels for the passenger baggage. We need a steady supply of good camels and drivers.

'I'm relying on you, Osman.'

It was a struggle to get Waghorn to wear his full dress uniform, but in the end I persuaded him that, Bedouin being what they are, the display of gold braid might swing the deal.

Big camel tribes are forever shifting around as they exhaust the desert's meagre vegetation. It took us several days to locate Ayd's camp. But we found him at last in a fold of the desert beyond the Wells of Moses and, in accordance with Bedou etiquette, I brought our camels to their knees, two hundred yards from the open side of the Sheikh's spreading black tent. Ayd and three of his sons came hurrying out to greet us, vowing that 'his house' was 'our house' and so forth.

In his new gold-braided glory, Waghorn looked an admiral at least. On the other hand, Ayd, a short and skinny fellow, a tautly strung, sun-blackened parcel of skin and bone, did not live up to Waghorn's idea of the 'noble Bedou'. I could see he was disappointed. Yet Ayd's dark lustrous eyes spoke of authority and pride, and his names unrolled in a pennant that seemed to stretch back to the prophet Musa and beyond.

'Tefaddal Tefaddal,' he said, gravely, as he escorted us back to the tent, extending his hand towards the guest mattress. We leaned back against its sheepskin-covered camel saddles, while he busied himself over the fire burning in a hollow in the tent floor. A decorated curtain closed off the women's part of the tent. Ayd sent his young son behind it to bring the coffee-beans and card-amon-seeds, and to honour his guests he personally roasted the beans on a long-handled spoon held over the camel-dung fire. It was a slow ritual, meticulously performed. The beans crackled and smoked, and were crushed and transferred to the coffee-pot. At last Ayd lifted it from the fire, pouring the bitter brew into tiny handleless cups, before embarking on the customary round of inquiries about our health.

I could see Waghorn was fast losing patience.

I whispered loudly in his ear that Sheikh Ayd was of the nobility of the Ahl Bil – the People of the Camels. I saw the little man swell with pride, so I added that the People of the Camels were not to be mentioned in the same breath as the Ahl Gaman, the sheep-keeping tribes – while of course neither were to be mentioned in the same breath as the miserable fellahin who dirtied their hands in the earth.

Tom couldn't contain his impatience any longer. Rising to his full height, and demanding that I translate, he delivered a fervent address on the coming wonders of steam power which – with the aid of the Sheikh's renowned camels – would cause the desert to bloom like the rose, while consummating the marriage of East and West.

I had no idea what Ayd made of all this, but the glint in his eyes told me he sensed there could be money in it; with hindsight, I fear the word 'marriage' may have given him other ideas, too.

The Bedouin have thirty words for camel and I reckon that afternoon Tom and I heard most of them. A *hirish* is a male camel over thirty years old, a *hadz waalad khafifa*, a three-year-old ridden for the first time, a *wadha* a white camel, a *safra* a fawn-coloured one . . .

I pointed out firmly that our concern was with the plebeian beasts – *jamai*s and *rahla*s – that could carry a load across the eighty miles of waterless desert between Suez and Cairo. These, it seemed, were out on the *hamdh* – the salting bushes and shrivelled shrubs they needed to nibble every ten days to survive. Ayd took us out riding to look them over.

'See how fat and solid are their humps,' he boasted.

So, at last, the bargaining started. I knocked Ayd's price down by a quarter, and advised Tom to wait. But Tom Waghorn was a man in a hurry.

I took over and haggled with Ayd for two *dhalul*s, riding-camels. Elegant, narrow-nosed, they looked down upon us superciliously.

'*El-hurra!*' said Ayd in a sort of awed whisper. 'Their feet are tough. They go like the wind. They will carry your letters between Suez and Cairo in eight hours, nay, less.'

Tom couldn't resist that. The price he agreed was twice what I would have paid. I had never seen Ayd looking so pleased. All the same, Tom seemed uneasy.

'Khawah?' he said. 'What is this *khawah*?'

I had to laugh. 'It is what at home they call "màl dubh" – the black rent. It's "protection money", an ancient Bedouin custom. It's to pay off the other tribes when you pass through their territory.'

Ayd had grasped the drift of the conversation.

'The Omran!' he said, with a look of horror. 'Without the khawah . . .' He drew a hand across his throat.

'The Overland will not pay tribute to brigands,' Tom announced. 'I know how to deal with brigands – I've dealt with them in Burma!'

'This isn't Burma,' I said. I knew, of course, that Mohammed Ali had settled the hash of the Omran years ago. But with the Bedouin you've got to respect tradition. 'Not blackmail – just the khawah,' I murmured.

'Never! Not one piastre!'

I could see big trouble coming. But I smoothed things over and Ayd insisted that our *bandobast*, as Waghorn called it, must be sealed with a celebratory dinner and a *mesamer* – a Bedou dance in the moonlight in the 'Admiral's' honour.

I was anxious to get back home to Jeannie and Rory, but a few hours would make little difference now. So I told myself.

I can recall to this day the look of surprise, turning to horror, on poor Tom's face as Sheikh Ayd reached over the mountain of rice soaked in yellow gravy and crowned by hunks of mutton, and picked out the fat of a sheep's tail to pass to his honoured guest, 'the Admiral'.

We lingered long over that great brass tray, and then, three hours after the sun had gone down, we passed from the gross to the exquisite.

I have seen many a Bedou *mesamer* in my time but never, I believe, one so beautiful – or so fateful. It began like a gentle stirring, a ripple of refreshing air over the surface of the desert. A party of Bedouin youths appeared in the open space behind the black tents and, forming a line, began to sing softly, in a plaintive minor key. After a while a gaggle of veiled girls emerged from the tents and ranged themselves in line, facing the men at about thirty paces.

One of the young men began to sing a single verse, which

returned again and again. He was interrupted by a sort of chorus, taken up all along the line, with much clapping of hands, leaping, swaying from side to side to the rhythm of the song.

Backwards and forwards the young men swayed, eyes glittering in the moonlight. Then two or three of the girls moved out of their line, advancing shyly towards the dancing youths, holding a blue cloth between outstretched arms. They moved delicately, on their toes, in time to the men's song: as they retreated, other girls came out, tripping towards the line of men.

The song of the men grew bolder. They danced more wildly, roaring out the refrains, crying out the words of command.

By now, even Tom Waghorn could recognise some Arabic camel commands. 'They're calling the girls by camels' names!' he protested. I tried to explain that it would be a breach of the code of modesty to call a girl by her own name. I translated:

'The poor camel is thirsty . . . Come and take your evening drink, o camel.'

The girl approached, then danced skittishly away.

'Come! Come!'

She approached again, the blue cloth held coquettishly before her eyes.

The songs grew more sensuous, the girls more daring. The Bedouin can neither read nor write, but in their songs they are the poets of passion.

Sometimes now, as his 'camel' came almost within arm's reach, a young man would throw down a kerchief or a scarf – even his turban.

Sheikh Ayd leaned across to Tom. 'Later he must go to her to redeem his offering – if she will allow.' As I translated, Ayd gestured towards a young girl – I would guess of about sixteen years – who was dancing with transparent delight towards the line of men. She had the great Hathor eyes of an Egyptian, with the sinuous grace and vitality of a Bedou.

'Is she not as sweet and as ripe as a pomegranate of el-Tur? Will not His Excellency the Admiral now join the mesamer and call the camel to her food?'

Tom recoiled in alarm.

'The Sheikh will be offended if you don't.'

'No! Tell him I'm not feeling well.'

I could see it was true. Raw camel milk is not everyone's drink. I put it as tactfully as I could to Ayd. He frowned.

I can't remember clearly what happened next, but I found myself on my feet, carried forward in the line of leaping, dancing men, borne along on plangent notes of songs of love and undying passion.

I saw the girl Ayd had pointed out, tripping swiftly towards me, blue *melaya* dancing on slender arms, dipping as she drew near to reveal sparkling brown eyes and leaping breasts. I let go my kerchief, and saw her scoop it up.

Out of the corner of my eye I could see that Ayd was watching me. I will confess that, even then, I had misgivings. No one knows better than I do how devious Bedouin can be. I had been carried away like some besotted schoolboy. Now honour demanded that I follow the ritual to the end.

Even Bedouin legs and throats give out in the end, but it was long after midnight when I found myself wandering through the exhausted throng seeking my 'camel', praying that she would permit me to 'redeem' my kerchief.

It happened that, among the usual presents one brings for exchange on such occasions, I had a Pharaonic *menat* – a sort of 'musical' bead necklace, sacred to Hathor, incorporating a kind of rattle which gave out notes when shaken.

Her eyes shone at the sight of the bright beads.

'A halter,' I said, 'for the neck of my camel.' Not bad on the spur of the moment!

Shyly, she took the *menat*, hung it around her slender neck, handed me back my kerchief – and disappeared. All I could learn was that her name was Nura. I noticed, though, that people pronounced it with a certain circumspection.

During the day, the men's side of the spreading Bedou black tent is sharply divided from the women's side by two or three brightly decorated curtains. But at night these are raised and the whole clan overflows the tent floor, a slumbering raft of human kind, stirring gently in the darkness. As best we could Waghorn and I fitted ourselves into this human carpet, lying down in our clothes like the rest. But I did not sleep. As outside the hobbled camels gurgled and, more distantly, jackals howled, and within men snored fitfully or some couple, fitting together, quivered in embrace, I found my thoughts turning again and again to my brown-eyed 'camel' of the *mesamer*, wondering where that lithe young body might lie, near or far, in that warm swell of recumbent humanity, and, more disturbingly, which of the young men I had seen at the dance might lie beside her.

It wasn't until late next day, when we were about to take our leave after the inevitable long exchange of fulsome compliments and presents, that I discovered that this girl, Nura, was in fact Sheikh Ayd's favourite daughter.

I got back from the desert trip with Tom, feeling well pleased with myself and the bright prospects opening before us, to find Rory lying dead in his cradle, and Jeannie beside herself with grief.

I recall every detail of that terrible day. No etching fluid bites deeper than a sense of guilt. At the very moment when I had been playing Bedouin love games with a sixteen-year-old, Jeannie, alone, had been desperately struggling to haul our son back from the brink.

Why had I, an experienced *hakim*, trusted that old fool Abbot? But then my experience had been with the children of Egyptian fellahin, who had the Nile in their blood. Notoriously, the infants of European parents born under the Egyptian sun cling to life by the slenderest of threads – as the Protestant cemetery in Cairo, where next day we laid Rory to rest, bears tragic witness.

I had to give her that, although I feared Christian burial must make my neighbours look askance. In fact, they could not have been more kind, although few could have had any idea of the havoc Rory's death had wrought in our lives.

25 The Fat Prince and the American Lady

It was worse for her, I won't deny that. My duties for the Overland Transit kept me busy. Whether it was seeing to the safe transfer of passengers' baggage and the mails from the Mahmudiya Canal to the Nile boats at el-Atfeh, or booking them into the British Hotel for the onward journey to the waiting paddle-steamers at Suez, or attending Waghorn's negotiations with Mohammed Ali – who was shrewdly insisting on control of the desert way-stations – I had little time for brooding.

But Jeannie, poor girl, had burned her boats. She refused to go crawling back to the Mission to be employed in some humble capacity suited to a penitent sinner. Refusing to wear a veil, she was effectively unable to leave the house I had provided for her in what every European save Burckhardt considered the dirty, smelly Turkish quarter. The quip about being my 'American concubine' which she had made at Luxor now seemed a sour joke indeed. The reverberating calls to prayer from dawn to dusk had no magic for her. Her only consolation was that Zobeida, in her generosity of heart, would now permit Aisha to make the short journey to the other house to resume her education at the Sitt Amerikani's knee. But the marriage-brokers were already hovering, for the daughter of that well-known *hadji* and dragoman, Osman Effendi, would be no small catch. This delighted Zobeida, but worried Jeannie, as indeed it did me. She demanded that I send the suitors packing. I could *make* history, she said, instead of just sitting around in my Mohammedan way submitting to it. It was hardly the time to point out that she had not been so brilliant at 'making history' herself. You might say she had had history made *against* her: we both had.

After all those bleak years, made endurable for me by my dreams of our reunion, I had led her into this dismal trap, beached high and dry between East and West.

It was the new British Consul-General, Colonel Campbell, who found the way out for us. Different in rank as we were, there was a sort of fellow feeling between Patrick and me. We were both old soldiers and Highlandmen. He'd served in the Artillery under General Macleod, and as soon as he found out my '*real* name' – as he put it – he sent for me. He was ten years older than I, a big fellow with side-whiskers and a bald pate, but we got along like a house on fire. It was he who came out with the crack about 'Clan Osman' – I'd never thought of it that way before, but rather liked it when I did.

'We Highlanders must stick together,' he said. So at a suitable moment, I told him our story, Jeannie Macdonald's and mine. It so happened that like Tom Waghorn, but unlike his master Lord Pumicestone, the Colonel was a great admirer of the old Pasha, Mohammed Ali, and was on excellent terms with him. He admired the driving determination with which this shrewd Albanian 'adventurer' was dragging Egypt out of the Dark Ages, and, almost alone, against endless obstruction, turning it into a modern state. And he knew that the thing that Mohammed Ali wished most dearly was to secure for his house the succession to Egypt's throne.

This wouldn't be easy, for in the eyes of the Grand Seigneur, the Ottoman Sultan, Mohammed Ali was a mere vizier, useful for paying the Tribute, but otherwise fit only to run alongside the All Highest's carriage. Worse was the problem of his heirs. His eldest son and heir, Ibrahim Pasha, born in Albania to his first wife before the adventure began, was now sick and had turned against his father. The next in line, Abbas, was a sadistic monster, hating the West and all its works. That left Mohammed Said as Mohammed Ali's best hope of perpetuating his dynasty. But Mohammed Said, his son by one of his Circassian concubines, was only ten years old.

The old man confided to Colonel Campbell that the boy was spoiled and and self-indulgent. He needed a firm hand; otherwise he would go the way of Abbas, ruined by being brought up in the harem.

'In Britain,' said the Consul, 'we have a well-known saying,

"Mens sano in corpore sano".' He ventured to suggest that the prince might perhaps be sent to England – or better, Scotland – to school.

Mohammed Ali looked thoughtful, then rejected the idea.

'No. He is too fat. He is disgustingly fat and flabby. He must not travel – he would bring shame upon our house.'

It was at that point, thank God, that the Colonel remembered the plight of Jeannie Macdonald.

'Your Highness should know that there is at present in Cairo a renowned American teacher, a woman it is true, but of Scottish birth, and a stern disciplinarian.'

'Disciplinarian,' said the old boy, stroking his white beard, testing the unfamiliar word on his full lips.

'In Scotland our schools employ an instrument of judicious correction called the tawse. It is made of leather, like the courbash.'

The Colonel wondered whether he might have gone too far. But no.

'Kindly inform your countrywoman that the best quarters in my Shubra palace will be prepared for her. Nothing shall be spared. If she is successful as a "disciplinarian", she will not find me ungrateful.'

It worked out very well for us – at first. Jeannie was able to get away from my house in the shabby old Turkish quarter with all its tragic associations, although I knew she felt guilty at leaving Aisha behind. As a dragoman, well known in the palace gardens by the Nile, I was able to come and go between the new governess's quarters and my work for the Overland Transit.

The luxurious accommodation promised by Mohammed Ali turned out to amount to a rickety table, a cracked and stained Louis Quinze armchair, a divan with the raw cotton-bolls bursting out of it, cracked floor-tiles and dirt-streaked walls. It was enough to break any European woman's heart, but with a liberal distribution of *bakshish* I was able to achieve damask curtains, a 'French' mirror, good carpets and rugs to cover the cracked tiles, and a large silk-covered divan with bright cushions. Jeannie hung up a framed drawing of her father, mother and elder sister, Isobel, and another of herself, done by one of her prize Cherokee pupils at Ross's Landing.

For the first time since I sailed from Fort George I had a feeling of being at home, and the presence of Jeannie's young charge even seemed to do something to ease the void that Rory's death had opened. The boy was lively and charming. Each morning, at the beginning of lessons, he would bow with a gravity which seemed strange in a ten-year-old, and present a large box of chocolates, 'from Paris for Madame'.

It was quite some time before Jeannie understood that these gifts were seen in the light of *bakshish* for which due payment was to be exacted in the form of permission to skip an irksome lesson, or ensure a blind eye would be turned to some disgusting indulgence. Even at the age of ten, the little monster had a highly developed idea of the Divine Right of Kings.

I remember getting back from a particularly hard day trying out one of the first of our new three-a-side covered horse-vans to find Jeannie more upset than I had seen her since Rory died. I found her trembling not, as I had thought, with fever, but with sheer fury at the inhumanity of man to man – or girl. The vision of the Equality of Man which had taken her to America had been violated once again, by this child who was her charge, and she found herself powerless.

The prince had been playing with some ingenious toy when a small girl-slave, in fact a half-sister, had picked it up off the carpet. He had flown at her like a demon, sinking his teeth into her leg, then sticking his fingers into her mouth, and tearing till blood trickled out. His expression bespoke the practised sadist. Jeannie dragged him off the girl, shaking him furiously. But the moment her grip slackened he was away, howling piteously, to the Pasha's harem.

After inquiring the cause of the boy's distress and receiving a flood of lies, one of Mohammed Ali's concubines sent for the little girl and commanded her to kneel down and beg forgiveness and kiss His Highness's feet. When Jeannie protested that it was the boy who had been the aggressor and should be punished, the princess's eyes opened wide. She lay back on the cushions, offering Jeannie a box of bon-bons, and shrugging her shoulders. Was not Mohammed Said a prince of the blood royal, in line for the throne?

Three hours later, when I got 'home', Jeannie was still incandescent with indignation, and determined to go straight to Mohammed Ali in the morning and 'give him a piece of my mind'.

As a 'piece of Jeannie Macdonald's mind' might include a diatribe on the evils of Mohammedan polygamy and the subjection
of women, I hardly dared contemplate the outcome. Nevertheless
it took me all of two and a half hours – with many storms,
reversals, returns to harbour and new bombardments – before I
was able to prevail upon her to acknowledge the folly of her
proposal. By that time we were both emotionally exhausted. The
flow of the Gaelic worked its usual magic; she was clinging to me
as she delivered her last diatribe. Our Highland daughter, Flora,
was conceived on the carpet of the governess's room in the Shubra
palace that night, and in due time was delivered and watched
over by the Royal Physican, Dr Antoine Clôt Bey builder of
Egypt's medical school and first hospitals. (According to our
agreement the child, being a girl, was a Macdonald, and named
after Jeannie's childhood heroine, the Prince's saviour.)

Jeannie's pregnancy brought no mellowing of the Royal
Monster's behaviour. Above all, he liked to play soldiers, with
himself invariably in command. He would press his playmates
into companies and drill them. Any who did not march briskly
enough would be beaten with a cane. There were many such
beatings.

Again the Governess wanted to go to the boy's father; again I
dissuaded her. We hardened the regime with the cold-water
ablutions that precede the dawn prayer and I recruited the stern
old sheikh who had commanded Sami and Giovanni's *kuttub* and
had now retired.

Still, it wasn't easy to keep the boy's nose to the grindstone the
way the Revd Macaskill did at home; the Reverend didn't have a
large royal harem to contend with. Said was always sneaking off
there and the ladies vied in stuffing him with sugary sweetmeats.

As Jeannie's pregnancy advanced, the battle of wits between
her and the prince and the harem became harder and harder to
handle. Then out of the blue, the way things so often happen in
the East, a peremptory message arrived, demanding the attendance
of the royal governess at the Pasha's *diwan* the following morning.

I confess I panicked. Had the boy already gone to his mother,
the beautiful Caucasian concubine, and spun a terrible tissue of
lies around Jeannie and me? Not least of my fears was that Jeannie
was still 'dying to give that old tyrant a piece of my mind'.

' "Dying" might be just what happens to us,' I told her, but of course she didn't believe me. Wasn't she, after all, an American citizen?

I rushed off to see Colonel Campbell and was lucky enough to find him in. He saw my point quickly enough and undertook to arrange that I, Osman Effendi, should be present at the interview as interpreter.

The old man's beard was white now, but still impressively full, and those eyes of his had lost none of their formidable power. I had managed to persuade Jeannie to envelop herself in a *habara* of glossy black silk as worn by the local ladies when visiting, although of course she still drew the line at the veil.

Mohammed Ali's eyes stabbed at me. He knew me well enough by this time. 'So this is the "dis-ciplin-arian",' he said.

She was furious, a volcano about to erupt. 'Those women . . .' she spluttered.

I leapt in, drawing a heavy curtain of Turkish over Jeannie's words. 'Indeed, Madame was famed as a disciplinarian at the American Academy . . .'

'But are not these Americans inveterate rebels? Have they not risen against their lawful masters yet again?' The old boy was proud of his knowledge of the world.

A pile of forms lay on a side table. He now turned to these. They were reports on Prince Said's progress.

'But what is this? Latin? . . . French? Good . . . but Madame, I do not wish to turn the boy into an English gentleman. There is but one figure here that interests me.' He stabbed a finger at an entry in the top right-hand corner and I recognised an innovation of Dr Clôt's, Said's weight, recorded weekly.

The Pasha took a sheaf of reports, reading out the weight figures slowly. There could be no argument: they were rising.

The old boy was merciless. 'Madame, I told you the boy was disgracefully fat, like some Bedou's favourite wife. Now he is even fatter. I avert my eyes. To rule Egypt he must wield the sword with vigour. With those flabby arms of lard he could not even hold it.'

He brightened. 'In your country you have, they tell me, a simple instrument called "a skipping rope". You will see that His Highness leans to skip.'

He leaned forward and drew reflectively on his long jewelled *chibouk*.

'My predecessor Salah el-Din, who built this Citadel, encircled it with walls. Yes, it is important that the boy learns our history. So he will run around them every morning. You will make sure, Madame, that he does not slack.' He took another pull at the *chibouk*. 'And since he may yet command my Navy, you will see that he regularly climbs the tallest mast of any of the ships tied up at Bulak.'

It was remarkable, but those eyes of his, focused upon her, had succeeded in reducing the Sitt Amerikani to silence. We were dismissed.

As Flora's birth was now only a few weeks away, it was obvious that I would have to take time off from the Transit to make sure that the Pasha's instructions were carried out in full. But where in God's name would I find a skipping rope? And even if I could, how would I ever induce that little monster to stick at it – or run round the walls at first light, much less in the midday heat?

Mohammed Ali had a powerful imagination in such matters, as every fellah knew. But he was not always practical. He was a man in a hurry, building his new navy of unseasoned wood, despite the incessant warnings of his French master shipwright.

'All those women!' Jeannie lamented.

It was a fair enough complaint. Unthinking, Mohammed Ali had put his governess's schoolroom close to the heart of his vast harem, full of idle, mischief-making concubines and their slaves. It was here indeed that Mohammed Said had received his early education. The boy and the women understood each other too well and now conspired together with malevolence and cunning to grind the 'American woman' into the dust. It took only a minute for Mohammed Said to wolf down a syrup-soaked *baklava*, even less to swallow a sticky slab of *halvah* – between skips, so to speak.

We began to dread the approach of Friday when the weekly ritual of weighing the boy took place. The little monster would smile angelically as he watched us shudder at the verdict of the scales. We redoubled our efforts. By dint of regular *bakshish* to the harem's eunuchs, and warnings of the terrible anger of the Pasha that would be visited on them, we at last managed to keep the boy out of the harem. As the weather grew hotter, he sweated so heavily on his runs round the walls that for a few weeks his weight actually dipped. I began to breathe more easily again.

But when the boy next sat in the pan of the scales, it went down with a bump. It was mortifying. Jeannie was now preoccupied with Flora, while I was hard-pressed trying to organise the supply of water from the Nile by Ayd's camels to fill the tanks at the way-stations – and here I was, a respected *hadji*, dragoman to the Earl of Belmore and many famous lords, being defied and even mocked by a flabby ten-year-old boy.

The gardens of the Shubra palace are extensive and in places much overgrown. However carefully we watched, Said managed to give us the slip. We questioned him, of course. But he just simpered: he was revelling in the situation, hoping to get his governess into trouble with his father.

I poured out my fears and frustration to Tom Waghorn one day after seeing off half a dozen vans from the British Hotel for Suez.

'Track him,' he said.

'I've tried, but . . .'

Tom thought for a moment. 'Haven't you a boy about that age?'

'Giovanni will soon be twelve.'

'Set a boy to catch a boy. Take Giovanni with you to the Shubra palace gardens tonight.'

Tom, as I've said, is a man of vision. It worked, not at once, but three evenings later, and Giovanni relished the job. He returned to report that Mohammed Said had a secret way out of the gardens which took him to a large white house which flew a red, white and blue tricolour. Mohammed Said had vanished inside the French Consulate.

Suddenly things began to fall in place. Ferdinand de Lesseps had arrived in Egypt the year before as France's junior consul in Alexandria. He was then a clever and personable young fellow of twenty-eight. Within next to no time he was Consul-General in Cairo, welcomed with open arms by Mohammed Ali.

'This young man's father made me what I am,' Mohammed Ali told the assembled consuls. Two years before the Ross-shire Buffs reached Egypt, Matthieu de Lesseps, Bonaparte's agent in Egypt, formerly victualler of his Egyptian expedition, had spotted this obscure but ambitious Albanian officer as a coming man, and had done all he could to support him. Naturally Matthieu's son, Ferdinand, enjoyed a position of peculiar privilege in Egypt. He was the only foreigner whom Mohammed Said was allowed to visit on his own.

I waited half an hour after the boy's disappearance. I knew just where to go. It was long after consular hours, of course, and the place was shut up and quiet, though some light came from the windows. I worked my way round the back, locating a window to some sort of kitchen. I felt a fool crouching to keep below the window ledge, not easy, given my height. As I looked cautiously over it, I was rewarded with a truly extraordinary sight: Mohammed Said, seated at a rough wooden table, spooning macaroni from a large basin into his mouth.

I made my way to the front door and rang the bell. As luck would have it, the dragoman there was an old friend of mine. When I explained that I had a message from Captain Tom Waghorn relating to the Overland Transit, I was quickly admitted to the young consul's study.

De Lesseps was engrossed in a thick, leather-bound volume, a report of some kind with many dog-eared maps.

I had only just embarked on my introductory remarks when Mohammed Said ran into the room, a comic figure, his snout smeared red with rich sauce.

His jaw dropped when he saw me. It was hard not to laugh, but I managed it. De Lesseps intercepted the look of distaste that passed between us, and decided to brazen it out: 'The poor child was hungry. The American woman starves him.'

That was too much. 'Mrs Macdonald is not an American woman. She is a Scot, a Highlander like myself.'

The boy stood in the doorway, malevolent stare fixed on me.

'He does not look starved to me,' I said. 'Mrs Macdonald, his governess, is under orders from His Excellency to reduce his weight. If he knew that . . .'

'Ah, Monsieur, but he is a mere infant. At such an age a boy needs beaucoup de nourriture, n'est-ce pas? Otherwise, how can he exercise? I teach him l'épée . . . I teach him to ride . . . We must cut the apron-strings.' He appealed to me. 'Man to man, Monsieur, I ask you, is this a task for a woman?'

Mohammed Said continued to glare from the doorway and the Consul became aware of him. 'Votre Excellence,' he said – I never knew when Ferdinand was joking – 'ce n'est pas gentil. Il faut se laver.'

The boy slunk away.

'A *Scots* woman,' I insisted, loyally.

'Yes, yes,' said de Lesseps, suavely. 'My cousin Maria's father came from Scotland, a Jacobite I believe, and settled in Malaga . . .'

He saw I was eyeing the battered old volume on his desk. He turned a page and unfolded a map.

'It is Lepère's report to Napoleon on his plans for the Canal des Deux Mers,' he said. 'Une merveille, n'est ce pas? They were fighting the Bedouin off all the time they were making the survey.'

Strange how things happen, how history gets made. It seems a man had died of cholera on the ship that brought young de Lesseps to his new post. The yellow flag went up in the harbour, the passengers were confined in Alexandria's *lazaretto*. Facing weeks of boredom, the young man appealed to his colleagues at the Consulate for reading matter, and among the books sent from their library was Lepère's report to Bonaparte.

De Lesseps' imagination was kindled by the detailed report. When promoted to Cairo he took the volume with him. He had been poring over it ever since.

'But didn't Lepère report that the Mediterranean here was thirty feet higher than the Red Sea, and that a canal would flood Egypt and turn the waters of the Nile salt?' I had heard all that from Tom Waghorn.

He nodded. 'But don't forget your Lord Nelson had destroyed the ship carrying his instruments.' It was an accusation.

'Not *my* Lord Nelson,' I said.

'But even then the mathematicians among Bonaparte's *savants* disagreed. And now one of my own countrymen, Monsieur Linant de Bellefonds, the Pasha's irrigation engineer, has made a fresh survey. He is sure they were right – and Lepère was wrong.'

He ran a finger over the old map from the Bay of Pelusium down to Suez. 'A hundred miles of sand and marshes. Nature herself has done half the job for us already. Think of it, Osman Effendi. A bridge between continents. One would be re-making the map of the world!'

I did indeed think of it. It was 'Mad' Tom Waghorn's vision writ large, and by a poet.

It was late by the time I got back to the Shubra palace, where

Jeannie was anxiously waiting. But by this time my mind had been completely possessed by this young man's vision: the Canal Between Seas, the hinge of Continents. Beside it, the antics of the fat prince seemed a ridiculous irrelevance.

I gave Jeannie a faithful account of what I had discovered, but by now I suppose my voice lacked urgency. 'Macaroni!' she shrieked. 'He gave him *macaroni?*'

I decided not to tell her of de Lesseps' insistence that the prince's education was work for a man. Already she was demanding that I go to Mohammed Ali first thing in the morning and report the heinous deeds of the Consul of France. Jeannie's outrage communicated itself to baby Flora, normally a peaceful sleeper, who sat up and howled half the night.

To complain to the Pasha about the French Consul befriending his small son would have been unthinkable; on the other hand it was plain as a pikestaff that if Ferdinand de Lesseps went on feeding bowls of macaroni garnished with rich sauce to the boy, his weight was likely to soar and we would appear to be flouting Mohammed Ali's personal orders.

We were boxed in, Jeannie and I, as surely as the Ross-shire Buffs had been at el-Hamed. She was thoughtful. 'What we need is a deus ex machina,' she said at last. Not having any Latin, I was baffled. I took down from the shelves Chambers *Information for the People*, and I read that a *deus* of this sort – and Heaven knows we have no shortage of gods in Egypt – means 'the intervention of a god', or some unlikely event, 'to extricate the clumsy author from difficulties in which he has involved himself'. I could see no clumsy author here save – forgive the blasphemy – Allah Himself. Yet, sure enough, the *deus* arrived in the nick of time, not from the theatre wings but out of the wastes of Central Asia.

The Great Plague of 1834–5 descended like a pack of ravening wolves through Turkey, cut a broad swathe of death and destruction across Syria, and around midsummer fell upon Egypt. People who had been strolling about in perfect health a few moments before were writhing on the ground, spilling out their bowels; a few hours later, they were dead. The real terror was that no one knew on whom the fatal contagion would fall next; only that fall it would. I returned to the Suk el-Zalat to find my friend the baker's door locked and barred and marked with the red cross and a seal signifying that the plague had struck. I watched food being taken in by basket, hoisted on a long rope to the top floor.

Coins in payment were dropped into a bowl of water to protect them from the lurking contagion.

Men called it the *taun*, the yellow wind; it entered our crowded narrow streets stealthily, then blew up a howling tempest as the dread sound of vomiting with which it announced itself grew. The streets were crowded with funeral processions, speeding the corpses on their biers to the burial ground lest they spread the infection. The terrible thing was that none knew how to abate or cure the disease. Even Doctor Clôt, late of Marseille, threw up his hands in despair. 'Flee,' he said. 'Flee early – and flee far!'

The rich pashas and bankers had already done so, taking refuge on islands in the Mediterranean. And thank God – or the *deus ex machina* – Mohammed Ali and his family and the Shubra harem had gone. Suddenly the threat of that malevolent boy was lifted.

But few Cairenes could make their escape this way, least of all Osman Effendi, for the passage of the mails by Waghorn's Overland Transit was now more than ever vital. What I could do – and did – was to send Jeannie and baby Flora off to Omar's village in the cotton fields of Menufiya, in the clear, clean air of the Delta. Zobeida, I knew, would never leave the old house on the Cairo canal to which I had brought her and where she had borne my children. As for Elena, whose eldest son was now seven and Theo five, Alexandria (where she now had her own establishment) with all the marshy lands behind it was a natural focus of infection. The upshot was that both wives, Ethiopian and Levantine, holed up in Burckhardt's old house, their children gathered around them, the front door double-barred against the rampaging beast outside.

Having done the best I could for my family, I made my way down to Alexandria, to the Waghorn office on the quay, where a mountain of letters and parcels, 'arrested' by the *lazaretto* authorities overflowed onto the floor, Each was hopefully rubber-stamped CARE OF MR WAGHORN. That meant that now each letter, each packet, had to be perforated to 'let the contagion out', then 'smoked', and packed with others in airtight tins. Larger parcels had to be encased in lead. No doubt about it, Waghorn's fame was growing. Faced with the tedious journey round the Cape, more and more Indian army officers and their families, returning from furlough, were taking Waghorn's 'short cut', even though the first stage along the winding Mahmudiya Canal was painfully slow, and collisions were frequent, with fearful entanglements of tow-ropes and sails. Despite all this, Lieutenant Waghorn's Overland Transit was becoming 'the latest thing'. I was working, I felt, in the very van of progress – as I intended to point out to Jeannie the next time I saw her.

'When I arrived in Cairo, I summoned Osman Effendi', Kinglake writes in that so-called 'masterpiece' of his, *Eothen or Traces of Travel Brought Back from the East.*

Let me tell you what *really* happened.

Two of Dr Clôt's young men stopped him outside the city – he was coming from Syria – and warned him to turn back since the place was in the grip of the plague. He refused. *Cordons sanitaires* were well enough for Turks and Arabs and Greeks and Italians and the like, but not for an English gentleman.

The next thing I knew he was hammering on my heavily barred door, demanding lodging, a fellow in his twenties, educated at Eton and Cambridge, an aspiring author.

'Poor Osman', he tells the world in that book of his, 'the fear of the plague sat heavily on his soul. He seemed as if he felt he was doing wrong in lending me a resting place'. *That* at least was true. From his pink, shining face I saw that he had come from the *hammam* at the end of the street, the first place a plague victim made for when dread sweats fell upon him, and a prime focus of infection. 'Poor Osman' was afraid for his wives and children, understand?

The young Mr Alexander Kinglake stayed with me nineteen days, and on each of them my fears grew sharper. He was, as he himself says, the only traveller still left in Cairo – the others had fled – but this did not stop him working his way through all the sights as the daily death toll rose from 500 to 1200. The howls of the mourners were ever in his ears. 'The sting of the fear of death', he tells his readers, heightened his enjoyment. He was indignant when his letter of credit was received with a pair of tongs. People died all around him: the donkey-boy who had carried him on his excursions around Cairo, his banker, the Italian doctor – the only doctor left in Cairo – who had examined his sore throat, the magician he had hired to demonstrate ancient tricks ... one by one the curse fell upon them, one by one they died. Not this young Englisman! 'The sting of the fear of death' exhilarated him.

Then he tells the world that I, Osman Effendi, *invited* him to see my harem. A lie! The fact is that with that obsessive curiosity that comes over English travellers when the word 'harem' is mentioned, he had been pressing me for days for a 'glimpse' within. For the sake of peace, I finally agreed, after having made quite sure that Zobeida and Elena were well out of the way.

He left at last, his notebooks replete with the peculiar ways of these Orientals, and, Allah be praised, I was at last able to get away to the Overland, where I knew Waghorn would have urgent need of me, for Tom's bluff 'seadog' style did not go down well with all the memsahibs.

I had to ride all the way out to the No. 4 station before I came upon him. No. 4 was what you might call the hub of the desert transit, forty-four miles out from Cairo, a one-storey building round a courtyard, with an underground tank of Nile water and facilities for refreshment, a few hours' rest, and a change of horses.

I saw Tom Waghorn at once, all six foot two of him, engaged in what looked like a furious altercation with a red-faced major in the East India Company service.

Lying on the desert sand just outside the circle of interested onlookers I spotted the cause of the trouble, a massive lead-lined travelling chest, its lid sprung open at the clasp, lying on top of a large, ornate bird-cage, squashed flat. As any experienced dragoman will tell you, the Bedou camel-driver, while master of his beasts' many and sometimes vicious moods, has absolutely no idea how to balance loads so that they remain stable on either side of a camel. The Major had now reached the point of promising to report Lieutenant Waghorn's 'insolence' to the Governor of Bombay, who happened to be his uncle. A few yards away, a pale young lady (whom I took to be the Major's bride on her first 'trip out') wept silently. The row had been going on for half an hour and seemed likely to continue. People sat around pretending that the whole thing was not happening, in that English way, while their ears remained pricked for every new insult. I knew there had already been letters in the London *Times* complaining about the Overland's battered suitcases or burst ink-bottles ruining the ladies' dresses. We needed no more: I had arrived in the nick of time. What these affairs require is the minimum of speech, at least in English, and the calm and dignity recommended by the Prophet, peace be upon him.

I straightened my robes, adjusted my turban, approached Waghorn purposefully and gravely informed him that an important message required his immediate attention. While he withdrew to our small office in the way-station building, I produced my *sebbah*, which the English call 'worry beads', and began to work slowly through the ninety-nine names of God.

This had its usual calming effect, so that we were able to get the Bombay-bound party stowed into the vans and off on time in the cool of the night. Normally we employ Maltese drivers, but on this occasion I took care to entrust the van bearing the Major and his young bride to Hill, our chief driver, an Englishman, the brother of the proprietor of Hill's Hotel in Cairo.

I forget how many days I was away in the desert on Overland's business, but it was too long. I returned to the house on the canal to find Zobeida not only struck down by the plague but already buried. The fear of the contagion was now so great that victims were being rushed to their graves the moment life was extinct.

I fear that 'the sting of death' – to quote Mr Kinglake – brought absolutely no 'buoyancy to *my* spirits'. I found myself overtaken by a great emptiness, which I had never experienced before, even after Rory's death. Unassertive, blending into the Cairo background, always there, faithful mother to Sami, Giovanni and Aisha, ever since that moment of sudden recognition in the Cairo slave-market, this woman had quietly built a solid foundation under my *renegado* life – and now, at a stroke, that was gone.

It was Kinglake who, in a sense, wrote Zobeida's belated epitaph. Back in England he spent the best part of ten years perfecting his 'Oriental' masterpiece. It wasn't until 1844, long after Anderson of the P & O had pushed in and Tom Waghorn had retired to England bankrupt, that I was able to read Kinglake's considered opinion of Osman Effendi's harem. 'The rooms of the hareem', he tells his readers, 'reminded me of an English nursery rather than of a Mahometan paradise. One is apt to judge of a woman before one sees her by the air of elegance or coarseness with which she surrounds her home; I judged Osman's wives by this test, and condemned them both.'

Poor Zobeida. Poor Elena.

Poor Osman, with his 'inextinguishable Scottishness' and his 'Edinburgh Cabinet Library'.

It was 1835, and Mr Kinglake was back in England honing his reminiscences, before the yellow wind blew itself out. According to my good friend Edward Lane, one of Robert Hay's company of tomb artists, more than a third of the population of Cairo had been swept away.

As the yellow flag came fluttering down from its pole over the Alexandria *lazaretto*, the pashas – Mohammed Ali among them – and their harems came rushing back from their bolt-holes to collect their rents from such of the fellahin as could still plough their fields.

It was now safe to travel again, yet there was still no word from Jeannie and Flora at Omar's village in the Delta. I could understand that she would not wish to get involved again in the grim farce of the prince's 'education', but then she would not need to, for it had just been announced that Mohammed Ali was placing his son, Mohammed Said, in his new Navy School. Young de Lesseps had been posted to the faraway Netherlands.

The continuing silence from the Delta worried me. Certainly in our strange alliance it had been agreed that if a child was a girl she would take the Macdonald name, but that didn't stop me from seeing Flora as 'my Highland daughter'. She would be taking her first steps, mouthing her first words, and I was not there to hear them.

As time wore on and there was still no message from Jeannie, my depression mounted, and I found it difficult to pay much attention to the Overland's straying luggage and vanishing camels. Even Waghorn noticed this at last, and asked what ailed me. When I told him, he insisted I take time off and travel down into the Delta to set my mind at rest.

'Grasp the nettle!' he said. 'I can always take Hill off the driving to see to the passengers.'

It was June and the time of the first picking. Long, wavering white lines of women and children combed through the dark glossy leaves of the cotton plants, wary on the one hand of the thorns that would tear their flesh, on the other of the long flicking cane of the overseer. I felt ill at ease. Herodotus said that Egypt is 'the gift of the Nile', and so it is, but it began to seem to me that this was a gift that was all too easily transferable.

I had not been down into Menufiya since Omar took Sheikh Hassuna's daughter to wife, a shrewd move as it turned out. Thanks to my apprenticing him to Alex Jumel, Omar was now an inspector and instructor in fine cotton cultivation, and Hassuna, the village headman, was clever at the accumulation of land in more ways than one.

I inquired for Omar from a couple of half-naked fellahin, covered in glistening grey mud, clearing out an irrigation channel. They salaamed. 'Sheikh Omar bin Osman?' they queried, deferentially, and swept an arm onwards as if Omar, like Allah, was omnipresent. It was evident that Fatima's boy had gone up in the world.

Set apart behind a wall, Omar's three-storey house of burned red brick seemed to me to tower over the mud-brick hovels of the fellahin much as, at home, the Dun of the Macleod dominated the black houses of us poor *màlairean* and crofters. The house was, in the vernacular, a 'palace', and Jeannie had been accorded as her territory the whole of the third floor. Small wonder she had been in no hurry to return to my odiferous surroundings in the Turkish quarter of Cairo.

I could see she had fallen readily enough into the familiar Egyptian role of 'mother-in-law': in one sense, it seemed to me, it might have been written for her. She looked up from a ledger of cotton yields on the various land-holdings put together to form the estate. She obviously felt at home here: I had forgotten the Carolinas grew fine Sea Island cotton and that in the South, cotton was king.

She received the news of Zobeida's death sympathetically enough, but showed no inclination to return to Cairo. She was still mad at me for my failure to 'report' young de Lesseps to Mohammed Ali and pressed me with questions about the young French Consul. I took pleasure in telling her he had been decorated by France with the Legion of Honour for his work during the Great Plague.

'My, my,' she said in that peculiar American way of hers.

'Anyway,' I assured her, 'Ferdinand has married and been posted to Rotterdam. That is probably the last we shall see of him.' (How wrong I was!)

Suddenly Flora, pulling free from the hand of a young fellaha in a flowered dress, was in front of me, staring at me fixedly. She stared for a full minute, then ran towards me, crying 'Abba . . . Abba! Papa!'

It was like a miracle, and what I saw in her eyes gave me new heart, renewed me.

The shadows lengthened, and Omar came in from the fields. Though he still wore the striped blue *galabiya* of the Egyptian fellah, he already had a certain embonpoint which spoke of money and authority. I had difficulty in recognising the lively imp to whom Alexis Jumel had handed the oil-can that day at his Bulak 'factory'. He was plainly his own man, and I was once more gratified to note those fugitive strands of blond hair that I was pleased to think of as my mark on him.

After some dutiful inquiries about the family back in Cairo, he took to explaining to his backward old father the economic beauties of the Jumel cotton-plant and the wonders he and his partner Sheikh Hassuna were performing with it.

Did I know that 400,000 bales were exported last year? Did I realise that cotton was now bringing in *seven times* as much as all Egypt's other crops put together?

'Just a pity people can't eat it,' I said.

That brought Jeannie into the fray. She gave me a pitying look. 'That's just the point. That's just why Mohammed Ali is ordering so much more to be grown – because the fellahin can't gobble it all up! It's a cash crop. They've *got* to sell it. So it irrigates the whole economy . . .'

'Supposing they're hungry? Supposing they can't feed their families?

This cotton plant, I've found, can do strange things to people. It bends them to its purposes. Planting, regular hoeing and watering and picking and fighting the cotton worms are only the beginnings of its exactions. The cotton-boll is full of hard, shiny black seeds deeply embedded in the fibre, hard to separate.

'Would you believe it, Donald,' she said, 'it takes an Egyptian fellah turning the handle of one of these *dulab* things seven *days* to clear a *cantar* of raw cotton, and even then it's full of dirt. At home, Eli Whitney's steam gin does it in as many hours!'

Flora was playing at my feet. 'At home', she'd said. No home of mine! I'd thought we'd shared one.

Omar was indignant. 'We've tried Whitney gins. They're no good for our Jumel. They rip it to bits. Liverpool would throw it back at us.'

I looked at him in amazement. Could this be the son of Adile Hanem's black slave-girl?

'Well, then, what are you waiting for?' she demanded. 'We had the same problem with Whitney's gin in the Carolinas. We didn't just sit around to see if God was willing. There's a young fellow named McCarthy. He's applied for a patent for a new kind of gin that works for Sea Island – you can't get finer than that! I'll write to my brother-in-law on his plantation down Wilmington way and find out what's happening.'

Her eyes were shining just as they had when she began to teach me English from the works of Tom Paine. She was a girl for Causes, and now she had a new one: the efficient manufacture of cotton. I preferred Tom Paine.

Before I left she took me aside to ask after Aisha, her prize pupil at the Mission, Aisha who, thanks to Zobeida's precautions against the Evil Eye, had brought us together again.

'Elena is looking after her.'

She threw up her hands in horror. 'That flibbertigibbet! The poor girl will end up on the streets.'

She was thoughtful for a while, then she spoke in her usual 'my-mind-is-made-up' style.

'It happens that Sheikh Hassuna's wife visited Alexandria and was carried off by the plague. He's been expressing an interest in Osman Effendi's clever daughter.'

My blood ran cold. Hassuna was old enough to be Aisha's grandfather; not only that, but he seemed to be just the kind of rich, ignorant fellah Jeannie herself had been warning me against as a suitor for my bright daughter.

I was shocked: was this another of the things the cotton-tree did to people? Yet, in the end, I had to admit that, as ever, Jeannie had a point.

'We must be realistic,' she said. 'If Aisha married Omar's partner, I would be able to watch over her and carry on with her education. It would all, so to speak, be "in the family" – a family in which money is not scarce. In any case, with the girl's mother gone, and her father fully occupied building up Waghorn's Overland Transit . . .'

I had to admit the force of her arguments. The cotton branch of 'Clan Osman' seemed to be flourishing.

And yet I was returning to Cairo with more misgivings than I had set out. Jeannie Macdonald had shown no sign of wanting to join me in Cairo. I felt doubly bereft. All my hopes were now centred on our daughter, Flora. But it wasn't easy to see how they could ever be realised.

27   Bedouin Hide and Seek

Once again I was saved from despair by my work. You might say, I suppose, that the age of the steamship grabbed me by the shoulders and shook me. I remembered the afternoon I had run into 'Mad Tom' as they called him in Hill's Hotel, and how anxious Hill had been to get rid of him. No longer. For in 1837 a new company calling itself the Peninsular Steam Navigation Company started a regular mail-boat service from Falmouth to Gibraltar, and the French Messageries Impériales began running Marseille to Alexandria, regular as clockwork. Suddenly, the Overland was 'all the rage'. Tom was advertising WAGHORN'S RENOWNED OVERLAND TRANSIT, CONDUCTED WITH THE AID OF THE VICEROY OF EGYPT. In London, people were flocking to the Colosseum to watch the diorama of Waghorn's 'patent English carriages' speeding across the desert, drawn by mettlesome horses towards the domes of Bombay and the East. There was even a new dance called 'The Overland Polka', its music cover decorated with palm trees, camels, cotton bales and minarets.

It was bound to happen, of course: I see that now.

I got down to the harbour one morning to see to the transfer of the Waghorn transit passengers to our track boats on the Mahmudiya Canal only to find that I'd turned out been beaten to it. It turned out that Hill, our head driver, who had taken over my duties when I was away in Menufiya, had used his time profitably. He'd seen all our books, learned all our secrets, taken a partner named Raven, and quietly set about organising a rival Overland Transit. The only difference was that their 'vans' were flat-topped while Waghorn's were hooped, but *theirs* had the advantage of operating out of Hill's brother's hotel, and commandeering the catering.

I could not believe such treachery. Tom, of course, shrugged the whole thing off. There was only *one* Waghorn's Overland: everyone knew that! He imported a small steamer for the Atfeh-to-Cairo passage on the Nile. But the *Jack o'Lantern*, as it was called, had to carry so much coal for the trip that she could only take ten passengers and she took so long getting up steam at el-Atfeh that people called her the tea-kettle. Then he imported a London horse-bus which was landed with its indicator still showing ENFIELD TO BANK. Alas, its wheels sank into the desert sand drifts. Hill and Raven were threatening to crowd us out of accommodation in the way-stations, so Waghorn had the brilliant notion of buying up the marquees from the great 'medieval' tournament at Eglington Castle in England. They arrived in a tangle of ropes and we never discovered how to erect them.

This rivalry brought a sparkle to the eyes of our Bedouin camel-drivers. It spelt opportunity. *Harami* – or nocturnal camel theft – was a much-admired art which brought spice, and cash, into their monotonous and otherwise cash-less lives. The baggage camels were the Transit's life-blood. For all Tom's talk of the wonders of steam power, it was these strange, durable beasts, bringing in water from the Nile, moving coal from Alexandria to Suez, ferrying the passenger's ever-mounting baggage, that kept the whole enterprise afloat. I congratulated myself on the deal I had made with Sheikh Ayd, of the Towra.

Alas, I congratulated myself too soon. One day, I was woken at dawn at the No. 8 way-station by our head camel-driver, pouring out a fearful tale of ten of our best camels being spirited away overnight. The beasts had been hobbled, as usual, just outside the tents. No one had heard a sound. Yet next morning the camels were gone, vanished into thin air. For all his indignant tones, the camel-man could hardly conceal his admiration of the *harami* who had pulled off the raid and was now, no doubt, many miles away.

Waghorn exploded. 'It's those bloody Bedouin of yours up to their tricks again. Hill and Raven will be laughing their heads off!'

Nothing would do but that we find Sheikh Ayd and demand an explanation.

Ayd put up a fine show, I'll say that for him. His brow darkened.

'The Omran,' he scowled. 'They have blackened my face! They have besmirched the honour of the Towra! They shall pay!'

He summoned his four sons and ordered them to take the swiftest mounts and not to return until they had the miscreants at the end of a rope.

Waghorn was impressed. But it didn't deceive me: the dreaded Omran had been exterminated by Mohammed Ali years ago. I suspected Ayd of having raided his own camels; I knew that the Bedouin look on all strangers as God-sent source of income, one of those crops which grow even in the desert, if with an uncertain yield.

Sure enough, Ayd took me aside and begged me to explain to the Admiral that for marauders such as the Omran the *khawah* – or protection money – simply wouldn't do. If he was to stop these impudent raiders, it would have to be doubled.

I did not consider this the moment to pass on Ayd's thoughts to 'the Admiral'. I embarked on the usual round of parting compliments while the Sheikh embroidered his denunciations of the treacherous Omran. Then he called for the *mukhbar*, to lend fragance to our departure.

And who should pass the incense-burner over the curtain but Nura, the lithe, brown-eyed favourite daughter.

Sure enough, a week or two later the camels bearing Ayd's *wasm* – two parallel lines branded high on the left haunch – mysteriously reappeared in Hill and Raven's camel train and were duly returned to us. Waghorn thought that his 'firmness' had triumphed. I suspected that this was not the end, but the beginning, of these Bedouin fun and games. I put guards on our camels night and day and saw that they were always tightly hobbled close to the tents. But the *haramis* just saw this as a challenge. They would spend hours lying in wait, crawling snake-like through the deepest shadows. They often struck at the most critical moments in our operations. Disgruntled passengers were deserting us for the Hill and Raven line.

With my father's tales of the exploits of Rob Roy and the cattle reivers still running through my head, I was willing enough to pay up. *Khawah*, after all, was a hallowed Bedou tradition. To Tom Waghorn, however, it was a betrayal of the British Empire.

'It is a matter of principle to Ayd, too,' I pointed out. 'The principle of Egypt is bakshish.'

'Not a penny,' he said.

'Ayd might take his camels over to Hill and Raven.'

'Let him!' There was no talking to Waghorn in this mood. I was at my wits' end. Camels were being lifted from within three feet of their sleeping drivers. This was an undeclared war we could not win.

Then, I had an idea. I knew that, outrageous as such Bedouin games may appear, they are regulated by a strict, unbreakable code. I knew Ayd was much impressed by the man he called 'the Admiral'. If Waghorn were to become a member of the House of Ayd he could not be robbed. What we needed was what diplomats called a 'dynastic alliance'. The name of Thomas Waghorn would enrich the splendid genealogy of the House of Ayd, and in so doing tie up our camel supply for ever.

'An alliance of East and West,' I suggested, tentatively. Tom seemed impressed, so I went ahead. 'I happen to know that Sheikh Ayd would be much gratified if the Admiral Waghorn were to take his favourite daughter, Nura, in marriage . . .'

He stared at me with unbelieving eyes. I rushed in with explanations. 'Marriage is not so serious a matter with the Bedouin . . . some of these girls are married half a dozen times. You could leave after a few days and you would still be a member of Ayd's House . . .'

He listened, open-mouthed. At last he stopped me. 'Osman, old chap, as you know very well, I have a wife in England already. I don't speak Arabic. Do you expect me to woo the girl in Bengali?'

My great idea to save the Overland collapsed like a pricked balloon. But Waghorn was back next day with some thoughts of his own. 'It was a brilliant idea, old chap, I see that now. I've been thinking: as a Mohammedan, you are permitted four wives. You speak Arabic like a native and you know these people's ways . . .'

'No,' I said.

'No one need ever know – the Bedouin live in a world of their own, as you told me. I hear you can marry today and divorce three days later.'

'No,' I said.

'You would be saving the Transit,' he said. 'Saving my life's work. Sheikh Ayd would be overjoyed to have the famous Osman Effendi join his house.'

'Out of the question!' I said, but I knew even as I said it that I was hoist by my own petard. I told myself that it was for Waghorn's sake, of course; desperate situations require desperate remedies. But I have to admit that the memory, recently renewed, of Nura's warm brown eyes, of her snatching up my scarf at that midnight Bedou dance, had more than a little to do with my response. The truth was, I suppose, that Tom had caught me at a moment of peculiar susceptibility. Zobeida's death had left the house on the canal without its centre. Elena was itching to get away to Alexandria, which she saw as her natural habitat, and my 'handfasted bride' and mother of my Highland daughter was showing no inclination whatsoever to rejoin me. In any event, I told myself, in the circumstances my obligations to Tom Waghorn must be paramount.

Fortunately, the formalities of Bedou marriage are blessedly simple. All I had to do was to appear in Ayd's tent in the presence of the Sheikh and his four brothers and the *mutawa*, the local blind man, well versed in the Koran, who asked me before these witnesses whether I was willing to take the girl, after which I presented the marriage portion, two dresses and a red quilt for the marriage bed, and the *mutawa* recited the prescribed prayers, received his fee, and was led away.

Unfortunately, I had not appreciated that the Bedou bride is expected to prove her purity by putting up a piteous show of resistance to the lusts of the bridegroom. The old women gathered around the marriage tent early, peering in lascivious anticipation through the open end, reliving ancient deflorations. I will draw a veil over this obscene pantomine, except to say that Nura did indeed put up an impressive display, cowering very prettily as successive garments finally fell. The women outside began one of those eerie ululations which spread and build up I prayed for a sandstorm; then I looked at Nura and saw that her eyes were shining and she was glorying in her role. Oddly enough, the girls of the desert in the normal way make little pretence of concealing their charms, but this was a special occasion. The performance concluded with a storm of weeping which would have sufficed for the death of a Pharaoh, and a searing shriek which finally induced the old women to depart.

It was about this time that my friend Edward Lane rendered into English what some call *The Arabian Nights*, more correctly *The Thousand and One Nights*, and some of my readers may feel that the story of what I sometimes dignify as the foundation of the Bedou branch of Clan Osman rightly belongs to those pages. Lane omitted the more indelicate passages, and so all I will say now is that Sheikh Ayd's favourite daughter's defence of her virginity was exceeded only by the enthusiasm with which she shed it, and the witness of the blood-stained white sheet, exhibited publicly next morning to conclude the ritual, was deemed satisfactory.

We remained at Ayd's camp only three days lest Hill and Raven steal a march on us. Nura never showed any desire to leave the world of the black tents, but our marriage was not merely the affair of a day. Whenever I was in the vicinity on Transit business, I would find the long red cotton *thaub* which is the Bedou woman's welcome flying from Nura's tent-pole. Thus were conceived my sons Mohammed, who I hope will become *imam* at the Company's new mosque at Ismailiya, and Thomas, head of the camel-drivers on the Canal works.

Now that I was of the house of Ayd, and a blood brother of the Towra, our camels were no longer stolen; it would have been an outrage against the unchanging laws of the desert.

With the Peninsular about to run regular services from Suez as well as Alexandria, the transit business was booming. The flow of passengers between England and India was broad enough to support two transit lines. Bonaparte had said that Egypt would be 'the most important country in the world' and now Waghorn, the John the Baptist of what he called 'Steam Intercourse', was showing just how right Bonaparte had been. Suddenly the old sand-choked land of the Ancient Egyptians, pillaged by those grotesque clowns the Mamelukes, was the bridge of Empire, the busy highway between England and the riches of India and Cathay. The writ of Mohammed Ali, the one-time tobacco-grower, now ran from the Sudan to the Taurus.

Or so we thought.

Waghorn, as ever, spoke his mind. He wrote a book. 'Egypt in proportion to its extent is the richest country on the face of the earth ... Turkey is fast verging on its downfall and Egypt in twenty years' time will assume her place ... Why should Egypt be made to render her monies to Turkey and thus pay for the thraldom that impoverishes her?' Hopefully, he dedicated his book to British Members of Parliament.

Like his gospel of Steam Intercourse ten years earlier, Waghorn's warnings fell on deaf ears. For the god of Europe's statesmen was the Balance of Power, and Mohammed Ali was the arch-unbalancer. Lord Palmerston avowedly proposed to 'chuck him in the Nile' if he gave further trouble. Waghorn, he barked, was just one of the Pasha's lobbyists. My old consul friend, Colonel Patrick Campbell, was recalled and replaced by one of Pumice-stone's lick-spittles.

Nevertheless, in that spring of 1839 it really did seem that Tom Waghorn's Egyptian vision was about to be realised. Egged on by England, Sultan Mahmud II at last steeled himself to send the Ottoman army across the frontier into Syria to teach his over-weening vizier a lesson. At the end of June came the news that the Ottoman army had been routed at Nazin by Egypt's new fellahin army and was in precipitate flight before it. The Turkish admiral thereupon took his fleet into Alexandria to join the Egyptian navy. Two weeks later Sultan Mahmud II died and was succeeded by Abdul Mejid, a boy of eighteen.

The road to Istanbul lay open.

Those were stirring times. They might, one would have thought, have shown up the vanity of mere personal concerns. In fact they seemed to underscore them. Down at Suez I ran into a passenger named Captain Macdonald, *en route* for Calcutta who, having learned that I was a Scot, mentioned that he had run into one of his clan, a Mrs Jeannie Macdonald, on arrival in Alexandria. A charming lady, a widow it seemed, looking for a suitable infant school in which to place her small daughter. I was plunged over-night into despair. My chances of seeing Flora again were receding. I felt that, somehow, my identity was being taken from me. And if *She* should learn of my Bedou wedding . . .

But how could she? I spent the weeks while the momentous drama of the Ottoman Empire's near downfall was played out around me, going over all the ways she might.

28 Shepheard's

It is not often given to a man to watch history being made before his eyes in the space of one afternoon.

I had gone down to Alexandria on the pretext of making sure we were still getting our fair share of the passengers as they came ashore, but in reality in the secret hope that I might somehow locate the school at which Jeannie had placed Flora. In the event, I found the place in such an uproar that all such thoughts were driven from my mind.

The flagship of the British Mediterranean fleet, HMS *Powerful*, Admiral Napier commanding, lay in the western harbour, her big guns trained on the Ras el-Tin Palace, Mohammed Ali's favourite residence, a sitting duck of a target, perched high on its seaward promontory.

A vast crowd stood around the harbour watching, mesmerised, as the bluejackets drove the ship's boat between the battleship and the palace steps, carrying the Admiral's messages to the Pasha and the old boy's replies. Whatever the ultimatum being put to him, he was obviously resisting strongly.

I knew that a few weeks earlier the Mediterranean fleet had pounded Beirut for days in an effort to get Colonel Sèves – Suleiman Pasha, architect of Egypt's New Army – to capitulate and cease 'threatening' the heart of the great Ottoman Empire. They say the British offered Sèves huge bribes to bring the Egyptian army out, with free sea transport back to Egypt. As anyone who knew the Colonel could have told them, they had mistaken their man. He had fought with Bonaparte during the Hundred Days. He knew the Turkish fleet had deserted to Egypt; he knew the Ottoman Empire was tottering. It only needed a final push.

So now Admiral Napier had come to the heart of things to drive home Palmerston's bitter message. I thought of the old boy up there in his favourite window-seat, overlooking the harbour, where David Roberts had painted him with Colonel Campbell and Lieutenant Waghorn and Roberts himself, discussing our plan for an Overland Transit. My heart went out to him.

The sailors' long oars cut the harbour water with an awesome precision, their blades glistening in the low afternoon sun. The crowd fell silent as Admiral Napier disembarked and, in full fig, ascended the palace steps.

I tried to imagine the scene in that room, but the mind boggled. Only later, when I was engaged with de Lesseps on the Canal, did I discover what really happened that day – from the pen of Napier himself.

Napier was a Scot, no Butcher Cumberland. 'I am a great admirer of Your Excellency,' he said. 'I would much rather be your friend than your enemy.'

He offered the old man what he knew he most ardently desired: the throne of Egypt would remain with his heirs to eternity. But the price was high: Egypt was to withdraw from Syria, cut down its army, and continue to pay tribute to the Sultan. Worse, he must return the mutinying Ottoman fleet.

The terms were humiliating; it was the return of the Sultan's navy that really stuck in the old man's craw. He raised himself from his seat to confront the Admiral.

'Never! Never will I return the Ottoman fleet. You may burn it if you wish! Burn Alexandria and drive me out! I will make my last stand in the powder magazine, and then, when all is lost – he threw up his hands – 'je sauterai!'

Napier waited for the storm to blow itself out, then told the old man that if he did not submit to the Powers' demands he would return to the *Powerful* and plant a shell 'on the very window-seat on which Your Excellency is now sitting'.

Like his hero Bonaparte, Mohammed Ali had met his Waterloo. But unlike him, he was a realist; he stopped short of his Hundred Days, his St Helena. For a moment it had seemed help might come from France, but Pumicestone saw to that: 'Tell Monsieur Thiers that if he throws down the gauntlet we shall not hesitate to pick it up!'

Might was right again. Tom's vision of what ought to have

been crumpled. He was furious. For weeks afterwards I had to keep him away from our passengers or they would have deserted *en masse* to Hill and Raven. As for myself, I was invaded by a sense of sadness. David Wilkie arrived in Cairo that year – Scots painters were now everywhere. He came straight from Istanbul where he'd just 'done' the Grand Seigneur and was set on immortalising Mohammed Ali. It is a fine portrait, but it is not of the man I knew, not the man we prisoners had paraded before in 1807, nor the reconquerer of Mecca who had suspected Burckhardt of being an 'English spy'. He sits, not cross-legged on his divan, *chibouk* in hand, but upright on a stiff-backed European chair, red cap decorous, pure white beard flowing, jewelled scimitar curving around his thigh. It is a pose of great dignity, but to me it is a man putting a brave face on things, a broken man. I happen to know that Wilkie's first sketch showed that scimitar raised in the old boy's hand. He told the artist to start again.

'The English have robbed me of my sword,' he said.

Disgust and anger drove from my head my plan to seek out Flora, and I made my weary way round to the Waghorn office on the quayside. Fortunate that I did, for I found there a great rawboned fellow waiting for me, or rather waiting for Waghorn: Arthur Anderson, managing director of the Peninsular Steam Navigation Company. He wanted to warn Mr Waghorn that they were about to add 'and Oriental' to the company's name to mark their regular service of steamships from Suez to Bombay and points east. It was their intention to provide the very highest standards of accommodation and service. Fine wines were to be served free at dinner. Naturally they would expect the highest standards from the Transit. He seemed worried that they might not be forthcoming.

It was all rather stiff at first, but then, as it will, my accent gave me away. It turned out, as I might have guessed from that great Viking prow of a nose, that he was a Shetlander. He'd started life as a fisherman's boy somewhere near Lerwick and joined the Navy at sixteen in 1808, the year after we'd been sold into slavery in Egypt – my 'Mameluke period', you might say.

Of course, now our paths had crossed, we had a lot to say to each other. But he was a serious fellow. His parting words were: 'Don't forget, I'm relying on you to impress on Waghorn that the

P & O's passengers will expect the very highest standards of service.'

That parting phrase regurgitated in my gullet like raw camel's milk. I knew all too well that Waghorn was so absorbed in his grand vision that he could not stoop to such 'trifles'. I knew that Suez was our weak point, our Achilles' heel. I dreaded to think what Anderson would say if he saw it. I dropped everything and went down there.

I found our Suez hotel deserted, everything under inches of blown sand. Several windows were cracked. Our last batch of transit passengers had sailed three days earlier. So I went to George's. STAVRIANOUS was the name you could still just about make out over the door, but to everybody in the Transit this was George's. As ever George rushed out from behind his counter to greet me, flinging his arms around me, moustachios quivering. Then he stepped back, furrows of anxiety running across his brow.

'Osman Bey! Where is Mr Waghorn? Something is wrong – no?' He lowered his voice to what passes with George as a whisper. 'I had that long-nosed one, Anderson, sniffing around here asking questions, many questions. I do not like it.'

He was pouring out two glasses of ouzo when I spotted an unfamiliar face behind the counter, a young fellow in his shirt-sleeves laying about him with a fly-swat.

George followed my glance. He shrugged. 'What could I do, I ask you? A ship's officer! An Englishman! No baggage. Only a shilling in his pocket! Put ashore, here in Suez! He says he's going to make my fortune for me . . .'

'Call him over,' I said.

He came out from behind the bar, addressing George, ignoring me.

'You've got no India Pale Ale. Don't you know the ladies have got to have their India Pale? No Hodgson's Tea, neither. Don't you know *anything*? And with all these military swells coming through, there'll be a call for Moet's mixture . . .'

George looked at me, and threw up his hands.

'You should meet Captain Waghorn,' I said. 'The Overland Transit needs someone like you.'

He jumped out of his skin. Obviously he'd taken me for just another 'dirty Arab'. It happens.

He eyed me suspiciously. 'Captain? Don't talk to me about

captains, mate.' He lashed out with George's fly-swat and splattered a blue-bottle on the table. 'Those East India Company fellows think they can treat English seamen like lascars. That bugger Watson . . .'

Slowly, as George's blue-bottles met sudden death, it emerged that the young man had been purser on one of Anderson's new steamers. But the crew's quarters were not quite so splendid as the passengers'. Water seeped in through the paddle-shafts, the ship's biscuits rotted, and when the men complained it was called insubordination. Faced with foul water in the furnace heat of the Red Sea, two stokers threw down their shovels and the Captain clapped them in irons. The Chief protested, the officers supported him. But when the Captain cried 'Mutiny', they all backed down – except Sam. The Captain put him ashore in a ship's boat at Suez without even paying what was due.

That was how Sam told it – and I believed him. Whatever else he was, Sam Shepheard was no liar. He was an orphan. His uncle owned the Crown at Leamington and apprenticed him to a pastry-cook. He didn't fancy that, so he ran away to sea. Cook's lad, ship's cook, purser. And now, like me, like so many of us, thrown up on the Egyptian shore, starting again, on the make.

I didn't run into Sam Shepheard again for a year or so, and by then he was working at Hill's Hotel. Not long after that, I heard he was Hill's partner.

That was only the beginning. Mr Kinglake notwithstanding. I don't suppose many people will ever have heard of Osman the Scotsman. But who hasn't heard of Shepheard's Hotel in Cairo? You might say that for a while Shepheard *was* Egypt, one Egypt anyway.

What a gallery of faces come swimming up into my mind when I hear the word Shepheard's: the fierce-eyed Captain Burton *en route* for Mecca – years after Burckhardt and me, for all the hullabaloo he made about it! Robert Stephenson, with his yacht in Alexandria harbour, taking guests over the Pharaonic sites and prospecting railway contracts; Auguste Mariette, newly arrived from the Louvre, officially to collect Coptic manuscripts, but all the time aching to get at the Pharaohs; and yes, Mary, dark-eyed Mary Rangecroft, a Windsor shopkeeper's daughter in her twenties, ringlets framing her face, travelling as a lady's companion to India. Sam thought she'd make a better companion for a man, especially a hotel-keeper, and snapped her up. He never looked back after that. Two years later he was proprietor of the British Hotel, and two years after that he was doing well enough to move out of the old Frankish quarter and into a bright new Shepheard's looking out over the grass and trees and cafés of Ezbekieh Square.

What a pity I didn't rope him into Waghorn's Transit that day at George's. Things might have gone differently if I had.

I wasn't sleeping well. Flora and her mother wandered disconsolately through my dreams, and now that long-nosed Shetlander, Arthur Anderson, intruded. He'd put a hundred-foot steamer, called the *Cairo*, on the Nile with cabins for fifty below decks. It made Waghorn's six-horse-power *Jack o' Lantern* look ridiculous. Anderson's presence had one good effect, though: Waghorn and Hill and Raven's transit lines stopped fighting each other and got together, working out of both the Great Eastern and the British Hotels. The scrambles to make up parties for the vans were worse than ever. I had to make them draw lots as the best way of keeping the peace. After that it went briskly enough: I would signal to the grooms holding the spirited horses and the grooms would let go, and off the vans would shoot as if from a cannon, careering round the Ezbekieh, a couple of footmen hanging on for dear life behind, through the Bab el-Nasr and out into the open desert where the footmen dropped off.

The number of passengers was mounting every week. We were doing very nicely; the camel thefts had stopped, Tom Waghorn seemed well content. But I had the deepest misgivings: I could not say we were maintaining the high standards which, according to Anderson, the P & O passengers were entitled to expect. Some instinct – I know not what – compelled me to go down to the No. 4 station, a pivotal point on the Transit where two contrary tides met: pale-faced recruits going out for 'a tour of duty', sun-bronzed loud-voiced 'Anglo-Indians' coming home on furlough.

All seemed much as usual. A couple of military 'swells' sprawled in the shadow of an unharnessed van. Chickens scratched diligently around the legs of two middle-aged memsahibs, who were sipping drinks under parasols. Yet as I crossed the courtyard to enter 'the salon', I experienced a feeling of foreboding.

The long table running down the centre of the room was piled high with greasy dishes, teapots full of dregs and empty bottles of India Pale Ale. Slumbering bodies were draped untidily over the divans that ran round the walls. One was stretched out precariously on the top of a sideboard. It was over a hundred degrees in the shade.

I looked around warily. Over by the bar at the end of the so-called salon, large as life, Jeannie Macdonald was in earnest conversation with Arthur Anderson. As I moved towards them, she spotted me and turned away.

Anderson is a slow speaker, articulating his words like a Kirk elder pronouncing judgement. I could hear him from yards away.

'We've been getting complaints, Mrs Macdonald. There was a letter in *The Times*. So I wanted to ask your opinion, as a woman – and an *American* woman. It won't do, will it? Not for the Peninsular and Oriental Steam Navigation Company's passengers.'

'No,' she said. 'It won't.'

By this time I had worked round so that I was three feet from her. She continued to stare through me, the way she had when I was a fourteen-year-old at my grandmother's waulking party, Macdonald confronting Macleod, 'crippled and clumsy, feeding on glass and coarse grass and mill-dust.'

She acknowledged me at last – in a manner of speaking.

'Ah, Osman Effendi, this gentleman is Mr Arthur Anderson, managing director of the famous Peninsular and Oriental steamship line.'

Anderson caught my eye and winked. I wondered then how much he knew about us and whether this was some new ploy of his.

'Mr Macleod and I are old shipmates,' he said. 'I have asked Mrs Macdonald as a lady from the Great Republic to advise me.'

As he raised his hand a great cloud of flies rose from a pile of chicken-bones on a stack of dirty plates. 'It simply won't do,' he said, 'Not for the first-class passengers of the Peninsular and Oriental Steam Navigation Company.'

'I shall talk to Captain Waghorn at once,' I said.

'I already have. In fact I offered him a good price – very generous – out of my respect for him. I *begged* him to take the money. You know what he said? "I'll see you damned first." '

'Yes,' I said. 'He would.'

I think I knew then how Mohammed Ali must have felt when he saw Admiral Napier's big guns trained on his window-seat.

Calm and affable as ever, Anderson pleaded urgent business in Suez. 'We're all Scots here,' he said. 'I don't doubt we'll be able to work out something... See you soon, Mrs Macdonald.'

He nodded gravely, and strode off on those long legs of his, leaving Jeannie and me face to face and on my own ground, so to speak, for the first time since I sent her down to Omar's village to escape the plague. Flora was still a baby then; Zobeida was alive.

Nothing much, it seemed, had changed. 'You're a fool, Donald, to stay with Waghorn. The man's a born loser.'

'Born loser?' I said. It was a new expression to me. It seemed to take us back to our days in the Kirk. 'You mean he's not of the Elect?' I said. A bad joke, I suppose.

'He'll drag you down with him,' she said. 'Anderson's a coming man. He'd pay you well. No saying where you might end.'

I said: 'Jeannie, Tom Waghorn doesn't just run the Overland Transit. Tom Waghorn *is* the Overland Transit. He built it from nothing when they were all jeering at him. "Mad Tom", they called him. The East India Company wouldn't give him any money. He risked his own. The British Postmaster-General snubbed him, wouldn't give him his mails. Now, when he's proved his case and changed the map of the world, Anderson comes along with his money and wants to buy him out. Do you really think I'm going to ditch Tom now?'

'You can't stop progress' was what she said.

I stared at her in disbelief. 'Progress? Isn't that what President Andrew Jackson said when he drove your Cherokees from their lands? Did that John Ross of yours call it progress?'

She fell silent and lowered her eyes. My heart went out to her.

She broke the silence at last, raised her eyes, seeking mine. 'Donald,' she said softly, 'Flora has been asking for you, asking for her father. Her best friend's father is with Briggs and Company and sells Mohammed Ali's cotton to Liverpool. Flora keeps on about his frock-coat. But she has no father to show off... she's asking me every day now.'

'I was beginning to think you might be making other arrangements,' I said and instantly regretted it.

'So I told her about where you lived on the island of Skye and the Macleod stronghold in Dunvegan Castle and the waulking of your aunts' plaid where we met . . .'

I was astonished – and touched.

'Well,' she said, defensively, 'now she has a story the other girls haven't got – and after all, her name *is* Flora Macdonald. It's her right.'

'So,' I said, 'I shall tell her how Flora Macdonald hid the Prince and Donald Macleod, the boatman of Galtrigill, though captured by Cumberland's men refused to betray him though offered a fortune, and how, as a boy, I lifted the Speckled Pipes for Donald MacCrimmon when he came back from Canada to pipe the Chief, back from India, into the Dun . . .'

'So what do we want with Mr Lane's *Thousand and One Nights*' she said.

We arranged a family tea-party.

I couldn't resist it. 'So you're not afraid to let your daughter near these dirty polygamous, superstitious, Mohammedans?'

'*Our* daughter,' she said.

Hill and Raven sold out to Anderson and the P & O took over the Overland Transit and I saw Tom Waghorn off to England a sick and ruined man. I was saddened and angry. And yet a crushing weight had been lifted from my shoulders. Hope was re-born.

5.30 a.m., 18 November, Lake Timsah – Noon, 19 November 1869, Ismailiya

Just after 5.30 p.m. the *Mohammed Ali* swung round into Lake Timsah, and Nubar gave the order to drop anchor. The low westering sun was beginning to gild that great mirror of water in true Second Empire style, throwing into high relief the Khedive's new 'Moorish' palace. Richly patterned marquees were erected in its gardens, often cheek by jowl with rough cornstalk shelters and Bedouin tents.

Heralding the entrance of *L'Aigle* a great explosion of cheering, counterpointed by the women's shrill, quavering cries, spread along the shores of the lake. The Empress on the bridge – de Lesseps at her side – acknowledged the shouts with waves of her handkerchief. One after the other, at five- or ten-minute intervals, the ships of the Grand Procession steamed into the lake, seeking anchorage where ships had never anchored before.

Even the British, consumed with envy as they were, had sent the Admiralty yacht, the *Psyche*. But the P & O's paddler *Delta*, with the directors on board, was hopelessly outclassed by the Messageries Impériales' crack liner, the *Peluse*, carrying the directors of the Canal itself. It was past midnight before the last of the ships found an anchorage.

It was a sight to lift the heart. Everywhere the navigation lights and deck lights and cabin lights of the ships riding at anchor spangled the dark waters, dancing in the light breeze.

Here was a new urban oasis, fed by the waters of the Mediterranean and the Nile: a palm-fringed quay along the lakeside, two hotels, five cafés, public gardens in the French style, a hospital, a mosque, a church – not to mention the 'magnificent natural port six times bigger than Marseille', to quote Ferdinand.

It was very late before Jeannie and I got ashore. In the Hôtel des Voyageurs every foot of carpet was occupied by sleeping bodies. The Khedive had erected over a thousand tents, in two lines, between the sweetwater canal and the town. All now occupied. I remembered then that I had a key to Ferdinand's modest chalet-office on the Avenue de Mohammed Ali. There we spent what was left of the night fitfully dozing in Ferdinand's cane armchairs. I put out my arm and held her hand, and she did not take it away. For a few hours the nightmare of the grandiose transit of the Canal faded.

At 8 a.m., not a hair out of place, radiant and eager for the events of the great day, that extraordinary woman the Empress was cantering off on horseback, accompanying de Lesseps to view the Kisr cutting to the north. She wore a light white riding-habit, her ladies following behind in two carriages, escorted by Bedouin guards in red and white on fine white dromedaries. I recognised my friend Ayd as they rode by. His sons rode proudly behind him: could the young Bedou bringing up the rear really be Nura's boy Thomas?

The afternoon was devoted to a *fantasia*. Forty thousand people, drawn from miles around, packed the streets of the little town. Tribesmen screamed by on galloping horses, rearing up suddenly, firing madly into the air. Fashionably dressed ladies from the ships stood on the seats of their carriages, craning their necks to watch horse races over the desert. I was pressed into service to help conduct the distinguished guests around the Bedouin encampments, new carpets for the tents having been supplied by the Khedive. I put myself in Ayd's good books by taking my party to admire his two Damascus swords. No sign of Nura, and Ayd seemed evasive on the subject, covering all in compliments as only a Bedou can. The Bedouin chiefs did Ismail proud, offering coffee, sherbet and pipes with lordly condescension. In the adjoining tents dancing-girls swarmed, with singers, jugglers and contortionists – East and West meeting after a fashion. Ismail Sadik Pasha, the Khedive's Minister of Finance, arranged a very private party on a houseboat on the sweetwater canal, promising to show what 'Oriental dancing' was *really* like. Thank God I had forbidden Wasifa to appear here.

My heart went out to Theo (Sam Shepheard's erstwhile apprentice), placed in charge of the catering. I tried to find him but couldn't. But Jeannie did get hold of the menu, which listed twenty-four courses, starting with *Poisson à la Réunion des Deux Mers*, and not excluding *Roast Beef à l'Anglaise*. A thousand waiters and valets in powdered wigs and scarlet livery had been engaged to attend the crowned heads' banquet, together with five hundred cooks from all around the Mediterranean.

The Palace was crowded to suffocation point. Ladies stood on the freshly imported Louis Quinze chairs, Prussian officers scrambled onto the new marble-topped tables to catch a glimpse of the Empress making her entrance in cerise satin, a magnificent coronet shining on her auburn hair, the Khedive on one side and the Emperor of Austria on the other.

No one danced at the Grand Ball because no one could move in that crush. They say that two thousand 'guests' had invited themselves. Even more, I reckon, had invited themselves to the Khedive's grand celebratory banquet, many Englishmen amongst them. The feast did not start until 1 a.m., but they were perched at the long tables, forks at the ready, from ten o'clock. For the humbler folk, whole sheep were roasting by the dozen along the shoreline and into the desert.

I'm afraid the distinguished French guests complained of the lateness of their promised feast. I feared for Theo and I confided my worries to Jeannie but she only laughed. 'Allah will provide,' she said, mocking as ever.

I suppose you might say Allah *did* provide – for us at least – because next morning Ferdinand sent a message suggesting that for the rest of the trip Mrs Macdonald and Osman Effendi might like to join the company on *L'Aigle*. She had held her grudge against him ever since the macaroni incident, but I could see she was flattered.

In the event, we didn't get up anchor until just before noon next day. *L'Aigle* swung round slowly, and headed for the south-eastern corner of Lake Timsah, leaving behind us, dancing on the waters as far as the eye could see, a long tail of empty bottles and tins.

I fear we have celebrated too soon. Six miles ahead, in the Serapeum cutting, lurks the deadly rock-ridge that still haunts my dreams. Did the underwater blasting go deep enough? The P & O's *Delta* has turned tail and gone back to Port Said.

Do the directors know something that I don't?

29 A Southern Gentleman

My heart sang. I was going down to Alexandria to meet my 'Highland' daughter, no longer clandestinely, but at our rendez-vous for tea at the Café de Paris.

On the way I ran into a sight that changed my mood. At first I could hardly believe my eyes, but there he was: the 'Old Pasha', Mohammed Ali, seated on a horse led by a single groom. No one else was with him. I salaamed, but he looked past me. Those penetrating eyes which had surveyed the Ross-shire Buffs prisoners at the Citadel almost forty years ago were vacant now, staring into eternity. Like the foundations of the great barrage across the Nile he had been in such a hurry to complete, the footings of the old man's mind had slipped again. The story was that at a state council in one of his last moments of lucidity he had risen from his chair to warn them against his grandson and heir: 'Beware of Abbas!'

The warning was warranted. I shall never forget the strange and fearful silence that fell across the land of Egypt that spring of 1849 when Abbas ascended the throne. All our futures now lay in the hands of a dark and malevolent recluse, thirty-six years of age, but already ancient.

'If I must submit to someone,' he declared at once, 'let it be to the Sultan-Caliph, not to the Christians.' Almost before his grandfather's body was settled in the great alabaster mosque-tomb he had built for himself atop the Citadel, Abbas had begun to tear down all Mohammed Ali had devoted his life to building up, creating a new Egypt. Clôt Bey's medical school, his modern hospitals, were shut down, their bright young doctors used as army fodder or turned into clerks. One after the other, all the brave, hopeful enterprises of the Old Pasha fell under the vicious axe of Abbas: the primary schools, the polytechnic, the cavalry school, the veterinary college, the shipbuilding yards, the cotton factories – even the great Nile barrage on which the old man had set his heart.

I remember the despair of those years. It was as if Egypt were returning to the shadows, disappearing again under the ever-lasting, blowing sand Giovanni and I had laboured so hard to clear. All the engineers and teachers and scientists Mohammed Ali had brought from Europe were packing their bags.

Jeannie and I and Flora went to the docks to bid farewell to Dr Clôt, helping him to get his collection of Pharaonic antiquities, gathered over a quarter century, safely stowed on the Marseille steamer. Both of us felt we owed him a debt we could never repay for the safe delivery of Flora, now a handsome, sprightly girl of fifteen or so – her mother's age when she began to instruct this callow drover's boy in the facts of life from the intellectual emi-nence of the Inverness grammar school.

According to our agreement, Flora Macdonald's education was under her mother's control, which meant that she was brought up among the Christian Copts, who claimed to be the direct descendants of the Pharaohs although the better-off families liked nothing better than to air their French, thus setting themselves apart from us poor 'Arabs'. I could still see a problem there, but I was heartened now to find that Flora resembled her mother in having a mind of her own. She was immensely curious to know how Donald Macleod from the island of Skye had become Osman Effendi, and my stories seemed to fascinate her just as my father's telling of our clan legends had long ago fascinated me.

While her mother was away on business among the cotton houses of Minet el-Bassal, I managed to take Flora up the Nile to show her the real Egypt. I took her into 'Belzoni's Tomb', as the Pharaoh Seti's vast mausoleum was still called, and she marvelled at all those brightly coloured little figures marching across the walls. I remember how excited she got at the recurring *ankh*s depending from the hands of the Pharaohs and the gods; she'd seen the same sign on old Coptic gravestones and her teachers had told her it was the origin of the Christian cross, a magical idea I was glad to fall in with.

I was still much of the time away on Transit business, under the P & O's ownership since 1847, but this merely made the moments Flora and I had together more precious to both of us, so that a father and daughter understanding grew up, a sort of secret conspiracy between us.

On her sixteenth birthday I gave her the much-thumbed old copy of Tom Paine's *The Rights of Man* from which her mother had begun to instruct me in the Sasannach tongue. I accompanied this with Burckhardt's copy of the Holy Koran, explaining how much it shared with the Bible, and that both harked back to Abraham and that Jesus ranked high among the prophets of Islam. I warned her, though, that it would be unwise to display the Koran among her mother's Alexandria Coptic friends. But being her mother's – as well as her father's – daughter I fear she ignored this prudent advice, giving rise to considerable scandal, which I must say warmed my heart. In this way Flora – Flora Macdonald – became a lifeline through the cold seas of the Abbas years.

It was just an accident that I happened to be in the street when Edwin de Leon, the new American Consul-General, escorted by a troop of cavalry, swept by in his carriage on his way to present his credentials to Abbas. I thought little of it at the time; consuls were always coming and going. It certainly never occurred to me for a moment that this man might be important in my life.

We saw little of Abbas. Terrified of assassins, he cowered in successive palaces he built in the desert, furnished like the tombs of the Pharaohs with false doors and cul-de-sacs to baffle pursuers. The only language he could speak was Turkish, and the only consul who spoke that language at the time was Colonel Murray, the Scot who represented Britain. It was in this way that Stephenson & Co. got the contract to build a railway from Alexandria to Cairo, the first in Africa, which pleased me greatly since I had apprenticed my son Giovanni to Galloway Bey, from the famous English iron-founding family.

Sam Shepheard did very well out of Abbas, too. He had two fine greyhounds, Ben and Bess, and when he heard that Abbas coveted them he presented them to him, and received in return the fine palace on the Ezbekieh, the Language and Translation School which had once been the headquarters of Bonaparte's *savants*, soon to find yet greater fame as 'Shepheard's Hotel'.

Sam had come a long way since I first set eyes on him wielding the fly-swatter behind the bar of George's in Suez. He was one of those men over whom Egypt seems to wave a magic wand. His name was already famous. His 'pickings', as he put it, were growing steadily. Yet Sam was not a happy man. Paradoxically, he was one of those Englishmen who, however far they travel, never really leave home. Bread and cheese in England, he was always telling me, were better than a feast of venison and champagne anywhere else. All he was waiting for was for his 'pile' to grow high enough to enable him to buy a manor house in Warwickshire, a coat of arms, and enough land to squire it over the English countryside. At this point Sam's bulldog would laboriously rise to its feet, walk three yards, and collapse onto the hotel carpet with a deep sigh.

There was another, deeper cause of Sam's despair. A year or so after their marriage a daughter was born to Sam and Mary Shepheard and christened Jane. But Sam was set on a male heir. Convinced that the next child would be a boy, he laid in extra stocks of champagne. 'Inshallah,' I prompted – and as it turned out God *was* willing. The boy was christened Joseph Campbell and the champagne flowed and Jeannie and I, remembering Rory, felt a stab of envy. Yet within a year JOSEPH CAMPBELL SHEPHEARD was just another name in the crowded Protestant cemetery. And in the torrid weeks of the *khamsin* the girl, Jane, too was carried off by a fever.

Sam was not a man to give up, but all he succeeded in doing was adding to the formidable number of infant graves in the Protestant cemetery in Old Cairo. These tragedies brought Jeannie and Sam's long-suffering wife, Mary, closer together, and, from time to time, when Mary was again *enceinte* or retired to England for the birth, Jeannie would take over her housekeeping duties at Shepheard's, rather to my astonishment, because Sam went through housekeepers like a McCarthy gin through cotton-bolls. I liked to think that Sam would now get as good as he gave, and I looked forward to seeing Flora's mother more often.

It did not occur to me that I was not the only person who might see her more often.

To mark the opening of his smart new premises, Sam put on a series of grand balls about this time. No place for a *hadji*, but to quiet the pleadings of Elena, who was pining for the 'civilisation' of Alexandria, I took her along one evening. And who should I find in a far corner of the room but Jeannie Macdonald, who had discarded her dark housekeeper's dress for a pink ball-gown. She was not dancing but in deep conversation with a handsome figure in a long blue coat decorated with oak leaves on the collar. She drew away when she saw me, then reluctantly introduced us.

'Oh, Osman Effendi, this is Mr Edwin de Leon, the American Consul-General in the Near East. He was, I believe, appointed to the post by President Pierce himself. He is also a distinguished author.'

De Leon bowed, his mutton-chop whiskers catching the light, the American eagles about to take off from his silver buttons. 'I have been fortunate indeed to find so charming a compatriot in my new posting.'

I corrected him. 'Mrs Macdonald is a lady from the Highlands of Scotland – as her name suggests.'

He ignored me. 'One does not expect to find a neighbour in so distant a post. Mrs Macdonald is from North Carolina, I am from Charleston in South Carolina. It is our mutual hope to extend the blessings of Freedom and Democracy in the Orient.'

I tried to catch Jeannie's eye, but failed.

My disquiet grew when, on my frequent visits to Shepheard's on Transit business, I kept finding de Leon – Edwin, as I now heard her call him – and Jeannie Macdonald in deep conversation, almost as if they were old friends. But what could an American diplomat and Shepheard's housekeeper have to discuss so urgently and, for that matter, so secretly?

Hitherto I had felt that our common roots in the Highlands, and above all Gaelic, our 'secret language', had constituted an indissoluble link between Jeannie and me, stronger than all that had separated us. It made her mine, uniquely mine. It was as if we were together in our own island. But now de Leon had called her a compatriot. Suddenly it came to me that she had lived as long in the American South as she had in the Highlands. De Leon and she also had a language all their own, a sort of whining drawl that I became aware of when they were together. I grew to hate the sound of it.

It was obvious now that the Transit's days were numbered. An

English engineer had plunged to his death inside the caisson of the bridge being built across the Nile. Not Giovanni, thank God. But despite such setbacks, the rails were now advancing inexorably southwards. Paradoxically, the Transit was busier than I had ever seen it. When the vans pulled up outside Shepheard's from Suez the stampede for beds was bloodier than ever. Using their parasols like sabres and their reticules like mortar shells, the seasoned memsahibs stormed up the stairs to the dim-lit corridors above, flinging open doors to stake claims to their beds, ejecting any male so ill-mannered as to be asleep there.

Labouring in their wake to attempt to see justice done one afternoon, I almost bumped into Jeannie, slipping out of a room, folded sheets under her arm. I would have ascribed this to her housekeeping duties – had not Edwin de Leon emerged a moment later, expelled by a furious memsahib.

Was it the *same* door? With the scrum surging around it was hard to be sure. The corridor was ill-lit, Sam being as parsimonious in such matters as he was generous with champagne.

What on earth was de Leon doing up there? What diplomatic business could he possibly have to transact in a bedroom?

In my head I could hear that insinuating Southern drawl of his. Ear now attuned, I could hear it on her lips too, when she was speaking English. I had never heard anything like it before. It was worlds away from the nasal yapping of Jacoub Barthouw, young Legh's dragoman, the Yankee. Whenever I saw them together now it seemed to enclose them in a soft intimacy, excluding me, mocking the Gaelic. De Leon had let it be known that he was a cotton-plantation owner in South Carolina; Jeannie's sister Isobel was married to a cotton-plantation owner in North Carolina. All of a sudden, I felt that all the bridges I had built up – *we* had built up – over the years were being destroyed. The despair I had experienced in Lochaber where it had all begun could be laughed off as calf-love. But you couldn't say that about the panic which now overtook me, a *hadji*, a respectable family man.

My mind having retreated into the past, I found myself back on the wards of our Gibraltar Military Hospital with my mentor, Surgeon Munro, cupping and blistering the backs of men taken by fever. It was my duty to heat the interior of the cupping glasses with a match before they were applied to the man's back. This plainly increased the sufferer's discomfort. So one day I asked Surgeon Munro why.

'The theory of the counter-irritant,' he said with a smile. Which seemed to mean the fever didn't feel so bad because the back felt worse.

Well, it may have worked, temporarily at least, in my case, because if the fever was high and delirious, the counter-irritant was worse.

At the end of May 1853, Tsar Nicholas of Russia ordered his army to march into the Danubian provinces of the Ottoman Empire to protect the Sultan's Christian subjects from persecution by the 'sick man of Europe' – the Tsar's phrase. Palmerston's 'balance of power' was being destroyed overnight. The British Navy was ordered to the Dardanelles to restore it.

The last thing I wanted in my situation was another war of 'the Cross and the Crescent', a new crusade fanning the hell-fires of bigotry. The only person not upset by the news was my son Sami, recalled urgently to his warship in Alexandria harbour. At last he seemed to have a chance of promotion. As for me, it was my duty to comfort his weeping wife, Nawal, a difficult task that would get more difficult. The Russian army was now well across the River Pruth, an army of occupation flowing over Ottoman territory.

Troop movements made the Transit busier than ever, and it was some weeks before I ran into Jeannie and 'Edwin' again in Shepheard's. This time they were seated at a table, forms and sheets of calculations spread before them, and there was a third person present, a clerkly young fellow wearing the blue turban of a Copt.

De Leon greeted me effusively, rising to his feet to show me a blueprint of what he proudly announced as the McCarthy Patent Cotton-Gin, the very latest model. As a cotton-plantation owner himself, he could tell me that this machine was going to revolutionise cotton production in Egypt and he sure was dee-lighted at having been of some assistance to his compatriot, Mrs Macdonald here, and her partner Mr George Girgis, in importing it.

At this point the young Coptic gentleman rose and held out a large, ornately engraved business card:

Mr George Jesus Girgis
The Counting House
Messrs Planta et Cie
Minet el-Bassal
Alexandria
Egypt

Like many Copts he was a book-keeper, or as he preferred to say a *comptable* or, better still, a *contrôleur*. In other words he was king of the Counting House in this noisome cotton port, where endless heavy horses hauled wagons piled high with bales, their great hairy hoofs forever slipping on the slimy cobbles paving its streets. The place seemed to me the great sump into which the sweat of the cotton-growing fellahin drained and was duly transmuted into gold.

If Jeannie and Omar and Hassuna needed a partner for the ginning venture, I had to admit that George Jesus Girgis, who had imbibed the secrets of compound interest with his mother's milk, was their man. (It never crossed my mind at that point that our daughter, Flora, might have been part of the bargain.)

I felt ashamed now of my jealous suspicions. De Leon had been doing nothing less than his duty in promoting the sale and export of American machinery (although I did still ask myself why business of this sort could not have been conducted at the American Consulate).

Although no longer needed, the 'counter-irritant' intensified. In October 1853, pushed by Palmerston, still desperate to 'maintain the Balance of Power', the Sultan declared war on Russia. The Turkish and Egyptian fleets sailed for the Black Sea. The Russian fleet was ready. On 30 November it caught the combined Egyptian and Turkish fleets sheltering in the almost landlocked harbour of Sinope. It pounded them to bits. MASSACRE AT SINOPE ran the headlines in the London papers that finally reached us. Hour after hour, they reported, the Russian warships had poured grapeshot into the trapped vessels, slaughtering the Egyptian and Turkish sailors struggling to climb up the steep sides of the harbour and get to safety. Few succeeded.

Poor Sami!

BOOK V

The Tarnished Rainbow

... to my right the east was already bright ... Suddenly, from that side, I saw a rainbow of the most brilliant colours with the two ends plunged from west to east. I admit that I felt my heart leap, and had to check my imagination which would have interpreted this as the success of my project today – the practical union of Occident and Orient, that sign of which the Scripture speaks ...

– Ferdinand de Lesseps, *Lettres, Journal, Documents* (1865)

The heat was terrible that summer of 1854. The narrow Cairo alleys were like furnaces. The pavements scorched the feet. People said it was the gates of Hell opening to receive our late ruler, Abbas. For on 13 July, in the sixth year of his reign, the assassins from whom he had been in continual flight had at last caught up with him.

As the shimmering heat haze lifted from the Nile we heard, first in a whisper, then in a great shout, that Abbas was dead, strangled overnight in his bath – or was it in bed? – by two of his own slaves whom he had threatened to bastinado in the morning (notoriously, Abbas liked to administer such punishments personally, even to the ladies of his own harem). Others said that the assassins were two young Mamelukes sent as a 'gift' by Princess Nazli, Mohammed Ali's favourite daughter, who had fled to Istanbul. However that might be, fast horses were waiting at the Benha Palace gates; the assassins were never caught.

A great weight was lifted from our minds. We felt that our lives could resume again. Except that mine was darkened by the fact that Sami had been posted 'Missing', and I had to spend much time trying to persuade his tearful wife that 'Missing' did not mean dead and that even then her husband might be recovering in some warm British military hospital.

The British and French armies had switched their effort to the Crimea and, by September were laying siege to the great Russian fortress of Sebastopol. Reinforcements were pouring through on the Transit from India. Sam Shepheard's pickings were soaring: the Hussar officers' consumption of champagne was awesome. Unfortunately, they tended to regard 'trademen's' bills as

importunities unworthy of a gentleman's notice. A large party left
for the front leaving their bills unpaid. Sam pursued them to
Alexandria. Too late: the party had sailed. He chased after them
to the Crimea and cornered the colonel on the battlefield. He
came back with all but fifteen shillings paid. The 'pile of tin' grew.

Returning post-haste from Paris, the new ruler, Mohammed
Said – none other than the fat boy who had so tormented us –
was by then in Istanbul for his investiture.

A few days later I heard from the Netherlands consul, a friend of
mine, that Ferdinand de Lesseps was following hot on Mohammed
Said's heels – at his special invitation. It was over twenty years
ago now, but would Mohammed Said remember? Would he still
bear a grudge? I remembered the malicious gleam in the boy's eye
and I shuddered. I rushed round to Shepheard's to warn Jeannie.
But to my astonishment, she swept this aside. What impressed
her was something quite different.

'My, my,' she said. 'Your friend Lesseps has been quick off the
mark. Now we shall see what a few bowls of macaroni slipped
to a hungry boy can do!'

De Lesseps, I pointed out, had had a dozen diplomatic postings
since Cairo. In any case, how could he have known that
Mohammed Said would succeed? Nevertheless, I begged her to
keep out of Said's way. As monarch, he would have many eager
artists of the cord or the *mauvais café* at his disposal. But she just
laughed and told me, once again, that she was an American
citizen. No foreign tyrant would dare touch a hair of her head. I
was glad at least that she did not tell me she was under Edwin de
Leon's protection.

I myself had come away with an excellent impression of Ferdinand de Lesseps after our brief encounter at France's Cairo
consulate all those years ago. I made it my business to be on the
quayside on 7 November when his ship docked. Though no longer
a diplomat, he was greeted by the Minister of Marine and was
conducted to the viceregal carriage; as Said's honoured guest, he
was to stay at a royal villa where, I happened to know, even the
wash-basins were solid gold. As de Lesseps moved towards the
carriage, he paused for a moment, looked around, and saw me.

He recognised me instantly. 'Ah, Osman, Osman Effendi!
Tomorrow I am to meet the new Viceroy, returning from his
investiture in Istanbul. I shall need a dragoman, a dragoman

renommé. Will you aid me? Be at the Gabbari Palace tomorrow.'
He passed on.

Next day, I donned my gold-braided dragoman outfit from my
days at the British consulate, and was very glad I had done so,
because de Lesseps was in his old diplomatic corps gold-faced
claw-hammer coat, knee-breeches, cocked hat and epaulettes, now
with the red cordon of the Legion of Honour.

Casting protocol to the winds, Mohammed Said advanced in
front of his assembled officers across the hall of the Gabbari
Palace, and flung his enormous arms around Ferdinand, a broad
grin splitting his red-bearded face. He was now a great bear of a
man whom I found it hard to connect with the petulant adolescent
I had caught, *in flagrante delicto* at the French consulate.

'Ah, mon vieux copain,' he chortled, airing his 'Parisian' French
as he pounded the ex-consul on the back with a hand the size of
a ham. 'What times we had together! Cette chienne americaine,
ma gouvernante! How we threw the dust in her eyes!' He shook
with laughter. De Lesseps looked mildly embarrassed. I made a
note to let Jeannie know that the Viceroy thought of her as 'that
American bitch'. But I was worried – was it possible that Said
would recognise *me*?

The two had settled down to coffee, pipes and reminiscences
of feats of horsemanship and the *épée*. At last, Said stood up. In
Cairo, he said, the Notables waited to salute their newly invested
Viceroy. He shrugged, French fashion. 'Well, let them wait! Voyez,
mon ami, nous allons faire l'école buisonière – we shall play
hookey. Tomorrow we go on manoeuvres in the desert. My regiments are already encamped nearby.'

Next day I found a fine white horse outside the gates of Ferdinand's villa. Its groom had brought it down from Syria, a present
from Said to his old *copain*. We were to ride to the sandy plain
between Alexandria and Lake Mareotis where ten thousand
troops were waiting to be reviewed by their new Viceroy.

Two days later we all moved out into the Libyan desert, where
Said set up his headquarters in a large van, furnished as a bedroom
and hauled by six mules. The soldiers were ordered to build a
loose stone wall around it with an embrasure for a field gun so
that Said could salute his troops as they marched past. Evidently,
he still loved 'playing at soldiers'.

De Lesseps put his white stallion at the stone wall and cleared it easily. Then he turned the horse and did it again. The soldiers cheered.

Next day Said set up a sharpshooter's target at 200 yards but none of the soldiers could hit it. De Lesseps took one of the men's carbines, demonstrating how it should be shouldered. An officer challenged him to try the target. He took aim – and hit the bull's eye. Said then sent for his own German rifle. De Lesseps shouldered it – and hit the target again. They begged him to shoot a third time, but he refused. 'I might have missed,' he whispered to me. 'I should have lost my reputation.'

We had been in the desert for about a week, and not a single word had yet been uttered about what I divined was the real object of de Lesseps' visit. Then came a morning when I rose early to find de Lesseps already at his ablutions. I remember how chilly it was before dawn; the camp was only just beginning to stir. Southwards the desert rolled away as far as the eye could see. A few thin spokes of light shot up over the earth's rim. Moments later, the sky was lit up by a brilliant rainbow, the most brilliant I think I had ever seen – an ethereal arch across the vault of the heavens from Orient to Occident.

Ferdinand had dropped his towel and was standing stock-still.

'Osman,' he said at last, 'do you recall the verse in the book of Genesis, after the Flood, when the water subsides, and a rainbow spans the sky?' He now had his 'sign'.

In the cool of the evening Ferdinand went over to Said's quarters to lay before him his tremendous project for the marriage of the seas. I am proud to say that I was there as de Lesseps' dragoman and interpreter, although in fact he had small need of me. At such close quarters there was a risk that Mohammed Said might recognise me as the accomplice of 'that American bitch'. If he did, he said nothing.

'This great work, the penetration of the isthmus of Suez,' announced de Lesseps, 'will shorten by more than half the distance between Egypt – and Europe and America – and the East Indies. No one knows the names of the kings who built the Pyramids, but the name of the prince who builds this great maritime canal will be known and blessed from century to century.'

The red beard twitched, the lips parted.

'Today, Your Highness, no operation, however difficult, is regarded by modern science as impossible.'

Said held up his hand. 'I am convinced. I accept your great plan. For the remainder of the manoeuvres we will concern ourselves with the means of putting it into effect.'

We had almost forgotten the world outside until a despatch arrived from Rashid Pasha, the Grand Vizier in Istanbul. The Russians were holding out in Sebastopol. A terrible storm had wrecked many British and Turkish supply vessels in the harbour. The winter in the Crimea was cruel; without warm clothing men were dying in droves from cold and exposure.

It was over a year now since the thunder-clap of Sinope – but still no word of Sami or his ship.

A Transit van from Suez skittered to a halt outside Shepheard's front door. As I went in to fix up our clients, I nearly collided with Sam, charging down the corridor with a clutch of bills in his hand.

'No go, Osman,' he said. 'Just can't do it, not even for you, old man. Every room's booked twice as it is.' The new railway was now halfway from Alexandria.

'I just wanted a word with your housekeeper, with Mrs Macdonald.'

'You're welcome to it – *if* you can find her.'

'She isn't here?'

'Skipped.'

'Where to?'

'How the hell should I know where they go?' He rushed off, clutching his bills.

It was not like her to leave Sam in the lurch. I looked around for de Leon, but there was no sign of him either. A hornet's nest of insane suspicions buzzed in my head. I made my way round to the house on the canal: Elena might know something. The two of them were fairly close, despite Elena's perpetual jealousy of Jeannie's freedom. The moment I entered the house I was treated to her usual diatribe about the unfairness of it all. Why had I abandoned her? Why had I been away so long playing soldiers with that clown Mohammed Said? When I inquired about Jeannie's whereabouts, she rolled out her big guns.

'She is in Alexandria, arranging the marriage contract of your daughter, Flora, to a certain Mr Girgis.'

Elena can beat Scheherazade any day of the week when it comes to fanciful stories.

'I don't believe it,' I said. 'If Flora were getting married, I'd have been the first to know.'

She raised her dark eyebrows and said nothing.

'And Mr Edwin de Leon?' I couldn't help it.

'He has gone to Alexandria, too.'

My anger owed much to a terrible feeling that she could be right. I hadn't seen Flora for some weeks, and this young Copt Girgis was personable enough and now Jeannie's partner in the ginning project. Not only could he or his family up in Asiut finance the purchase of the new American gins, he could also buy the things a young girl would fancy.

I must apologise: my readers may not understand the reasons for my distress. The fact is that though the Copts and the Moslems are equally Egyptians and have rubbed shoulders, speaking Arabic, in this land for hundreds of years, they do not mix well. Do you know what we call a Coptic church? A *kamish* – an idol house. They've hated us – those we couldn't manage to gather into the House of Islam – ever since the army of General Amr took Egypt in the name of the Prophet, and that was in AD 641. They hate us because we won. Even now, if a Coptic girl takes a Moslem husband, or a Moslem girl a Coptic husband, most likely it will end in throat-cutting and bloody feuding. Respected as my name might be, there would be no place for me at my own daughter's wedding.

'I don't believe a word of it!' I yelled at Elena, and stormed off, slamming the door.

Back from the desert 'manoeuvres', de Lesseps had now been lodged in the Palace of Strangers on the Ezbekieh, with a gilded state coach, a barouche, a 'milord' and ten fine riding-horses at his disposal.

About ten days later, I was summoned to escort him in the coach to the meeting at the Citadel where Mohammed Said was to receive the congratulations of the foreign consuls on his accession.

One by one, each stepped forward in all his glory, each vying with his predecessor in unctuous compliments. It took a long time. But the moment the last gilded diplomat subsided, Mohammed Said was on his feet, announcing that he was resolved to pierce the isthmus of Suez with a great canal. He gestured towards de Lesseps, who was standing on his right.

'I have chosen the distinguished man of affairs, Monsieur Ferdinand de Lesseps, to form a company to which I have granted the right to carry out the work. Of course, it will be open to receive capital from all the Powers represented here today.'

An audible gasp arose from the gilded assembly. Mohammed Said turned towards Ferdinand like a small boy seeking approval – or another plate of macaroni! 'Is that not so, Monsieur de Lesseps? Isn't that what we are going to do?'

Sir Frederick Bruce's jaw fell. His expression was a study. I felt sorry for him, reporting to Palmerston as he would have to do.

Ferdinand, I knew, had not been expecting this. But he rose to the occasion magnificently, crediting the illustrious and far-sighted Viceroy of Egypt with the entire idea.

Looking for support from the flabbergasted representatives of the European Powers – and not receiving it – Said turned to the American Consul-General in his sober blue oak-leafed uniform. 'Eh bien, Monsieur de Leon, so we are going to give you competition with your canal-building in the isthmus of Panama! I promise you a warm contest.'

So de Leon had *not* gone to Alexandria. Elena had lied to me. As soon as I had escorted de Lesseps to the Palace of Strangers, I made my way back to the old house on the canal to have it out with her. But save for Sami's wife Nawal and her children, the house was empty. I looked into all the *armoires*. Elena's dresses had gone. So had her jewellery.

I questioned Nawal. 'She has taken everything.' Nawal shrugged, resignedly, her mood ever since Sami had been posted missing.

'Did you see her leave? What did she say?'

'She just said, "What's the use? The old fool will not believe me," and she said to give you this.'

One of the children was playing with an envelope. Nawal took it from him and handed it to me. It was addressed to me, but it had been torn open, the letter roughly stuffed back inside. I was outraged: the private compact between Highland daughter and Highland father had been violated. I took the letter out and tenderly smoothed it on the table.

'Dear Hadji,' my daughter wrote – it was a sort of private joke between us –

> Mother says it will be better for all concerned if I don't tell you yet. But I couldn't do that. The truth is that I'm going to be married to Mr George Jesus Girgis on the 29th of this month – Hatur in the Coptic calendar. As you know, Mr Girgis is Mother's new business partner, and a Copt, which is very picturesque and exciting. He is a very kind and clever man, and his family is well-to-do and distinguished. Mother says he will be a tower of strength in the new cotton-ginning company.

I couldn't read any more. My daughter was being stolen from me. She was being delivered to the usurers, lock, stock and barrel.

There were three or four more pages of Flora's letter. I picked them up again –

> ...Mother says that the Copts are true descendants of the Pharaohs. George can't speak the Coptic language, but says I can read it from hieroglyphs in the Pharaohs' tombs. I remember when you took me down into your friend Belzoni's Tomb at Thebes – how hot it was down there! – we saw that goddess with a feather in her hair. She was passing an *ankh* under the Pharaoh's nose, and you told me she was giving him the breath of life. Not long ago dear George showed me one of these *ankh*s on a gravestone of one of his own forebears. So I feel as if I'm getting the breath of life, too...

I laid the letter down again. When I'd taken her up the Nile she'd been a little girl of – what? Five? Now she was a handsome woman with her mother's dark hair and eyes. She spoke Arabic 'like a native' – which indeed she was – and English with an odd accent, though thanks to her father she did not say *clothes-es*, like so many Egyptians. I couldn't sully her with this word 'Levantine', and I had to admit that if she married a Moslem, she would face Elena's dilemmas. In truth, marriage to a well-to-do Alexandrian Copt might give her the best protection: *eau de Nil*, you might say.

> ... so I am wearing *el-Shabka*, the great golden engagement ring, which George sent me by the priest – it is their custom – and we shall be married in the Cathedral of St Mark here in Alexandria, by the Patriarch of Alexandria, Pope Cyril, who they say is the 102nd in the descent from Saint Mark who converted the Egyptians to Christianity 560 years before the birth of the Prophet Mohammed.
>
> Whatever Mama may say, I hope, dear Hadji, that you will come. As you told me, we all worship the same God, the one God – though not everybody seems to understand this. There will be difficulties. But whatever happens, I shall understand and you will have my love always.
>
> Your affectionate daughter,
> Flora

Self-pity isn't an emotion encouraged in Islam, nor are we permitted the indulgence of the confessional box, as it now occurred to me (with some distaste) Flora would be. Nevertheless, I have to admit that as I put down her letter a great wave of self-pity engulfed me.

The Girgis family would spare no expense to mark the marriage of one of its sons to the daughter of the illustrious 'Sitt Amerikani'. The consuls would be there, resplendent in their uniforms, the cotton merchants and the bankers of a dozen nationalities, the entire *haut ton* of that now booming Mediterranean city, founded by Alexander the Great three hundred years before the birth of Christ. In short, everybody would be there – except Osman Effendi, the bride's father, the well-known *renegado*.

I brooded long over Flora's letter, snapping at poor Nawal with her endless wailings over Sami's fate. Then I thought: did I really have to drain the poisoned cup held out to me? Did not the Prophet Himself – blessed be His name – instruct True Believers to respect Christians and Jews, 'the People of the Book'? Was not Jesus Christ high among the prophets of Islam? I took up the

Holy Koran and turned to Sura 2 and there it was, plain as a
pikestaff, in verse 136:

> We believe in Allah and that which is revealed unto us, and
> that which was revealed to Abraham and Ishmael and Isaac
> and Jacob and the tribes and that which Moses and Jesus
> received . . . We make no distinction between any of them,
> and unto Him we have surrendered.

It seemed to me then that bigotry is as corrosive and debilitating
as jealousy: it was like the water worm Dr Bilharz had just discovered that bored into the fellahin's skin, travelled to the portal
vein, there to deposit three thousand eggs in a single day.

I looked at the date on Flora's letter. Evidently it had been
written at the last moment; she had had a struggle of her own.
Coptic weddings, I knew, always took place on Saturday nights.
Three days away! I had shilly-shallied too long. I hadn't a hope
of getting to Alexandria on time.

Then I remembered the railway. The bridge at Benha still wasn't
open, but the line itself was now quite close to Cairo, and my son
Giovanni, the engineer, was continually boasting about the speed
of the Stephenson locomotives.

I rushed round to the railway construction headquarters, and
found him with another young man poring over a blueprint of
the Benha High Bridge that will carry the trains over the Damietta
branch of the Nile.

He introduced his colleague: 'Mr George Robert Stephenson,
the nephew of our great railway engineer.' They were a new tribe,
a special clan, these men – or would be. 'All the girders, tubes,
iron piers and the rotating machinery of the high bridge have
come from the Stephenson foundries, in England,' I was informed.

'Truly, it is a miracle!' I said, eager not to fail my son.

'My father was a partner of the late Captain Waghorn, founder
of the Overland Transit,' Giovanni explained.

Young Stephenson beamed upon me. 'Oh, yes, the camels.'

I managed to draw Giovanni aside long enough to explain my
problem. He looked doubtful for a moment, then accepted the
challenge. 'Fine, we'll meet around dawn where the line runs out
just north of Cairo.'

On the way home, exhilarated now that the die had been cast,

I suddenly remembered that the Monday following the wedding is the day on which the bride receives relatives and friends bearing gifts, and in acknowledgement gives each a handkerchief she has embroidered by her own hand. How terrible, if of all that company, the bride's own father should have no gift to offer!

I had very little time, but as it happened another son, Ibrahim, had an 'Antikas' shop near Shepheard's.

In his late twenties now, Ibrahim was, I suppose, the one who had most nearly followed in his father's footsteps. I'd got him a job with my friend Auguste Mariette, late of the Louvre, excavating the vast burial galleries of Apis, the sacred bull, at Sakkara. So Ibrahim had caught the bug of 'Egyptology', which is what they call it these days. After that, to his master's disgust, he'd gone off and opened a now famous shop for the sale of 'the treasures of the Pharaohs'. He was in touch with Belzoni's old pals, the tomb-robbers of Kurna. The 'spoliation of Egypt', Mariette called it. I saw his point. But then I knew it had been the height of respectability not so long ago. Mohammed Ali was handing out obelisks right and left then, a sort of *bakshish* for favours done or anticipated. So I couldn't see that my boy was committing any great sin.

As I parted the bead curtain over Ibrahim's shop door, I saw that he was on the point of making his usual 'great sacrifice' by letting an American woman have a mummified ibis, 'absolutely intact', in its sealed jar for 'a give-away sum'. The mummy, he was telling her, was sacred to the ibis-headed god, Thoth, the scribe of the gods – and she wouldn't find another like it. The first statement was true enough, but I blushed for the second. I could find thousands just like it, neatly sealed in their pottery jars in the catacomb at Sakkara.

Instead of jumping at Ibrahim's 'special price', the American woman was preparing to haggle. Evidently she had been reading Herr Baedeker's advice on 'how to deal with Orientals'. I could see it was going to be a three-cups-of-mint-tea job, so I nodded to my son and looked around his shelves for myself.

There was the usual profusion of amulets, gleaned from wrappings of mummies. There was a fine bronze of Bastet, the cat goddess, boldly holding a sistrum in her right paw, with four kittens at her feet. That looked like one of Ibrahim's real treasures, expected to bring a big price from some museum. I passed it by.

I was drawn to an exquisite wooden cosmetics dish, the handle a swimming girl, legs stretched straight behind her, gliding. Then, an *ankh* in shining green attracted me – and a delicate stone figurine of Isis with her infant son Horus at her breast. I had heard claims that this was the origin of the Coptic church's veneration of the Virgin and Child, long before the other churches focused their adoration on the Virgin – one more proof, to my mind, that religions do not exist in water-tight compartments.

Ibrahim, I could hear across the shelves, had reached the stage of throwing in an 'absolutely priceless *ankh*'. My son was a master of his craft: the 'breath of life' – thrown in *gratis* – was a notion which overcame the most resistant ladies.

It was at this moment that my eye lighted on the jolly little figure of Bes, the dwarf god, bandy-legged, with the ears of a lion, and the body of a man. He carries on his back, rolled up like a Highland soldier's plaid, the hieroglyph for 'Sa', which conveys a shepherd's rolled-up shelter, and promises protection. And protection, it seemed to me, was what my daughter was going to stand much in need of.

Ibrahim was still engaged, so – sure that Flora would delight in this cheerful little imp with the lolling tongue and the heart of gold – I held up the small figure of Bes for him to see and hurried away.

The rail tracks had reached Kalyub, six miles short of Cairo. I got there on a donkey soon after dawn, and found Giovanni waiting, although at first I didn't recognise him in his blue 'dunga-rees'. The dress of new Egypt, he said – the *galabiya*'s sleeves caught in the machinery. He looked doubtfully at the dragoman outfit I had judged it best to wear. Five hundred yards down the track, a sort of small platform on wheels waited.

'The line is all clear to Benha,' Giovanni said, hauling me up onto this contraption and pushing down the crossbar of the lever that ran through the floor.

The platform began to move. Very slowly at first, then more quickly, until we were flying through a blur of mud-walled vil-lages, while the iron way unrolled at frightening speed behind us. The wheels click-clacked as they sped over the joints in the rails

– a new sound in this ancient land, counterpoint to the perpetual squeal of *sakiya*s raising water.

It was my first experience of rail travel and I found it exhilarating. By the time the Nile and the railway works barred our path at Benha, the sun was up and hot on our backs. Still unfinished, having claimed more than one life, the great tubular bridge reared up in front of us.

'Our new pyramid,' boasted Giovanni. 'See that central pier? It contains six cylinders, each seven feet wide, filled with concrete and driven thirty-three feet down into the river bed. The Nile is strong, but we engineers are stronger!'

I was proud of my son, offspring of an ignorant Highland drover-lad and an ailing Ethiopian bought at a knockdown price in the Cairo slave-market.

'But how can you ever open a swing bridge of such weight?' I asked, dutifully playing the role of the antiquated parent.

'Gearing,' he said. 'Gearing and steam power.' He looked at me indulgently. The crumbling palace where Abbas had been strangled by his young Mamelukes rose just behind us. I found it hard to believe that had only been a year ago.

Steam power, Giovanni explained to me, was the *jinn* conjuring up a New Egypt. Where had I heard that before?

And yet the vital bridge was two years late and still not open. The Old Egypt, it seemed to me, was far from dead. *Malish!* Never mind! Why worry? We crossed the Nile the old way, by ferry, to where a single railway carriage, hitched to a tall-stacked Stephenson locomotive waited, wreathed in white vapour.

'She's "getting up steam",' explained Giovanni and introduced Joe Oakroyd Effendi, the English engine-driver.

Joe eyed me curiously, as well he might, and told me we should be leaving in ten minutes. It was another trial trip. I said goodbye to Giovanni and climbed uneasily into one of Oakroyd Effendi's new carriages. Giovanni's 'science' was fine, but it would do little to dissolve the ancient feuds and festering suspicions awaiting me in Alexandria.

It was less than sixty miles to the crossing of the Rosetta branch of the Nile at Kafr el-Zaiyat, but Stephenson's engine was continually stopping to quench its thirst from overhead watertanks. I would have done better to take one of Sheikh Ayd's fast dromedaries. And at Kafr el-Zaiyat the engineers were still working on the chain bridge that could be raised or lowered according to the level of the Nile. I had to take a *dahabiya* to the west bank to get to the bright new railway station, from which a regular passenger service was now running into Alexandria.

It was almost 11 p.m. before we clanked morosely over the shallow waters of Lake Mareotis and jerked to a halt in Alexandria's Bab el-Kedid station.

I took a firm grip on good old Bes in his wrappings and, invoking his impish protection, climbed down into a world that every year seemed more alien to me.

31 The Idol House

'Dove, ya Bey? This donkey, she very fine runner. Molto buono! Vite, très, très! Montez, monsieur!'

The flying phrases of a dozen tongues impaled like kebab on an Italian skewer, well done, possibly charred a little: in Alexandria, even the donkey-boys are multi-lingual. Nothing is quite what it seems here.

'Imshi!' I yelled, raising my stick above my head and, as ever, they fell back. That, if you want to know, is the real *lingua franca* of Egypt, going back to the Pharaohs, the mace, the *nabbut*, the *courbash*, the cane, the cudgel, any old stick, the bastinado. As Monsieur Flaubert put it: everybody in clean clothes beats everybody in dirty clothes.

Before the donkey-boys could re-form for a new assault, I set off boldly for the Square, the immense oblong space which Mohammed Ali opened up in the heart of the town, officially known as La Place des Consuls, but known to its Arab habitués as 'the Franks' Square'.

But in the Rue de la Poste Française my resolve faded. I sank into a chair on the terrace of the Café Paradiso and ordered a café *masbud*. Café Paradiso is the proper name of the place, though it is known to one and all as Aristides'. Late as it was, the place was garishly lit with innumerable oil lamps and naphtha flares. Aristides' was in its usual nightly uproar, swollen by the corncrake voices of the waiters bawling their orders. All the languages of Europe, as well as the Alexandrian *olla podrida*, were being spoken at the tables as the inhabitants touched up old scandals, started new ones, fabricated swindles and clinched deals.

Since the Frenchified Mohammed Said had let it be known that he welcomed foreigners as cordially as Abbas had detested them, fortune-hunters had been pouring into Alexandria by every ship. A few sought their fortunes by honourable means; many others, the dregs of society, resorted to swindles and villainies that would not have been tolerated in their own countries, but in Egypt received the protection of their national consuls.

A few tables away I spotted a well-known Maltese brothel-keeper in animated conversation with a Greek money-lender. The Greeks were steadily taking over in Alexandria, beating the old English merchants at their own game. Greeks stood together through thick and thin: Greeks against the world.

A lamp flared up, illuminating a distant corner of the terrace. It revealed Elena, my errant wife Elena, sitting alone at a table, without a vestige of a veil. A glass of raki stood in front of her and, as I watched, she raised to her lips one of those long Russian paper tubes of tobacco which our soldiers brought back from the Crimea.

I went over and took the vacant chair facing her. 'Anyone may sit here, if he has the price. Is that not so?'

She looked me brazenly in the eye and said nothing.

'Osman,' she said at last, 'you should hang your head in shame. That poor girl, Flora. She weeps, your daughter. She is deserted by her own father on her wedding day. Is that not terrible for any girl – and after she wrote to you and begged you, implored you . . .'

I was taken aback by Elena's attack.

'I pity the poor girl – I know just how she will feel. So I must leave all in Cairo, and run down here and tell her her father is so busy playing soldiers with that comedian, Said, that he cannot bother about his own daughter's wedding.'

Her voice was rising. I looked around anxiously – Said's spies were everywhere. Knowing how difficult it is to silence Elena when she gets in this mood. I resorted to counter-attack.

'Must I tell your son Ibrahim how his mother flaunts herself in Iskanderiya like a dancing-girl? It is a matter of public scandal. I should tell you to "cover your face".'*

She just laughed. 'I am not a dirty Arab you can shut up in

---

* This expression implies that a husband is about to send his wife away in disgrace before divorce. – F.M.

your harem. I am a Greek. This is my city. In Iskanderiya even the Arab women do not wear the veil. It is not healthy. We are civilised here.'

I let that pass. I have found it is useless to argue. But I could see that Elena could be my ally, a bridge – if rather a shaky bridge – between the shuttered world of Cairo and this brazen, steam-driven new world of Alexandria which we Arabs, often with a lift in our voices, call Iskanderiya.

Fresh breezes blew off the sea. A hint of salt on the night air. I ordered two coffees. 'Have you seen Flora? Is she happy with these Copts? Really happy? Tell me truthfully.'

'Of course I have seen her. Am I not staying at her mother's house? Did I not take her with the others this morning to the *hammam* in accordance with the custom of these people? And tonight there is to be a great reception before the wedding ceremony tomorrow.'

'Well then? Is she happy?'

'How can I say? She is a strange girl. She keeps her own counsel. She is cold like her father. Mon Dieu! She talks all the time of the Copts being descended from the Pharaohs. George Jesus Girgis – a Pharaoh! It is too much!' She threw up her hands.

I ordered two more coffees.

'Mr Edwin de Leon – the American Consul – is he at the house?'

She gazed at me coolly. 'Naturellement,' she said, smiling maliciously.

The woman knew too much. She knew de Leon's presence would throw my mind into turmoil. He was Christian, of course, besides being American – an Episcopalian, I think I'd heard him say. Jeannie could so easily pass him off, if not as the father, at least as the 'guardian' of the bride, usurping my rightful place, avoiding the awkwardness of a *renegado* father. Together they could charm the company with tales of life under the Carolina sun in that land where all men were equal – except of course the 'blackamoors' and the Red Indians.

'What can I do?' I said, half to myself. 'If I attend the wedding in church I shall cause a scandal. If I don't, I shall let my daughter down unforgivably. I shall ruin her wedding.'

Elena sat back in her chair. 'I have arranged,' she said. 'I have arranged all.' She produced a large rusty key, and laid it on the table between us. She was good, I remembered ruefully, at keys.

'I do not know why I do this for you, but I do. You must go to the Rue de l'Eglise Copte, which runs off the Boulevard de Rosetta. There, in a garden, you will find the cathédrale of the Copts. Do not seek to enter by the porch. Go round to the south side. There you will see a door overgrown by ivy. It has not been used for many years.'

She fingered the key.

'This will unlock the door – push hard. You will find stone steps before you. Ascendez. They will take you to a gallery over the south side. Once it was for the women, but now they are behind the screen below on the church floor. You will see all . . .'

'If they see me, there will be murder done!'

'They will not see you. Go early in the morning. Keep your head down.'

I palmed the rusty key. Right then I forgave her everything. I insisted, though, on escorting her back to Jeannie's house – villa, as she insisted on calling the place – on the verdant edge of the Mahmudiya canal. Draped with flags and bunting, the house was ablaze with light, the party evidently in full swing. This was the night when the Girgis clan would present the bride with a candle exactly as tall as herself. It would burn in Flora's bedroom throughout the night before the wedding.

'All those old aunts and uncles from Asiut,' sighed Elena. I could feel her grimace in the dark. 'There are so many. Too many! I suffocate . . .'

She retreated up the path towards the house.

For some minutes after she'd gone, I lingered there in the shadows, savouring the bitterness of exclusion from my own daughter's wedding feast. I could feel the heavy key in my pocket, pressing against my thigh. My daughter, my Highland daughter, was somewhere in there, hemmed in by these pretenders. Was that the tall figure of de Leon, briefly silhouetted in the window? I was like a moth drawn to the flames.

I got to St Mark's very early. Everything was just as Elena had said it would be. I pushed away the ivy gently so that it would fall back into place once I was inside. The rusty key turned with wonderful ease in the lock: she must have oiled it. Clouds of thick dust rose under my feet as I climbed the stone steps that led to the disused gallery.

Most of the gallery had been walled in years ago. But in the derelict chapel at the east end there was a break in the stone tracery commanding a view over the whole church, from the high altar to the entrance porch. I could see, but not be seen.

It was dim down there. A solid, richly carved screen, broken by three heavily curtained openings, separated the body of the church from the *heikal*, the high altar, the holy of holies, the secret heart of the ancient mystery. This lay just below me. At that time of the morning it looked merely sad and tawdry; an empty stage. Further back, other latticed wooden screens divided the body of the church, in descending orders of holiness, as you might say: the first division for the choir, the acolytes, the assistant priests, next the men of the congregation, and, beyond that, last, the women.

As I looked down, a solitary black-clad old woman crept in, genuflected towards the high altar, invisible behind the screen, and, advancing across it, kissed the central curtain, kissed the picture of the Virgin and Child, placed her lips devoutly against the toe of a dark-visaged 'St Mark landing in Egypt', kissed a wide-eyed, winged Angel Gabriel, and kissed Mar Girga – Saint George on a rearing horse, sword raised to slay the dragon.

Having made her devout round, she shuffled slowly out again. I hoped the saints would help her, but I thanked God for the Prophet who cleared the idols from the Kaaba, and I wondered how Jeannie Macdonald, brought up a good Calvinist, could bear to condemn Flora's free spirit to such debasing superstitions.

I lost count of the hours I spent up there. At last, the distant sound of music roused me from my reverie. Two bands were evidently approaching, leading the bride and bridegroom's processions. Just outside the church door the merry shrill of the *nai* was swallowed in a long bleat of terror. In my mind's eye I saw the sheep's blood, a bright scarlet stream across the path. The bride and groom must step through it into the church.

As the white-robed priests, singing the Ave Maria, escorted her, it seemed to me that Flora looked terribly pale.

Was it just my imagination, or did she look up, momentarily, at my south gallery eyrie, and smile? Behind her, wearing the black veil of the matron, Jeannie Macdonald looked grim as the chanting priests ushered bride and mother to their allotted places behind the women's screen.

Majestically black-bearded, Pope Cyril IV, 'the Most Holy Pope and Patriarch of Alexandria and of all Egypt', made his entrance last, jewels gleaming in his high silver crown. He vanished into the secret world of the *heikal*.

The heavy scent of incense drifted upwards. Peering down, I saw that the Patriarch had re-emerged, surrounded by monks, priests and acolytes swinging silver censers as they wove an intricate tapestry of sound, kyries, hallelujahs, psalms.

Accustomed as I was to the austerity of the mosque, I felt ill at ease. I saw Girgis, arrayed in a white silken tunic that fell to his feet, conducted down the church to where Flora was waiting. The Patriarch bade him place the ring upon her finger, and, inclining their heads together, he led them back, side by side, to the entrance to the choir.

This time there could be no doubt about it. Flora looked up at the gallery, and I saw a smile of recognition flicker. I couldn't stop myself: I rose to my feet, throwing up a cloud of dust which made me cough and splutter. I dropped back behind the stone screen, as frightened, I think, as I ever was at el-Hamed. I waited, not daring to look. Minues passed. But nothing happened.

By the time I dared look down again, the Patriarch was giving his blessing, anointing the couple on wrists and foreheads with holy oil, signing them with the sign of the cross at every mention of their names. More prayers now, in that strange mummified language, embroidered by music hardly less ancient – and then the moment of the crowning, the placing of the silver diadems upon their heads, Pope Cyril IV crying out in a sonorous voice that echoed in every corner: 'With Glory and Honour the Father has crowned them, the Son blesses them, the Holy Ghost comes down upon them and perfects them.'

Clouds of incense rose from behind the iconed screen as the Epistles were read in Coptic. There was nothing left for me here. It was as if my daughter, my closest daughter, part of me, had passed behind the stone screen and was lost to me.

I felt myself choking. Creeping down the stone stairs, I edged open the old door, and, pushing the ivy aside, escaped into the sunshine.

32 Wasifa

The following day was the day of the great feast at the bride-groom's house, where the bride would receive her guests and gifts. All the world would be there. Even a *renegado* named Osman might find it possible to exchange a word with his daughter.

I had no difficulty finding my way to the Villa Girgis. The sound guided me from half a mile away, putting me in mind of a swarm of locusts devouring a ripe cornfield. The usual red embroidered marquee, one side open, half blocked the street. Within, a party of *khawals* with rouged cheeks and kohl-black-ened eyebrows gyrated their hips lasciviously, eyes flashing in unsmiling faces. The Girgis family was evidently of the school which found dancing-girls not *comme il faut* on such occasions, engaging instead these epicene young men, who wore their hair in long braids over tight embroidered vests and petticoats.

As the pulse of the drums quickened, the ripples coursing over the *khawals'* bare bellies swelled into waves, and the tremulous *nai* rose to ever more excruciating heights.

'Allah! Allah! Allah!' yelled the rapt crowd.

'Oh, la-la!' A party of French travellers was watching, goggle-eyed. And then I heard a familiar voice, milord Bankes's old dragoman, Giovanni Finati – Mohammed Effendi – assuring his French clients that *tout le monde* was invited. Providential! I could escape notice if I tagged along behind them between the imperial stone eagles that surmounted the gateposts.

'Buona sera, my friends. Marhaba, marhaba. Soyez bienvenus, mes amis!'

Face flushed, Flora's husband – I found it difficult to think of him as that – rushed forward to welcome the French party. He led us over to a long table loaded down with Turkish sweetmeats, French-style canapés, Spanish sherry, bon-bons from Paris, Greek brandy, and enough bottles of Moët's champagne to stock Shepheard's bar for a fortnight.

Girgis waved a hand over the table. 'My house is your house, gentlemen.' He disappeared through a small gap which had opened in the press around the comestibles.

In the swell of consular gold braid and coruscating orders and sashes, I caught sight of Sir Frederick Bruce drinking sherbet with one of the Sultan's viziers, perhaps warning him against the delusive scheme of that French speculator, de Lesseps. I looked around anxiously for the republican blue of Edwin de Leon, but could not find it. More disquieting still, I could not see Flora.

The attention of the French party had been captured by two large white globes at the end of the table. Faint, querulous sounds issued from within. From my dragoman days, I knew exactly what was going to happen next: Coptic weddings are always a good show. Formed from hard-baked white sugar, each globe contained a live Egyptian pigeon. The birds were first made dizzy and docile by whirling them through the air by the feet, then inserted into the globes by a hole in the bottom. Judging by the sounds now emerging, the pigeons had recovered from their stupor and were preparing to peck their way out.

An old Copt in the traditional blue turban was loudly lamenting the loss of his two sons to the army's press-gang in an Alexandria street. Hitherto, the Copts had been free from military conscription, but Mohammed Said, hard-pressed to replace losses in the Crimean war, had fallen upon them, 'good families' and all.

I passed through this sea of lamentation and reached the other shore, suddenly spotting Edwin de Leon's plentiful sidewhiskers, outlined against Jeannie's black – still black – hair. Girgis, I was relieved to see, was on her other side. Evidently they were still talking cotton, cotton gins, and dollars. Om el-Arusa – the mother of the bride – was losing no time in putting the new family money to work. But where was Flora? Where was the bride?

At that moment the first of the white globes cracked. A pigeon climbed out and took off, circling the ceiling, the little bells attached to its wings tinkling prettily. Three seconds later its fellow prisoner made its escape.

The knot of middle-aged women in front of me suddenly broke apart, revealing my daughter.

I saw that the women were of the Girgis clan, the aunts' and brothers' wives, down from Upper Egypt, where the family had extensive lands, accumulated over the years out of taxes collected for the Mameluke beys and after that for Napoleon Bonaparte himself. It was said that George's grandfather – or was it great-grandfather? – had 'lent' Mohammed Ali the forty thousand purses he needed to buy off the Turkish admiral sent from Istanbul in 1806 to oust him from the Citadel.

The tinkling of bells had ceased. The pigeons had come to rest, perching messily on the arms of the two Italian-made 'Louis Quinze' chairs. A bad omen. The eldest of the aunts signalled urgently to the musicians.

The *ud*-player, a wizened old Armenian, with a half-finished glass of brandy in his hand, was followed by a young fellow in a blue *galabiya* with a *zummara* – a double-reed pipe. Then a boy with the inevitable *darabukka*, and a *tar* – which in Europe would be called a tambourine. There were others. I forget.

What I do remember – with every reason – was the entrance of the singer Wasifa, who walked with the easy grace of the south. She might indeed, it seemed to me, have been carrying a water-jar from the well, as indeed everyone knew she had been doing not so very long ago.

For Wasifa was the daughter of a village *ghafir*. She had been an ordinary fellaha of fourteen or so when the old Armenian *ud*-player had come upon her, singing Arab love songs at a village feast and had been struck by the vibrancy and latent passion in her voice. It was something that happened from time to time in Egypt – as if Allah, in witness of His omnipotence, had chosen to pour out the essence of life on earth and all its innermost secrets into the body of some unlettered child. By the time she was seventeen, as she now was, the name of the new *alma** was on every tongue.

---

* My father has neglected to explain that an *alma*, literally a 'learned woman', implies a respected and distinguished singer of classical Arabic compositions, as distinct from a *ghaziya*, a singing-dancing girl of low morals. In view of my father's relations with Wasifa, it is important that the reader understand this. – F.M.

A hush fell upon the room as, sitting cross-legged on the carpet behind Wasifa, the old Armenian drained his glass, cradled the full-bellied lute, and struck three plangent chords which hung quivering in the air. In a deep and vibrant voice the girl – and it began to seem vaguely improper to call her a 'girl' – launched into a poignant requiem of unrequited love.

> And why, O eye, has thou ensnared us
> And with glances wounded us?

The *ud* shed a long, slow tear: the black silk kerchief depending from Wasifa's wrist drooped as she exhaled a deep breath that was also a sigh. Racked by emotion, Wasifa's voice cut off abruptly. The room shook with paroxysms of applause. She bowed, but remained aloof, a faint smile playing on her lips. I was reminded of a quartzite head of Nefertiti that I had held in my hand in Ibrahim's shop.

The *zummara* emitted a long, convoluted lament, and for a moment, in the eerie half-world it conjured up, I saw my brother Angus the piper out in front of the drove in the slashing rain. Then Wasifa's voice burst through, peremptory, irresistible –

> Ya dema eini alkunkudeyed men hallek . . .
> O tear, who drew thee forth across my cheek . . .?

Like the rest of the company, I found myself entranced, transported into an Arab paradise throbbing with sensuality yet cooled by limpid streams, a world at once magical and eternal and sacred, like texts from the Koran cut in Kufic into the marble of mosque walls.

At last the voice died, releasing us.

In the tempest of applause, of huzza-ing and bravo-ing, and Allah-ing, and showering of the silver coins, deftly garnered by the old Armenian, I glanced across the room and saw Flora, deserted and disconsolate. She held out both her hands to me. I saw that palms and finger-tips were stained deep orange. I don't know why this should have so disturbed me. After all, Zobeida had used henna all the time, and so did that sophisticate, Elena, on occasion. But it did disturb me.

I took the hennaed hands in mine.

'So you came!' she said. 'I knew you would.' She was gripping my fingers as if she did not mean ever to let go.

'Your mother . . .' I began.

She dropped her eyes. 'I know.'

'He is good to you?'

She nodded expressionlessly. A long table, displaying many costly gifts of gold and silver and richly woven fabrics, stood on Flora's left. I nodded towards them and extracted the parcel from my pocket. As I began to unwrap it, I felt some misgivings. I heard my voice as though it belonged to someone else.

'I remember when you were a little girl how you used to love the figures on the tomb walls. I remember how you used to laugh at funny old Bes, the dwarf god with the bandy legs. "Old Bandy-Legs" you called him . . .'

I saw that a vacant look had come into her eyes. I ploughed on. 'So when I spotted a fine figure of Bes in Ibrahim's shop, I remembered that he's the god of protection . . . He'll look after you through thick and thin.'

I unwound the last furl of wrapping, and the grimacing features of the bandy-legged dwarf glared out, tongue lolling, guardian knife poised to strike.

I felt the grip on my hand loosen as Flora slid to the floor in dead faint.

I don't know where Elena had been standing, but she was at my side in a trice.

'It's the heat,' I muttered.

She saw Bes leering up from his wrappings. 'Get out of here, you fool,' she said.

Out of the corner of my eye I caught sight of the aunts descending on us in a phalanx. I didn't hang about. I took Elena's advice.

Mohammed Ali's Alexandria turns her back upon the sea. Old memories stirring, I plunged wildly into the narrow alleys of the old Arab quarter within the ancient walls and, half running, half walking, emerged on the Mediterranean shore beside the two 'Cleopatra's needles' where we used to go swimming in the warm waves in those carefree days before Rosetta.

The fallen obelisk lay just as I remembered it when nearly half a century ago, Colonel Macleod came by and brushed away the sand to give Tom Keith and me and the Macraes our first sight of a hieroglyph. The thought brought tears to my eyes as I sank onto the fallen obelisk.

Since then I had narrowly escaped death a dozen times and come through. So why had I capitulated so shamefully in the matter of the marriage of my own daughter? Why had I failed her at this critical moment of her young life? In Cairo, Osman Effendi, Hadji Osman, was a much-respected man: people came to me for counsel or to settle their disputes. And yet confronted by Jeannie Macdonald, all that fell apart and I was as confused and helpless as that fourteen-year-old boy at my grandmother Beaton's waulking party at the beginning of it all.

Mektub! Was that, too, 'written'? I could still hear in my mind that crystal-clear voice:

> ... the race of the Macleods, crippled and clumsy
> Feeding on glass and coarse grass and black mill dust...

For 'mill dust' should one now read 'sand'?

I don't know how long I sat there brooding, staring out over the dark, sparkling, phosphorescent Mediterranean, pondering these mysteries. All I know is that some time before dawn I dragged myself to my feet and found my way back to that new wonder of the East, the railway station. After all, I still had my old house in the 'native quarter' of Cairo.

I awoke to a great clanking of chains. As I climbed out of the sleep of exhaustion, I imagined for a moment that I was back in the great dark barracks below the Citadel. Then the clouds of steam cleared, and I saw that I was in a railway carriage clanking to a halt by the Nile crossing at Kafr el-Zaiyat.

The chain ferry still wasn't working. Dismayed passengers drifted up and down the Nile bank, seeking passage to Cairo. Heavily swathed against the night air, a wizened old man was offering ever-mounting sums to the *reis* of a barge loaded high with ballooning sacks of raw cotton. The *reis* indicated the cotton and shrugged.

'Throw it overboard,' yelled the old man. 'I will pay. It is for

Wasifa that I ask – she sings at the nuptials of an important bey in Cairo.'

I recognised then the *ud*-player of the Villa Girgis, who had been so deft in scooping up the coins. I looked around and saw, a few yards back from the bank an untidy heap of drapery propped against a palm-tree. At the sound of raised voices it stirred, and the form of a girl emerged.

To my astonishment, it was Wasifa. She no longer put me in mind of Nefertiti. The ethereal creature of a few hours ago was now a tired, bedraggled village girl again, the watchman's daughter. The kohl crept in a zig-zag course down her cheek, and she had been too weary to wipe it away. It looked as though she had been crying.

As it happened, the *reis* the Armenian had been cajoling was a friend of mine. It was his boat that had brought Bankes's obelisk down the Cataract from Philae. The cotton sacks were pitched out onto the bank for collection later. The boat was turned round, the *ud*-player, Wasifa and Hadji Osman taken aboard. The boat had a small cabin at the rear, and into this the girl retired without a word. I could see that she was at the end of her tether.

Like most musicians, the old Armenian was a confirmed *hashash*, and as the boat headed back towards Cairo he applied himself to his cane-stemmed water-pipe in which the intoxicating fumes were already stirring. In gratitude he pressed the *hashish* upon me. But I had strange enough dreams already, so I borrowed a *nargila* from the *reis*, and filled it with *tumbak*, my favourite brand of Persian tobacco. Companionably, we smoked together as the north wind filled our sails and bore us towards Cairo.

His name, the Armenian told me, was Yussef – Yussef Boghos – and he claimed to be a relative of Boghos Bey, who had been Mohammed Ali's right-hand man and minister of all work. Whether that was the *hashish* speaking I never discovered, for, taking a long pull on his pipe, Yussef embarked on the clearly oft-told tale of how he had discovered Wasifa, singing at a wedding feast in the remote village in the South.

'She was just an ignorant, bare-footed young fellaha in a gaudy *baladi* dress when I found her singing at the feast. She had a rough, uncultivated voice, but underneath I, Yussef Boghos, could hear the voice of an angel. I knew then why God had brought my musicians to that place.'

To cut a very long story short, Yussef had gone to the village watchman and put down a deposit on his daughter, garnished with promises of more, much, much more.

'The ghafir agreed. I took her away that very night before he could change his mind.'

The *hashish* smoke curled up through the cane mouthpiece and spiralled down into the old man's lungs, making him cough, but his black eyes glittered as he told the story of how, from this rude clay, he had fashioned, no mere *ghaziya*, but a true and rare *alma*, fit to rank with the greatest. It had been, he implied, an infinite labour. He had to teach her not only such mundane matters as the proper dresses to wear and how to behave on ceremonial occasions, but also how to respond to the musicians, how to ride with the flights of the *nai*, how to conspire with the *darabukka*, raising the pitch of expectation, how to conduct a tender dialogue with the *ud* under his own cool fingers. He had, in short, taught her everything. Wasifa was his creation.

He took another long pull at his pipe. Alas, it had all been too good to last. The girl had become spoiled, sated on applause (and, I thought, very possibly sick of watching the offerings rained upon her disappearing into that Armenian's pockets). She had fallen in love with a handsome officer, a sheikh's son from a village near her own in Upper Egypt. The two Saidi were resolved to marry. Then the officer was posted to the Crimea to fight the Russians.

He did not return.

For a while, said Boghos, there was a new poignancy in her recitals. Her fame grew. Then, suddenly – he raised his arms – the voice had become merely ordinary, dull. There were still times, like the one I had witnessed, when the old power, the old magic, came surging back. But there were also days when Wasifa – the ingrate! – would not perform at all.

The night passed, and as dawn broke three puny triangles appeared, floating in a cloudless sky: the Pyramids. Refreshed by sleep, the kohl washed from her cheeks, Wasifa emerged from the cabin and began to heap complaints on the Armenian's head. Well-worn complaints, evidently. How could she be expected to perform when she had no decent place to lay her head in all Cairo, when he was too mean to offer her anything but a room in the slum quarters inhabited by his musicians? What *did* he do with all the money he was stealing from her?

Boghos, crouching cross-legged on the deck, looked at me and shrugged. But if he expected me to commiserate with him, he was disappointed. My heart went out to Wasifa. Like so many in this land she was a victim of relentless greed, greed that was like a force of nature, like the flow of the Nile.

It occured to me at that moment that the house on the canal, Burckhardt's old house, to which I was now returning, was empty save for Sami's grieving wife and her small children. Zobeida was long dead, the children had gone their various ways, and Elena, it seemed fairly clear, was not going to return to what she called my 'cage'.

On impulse I went over to Boghos, who was looking distinctly wan in the morning light, and put my house, or some part of it, at the disposal of his young singer.

He looked at me curiously. She was, I pointed out, young enough to be my daughter, and I would indeed treat her as such. He winked, and slapped me on the back. 'Bravo, mon vieux,' he said, but I could see he felt he was in no danger of losing his valuable investment.

In this, however, as things turned out, he was in error. Wasifa made herself at home in the crumbling, untidy house, which reminded her of her long-lost village. The refinements Boghos had been at such pains to instil in her faded.

When I got back from what Ferdinand called his 'first knocks on the desert', I found that the great *alma* of the Villa Girgis had become an earthy Egyptian girl again. She needed no *ankh* to restore the 'breath of life' and was eager to show her gratitude to her 'rescuer'. At that point we were both, I suppose, bereft. She had been sold by her father and had had her lover taken from her by war. As for me, Jeannie Macdonald seemed lost to the McCarthy Patent Cotton-Gin and its purveyors. Elena had deserted me for the bright lights of Alexandria. I had caused a scandal at Flora's wedding party that by now must be the talk of the *ton* of Alexandria. And Nura? Nura remained faithful as ever to the black tents somewhere in the Sinai desert, following Ayd's camel herds.

My roots had struck deep into the rich black soil of the Nile valley, and it seemed only proper that this should be acknowledged, if belatedly, by marriage to a true Egyptian. This refreshment, as one might say, of my harem had the whole-hearted approval of my neighbours of the Suk el-Zalat, who found it only fitting that their respected Hadji Osman should form an alliance with a famous *alma*.

I did wonder what my distinguished memorialist, Mr Kinglake, would have written had he known that Osman Effendi had chosen at his advanced age to enlarge his harem. 'Poor Osman', no doubt.

Whatever he would have written, it would certainly have been irrelevant after Wasifa's boy, Aziz, and Flora's girl, Leila, were born within a week of each other in 1856, a year after the great Russian fortress of Sebastopol fell at last, and Sami came home from a long stay in the British military hospital at Scutari, his wounds healed, and, to Nawal's infinite relief, sound in life and limb.

As for Wasifa, motherhood lent her new authority. 'Om Aziz'* was judged to plumb new emotional depths. Her career as a great *alma* had not ended: it was only just beginning.

* 'The Mother of Aziz', an Egyptian honorific. – F.M.

3 p.m., 19 November 1869, Kilometre 85, aboard
SY L'Aigle

Captain Surville informed us that he expected to drop anchor in the Great Bitter Lake around seven o'clock in the evening. Knowing what I knew, I thought him more certain of this than he had any right to be. The underwater rock-ridge at Serapeum was now only five kilometres ahead. When they found it, only a fortnight before the Grand Opening, the rock rose so far in some places that it gave only a ten-foot clearance.

I remember the savage clang when the excavator bucket hit. They had used gunpowder there since then, but had they cleared enough? What worried me even more – if they could miss something as glaring as that, what else might they have missed in this section?

Even as I listened to the gracious words of the Empress Eugénie, who had at last emerged from her cabin (Jeannie and I having been presented to her informally by de Lesseps), my ear was straining for that first scrape of the keel on rock, then the terrible wrenching, tearing sounds I knew would follow.

I couldn't forget what had happened to the *Latif* near el-Kantara – and, even worse, I could not understand *how* it could have happened. All I knew was that Sami had vanished. In the way of the Orient after such things, he had become a non-being. It was as if he had never existed.

I marked off the kilometres. Four more now to the Serapeum ridge, lying in wait like a crocodile with open jaws.

Then I realised that the vast man-made – de Lesseps-made – sea of the Bitter Lakes lay just ahead of us.

De Lesseps flung a copy of the London *Times* down in front of me. It was folded back at a column headed 'Parliament: The French Canal'. A passage was ringed in red crayon, not once, but again and again.

> Lord Palmerston said that this was just another of those
> bubble schemes so often formed to induce English capitalists
> to part with their money, the end being that these schemes
> leave them poorer, though they may make others richer.

In the debate that followed, Robert Stephenson rose to declare that, as an engineer, he shared the view of the noble lord. A railway was all that was required.

Ferdinand was distraught, pacing about the room like a madman.

'Your Palmerston – he accuses me of being a common swindler!'

'Not *my* Palmerston,' I said. 'He's an Englishman!'

'I shall call him out! I send my seconds to London tonight.'

I had seen that de Lesseps was a brilliant marksman and heard that he was deadly with the épée: Palmerston was in his seventies. I tried to calm my friend down, but he paid no heed.

'I have no choice. He has insulted my honour.'

No use to tell him that the English had given up honour, since you can't price it. I concentrated on the unfortunate consequences that might follow killing the Prime Minister of Great Britain.

'Very well, I will send my seconds to Stephenson. Did he not say he agreed with Palmerston about my "bubble" scheme?'

I think I may have saved the Canal that day. Pumicestone might have picked up the challenge but, as I expected, Stephenson just sent back a note saying he had been entirely misunderstood. Not that it was plain sailing after that: in fact, it was just the beginning of an undeclared war.

That summer of 1858, driven forward now by the rush to get troop reinforcements to India after what they called 'the Indian Mutiny', Robert Stephenson's overland railway reached a point twenty-five miles short of Suez. Out of deference to Egyptian national susceptibilities, suddenly discovered, the British troops discarded their uniforms for whites in Alexandria. Red-faced, white-clothed, the reinforcements for Delhi and Lucknow and Cawnpore would steam up to the No. 5 Station of the old Transit, then pile into vans for the remainder of the trip to the waiting troopships. A good time was had by all, especially Sam Shepheard, who had the contract to feed the soldiers in transit. Sam fervently hoped that Lord Palmerston would continue introducing the natives to 'the blessings of civilisation' – a favourite phrase of his.

Six months later, in mid-December, the gap in the Alexandria– Suez rail lines was finally closed. The vans which had ruled my life for a quarter of a century gathered dust at Suez, their hoods ripped and torn by the winds off the Red Sea. Progress? Maybe, but a melancholy sight.

I ran into Sheikh Ayd about this time, disputing his rightful dues with an engine-driver, a big blunt man of the Tyne. It is difficult to collect the *khawah*, however obligatory, from a locomotive that can outdistance the fleetest dromedary. I tried to console the poor fellow, telling him about de Lesseps' grand project and the great ships that would ride across the desert, coming from all over the world. I fear he did not believe me. He was strangely reticent, too, about Nura. I wondered about the young man who had partnered her in the midnight *mesamer*. I even wondered whether Thomas, working with Ayd's camels transporting water from the Nile, was really my son. The first boy, Mohammed, I'd taken under my wing of course. He was nineteen now, a short, slender fellow with black eyes and doing well at el-Azhar. The idea of an *imam* from the desert, where Islam was born, appealed to me.

Ferdinand de Lesseps' sudden reappearance in Egypt in the winter of 1854 had turned out to be remarkably timely for me – almost as if it were part of some grand design. Switching from the Overland Transit to the service of de Lesseps and the Compagnie Universelle was a natural progression. What neither de Lesseps nor I had appreciated was that though the Canal project seemed inevitable, in the interests of all mankind, it would have so many ruthless enemies. Mohammed Said might have signed the concession, but his Turkish suzerain, Sultan Abdul Mejid had not, and if Lord Stratford de Redcliffe, the British ambassador at the Sublime Porte, had anything to do with it, he never would. De Lesseps travelled to London, and bearded Palmerston in Downing Street. He got short shrift.

'Tell me, Monsieur de Lesseps, why should I support a canal which will open India to the French? Why should I support a canal which is against England's interests?'

Dumbfounded, de Lesseps resolved to appeal directly to the people. He addressed crowded and enthusiastic public meetings, presided over by local worthies and merchants at Birmingham, Liverpool, Aberdeen, Manchester, Belfast and Dublin. At Liverpool a Mr Gladstone, a banker, took the chair; his kinsman, later Chancellor of the Exchequer, was in the audience. Both spoke of the benefits to humanity that would flow from the Canal.

'I thought then,' Ferdinand told me, 'that I had won.'

He did not know England, poor fellow. A meeting chaired by the Lord Mayor was to be held at the Guildhall, where the City's enthusiasm for the great project would crown de Lesseps' triumph. At the very last moment a letter was received from the Lord Mayor regretting his inability to preside. In its wake came an invitation to tea at Downing Street from Lady Palmerston. Gratified, de Lesseps was received by Palmerston himself. 'So, you are working up England and Scotland and Ireland to agitate for a Suez Canal, Monsieur de Lesseps?' Palmerston said. 'You have decided to make war on us . . .'

'Make war on you?' De Lesseps could hardly believe his ears. 'I thought England was the land of free speech!'

Boldly, de Lesseps wrote to President Buchanan of the United States, informing him that an allocation of shares was being set aside for him. But in the end it was the 'little men' of France who saved the situation, in the sour words of the London *Globe*: 'hotel waiters who have been deceived by newspapers, petty grocers beguiled by puffs, the priesthood, and day labourers who have been induced to pool their savings'. The *Globe* was Palmerston's paper.

There was a moment, it is true, when it looked as if at Istanbul the Grand Vizier, Rashid Pasha, was going to persuade the Sultan to issue a *firman* approving the Canal. Two weeks later, he died in convulsions after taking coffee.

For some weeks after that, I kept a close eye on Ferdinand's coffee-makers. It was evident that we had powerful enemies. The key to our great project was to bring the water of the Nile to the desert. The Canal Between Seas must march with a sweetwater canal. But we were harassed by parties of *bashi-bazouks*,* directed by a mysterious Turkish officer. Our camel-drivers were waylaid, roped, and carried away. Villagers who gave us food were threatened with terrible retribution. It became evident that actually digging the Canal Between Seas would be the least of our problems.

I remember going down to the Alexandria docks to sort out a big consignment of wheelbarrows we were importing from Marseille. The wheelbarrow had never been seen in Egypt before. I should have known that no fellah would ever consent to use one, preferring to scrabble around with his old wicker basket. I suppose I had allowed all Giovanni's talk of 'engineers' to go to my head.

A ship stood out in the harbour, flying the American flag, and offloading big crates into barges. One barge was already at the quayside, and beside it, none other than dear Edwin, the American Consul. He hailed me in the friendliest of fashions, and I went over. Two slats, I saw, had been knocked off a crate.

'The new McCarthy Patent Cotton-Gin,' de Leon announced proudly. 'One of our latest American inventions. As a plantation-owner myself I can assure you, sir, there's a fortune to be made with that machine in this country. Mrs Macdonald is a mighty shrewd lady.

'See that roller down there? That's walrus hide, real walrus hide, so it holds the lint kindly – doesn't rip it like old Eli Whitney's gin does.'

I peered into the packing-case.

---

* In Turkish *bashi* means 'head' and *bazouk* 'out of order.' – *F.M.*

'Now see those two long knives moving across the rollers. Those, sir, are what we know as "the doctors" . . .'

'The doctors': the words reminded me of those filthy monks at Zawiyet el-Deir and the long lines of young boys being led in for castration, roped together, from the *gellabs'* boat moored at the Nile bank.

De Leon nodded towards the ship. 'Mrs Macdonald's out there checking the inventory. She has a fine head for figures . . . The captain has invited us to partake of some liquid refreshment. Perhaps you would care to join us? I can assure you, sir, Captain Johns serves an excellent Bourbon.'

I wondered how much he knew about Jeannie and me. He might have seen me at Flora's wedding. Could this solemn fellow be laughing at me? I felt, as she says, 'sick to my stomach'. I tried to look him in the eye but he evaded my glance.

'I thank you, sir,' I said, 'but I am, as you may know, a Believer and our Holy Koran forbids strong drink.'

'Our great patron,' de Lesseps declared, 'is hiding behind a tree again.' Intimidated by the Sultan-Caliph and the British behind him, Mohammed Said had lost his nerve and ordered all work to stop until the Grand Seigneur's permission was received. In truth, little work had been done; the Canal Between Seas was still a glorious mirage conjured up by de Lesseps' powerful imagination.

At this point Ferdinand had one of his great ideas. Authorised or not, funded or not, he would start work on the canal at Port Said: the mirage would become a reality – of sorts. He would make, as he put it, some 'knocks upon the desert'.

I am proud to say I was there and helped him to make them.

A solitary Egyptian flag fluttered from a pole on the long spit of gravelly sand that extends like the rim of a cup between the Bay of Pelusium and Lake Menzaleh. Out on the ocean four ships waited, loaded with the iron parts for 'Port Said's' new lighthouse. South, from the seashore, two parallel lines of pegs, three yards apart, receded across the sand until halted by that vast salt lagoon where the Nile delta slides into the Mediterranean sea.

No consuls or foreign dignitaries were present on this occasion. Our position was too precarious for that. It was just Ferdinand de Lesseps making a commitment, as his father had made one to Mohammed Ali, a commitment to a great canal that would transform the map of the world.

Ferdinand raised a pickaxe above his shoulders and brought it down near the first peg in the line. He dug out half a square yard of sand, then passed the pickaxe on to Laroche, the chief of the French engineers. Then he gathered the hundred and fifty workers, already living in tents on this spit of sand, and made a little speech:

'The first sod of the Suez Canal has been turned. From this place we shall open up the East to the commerce and civilisation of the West. Remember, my friends, you will not just be moving earth – you will be bringing prosperity to your families and to your beautiful country. Honour and long life to His Excellency, Mohammed Said Pasha!'

When the cheers had died away, the pickaxe was handed to the most senior of the workmen to cut his 'sod', and from him passed to the next most senior, and so on until the youngest had 'made his knock upon the desert'.

At that stage the men were all volunteers, men of many races: Druzes from Syria, Maltese from Malta and Alexandria, Italians, Egyptian fellahin, even Bedouin. Inspired by de Lesseps, they plied pick and shovel with a will. Soon the trench which was to become the pilot channel – the *rigole de service* – described a dark, straight line through the burning sand from the ocean's highwater mark to the majestic mirror of Lake Menzaleh.

The canal was begun. True, there were twenty miles to be excavated under the gluey bed of Lake Menzaleh, two high ridges to be cut through in the desert, swamps to be turned into three lakes, nearly a hundred miles of deep ship canal to be created. But it was begun.

Port Said, I ventured to point out, had no buildings, no food, no stone and, worst of all, no water.

De Lesseps swept that aside. 'We will make the stone from sand, lime and salt water, and fetch the drinking water by barge from Damietta. Lake Menzaleh is alive with fish for our labourers and all this salt-wort on the dunes will give us cooking fires.'

'Inshallah!' I said.

That was the one thing that worried me about Ferdinand. He took it for granted that Allah would be willing. In this he resembled Jeannie Macdonald. I had not sought her out since the wedding party for fear of wrecking the credit of Macdonald, Girgis, Hassuna and Company, Cotton-Ginners, at this delicate stage of their fortunes. But I was vastly comforted to find that Flora, after her marriage, remained very much her own woman and came up to Cairo to see me whenever I could get away from my work at Port Said. She often brought with her my small granddaughter, Leila, who took a particular fancy to me, and was taught by her mother to call me 'Donald'. I think perhaps I constituted a sort of escape route for Flora, as indeed she did for me. Since Wasifa was often away on her 'recitals', Flora took her boy under her wing and Leila and Aziz became firm friends. This new alliance between the 'Arab' and 'Highland' branches of Clan Osman renewed my hope for the future.

Down from Port Said and still trying to tackle the problem of the water supply, I dropped into Shepheard's to have a word with Sam, and ran into de Leon and Jeannie sitting at a table covered with pencilled calculations as usual. An American newspaper lay between them, a black headline blazing from its front page: LINCOLN ELECTED PRESIDENT.

I knew little about this man, except that apparently he had been born in a log cabin. Yet he had become a bone of bitter contention between Edwin and Jeannie. Both were eager to enlist my support.

'Hadji Osman,' she asked, as if I were once again her dragoman, 'would you please tell Mr Edwin de Leon what the Koran says about slavery?'

I made a quick search of my mind and quoted Sura 2, verse 177: 'Righteous is he who sets his slaves free'.

She sat back for a moment, savouring de Leon's discomfiture. 'You've got to face it, Edwin, Abraham Lincoln has only been saying what even the Prophet was saying hundreds of years ago ... what Christianity is saying now. You can't defend the institution of slavery ...'

But he could, and did. The way he went on you might have thought slavery was at the heart of the Constitution itself, that America would collapse if it were abolished, and that the new president was the Devil incarnate.

'What does a half-illiterate Illinois backwoods lawyer know

about the civilisation of the South?' de Leon demanded. 'What do those Yankees know about our way of life? Our cotton sustains America. On my plantation every black and his family have their trim cabin and plot. Set them free and they won't know where to turn . . .'

'Nor will you,' snapped Jeannie.

I was astonished. This was the Jeannie I remembered. It had not occurred to me that 'Americans' – even from adjacent states – could sing such different tunes. It was a discovery that cheered me immensely.

I met her again not very long after that, at a farewell party. In the twenty years since he had been put ashore at Suez with nothing but a shilling in his pocket, I had watched Sam's 'pile of tin' growing inexorably, year by year. Now it was high enough to purchase the manor house in Warwickshire that he had set his heart on, and he had sold out to Mr Zeck of Alexandria. He had secured an immortality as durable as the Pharaohs'. But he had left it too late: he was crippled with arthritis. His famous bulldog had died in its sleep. We helped him get aboard three gazelles, four Muscovy ducks and a white Egyptian donkey for his park at Eathorpe Hall. As we stood side by side on the quay, watching his ship getting smaller and smaller, I felt unfathomably sad. Sam at least had a home to go to. I stole a glance at Jeannie, for she too was now without a country.

That same December Edwin de Leon was showing a party of American tourists round the ruins of Karnak when a message arrived by runner from the Viceroy to inform him that South Carolina had seceded from the Union.

'My duty', he tells us in his memoirs, 'was clear.' He at once returned to Cairo, resigned his post and took ship for Charleston: 'My mind is made up. I must share the fortunes of my state and friends in the terrible struggle that I see is coming.'

I don't know whether Jeannie ever tried to dissuade him. Her own state, North Carolina, had not then joined the Confederacy. What I do know is that she wasn't on the quay when the Southern gentleman sailed away in a grubby little mail-boat named the *Atrato* whose holds (I happened to know) were packed with rifles and ammunition for the rebels.

I won't pretend I was sorry to see the back of him.

The western harbour in Alexandria was more crowded than I had ever seen it before, a forest of funnels and masts flying the flags of many nations. Some flew the red duster and bore the name of Liverpool across their sterns. But I saw others out of Bristol and London and Rotterdam and Le Havre and Hamburg. There was one tall-masted sailing-ship flying a flag I had never set eyes on before: five horizontal bars, three white, two red across the whole, and up in the corner, on a blue field, eleven white stars.

I ran into the harbour-master who was very agitated. The eleven stars, he told me, stood for the eleven rebel states of America. This was the flag of the 'Confederacy'.* 'Unauthorised!' he muttered. Mohammed Said had already given orders for the ship to up anchor and leave. A Union warship might turn up in pursuit, and the last thing His Excellency wanted was a naval battle in Alexandria harbour.

Mrs Macdonald, the American lady, the harbour-master confided, had been on board. Had she been seeking news of Edwin de Leon? His brother was Surgeon-General of the Confederate Army. I felt a sharp twinge of returning jealousy, but told myself that she was probably inquiring about her own family – her sister, Isobel, was married to a Scot who owned a plantation south of Wilmington.

I was swiftly disabused of any idea that Jeannie might have warmed to the South's cause when I ran into her a few hours

---

* What my father accurately describes here was the *first* Confederacy flag. The more familiar verson, with white stars embedded in a blue St Andrew's Cross, appeared later. – F.M.

later, seething with indignation. She thrust into my hands a crumpled copy of the *New Orleans Picayune*, pointing to a column where she had ringed the speech of a Southern Senator:

No power on earth can make war on the Southern states. Cotton is King. Without firing a gun we can bring the whole world to our feet. What will happen if we furnish no cotton for three years? England would topple headlong . . .

'Silly old windbag!' she said.

The blockade of the South's ports by the Union Navy did indeed silence the cotton mills of Lancashire for a while, but the senator had overlooked the fine long-staple cotton-bush Alexis Jumel had found decades ago in a Cairo garden – and my son Omar's dedication to its cultivation in the deep black soil of the Delta, under the Egyptian sun. Cotton was indeed King, but as I looked out over Alexandria harbour, packed with ships waiting impatiently to load, it was evident that day that the King had changed his throne.

The white gold was flowing down the Nile. The Sitt Amerikani, George Jesus Girgis, Omar and Hassuna had chosen the right time to import their new American gins. I ought to have rejoiced, but somehow I could not.

Some weeks the water-kegs unaccountably failed to arrive from Damietta. Salt spray blew in a high wave over the sandspit now to be called 'Port Said', and the men's tongues swelled in their mouths so that they could not swallow. De Lesseps would rush off to complain to the provincial governor and find that he had taken to his bed to escape him.

'The dogs bark, but the caravan moves on!' Ferdinand used to say. It was an old Bedou saying he had adopted to keep our spirits up, and certainly we were in sore need of it. Mohammed Said was pledged to supply the labour for the Canal. But when it came to it, he was afraid to sign the call-up orders. Whenever he heard that de Lesseps was on his way to tackle him on the matter, he would rush off to some inaccessible spot in Upper Egypt. 'Hiding behind trees' was what de Lesseps called it.

When he did at last bring himself to sign the call-up, 'the

barking of the dogs' was deafening. England stirred up an immense outcry about 'forced labour', although undoubtedly forced labour had been used on Stephenson's overland railway only a few years earlier. There's no hypocrite like an English hypocrite.

At last, fitfully, our caravan moved on. Twenty-five thousand Egyptian fellahin scrambled like so many ants over the vast sand dunes that lay athwart the Canal route, gathering up the fine sand, pushing it into the little wicker baskets they had used since the days of the Pharaohs.

My role was to preserve the peace. The Egyptian fellahin were quicker to explode in anger than even the memsahibs on the Transit but the upraised *fas* was more deadly than the flying handbag. I saw to it that the water-kegs were deployed at judicious intervals, but a raging thirst does not make for forbearance. I had just succeeded in patching up a deal between two rival parties set on murdering each other when I became aware of a tall boy of fifteen or so hovering on the edge of the dispute. He held in his right hand a large white envelope, and this he awkwardly thrust upon me. My first thought was that it was one more petition from a village, pleading for the return of its men to get in the crops before they rotted.

'I am Yussef,' he said in the simple way of the young, as though the mere name would explain everything.

I opened the envelope. A card with gilt lettering, in the French language, requesting the pleasure of the company of Osman Effendi at a reception to celebrate the inauguration of the McCarthy Patent Cotton-Gins of Messrs Girgis, Macdonald et Cie, RSVP.

'Grandfather,' said the boy, 'my father has sent me, the youngest of his sons, to invite you. Prince Hilmi will be there and other great persons.'

I looked at him and was startled to see the broad Nubian grin, guileless yet knowing, outshining the sun, that had been Fatima's, passed on no doubt through Omar, his father. Another world!

Suddenly I was ashamed that I had not known my own grandson. I knew of course that Omar had ten children, all boys, by Hassuna's daughter. I had heard that they had followed their father by marrying into land. All, that is, save Yussef here – a counter, you might say, still to play.

An unworthy thought. But it seemed to me that there was something about *Gossypium*, the cotton-bush, whose dark glossy leaves concealed cruel thorns, which of its nature gave rise to unworthy thoughts. 'King Cotton' was no benevolent monarch but a tyrant as grasping as any Mameluke bey, ever demanding, enslaving and, yes, finally debauching. An illusionist that had already divided the great American republic against itself, torn up its Constitution, made mock of its proclaimed equality, and embroiled Americans in a bloody war that divided families, setting brother against brother in a tide of blood.

I made sure that my new-found grandson had a good meal before he set off on the journey home. The RSVP I would deal with later.

In Louis's old room in the house on the canal the invitation card summoning Osman Effendi to *l'Inauguration* glared at me from the top shelf of my Edinburgh Cabinet Library. The sweetwater canal had now advanced near enough to Lake Timsah to make it possible to sail down to the Nile in comfort. I was deprived of my last excuse. I hired a horse at the river, crossed by the Benha Bridge and was soon in Omar's rich province, where the black soil, piled down the centuries, lies thirty to ninety feet deep on the land.

Menufiya swarms with people blackened by the sun, black against the black earth, barely visible, just *there* as they have always been, strong arms, indomitable legs, rueful belly laughter making the best of a bad job ... *Malish!* ... *Inshallah!*

The McCarthy gins declared themselves from far away. Fellahin were converging from all directions, driving donkeys and camels which were almost lost to view beneath great sacks of cotton-bolls. The second picking was coming in.

As I came nearer, I could distinguish the elements in that roar; the dervish howling of the drive-belts, the scream of the rollers, the swish-swish-swish of the cruel 'doctors' – for so I thought of them – the yelling of the labourers as they fed the voracious hoppers, the tattoo of the hard black seeds, torn from their white cocoons, rattling down upon the waiting pans beneath.

Dust motes by the million danced in the bright light around the gins. A 'snow' storm raged, carpeting the earth white. (How many years was it since I had felt real snow crunching under my feet?)

This 'snow' did not crunch, but nestled like down, ruffled by my boots. The price of 'Best Fair' in Liverpool had reached half a crown per pound. The gins would throb through the night. The upper storage floor had long since been packed, and walls of sacked cotton-bolls towered high around the vibrating shed.

In the huddled village, mud on mud, flat roofs were heaped with piles of dried maize-stalks for kindling, old cotton-bushes, and gigantic jars storing beans. Omar's villa of burned brick stood out – as the English say – like a sore thumb.

A wall surrounded it. A couple of watchmen saluted obsequiously as I passed through the iron gates. Waiters with great circular brass trays, loaded with sweetmeats, were passing up the steps and into the house. At the top I almost collided with a darkly handsome fellow in a white coat and chef's hat. It was several moments before I realised that he was my son, Theo. He seemed taken aback by my presence.

'Mother is here,' he said, nodding towards Elena, who was talking her head off as usual in a far corner. 'In fact tout le monde is here – Mrs Macdonald, and Mr Ross from Briggs and Co, and Monsieur Jules Pastré, the Prince, of course, and Mr Girgis and his relatives from Asiut.'

'And Mrs Girgis?' I asked, hoping that Flora might save me.

He shook his head. 'I haven't seen her.'

'And Sami?'

'I hear his ship is at sea again.'

'And Giovanni?'

'He's working on the Canal, isn't he?'

'*Le tout monde?*' I said, intending sarcasm, but he agreed enthusiastically. 'Since Prince Hilmi is here Sheikh Hassuna has spared no expense. We have engaged Om Aziz . . .'

'Really!' I said.

He broke off to pronounce his benediction on a waiter's tray, sweeping his hand over it – *petits fours . . . glaces . . . langues de chat . . . babas . . . poires belle Hélène.** I offered my paternal congratulations and thanked God that Giovanni was an engineer.

---

* I find that M. Offenbach's opera, which inspired this elaborate sweet, was not in fact performed until two years later, 1864. Perhaps my father is confusing this with some subsequent Suez Canal celebration. – *F.M.*

I plunged into the crowded room in search of Omar, but failed to find him. The old divans had disappeared. Gilt Louis Quinze armchairs, imported from Italy, now stood against the walls. Four or five token fellahin stood together at the long table, in their best *galabiya*s and embroidered skull-caps, wolfing platefuls of *poires belle Hélène*, furtively licking the vanilla syrup from their moustaches. I would have joined them, but at that moment I spotted Omar. He was wearing a red tarbush and a new *stambouli*, and was talking to the Prince and two Alexandria bankers, as they call the money-lenders these days. He caught a glimpse of me out of the corner of his eye and quickly turned away, then thought better of it and came over.

I had always thought of Omar as my 'fellah' son. That was difficult now, although the rich damask waistcoat did not sit comfortably with the memory of his beaming black face, which used to cheer me when I was weary. All that seemed to concern him was any news I might have of the civil war across the Atlantic, not because he cared about either side but because changes in the tide of war brought swift fluctuations in the cotton price. Omar had been caught out already by one rumour of the Union's defeat. He did not mean to be caught out again if he could help it. It worried me.

I had brought him up to live by the precepts of the Koran, but under the tuition of Hassuna, Jeannie and George Girgis he had embraced a new creed, no less demanding, but without compassion or charity.

As the day advanced, I became chillingly aware that the prophet did well to warn against the vice-like grip of compound interest, that witherer of the human heart. In this new world of 'Steam Intercourse' which Tom Waghorn had foretold and which was now upon us, youth no longer deferred to the superior wisdom and experience of age. This much I had already discovered. But while I was amused by Giovanni's indulgent condescension, Omar's unease in my presence, the formality and distance he put between us, dismayed me. In the black poll of the small boy I had taken to the *kuttub* to master his Koran there had been a streak of white which I liked to regard with pride as my contribution, my mark, so to speak. No doubt this was vainglorious of me. I noticed, with a shock, that there were no stray blond hairs now. The dye bottle or the barber's clippers? As Omar turned away to resume his conversation with Prince Hilmi, I could not help staring. Trivial as the thing was in these circumstances, the absence of fair hair was like a slap in the face, a rejection of me and all I had stood for. My suspicions that something was badly wrong came flooding back. Why, for instance, had I seen no sign of my daughter Aisha, now the wife of Sheikh Hassuna. Surely she should have made at least a token appearance?

I detached Omar with difficulty from the Prince and the bankers and tackled him. He tried to conceal his embarrassment, but failed miserably.

'She is not interested in these matters.'

'But where *is* she?'

'She is in the women's quarters – in the *haramlik* across the courtyard.'

I accepted my dismissal, but with rising disquiet. I crossed the courtyard, passing from this false façade of French sweetmeats and Louis Quinze armchairs to the Egypt I knew of shabby divans and sweet, stewed black tea in small glasses.

I entered the *haramlik* without notice – it was, after all, my daughter I was going to see.

Aisha greeted me with a cry of startled recognition. She had aged terribly; I found it hard to recognise in her the bright, bubbling girl who left the house on the canal, sought – and given – in marriage to the well-to-do, highly respected cotton-planter Sheikh Hassuna.

To my astonishment, Jeannie was in the room.

'I warned you, Donald,' she said. 'I told you what would happen – and it now has. That clod Hassuna has put Aisha away. She's borne him eight children, and now he's put her away.'

I was dumbfounded. It was she herself who had suggested the marriage, partly on the grounds that it would enable her to continue her prize pupil's education. I started to protest.

She switched into Gaelic, as she often did at moments of crisis. 'They were all girls. The old devil says that she hasn't given him an heir, and now that he's rich he feels entitled to buy a young Circassian beauty – God knows where he got her from. And now *she* is pregnant. If the child is a boy, poor Aisha will be out on her ear. *Talak! Talak! Talak!* You're no more my wife.' She laughed bitterly.

A younger woman sat beside Aisha on the grubby divan, her

face stained with tears. Two small children crawled around her feet. I nodded towards her. 'Who's she?'

Jeannie laughed again. 'So the great Osman Effendi doesn't even know his own granddaughters? She is Aisha's eldest child, Kadra. She is the wife of Abdul Hadi.'

'So where is Abdul Hadi? Is he at the celebrations?'

There was a touch of hysteria in Jeannie's voice. 'Kadra doesn't know. Nobody does. Kadra's come to see her mother to beg her to plead with Hassuna. But with that woman in his bed . . .' She shrugged.

I was baffled. 'How does Hassuna come into this?'

'He owns Abdul Hadi's farm. At least, he does now. You might say he owns Abdul Hadi.'

She didn't seem too concerned. 'The man's a fool', she said. 'Obstinate as an ox. He and Kadra could be doing fine, if only he'd listened to us. We offered him well over the odds to bring in his cotton crop to our gins – after all, he's "family". But the man's been mortgaging his crop to Greek money-lenders for years, and he insists on going his own sweet way, even though Hassuna gave him a daughter in marriage. Then Omar had to warn him against using unauthorised seed. He warned him twice. But the fool paid no heed.'

'A proud man,' I said. 'He likes to be his own man.'

'His own man!' she snorted. 'He's those Greek bloodsuckers' man. They have him by the throat.'

'I thought it was Sheikh Hassuna who had him by the throat.'

She made an impatient gesture. Look, Donald, we need a reliable supply for our new gins. We can't afford the Abdul Hadis.'

This much I gathered, little by little. The day came when, inexplicably, water ceased to flow through the irrigation channels of Abdul Hadi's holding, even when it was the due time. New furrows, prepared with much labour to spread the life-giving Nile flow, were found to have mysteriously caved in overnight. Abdul Hadi took his complaints to the village *omda*, who happened to be Hassuna, and the *ghafir*s were sent for and ordered to keep watch day and night. For a few hours after that the blessed water flowed through the furrows, darkening the parched earth. Then once again the flow was reduced to a trickle, and died. The leaves on Abdul Hadi's cotton-bushes curled up. The cotton-bolls fell to the ground. Even the clover failed, so that the gamoose gave no milk and was too feeble to pull the plough.

Abdul Hadi had sold his cotton crop in advance to the Greeks. Now he had no crop. They lent him a little, as an old customer, then took it back again with interest, or tried to. While the other fellahin were eating white bread and meat and even buying wives, Abdul Hadi faced ruin.

'Your father,' he complained to Kadra, 'is like the saw that cuts coming and cuts going.' He implored her to beg her mother, Aisha, to go to her brother, Omar Bey, and plead with him to open the sluices to save his family.

But in this ancient land, ever since the days of the Pharaohs, the power to control the flow of the Nile's water has been absolute power. Those who possess it feel themselves gods, Pharaohs. Omar turned a deaf ear to his sister's pleas and sent her away.

In the *haramlik* Kadra's children tugged at her skirts, grizzling. Theirs was the only sound. I looked across at Jeannie Macdonald, the Sitt Amerikani, erstwhile disciple of Tom Paine, champion of the Cherokees, the 'native Americans', but she gave no sign. Then, into the heavy silence of that shabby room crept the rub-dub-a-dub and whine of the McCarthy gins, growing ever more insistent, and from across the courtyard came a roar of applause which could mean only one thing: the incomparable Om Aziz was making her entrance.

Much troubled by what I had learned, I left Aisha and made my way back to the reception. Such was the demand for her 'recitals', it wasn't often these days that I had the opportunity to set eyes on my Egyptian wife.

The room was hushed, gripped in reverential expectancy. I was astonished to see Yussef Boghos in his accustomed position, sitting cross-legged on the platform, cradling his *ud*. His skin was like thin parchment now; he was not so much old as ancient. I wondered whether he still had the strength to gather in the gold and silver that rained down in tribute. But perhaps that ritual was considered vulgar now, for the tearful child to whom I had given shelter was transformed. By general agreement Om Aziz plumbed the depths of the Arab soul, gave rise to ecstasy that soared even above the peaks of the Liverpool Cotton Exchange.

She began slowly, barely audible, yet commanding the total attention of the crowded room. Then her voice deepened, gathering authority and power until it seemed to transcend the merely human: 'Every night my moaning ceaseth not, for a solitary gazelle that has taken away my soul . . .'

To translate Arab poetry into English is to insult it. That sober language cannot encompass the emotional spectrum, the intoxicating rhythms and rhymes. The voice grew more sonorous, more urgent, throbbing, possessing the whole audience as it mounted to its climax.

Then the voice dropped away and in the awed silence that followed I became aware of the distant howl of the ginning machines before that, too, was drowned in paroxysms of applause.

'Allah! Allah! Allah!'

But I must confess I was in no mood for Arab poetry that evening. My daughter, once such a bright child, had been made wretched, cast aside; and my granddaughter was being plunged into penury through no fault of her own.

As Om Aziz ran through her classical repertoire I asked myself what I had done wrong. How had I failed them? Immersed in these broodings, at first I failed to notice that an interval in the recital had been reached. Then, as I pondered what course I should take, I became aware that something was missing: the faint ground-bass of the distant McCarthy ginning stand we were assembled that day to celebrate. It had reasserted itself in the previous intervals, but now it was absent, although I knew the machines were working round the clock. Perhaps, I thought, the wind had changed. Looking at Omar, I saw that he, too, was listening intently. Jeannie came over and whispered urgently in his ear; they made their excuses to the Prince and went out together.

When they had not returned, and a deep hush indicated that Om Aziz was about to resume, I slipped out after them.

I found them standing together outside Omar Bey's double iron gates, staring in the direction of the ginning stand.

'No question about it,' she said, angrily. 'They're out again! That's the sixth time this month – and today of all days. You're supposed to run checks on them!' In the moonlight Omar's *stambouli* looked ludicrous, a cruel caricature. He seemed to shrink within it.

'The engineer is working on the Benha gins,' he muttered unhappily, 'I could send for him tomorrow . . .'

She exploded. 'Bukra! Bukra! It's always tomorrow, never today! Look, Omar, have you any idea how much this company is losing every hour those gins aren't running?'

She had, I'm sure. The son-in-law would have worked it out to the last piastre. I recalled how people had laughed at Tom Waghorn's Greenwich Chronometer. How things have changed! This is a new world in which, as she is fond of saying, 'Time is money'.

It was something I did not much care to hear. I fear that before long it may become: 'Life is Money', or 'Money is Life'.

'I could go myself,' said Omar, miserably. 'See what I can do . . . when it's light, bukra . . .'

'Not tomorrow, *now!*' Jeannie almost shouted.

I could understand her irritation, of course. I've seen Europeans driven almost crazy when they first come out here. The sensible ones learn. Egypt is the land of the camel, and you need the camel's patience and endurance to survive. What a pity she never learned to say *malish* once in a while. I've found it rarely does, you know – *matter* all that much.

I made my way back to the room where Aziz' mother was again plumbing the depths of the Arab soul. I would speak to Omar about Abdul Hadi's plight and my daughter's tragedy next day, though there seemed little enough I could do for either of them. King Cotton's 'white gold' contained too much dross. The recital ended in thunderous applause, which my wife graciously accepted as her due.

Even now the show was not over. Incongruously, the gilded armchairs had been set out for the Notables on the edge of a burgeoning cotton-field. There was to be a firework display such as the province of Menufiya had never seen before to mark the triumph of the houses of Girgis, Macdonald, Omar bin Osman and Hassuna, and also to serve as a salute to that latter-day Moloch, the McCarthy Patent gin.

As ever, the show was late, very late, in starting. Meanwhile a crowd of excited fellahin drifted in from the surrounding villages and took up positions on the ground at a respectful distance from the Quality. At last a single Catherine wheel began to turn, tracing a circle of spluttering light in the deepening darkness; gathering speed, it was spurred by another, and then others, until an incandescent line of spinning wheels lit up the earth, imprinting itself on the eye.

'Allah! Allah!' cried the fellahin. The Prince, a provincial governor on either side, applauded decorously. My thoughts were of Omar, somewhere out there, struggling to find and repair the fault in the gins. I strained my ears for a sound that would indicate that he was succeeding. Om Aziz had pocketed her fat fee and departed. A crescent of red and yellow and green shot across the night sky, spanning the spectrum, emulating the rainbow that had been de Lesseps' 'sign'. The grand finale was a rocket that rushed off with a roar that made some of the fellahin leap up in consternation. It exploded high in the sky. A golden rain spilled over the vault of Heaven, drifting earthward, until slowly, one by one, the bright stars paled, flickered and clicked out.

The show was over.

The gilt chairs were pushed back; the fellahin got up and began to wander back, chattering, towards their villages. Then a couple of them stopped, pointing excitedly towards the horizon. A faint pink glow had appeared, as if the fireworks display was about to resume. The glow grew with astonishing speed. Pink turned to yellow and then to orange. A shaft of yellow light fell across the whole vast cotton-field, eerily illuminating the bursting white bolls.

A woman yelled, 'It's the ginning stand! The cotton's going up!' It was Jeannie's voice. Jagged yellow tongues of flame leapt skyward.

'Omar! Omar!'

I heard my own voice. I looked round and saw Omar's youngest son, Yussef, coming up with two horses. Without a word we mounted and spurred our horses down the road that led to the ginning-shed.

We could feel the heat of the fire on our faces from half a mile off. The hundreds of sacks of raw cotton stacked around the gins were walls of flame. It was impossible to get near. If Omar had been in there, he wouldn't have had a chance.

It was late next day before the ginning-shed had cooled enough to allow us to search. We found Omar's body – or the poor charred bones that were all that remained – near the engine-house, where he had evidently been working when the cotton went up.

The workers had gone home long before, well content to leave any repairs for the next day.

The cause of the fire was never discovered. Abdul Hadi never returned to the village, nor was his body ever found. Kadra's family was fatherless and landless.

The manner of Omar's death haunted me. For weeks afterwards I dreamed of those leaping flames against the night sky, turning from crimson to orange and then to yellow, howling, devouring like jackals, and I would think of the flames of Hell promised in the Koran for the wicked and those who 'chooseth the pomp of life ... They are those for whom no other reward is prepared in the next life except the fires of Hell.' I came on that in Sura 11, entitled 'Hud', revealed at Mecca. Certainly my son had been led to 'choose the pomp of life'; Omar was weak, vain perhaps, but I could not believe he was wicked.

'Sad, very sad,' said George Jesus Girgis, But the firm had other American gins, well placed around the country. The fire damage could soon be repaired.

Girgis could restore the cash-flow, but he could not bring back my son, my first-born, the smiling boy who had come to me ready-made, so to speak, with the name of second caliph of Islam already attached.

For the first time in my life I began to understand what was meant by that curious expression, 'the weight of years'. They pressed upon me. I turned to the pages of the Holy Koran, seeking comfort and consolation, but I did not find them. Perhaps I am not a good enough Moslem. Islam, after all, means submission, submission to the Will of Allah. Are we not told in the Holy Koran, Sura 37, revealed at Mecca, as well as in the Holy Bible in the first chapter of Genesis, that as a trial, the Lord ordered Abraham to offer his only son, Isaac, in sacrifice, and that with a heavy heart Abraham went to the mountain, steeling himself to obey his Master's command, laying the boy 'prostrate on his face'.

But then Allah, in His compassion, relented. I myself, on my pilgrimage to Mecca with Sheikh Ibrahim had seen the deep cleft in the rock of the Mount of Mercy made by Abraham's knife, deflected by the angel of the Lord.

So why had not Allah sent a strong wind to turn the flames

from the ginning-shed, or, for that matter, a thunderstorm to douse the flames? That should not have been difficult. Come to that, why was it my poor Zobeida who died from the plague, and not Mr Kinglake who had done everything to spread the contagion? Come to that, why had Allah allowed that good Moslem and Koranic scholar Jean-Louis Burckhardt to perish at thirty-three, leaving his great work unaccomplished?

Malish! A good Muslim should not ask such questions. But this time the *malish* died on my lips. I *did* mind.

I minded in every bone in my body.

How glad I was to be away from those endless cotton-fields and mud villages, back in the clean air of the desert. Under its vast sky, little by little, but surely, I recovered my faith. Out here it was impossible not to believe that God was great and had work for me to do.

Despite all the English had been able to do to stop us, the *rigole* was moving slowly forward, a glittering line of salt water cutting through the great sand dune to the edge of the Timsah morass, where our labourers had built an earth dam.

An important stage in our advance had been reached, and de Lesseps was determined all the world should know about it. The date was 18 November 1862. At 11 o'clock the workmen began to nibble away with their *fas*es at the top of the earth wall. As it crumbled, and sea-water and fish and earth came spewing forth, de Lesseps produced an illuminated scroll and read from it:

'I command the waters of the Mediterranean to flow into Lake Timsah in the name of His Highness Mohammed Said.' A military band struck up the national anthem, the sheikhs of el-Azhar called down Allah's blessings on the great work, while the Grand Mufti of Egypt delivered himself of a *fatwa* to be read in mosques throughout the land, thanking Allah for having willed this beneficent enterprise by this noble Frenchman, the elect of God, who had done His will.

It should have been a moment of triumph, the culmination of six years' work and struggle since that extraordinary day when de Lesseps saw his 'bow in the sky'. But for me, the cheers rang hollow. As the Mediterranean spilled out into the mid-desert, what I saw was Omar's small head bobbing in the churning Nile

water as he dived for the gold and silver coins hurled in by the
Governor of Cairo to celebrate the 'Bride of the Nile' occasion.
'My' blond streak was still in his black hair then.

Slowly spreading out, forming a sheet of shimmering water
mirroring the steel-blue sky, the Mediterranean reclaimed me.
They were cheering now for the Viceroy, for Mohammed Said.
The Grand Mufti sought Allah's protection for the life and reign
of this ruler 'who day and night worked for the happiness and
prosperity of his people'.

The truth, unfortunately, was very different. Despite all the efforts
of his Scottish governess, Mohammed Said was at heart little
changed from the self-indulgent boy prince we had known.
Exhausted by his debaucheries, he was at death's door. In January,
his doctor sent a message warning de Lesseps that he might not
last the night. Before Ferdinand could reach Alexandria, he was
dead.

On the Paris *bourse* the Canal company's shares plunged. The
concession had been peculiarly Mohammed Said's affair. No one
knew which way his successor would jump. Already a British
envoy was at Ismail's side, whispering that France was scheming
to take control of Egypt through the canal, and urging him to cut
loose while there was still time.

Just at the moment when our mirage seemed about to become
reality, Fate had dealt us a crushing blow.

Our coffers were almost empty. Half the company's shares had
been 'reserved' for Mohammed Said, but Mohammed Said had
never paid up. Our operations were unlawful, as the Ottoman
Sultan still withheld his permission. We were at the mercy of the
new ruler.

Grandson of the 'Old Pasha', Mohammed Ali, Ismail was thirty-
eight when he succeeded, the fourth member of the extraordinary
'home-made' Albanian dynasty that commanded all our lives.
They were to call him 'Ismail the Magnificent' in the end, but
never, I think, very seriously: he was the runt of the litter. Short
and portly, he walked with a rolling gait: you would never have
guessed that he had been through the French military college of
St Cyr. Sprouting in all directions, his eyebrows concealed 'shifty'
eyes (in fact the result of a childhood bout of ophthalmia).

Our summons to the presence was not long in coming.

The new Pharaoh laid a hand on Ferdinand's arm. 'Mon cher Lesseps,' he began in his perfect French, 'you need have no fear. Je suis canaliste.' His left eyelid shut down, while the right eye opened wide and focused on de Lesseps in a manner I found disconcerting.

'Peut-être plus canaliste que vous,' he continued, the left eyelid re-opening like a theatre-curtain rising. 'Oui, c'est vrai, je suis canaliste. But there is one thing you must never forget. This canal is created to serve Egypt, not Egypt to serve the Canal Company!'

Both eyes were now fully open. He was shrewder than I thought – or was he just echoing the English special envoy? Palmerston was Prime Minister again and, although now over eighty, as powerful as ever.

Sure enough, the Grand Vizier in Istanbul despatched a note to Ismail:

> The Sublime Porte, keenly interested in the progress of Civilisation in the East, cannot allow this great work [the Canal] to be accomplished by a system of labour severely condemned by all civilised nations.

Ismail capitulated. From having 20,000 workers, all of a sudden we had none. The London *Standard* was jubilant: 'What will the poor shareholders say now? Those poor speculators in France, Egypt and Turkey? They will be ruined. De Lesseps and the adventurers who are supporting him will do well to withdraw.'

Adventurers? I had never thought myself as an adventurer. But, all things considered, perhaps I was. The obstacles we faced, though, were not so much those of Nature as human avarice, suspicion and envy.

Ismail, the *canaliste*, took up and actually arranged to pay for the shares that had been reserved for his predecessor, Said. This was encouraging – but did it perhaps point to some deeper game? Ismail had sent Nubar Pasha to the annual general meeting of the Compagnie Universelle in Paris, where the Duc de Morny, a notorious speculator, was plotting to take over the company, panicking shareholders into selling, then smartly buying in the fallen shares.

I was out of my depth – but I did not sell my humble holding.

'The dogs bark, but the caravan moves on,' repeated de Lesseps, and with characteristic boldness he proposed to invite 200 representatives of chambers of commerce from all over Europe, and some from America, 'to make the voyage across the isthmus from sea to sea'. Unfortunately, he omitted to mention that for much of the way the water in the canal would not be more than three feet deep: the 'ships' would be flat-bottomed barges hauled by camels.

Explaining away little matters like that was the duty of that famous dragoman, Osman Effendi. (I will admit, though, that it was Ferdinand's energy and enthusiasm that saved the day.) A sumptuous banquet was provided in the desert, and a famous American businessman named Cyrus W. Field, who had financed the recent laying of a telegraph cable beneath the Atlantic, made a speech. That very spring, he told us, railway lines from the east and west coasts of the United States had linked up. Steam power, he opined, was making history, transforming the world.

It struck me that Mr Field was at one with Jeannie in this 'making history' matter. I've lost count of the number of times that, rebuking my 'fatalism', she's told me, 'Donald, Osman . . . it is *not* written; *we* write it. History is what we make, you and I, and the rest of us. You're building this canal aren't you – from sea to sea?'

'Inshallah,' I added hastily.

I have to smile when she goes on like this. My whole life – hers, too, for that matter – gives the lie to her argument. Was it of my own free will that I enlisted in the Ross-shire Buffs at the age of fifteen? Did I *ask* to be sold into slavery – or did it happen because the departure of the French had brought anarchy to Egypt? The tides of history fling us about like driftwood, hurl us up on the beach, as they did me in 1807, sap us even as they eat up our coastlines.

I made a trip down to Alexandria, eager to refresh my spirits with the sight of my half-Highland granddaughter, Leila. But I was brought up short by the American flag – the 'stars and stripes' – flying at half-mast everywhere. I rushed to the consulate. It seemed that a madman had entered the box at a theatre Abraham Lincoln was attending and shot him in the head. It was just three days after the Confederacy had surrendered. The long, cruel war was over – and now the President of the Union lay dead of a fanatic's bullet. Everything was thrown once more into the cauldron.

So we make history, do we?

Despite Lee's surrender, fighting was still going on in some places like North Carolina, the Consul told me. I thought of Jeannie at once, of course. I knew from her angry words with de Leon how much Lincoln meant to her, how much she admired his stand against slavery and the hypocrisy which proclaimed the equality of men with one hand while denying it with other. I felt I had to seek her out as, with Aisha's help, she had sought me out so long ago in Cairo. There was much to say, but there was also much that could not be said, and much that we did not need to say because it was part of us: the history that made us.

We talked of the ending of the Union's long blockade of the South's cotton states. It had made Ismail – and a few others – rich beyond their wildest dreams, and now it was threatening bankruptcy. At 1s 11d a pound in January, Egyptian 'Fine' was down to 1s 2d by April and still falling. A fanatic's shot, many thousand miles away, was determining Egyptian destinies.

'Don't panic, Donald,' she said. 'It will be years before the South can come back. Their slaves – and they can do nothing without them – have been freed or enlisted. The plantation owners are on their uppers, ruined – or dead.'

Her voice tailed away: the tragedy of the South engulfed her.

In my infantile jealousy and suspicion of Edwin de Leon, the late American consul, I had forgotten how deeply she was involved in that bitter conflict of irreconcilable philosophies. She had chosen the North's, but she was still willy-nilly of the South; its humiliation was hers, too. And not merely humiliation. Isobel, her eldest sister, had been on the Ladies' War Committee feeding the starving Confederate soldiers at the railway station and, I learned, had been carried off by the yellow fever that swept the place. Their house had been burned down in Sherman's merciless march to the sea, their slaves taken off, her husband killed in the act of firing his own cotton to keep it out of the Yankees' hands.

I remembered Isobel. I could still see those cool, appraising eyes as she played the 'mother' role on the shieling, determining whether I should be allowed to stay the night up there with them.

Supposing she had said no? Our histories – mine, at least –

might have been entirely different. I might still be up there, driving the cattle down to the Tryst.

But Isobel did not say 'no'.

Was that wholly chance? Or was it written? *Mektub* – or Kismet, as the English mutilate our language.

Otherwise, how do you explain that just at the moment when the Canal seemed to have been brought to a full stop by our 'barking' enemies, the 'caravan' began to advance with unprecedented speed. A *deus ex machina* of a more literal sort, a series of sand-eating juggernauts, had been designed by the French engineering firm of Borel, Lavalley et Cie and built in the desert. They opened up a fine new career for Giovanni, now that Stephenson's overland railway was finished. I remember the pitying look he gave his antediluvian parent when I ventured to bemoan the withdrawal of our thousands of labourers.

'Better off without them,' he said. 'You don't believe me? All right. Come on, I'll show you.'

We rode over to a high slab-sided workshop the contractors had erected in the desert. The clang of metal on metal cut eerily through the clear, dry air. Inside, men in blue dungarees were moving about their tasks with an urgency startling in the Orient.

Giovanni took me over to a spot where a huge iron frame was being hammered and bolted together. 'The long *couloir*,' he explained. 'Borel and Lavalley designed it specially for this canal job. It will rest on the deck of a barge ninety-six feet long. See that iron pipe? Five feet diameter. It will suck up the sand from the dredger and put it down on the bank seventy-five feet away.

'Suppose the bank is already well up. Then you use the élévateur over there. The cable hauls small trucks up the incline; at the top, the end opens, and the mud drops on top of the bank wherever you want it.'

He was triumphant: the voice of the future against the voice of the past.

'And remember,' he said, 'those machines don't stop to eat or pray.'

'Very clever,' I said, 'but one of these machines will cost thousands of times the hire of the fellahin – and the company is bankrupt already.'

He had his answer pat. 'They cost six hundred thousand francs a piece and each will shift two million cubic metres a month. We'll have sixty at work before long. Lesseps says we'll excavate enough earth and sand to cover the whole of the Champs-Elysées in Paris from the Place de la Concorde to the Arc de Triomphe.'

Trust Ferdinand! I could see that in my son he had an apt pupil. *Whizz! Whizz! All by Steam!* I thought of our endless fight – Belzoni and Burckhardt and Henry Salt and I – against the ever-encroaching sand, filtering back to entomb again the colossi of Abu Simbel.

Sometimes now the entire earth seems to be opening under my feet. I don't much like the sensation. Am I a natural stick-in-the-mud like my father – or just getting old?

The entrance to the Canal immortalised the fat boy prince, Said. Naturally the mid-way point, the company 'capital' on Lake Timsah's western shore, had to be named Ismailiya after our new pharaoh, Ismail.

His Excellency accepted the dedication with enthusiasm and was already working on lists *de la qualité* to be invited to the Grand Opening which would establish, once and for all, that Egypt was no longer some noisome Oriental *suk* but – as Ismail insisted – 'a part of Europe'. The lists were long and comprehensive: poets and painters, playwrights such as Alexandre Dumas, critics including Théophile Gautier, young journalists, Emile Zola among them. All expenses found: liberal pocket-money on application to the Chamberlain. Ismail's pockets were deep, or he thought they were; the foreign bankers pressing loans upon him had shown him how to raise unlimited sums through a new sort of *hegab** called a bond.

As a prelude, Ismail embarked on a grand tour of the courts of Europe personally to invite their crowned heads to the Grand Opening. A high point of this was to be a visit to the Paris International Exhibition of 1867. The only problem was that, despite the doubling of the Tribute and the despatch to the Sultan by special frigate of the most beautiful Circassian odalisque from Ismail's own harem, the new title Ismail considered indispensable

---

* A *hegab* is a charm written on a strip of paper, widely used in Egypt. – F.M.

to his new status had not arrived by the time of his departure. Nubar had to go racing after him to Paris with it.

Divested of its wrappings, it proved a sad disappointment. 'Khedive' was Persian in origin and ancient (indeed obsolete), though Nubar – crafty as ever – pointed out to his master that he would enjoy the distinction of being the only Khedive in the entire world.

I was not, unfortunately, present on this trip. But Sami was. Recovered at last from the wounds inflicted by the Russian guns at Sinope, he had been placed in command of the twenty-four-oar *dahabiya* transported to Paris and floated on the Seine.

In this way we received from Sami inside information on the Khedive's new enthusiasm for opera. A Paris opera house was presenting Offenbach's latest, *La Grande Duchesse de Gérolstein*, and our squint-eyed ruler was attending every second night.

His dedication proved to be not so much to the music of Offenbach, delightful though that was, as to the opera's star, Hortense Schneider. As Sami told it, his infatuation with the lady was shared by other crowned heads who flocked to Paris for the Exhibition. So much so that the long corridor leading to the star's dressing-room had become known as *le passage des princes*.

Whether it was the charms of Hortense Schneider, or my old friend, Mariette Bey, newly appointed Director of Antiquities, who put the idea of a grand opera of Ancient Egypt into the Khedive's head, I never discovered. Hortense herself had hardly the figure for Aida, but Mariette, I happen to know, had to hand a story of doomed love among the Pharaonic tombs and temples, and he rather fancied himself as a literary man.

I warned him that he might be making a rod for his own back. The trouble was that for such an occasion the Khedive insisted that none would suffice but the greatest composer in the world. Maestro Verdi was approached, but no reply came. A libretto was prepared by one of Verdi's regular librettists. But still the Maestro would not commit himself.

'Tell the Maestro he can name his own price!' ordered Ismail. Auguste was already working on the designs of the Pharaonic costumes, meticulously copied from the tombs. But Verdi was engaged on other operas.

Time was running out.

'The Maestro works fast, very fast, once he starts,' Auguste said.

'He'd better,' I said. If Ismail took it into his head that he had been insulted, it would go hard with Mariette, distinguished international figure though he was.

Mariette changed the subject abruptly.

'That boy of yours – Ibrahim, wasn't it? He worked with me at Sakkara, excavating the avenue of the sphinxes, remember?'

Did I *remember*? It was I who got him the job on the strength of my own work with Belzoni.

'Good worker, Ibrahim, and never slipped any of our finds in his pockets – as far as I know.' This was a sore point with Mariette, who had sworn to stop what he called the 'plundering of Egypt', whether by grave-robbing fellahin or by pashas.

'So what is he doing now?'

As if he didn't know! 'He's running an Antikas shop for foreign tourists near Shepheard's. He's doing well!'

Mariette grimaced. 'We're just about to enact a law to stop this plunder. I was hoping your boy would join me. Poacher turned gamekeeper, as the English say. I'm relying on you to use your influence, Sheikh Osman.'

I said, 'He's going on forty and has a family to feed.'

'It would be a post of much honour – Deputy Director'.

I shook my head doubtfully. 'I'll put in a word. But he has a mind of his own.'

In the end it was Mariette himself who put in the 'word' that mattered. He went into Ibrahim's shop without notice one day and took possession of that exquisite bronze of the cat goddess, Bastet. He claimed that he could prove that it had been taken – against the new law – from the temple at Bubastis. Ibrahim could be gaoled for a year, unless of course he chose to restore the ear-ringed creature to its proper place – which was in the Egyptian Museum – and accept the post of Deputy Director into the bargain.

There are days when it seems to me that it's blackmail that makes the world go round.

But those are my bad days.

They aren't all bad days. That April I saw Edward, Prince of Wales, a tubby little man not unlike Ismail, with a tall stately wife, Princess Alexandra, at his side, open the sluices which let the waters of the Mediterranean into the Bitter Lakes. William Russell, the famous English war correspondent, was there and told the world of our remarkable accomplishment 'in the heart of the Egyptian desert', and the Prince of Wales made a speech saying that it was a great pity that Lord Palmerston had not been more far-sighted.

I wished that Tom Waghorn could have been there to hear him.

10 a.m., 20 November 1869, el-Shallufa, aboard SY L'Aigle

The engines turn slowly, thrusting against the incoming tide from the Red Sea. Suddenly, the sky opens. We are out of the Shallufa cutting. We are *through*. To starboard the sweetwater canal swings in towards us, a green garland from the Nile to Ismailiya to Suez, life to the desert.

Ten more miles to go. Bright as the sky is above, the question of Sami's fate still hangs like a thunder-cloud above my head. In this great moment of triumph the Khedive might forget, even forgive. But he is a vengeful man – and I have been able to get no word of Sami.

I look for the old Overland route, which I know must come in very soon. Thirty years now since I took Tom Waghorn over it for the first time, his Greenwich Chronometer in one hand, log-book in the other.

But what I see is a trail of smoke, a glint of sun on rails. *Whizz! Whizz! All by Steam!* Stephenson's engines put paid to our vans, and now de Lesseps' with his 'mere stagnant ditch' will eclipse Stephenson. A more satisfying retort than that duel Ferdinand wanted to fight.

Standing by my side at the rail, Jeannie sums up my thoughts: 'London to Bombay or Calcutta without having to transfer your luggage, or even leave your cabin.' She hasn't entirely forgiven de Lesseps, but she knows 'the bottom line', as she puts it.

Now the jagged peaks of the Ataka Mountains, south-west of Suez, blaze out before us as we plash steadily on towards the Gulf of Suez, putting me in mind of the Cuillins, seen from Drynoch, as we started out with the drove.

Every time I come into Cairo on Canal business the place seems in the grips of a perpetual *khamsin*. Thick veils of ancient stone dust dance in the air as el-Kahira's medieval buildings come crashing down. If any, erected perhaps by some formidable Mameluke mason, hold out against the demolition gangs, Ismail brings in the army's siege guns. He hasn't much time left to prove to his distinguished guests that Egypt is 'a part of Europe'.

On his visit to Paris the Khedive had talked to Baron Haussmann as well as held hands with Hortense Schneider. From the northern corner of the old Ezbekieh he plans to drive his Mohammed Ali Boulevard straight through to the Citadel. From the Place Sultan Hassan on the old Ezbekieh's north-west corner, where the Place de la Bourse is to be located, he plans to run the Boulevard Clôt Bey to culminate at Cairo's Rond Point by the new railway station.

Though Baron Haussmann remained behind in Paris, cursed by the population, Ismail had managed to recruit some of his famed collaborators to rub their Aladdin's lamp for him – among them Monsieur Jean-Pierre Barillet-Deschamps, late chief gardener of imperial Paris. The grand old sycamores, under which I had enjoyed countless cups of coffee, came crashing down under that godless Frenchman's axe. It was like blasphemy: every blow hurt. Islam forbids graven images. But fine old trees like this are among the greatest of the works of Allah, a daily declaration of His Oneness and benignity.

The fact is that this fellow, Barillet-Deschamps, turned our old Ezbekieh – the Place Ezbekieh now, of course – into a 'chic' Parisian tea-garden: artificial mounds, trim flower-beds,

picturesque grottos, exotic trees ... DEFENCE DE MARCHER
SUR LES PELOUSES. It isn't ours any more. It used to be the
place for magicians and snake-charmers and *Abu Zeidiya*, spinning endless yarns. Now it's going to be *cafés chantants* in place
of rough-and-ready shadow plays. The *galabiya*s are in retreat
before the frock-coats and *stamboulis*. I don't feel comfortable
there.

Elena, of course, loves every minute of it. You might say she's
coming into her own at last – or what she considers to be her
own. Jeannie calls me a mummified old *bodach*, an interesting
mixture of Pharaonic and the Gaelic, and tells me that what with
gas-lighting and the McCarthy gin the Khedive's Egypt is moving
forward in the van of progress. But young Aziz feels as I do, and
wept at the felling of those majestic old sycamores. I'm sure he's
going to make a fine doctor.

Mohammed Ali used to say that as long as his successors took
care to reside in the Citadel, Salah el-Din's fortress on its rock
under the yellow Mokattam Hills, the dynasty he had founded
would continue to rule over the land of the Pharaohs. But the
Khedive does not warm to this cold place. He could hardly wait
to move into the new Abdin Palace Italian architects had designed
for him, two great wings and a courtyard, near the modern quarter
of Cairo. It is whispered that he spent more than a million pounds
on furniture for the drawing-room alone. Said was a big spender,
but Ismail is a bigger one. He told a visitor: 'Everybody has a
mania for something, and mine is stone and mortar.' He has built
seven new palaces in addition to the Abdin, including the cast-
iron 'Moorish' Alhambra, contrived by Franz Bey, a German, and
set down on an exotic island in the Nile for the reception of
Ismail's most glamorous guest, the Empress Eugénie.

Alas, Cairo was now neither old nor new, but a gap-toothed
chaos. But then our Khedive had a splendid idea. He would *give*
building plots in the quarter between the Abdin Palace and the
Nile on condition that those who took up his offer agreed to erect
a new villa, spending at least 30,000 francs and finishing the job
inside eighteen months. Thus a splendid new quarter, to be called
Ismailiya, would greet the crowned heads and *invités* when they
streamed down the gangplanks.

Though the cotton bubble had burst, centuries of tax-collecting
and keeping the books had left the Girgis clan with plenty of fat

on its bones. My son-in-law and his aunts lost no time in putting their heads together and taking not one but three of Ismail's free plots, cunningly choosing those near the splendid mansion being erected for Mr Remington, an American engineer who was supplying his patent breech-loading rifles to the Egyptian army.

It was no place for an old *renegado*, even if he had the money, but it had the welcome effect that Flora and Leila came to live in Cairo, and – when not tearing about the cotton-fields, tying up village sheikhs in ginning deals – Flora's mother came to live next door to them. And what could be more natural than that in the fullness of time the third villa should be taken over by my celebrated wife Om Aziz, thus providing a suitable shrine at which her admirers might worship?

The happy effect of all this was that I could meet Flora more often and at last really get to know Leila. I met them on the neutral ground of Monsieur Barillet-Deschamps 'Tuileries' – much as I detested most of his works, I was grateful to him for that. There was a certain table underneath a jacaranda-tree where we used to sit, and escaping from the endless chatter of raw-cotton prices and new bond issues I would tell them of my boyhood in the island of Skye and of the drove of black cattle and my grandmother Beaton's house – and potstill – where I had first set eyes on Jeannie. Flora has long had a consuming curiosity about this far-away, sea-girt land and this she has passed on to her daughter, who somehow found a map of Great Britain and demanded that I point out the island of Skye. She was fascinated by the strange starfish shape of it. The *Eilean Sgiathanach*, I said, the 'Winged Island', and after that it became a magic place for her, and she and her mother plied me with questions.

And so as we three sat around the genteel tea-table, we would be transported to our black house at Bracadale with its glowing peat fire and, like my father before me, I would tell old stories of the Dun, the ancestral stronghold of the Macleods, and of Rory Mor's half-gallon drinking-horn – to be drained in one draught by each new Chief – and of the 'elf-spotted' fairy flag brought back from the Crusades, and of Donald Macleod, the boatman of Galtrigill, who would not betray the Prince even for £30,000, and of my half-brother Angus, the piper, whose mother had been of that great piping clan, the MacCrimmons, and of my half-brother, Dugald, who enlisted in Fraser's and was taken prisoner at Yorktown, and of the black cattle we 'swum' over the Kyle.

I felt miraculously renewed and in my mind the mists rolled back from Macleod's Tables and I saw, clear as day, surf breaking over Macleod's Maidens, the three dark pillars of stone off Idrigil Point, the tallest, the Mother, weaving her web of Fate, her two daughters (some say) preparing to cut it.

On the south-west corner of the old Ezbekieh, the master architect of Paris-on-the-Nile, set down his Place de la Bourse, and on the north-west corner – his Place de l'Opéra. All that year, after an afternoon around the tea-table we would pause to watch the Khedive's pride and joy, the Cairo Opera House, taking shape before our eyes. It was modelled on La Scala in Milan, but its frontage was stone for only half of its height, then wood, plastered and painted white, it having been impressed upon the Italian builders that speed was of the essence.

Indulgent to children as Italians are, they let Leila look inside and she was fascinated by that exotic 'bird's nest' of a place, the three tiers of the circle, picked out in gold, the crimson and golden drapes, and – as the work advanced – the Khedive's box. Opposite this, behind a lacy metal screen ornamented with golden flowers, came a sensational innovation, boxes for his harem. I happen to know that Ferdinand had informed the Khedive that until Egyptian women could move about freely, Egypt would remain 'a nation walking on one leg'.

I remember that one afternoon, after discussing the endless murderous feuds of the Macleods and the Macdonalds over tea, we stopped by the Opera House and found the workmen installing the front two rows of Louis Quinze armchairs for the pashas and beys. Beyond, phalanxes of red plush stalls rolled back into the distance. Behind the proscenium arch, framed in playful cherubs, the stage lay empty, expectant. But with her exuberant child's imagination Leila had already peopled it; applause exploded from the *fauteuils* and swept back to the uppermost recesses of the circle. I suppose that must be the moment at which my granddaughter became stagestruck. She would have been about thirteen at the time, tall for her age, with her grandmother's dark hair. I wondered what fate awaited her in this new Egypt which was 'part of Europe'.

*

They began to descend like locusts, jaws champing, weeks before the date set for the official opening. Two shiploads from Marseille, poets, scientists, painters, dramatists, sculptors, historians, philosophers. In fact, it seemed to me that the only person *not* invited on this momentous occasion was the person most entitled to be there, the Sultan Abdul Aziz, God's Shadow on Earth, Caliph of All the Faithful. Despite the fact, that in March 1866 the Grand Seigneur had at last issued a *firman* describing the Canal – which he had fought for ten years – as 'a great work of civilisation'. (Was it altogether a coincidence that Lord Palmerston had died, aged eighty, the preceding year?)

It was agreed that Mariette, as Director of Antiquities, would escort the Empress Eugénie, her nieces and her suite of two hundred ladies over the Pharaonic tombs and temples of Upper Egypt, while I, as a senior dragoman of unrivalled experience, would display the sights to the distinguished guests and minor princes.

Mariette had much the best of it. For instance, he didn't have to deal with Théophile Gautier, who rejected his room in Shepheard's as a 'cold monastic cell' in a 'dark English barracks'. I wasn't exactly sorry when, walking down one of the 'barrack' corridors, opening doors, he fell into a coal-hole and broke a leg. As for Madame Colet – a poetess, I'm told – she complained endlessly about the objectionable behaviour of her donkey, until one day – and who can blame it? – it refused to budge an inch. I had to have two fellahin carry her to our Nile boat in a sack.

We had the usual push–pull and heave-ho up the Great Pyramid. As ever, they were astonished to find the 'apex' flat, littered with great blocks of stone on which pilgrims going back to the ancient Greeks had made their bids for immortality. My French charges were excited to find the 'signature' of Chateaubriand, and then of some of Bonaparte's *savants*, dated in new republican style *Anno IX*.

I took some pleasure in pointing out, crisply carved, the name of General Abercromby, who threw the French army out of Egypt in 1801 and in the process came upon a string of names from the past which leapt back into my life.

BELMORE . . . JULIANA . . . ROBERT RICHARDSON MD
CAPTAIN LOWRY CORRY RN
LORD CORRY . . . THE HON HENRY CORRY . . . ROSA

One of the French clients noticed my absorption.

'Ah, la belle Rosa! You knew her, monsieur?'

I nodded. I did not tell him she was a King Charles spaniel bitch with a keen appetite for fellahin's ankles, and one of the many crosses poor Miss Brooks had to bear. I looked for Brooks's name here on the top of the Great Pyramid but failed to find it.

By this time the French had their knives out and were busy making their marks on History.

A couple a weeks later I ran into Mariette near the Colossi of Memnon on the west bank. I was waiting for one of my artists to finish his sketch. Mariette was taking the opportunity to have a word with one of his inspectors at Kurna, capital of tomb-robbers through the ages.

'Where is she?' I said.

'Where she always is when there's a telegraph station – on the wire to Paris to find out which lady the Emperor's taking supper with tonight. If the reply doesn't come whistling down the line, she's complaining to the Khedive, poor woman.'

'Poor woman?'

'This is her last hour of glory – and she knows it. The Prussians are on the move . . . Bismarck is ready to call the Bullfrog's bluff.'

Like seasoned dragomen, we fell to comparing notes. I contended that I had had the worst of it. I had this painter, Léon Gérome, demanding to be smuggled into a *hammam* when the towel was floating outside to indicate ladies' day. He had an idea for a picture to be entitled 'White Circassian being washed down by her Black Slave'. He insisted that it must be done from life. Mariette's charge, the Empress, by contrast, was already well informed about the Pharaohs, and had been giving lectures to her ladies as their steamer moved up the Nile.

Mariette grimaced. 'All too well informed,' he said – and he told me that the Egyptian Museum had nearly lost one of its greatest treasures when the Empress had asked to see Ashotep's turquoise necklace and golden bracelet. She held them in her hands and spent ten minutes gloating over them. The Khedive would have presented them to her like a shot.

I looked around nervously. Mariette is a big man and tends to boom; but the great stoney plain, running back to the bleak yellow cliffs, was empty.

'It was a good thing Ibrahim was on duty at the museum that day.'

I was astonished. 'Ibrahim?'

'He's a fast thinker, that boy. He took one of the Empress's ladies aside, and casually mentioned that Queen Ashotep's necklace carried a terrible curse.'

'A curse? What sort of curse?'

'That any woman who wore it would lose her home and everything she possessed. Ibrahim reads the French papers, you see. That boy of yours will go far.'

Flora and Leila and I watched the last lick of white paint being applied to the Opera House, the last curlicue of gold leaf laid on, ready for *Aida*, the world's first grand opera of Ancient Egypt, to be performed in the presence of the crowned heads of Europe. Alas! Maestro Verdi had not yet written a single note. Wagner was suggested as a substitute, but it was too late. Draneht Bey, the opera-house manager, fell back on an old Verdi favourite, *Rigoletto*, and got away with it – Draneht always got away with it. Seventeen days before the Grand Opening of the Canal the curtain rose on the celebratory performance. I was away at Serapeum, where that rock-ridge had just come to light. But I had a full account from Flora who – to the annoyance of her husband – had been pressed into service as wardrobe mistress.

The critic from the London *Daily Telegraph* announced to the world that 'this is quite the prettiest and lightest opera house I have ever seen.' The Khedive, much gratified, beamed down from the royal box on the forty young Italian girls of the *corps de ballet* who enliven Act I.

But Cairo was chock-a-block. Overnight accommodation could not be found anywhere for the sparsely clad Italian dancers. Draneht Bey was in a panic; scandal was the last thing he needed. In desperation he appealed to his wardrobe mistress. Flora is a woman of resource. Across the road was a police station. She led the girls over, and they were made comfortable for the night in the cells. Draneht Bey was so relieved that he insisted on putting Flora on the pay-roll.

There was another consequence. The ballet girls made a great fuss of Leila, letting her try on their pretty tutus, so that she became more stage-struck than ever. Nothing would do but that Verdi provide a small part for her in *Aida*.

Her father strictly forebade it. But her mother, I've always suspected, encouraged her, if she needed any encouragement, which I very much doubt. There's good Highland blood there, even if it is third-generation. Interesting to see if, in due course, she brings about the 'marriage of East and West' announced by the Empress's chaplain, Monsignor Bauer, at the Grand Opening. She'll be living in Paris-on-the-Nile, of course, a long way from Burckhardt's old rickety house on the stinking canal where Drummer Donald Macleod finally became Osman Effendi.

'Poor Osman!' as Mr Kinglake had it.

Ah well, *malish!**

---

* When I examined my father's story, it broke off abruptly here. However, as his editor I felt that the final entry in the journal he kept of the first transit of the Canal would make an excellent conclusion. – F.M.

Midday, 20 November 1869, Suez Roads

Jeannie and I leaned over *L'Aigle's* starboard rail, side by side, sharing our mounting excitement, lifting into exhilaration as the white walls and houses of Suez sprang into view across the marshes, shining in the morning sun.

'Tìr nan Og,' I said, half to myself.

'Yes,' she said, 'the Land of Eternal Youth.' She laughed, but not bitterly, and the silence enfolded us again, broken only by the steady, reassuring plash-plash of the imperial yacht's paddle-wheels.

For its last dozen or so miles the Canal makes a scimitar-swing eastwards so as to emerge into the Red Sea just south of the roadstead of Suez. In unspoken agreement we moved over to *L'Aigle's* stern where a strange, never-to-be-repeated, sight unfolded; the ships of the monarchs and nations of Europe, threaded on a bright necklace of water. The white No. 2 flag fluttering from her mainmast, the *Greif* had fallen four hundred yards behind us, but we could still see the Austrian imperial eagle flapping at her stern.

Three weeks ago I had watched the Emperor Franz Josef being heft up the Great Pyramid at Giza like a sack of potatoes. I suffer from inappropriate thoughts: it occurred to me now that the bruising he may have incurred then must have been trifling compared to the humiliation inflicted earlier by occupants of the ships fore and after, Bonapartist in front, Prussian behind. But as Mariette said, the French 'Emperor' too would soon get his come-uppance: Bismarck was moving in to take all.

Is that why Empress Eugénie was sobbing down below in her cabin yesterday? She is her own proud self again today, back at her place on the forward deck in yet another new Worth creation of cascading silken flounces.

We are out!

Deafening cannonades from ships in the roadstead as we slide past the Quai Waghorn at the Canal's mouth. I point out to Jeannie the bust of 'Steam Intercourse' Tom, still shrouded in canvas at the end of the quay. The Empress is going to unveil him this evening, for, as Ferdinand puts it, 'He opened the route, we followed.'

L'Aigle takes up her allotted position in the roadstead and the anchor rattles down. As the bands on the ships in the harbour blare out the new French national anthem, '*Partant pour la Syrie*', I observe the dumpy figure of Ismail, putting out from the Suez shore in the state barge, manned by thirty-six oarsmen. Ever devout, the Empress has announced her intention of riding out to the Wells of Moses, eight miles down the Red Sea's Asian shore (where the water was called forth from the rock by the rod of Moses – or was it Aaron?).

As the curtain of gun-smoke lifts, the fearsome peaks of Jebel Ataka glare down upon us, raw pink in the early afternoon sun, and are answered on the Asian shore by the long yellow flank of Jebel el-Raha. Again, another world.

Announcing urgent business on shore, Jeannie had herself rowed the couple of miles through shallow water to the now booming little town of Suez. I suddenly felt old and tired. I went below and collapsed on a bunk in an empty cabin. I was still desperately worried about Sami. To have come through the Crimean war, surviving even the holocaust of Sinope harbour, and then to come to grief hitting a sand wall in a straight-as-a-die canal – under the eyes of half the world!

Long after everybody else had gone ashore, I lay in that hot cabin, going over and over things in my mind, examining my conscience in a manner which, I grant you, owed more to John Knox than to the Prophet, until at last I fell into an exhausted sleep. My dreams were not of Paradise, of the 'gardens beneath which rivers flow', but of the flames of Hell. Into my mind came those terrible verses of Sura 9, called 'The Repentance', warning of the fate of those who 'hoard up gold and silver and spend it not in the way of Allah'. That was a good description of the Khedive's 'New Egypt'. Already, as the loans multiplied, I could smell foreclosure on the air, cloying as the miasma around one of Ismail's proliferating sugar factories.

I woke up soaked in sweat and, after a few minutes to get a grip on myself, made my way up on deck. The sun, slipping down behind Mount Ataka, made its peaks glow molten purple and stained the sea. By this time the roadstead was crowded with the ships of many nations, and others from the grand procession were still emerging from the canal.

I hailed a passing boat, and was rowed ashore. I found Admiral Milne already at the telegraph station, reporting to his masters in Whitehall. The telegraph operator, who knows me well, showed me a copy of the message:

Empress, *Psyche, Newport* arrived. Canal great success . . .
The arrival of thirty-five ships in the Red Sea from Port Said
has established the passage of the Canal, a work of vast
magnitude, conceived and carried out by the energy and
perseverance of Monsieur de Lesseps.

Well, better late than never.

I was hoping to watch the Empress unveiling Tom. But she was so late getting back from her trip to make the acquaintance of Moses that the ceremony had to be cancelled.* Poor Waghorn was out of luck again.

I made my way down to Theo's headquarters at the Hotel Suez. He was still away at Ismailiya, superintending the clearing-up after the feeding of the five thousand, so I wandered into the restaurant. Immediately my eye was caught by something which sent my mind racing back to that first morning in Port Said, all of five days ago. An outsize white solar topee hanging from the hatstand – and, seated below it, the *kukucki* who had taken me for a Thomas Cook's courier and asked to be directed to the *danse du ventre*.

---

* M. Ferdinand de Lesseps himself unveiled the bust a day or two later. He said: 'In his own country, Thomas Waghorn passed for a man with a craze . . . but when English seamen pass this memorial, erected by the French, they will remember the close alliance which ought to exist between the two nations at the head of the world's civilisation, not to ravage, but to enlighten and pacify.' – F.M.

Facing him across a paper tablecloth covered with scribbled calculations was Jeannie Macdonald, who took the situation in her stride.

'Osman Effendi,' she said, 'this gentleman is Alderman Isaac Birtwistle, proprietor of the Trafalgar Mills of Oldham in the county of Lancashire.'

'I do believe the Alderman and I have already met,' I said. Whether he blushed or not was impossible to say for, despite the pith helmet, his face had been baked brick-red by the sun. Certainly he looked a little sheepish.

I pressed my advantage. 'I am surprised to find you in Suez, Alderman. Did you not inform me that the Canal was blocked, that the ships could never get through, that Monsieur de Lesseps was' – I was going to say 'off his head', but he cut in hurriedly:

'Wild rumours, Mr Osman. What I've found, Mr Osman, is that the Arab mind cannot understand the difference between fact and fiction . . .'

'Wallah, ya Bey! It is the truth Your Excellency utters.' I salaamed deeply, catching Jeannie's eye as I did so. She was not discountenanced.

'Osman Effendi,' she told the mill-owner, 'is my most trusted dragoman. When you return to Alexandria, rest assured he will take care of your accommodation and other needs.'

She turned to me. 'Alderman Birtwistle wishes to inspect a consignment of "Best Maho" from our gins.'

The Alderman got ponderously to his feet, more elephant than camel. 'Aye, that's it. If your ginned long-staple's all you say it is, mebbe we can do business. Now you must excuse me . . . His Highness has invited me to the fireworks . . .' He lifted his white sun helmet from the hat-stand and set it on his half-bald head with great deliberation.

I wondered what he would have said if he had known our real relationship. I was just about to put this point to Jeannie when, as ever, she got in first:

'Donald, my dear, I'm so glad for you. Isn't it wonderful? Having Sami back – and no charges against him.'

I looked blank.

'Oh, Donald, you mean you don't *know*? Nobody's told you?'

'You mean the *Latif* is *here* in Suez?'

She seized my hand. 'Come and see for yourself.'

We went out from the Hotel Suez, past the mosque, and on to the spot on the waterfront where I'd stood a long time, watching the retreating figure of Tom Waghorn, and then, arm in arm still, we walked to the end of the long stone pier which runs two miles out from the town. She pointed out the familiar outline of the *Latif* at anchor in the roadstead, her rigging picked out in lights like the rest.

Just then the fireworks started up behind us, and, in the light of a slowly falling flare, I saw, clear as day, my son Sami, Lieutenant-Commander Sami bin Osman, pacing the deck, resplendent in his Khedival Navy uniform.

'Sami!' I yelled. 'Sami!' Of course he could not hear me.

'Mo chridhe,' she said, 'I am glad for you. Sami had to return to his ship, but you will talk tomorrow. You will hear the whole story.'

Very early next morning, *L'Aigle* weighed anchor and began to steam back northwards along the canal. The Empress was eager to get back to France. 'Le vin est tiré,' she had been heard to say; 'il faut le boire.'

A brave woman. She has Highland blood in her veins. She understands about history. *Mektub*. It is written. The wine has been opened: we must drink it.

Postscript by the Editor,
Flora Macdonald (Mrs G. J. Girgis)

My father – I cannot write my 'late father' because even now he still stands before me – died on 24 December 1871, while attending the first performance of Maestro Verdi's great new work, *Aida*. The doctor said he died of a 'Visitation of God', which I think Donald would rather have liked, but it seemed to me that what he died of was grief: he had not been the same man since Mother died six months earlier in the furnace heat of the cotton-fields, inspecting the new crop. His grief was as many-sided as his life – and yet it somehow all turned around her: the anguish of the long separation which seemed to him a betrayal; the bitter-sweetness of their reunion, only to find themselves separated again by the towering wall of religion and the sudden death of the son who would have carried on the name of Macleod. In me he found the best substitute, a 'Highland daughter', only to have her snatched from him by Mother's marrying me to a Copt; and, most shattering of all, Omar's immolation in that great gin fire while, as he saw it, Egyptians worshipped the Golden Calf.

For him there was an awful inevitability about it all; as the old Cairo crumbled, Allah was being challenged by new gods. He would often quote the Hadith in which the Prophet says: 'Cursed be the taker of Usury, the writer of Usury and the witness of Usury, for they are all equal.' That, he told me, would embrace a large part of the Notables of the Khedive's Paris-on-the-Nile, as the foreign money-lenders swarmed like hornets, pressing yet more new loans on the Khedive to enable him to pay off the loans he already had – at an enhanced rate of interest, naturally. Life had taught my father that Greed is the supreme Evil. As a boy he had seen it drive the Highlanders from their clan lands; in the

New World it had robbed the Indians of their farms and rights; and in Egypt it was battening on the fellahin. It had destroyed his first-born, Omar. My mother would tell him that he did not understand business: he was just an old 'Mohammedan stick-in-the mud'. That was another grief.

In the two years that have passed since the Grand Opening of the Canal and the collapse of the great cotton boom, many of the misgivings expressed in my father's latter-day writings have turned out to be all too well founded. Within less than a year of the imperial yacht's heading for home, the Empress Eugénie was a refugee in England, and the Emperor was Bismarck's prisoner.

Donald's great work was over. But he had given a solemn promise to my daughter, Leila, to attend the première of *Aida* to see her appear as one of Princess Amneris's fan-holders and Moorish slaves. On account of the Prussian siege, M. Auguste Mariette – in Paris to supervise the production of the costumes for *Aida* – found himself only able to communicate with Signor Verdi by balloon mail. It wasn't until September 1871 that we in Egypt at last set eyes on the complete libretto, settings, costumes and music.

The dress rehearsal on 23 December went on until three in the morning. Having been again pressed into service as wardrobe mistress, I can testify to the many problems of staging the Pharaohs; so many styles of headcloth, so many long wigs to be curled and combed, the Pharaoh's great gold crown to be kept burnished, so that its gleams penetrated to the back of the stalls. My father's great friend, Monsieur Mariette, had insisted on accuracy in every detail which sometimes led to difficulties. The Ancient Egyptians were close-shaven; the Italian male singers did not take kindly to shaving off their moustaches and beards, I can tell you!

As editor of Osman Effendi's life story, it is my sad duty to give a brief account of the circumstances of this remarkable man's death, which occurred in public and in the presence of many people, yet was observed by few.

That night the pretty little opera house was packed from floor to ceiling. Seats were commanding fabulous prices. 'Everybody' was there, except, as Donald remarked, 'the real people of Egypt on whose backs we all lived'. His, I believe, was the only turban in the house. With reluctance he had agreed to wear a frock-coat, since the Khedive was to be present, but he drew the line at the tarbush, 'that red plant-pot', as he called it. The real reason for the turban, I suspect, was to cover his still flaxen hair and the thin blue scar from el-Hamed high up on his brow, which were apt to provoke impertinent demands for his 'story'.

A year or more before the much-delayed première, when my mother was still alive, Monsieur Mariette had arranged that the middle of the third row of the *fauteuils* should be reserved for his old friend and collaborator Osman Effendi and his 'clan'. I sat on my father's right, where Mother would have been, while the seat on his other side was occupied by his youngest son, Aziz, who was just about to enter the medical college at Abu Zabel. Om Aziz – the Egyptian Nightingale – was away, giving one of her passionate recitals. But to Donald's great satisfaction his eldest son, Lieutenant-Commander Sami bin Osman of the Khedival Navy, was present, his gold braid outshining the consular corps; unlike them, he had been unable to bring his 'lady'. Nawal shrank from thus 'flaunting' herself. This was no problem for Elena, who now considered herself of the *ton* of Alexandria. Flanked by her sons, the famous hotelier, Theo, and the new Deputy Director of Antiquities, Ibrahim, she had taken up her position further along 'our' row. Donald had brought both boys up to know their Koran, but whether they ever went to the mosque now, even on Fridays, I do not know.

The curtain rose on the mighty colonnades of Karnak. Little squeals of delight came from behind the golden grilles of the harem's boxes. I doubt whether Donald heard them, so totally was he absorbed in the scene unfolding on stage.

It wasn't until Signor Pietro Mongini, in the role of Radamès, the Egyptian commander, was well into his great aria, '*Celeste Aida, forma divina*', that it began to dawn on me how closely Verdi's great new opera mirrored my father's own life and that it might bring painful memories. Although I never met her, of course, I knew that his first wife – that is, Omar's mother, Fatima – had been, like Aida, an Ethiopian, dragged from her native land and sold into slavery in Egypt – like Donald himself. I knew too, that, like Aida, she was beautiful and faithful unto death. Donald never forgave Alexander Kinglake for the aspersions cast upon her in *Eothen*. When the Pharaoh's daughter, Princess Amneris, vowed vengeance on Aida,* singing, 'Oh slave, beware my anger,' I began to worry that at my father's age such excitements might be unwise.

However, Act II brought what we all had been waiting for – Leila's début in the 'Dance of the little Moorish slaves'. Donald started to applaud the moment he spotted her in her filmy white dress, and Signor Bottesini turned round on his rostrum and glared. All the same the dance, performed while Princess Amneris was dressed for the victory parade, was a great success, and despite my husband's objections to Leila's appearing, the row of Girgis aunts at the front of the dress circle unbent and applauded.

Donald gripped my hand tightly, but before we could speak, we were swept up with the whole house in the victory march, helmets blazing, soaring trumpets – each exactly one metre forty-eight centimetres long, as on the tomb walls. For eight minutes the stage shook to the tread of the triumphant Egyptian army, then a sudden change of tempo as the bedraggled Ethiopian prisoners were driven across the stage, roped yet defiant.

'*A morte! A morte! a morte!*' intoned the High Priest, Ramfis. 'They invaded our land. O Pharaoh, they must die!'

I stole an anxious glance at my father, for the scene before us seemed all too reminiscent of the humiliations he and his wounded comrades had undergone when they arrived on these shores. I saw that he had fallen into a reverie, from which he did not emerge until the curtain rose on Act III, moonlight playing on the Nile; a temple rising from the granite; the holy island of Philae which, I recalled, he had taken me to see as a small girl. Whispering urgently in my ear, he was eager to point out the very obelisk which he and his friend Mr Belzoni had recovered and sent down the Cataract on its way to Mr Bankes's park at Kingston Hall in Dorset.

The people in front of us were shushing indignantly as the opera moved on to the deeply moving moment when Aida embarks on her poignant aria '*O patria mia*':

Oh, how I yearn to see my homeland
O verdant meadows, autumn flowers

---

* The Ethiopian name is in fact *Aita*, but Signor Verdi insisted that Italian singers would not be able to get their tongues around this.

> O *patria mia*, shall I ever set eyes on you again?
> O *verdi colli*, O *profumate rive*

My father's eyes were closed. Was he once again high in that mountain meadow in Scotland where the two of them, my father and my mother – boy and girl then – had been handfasted in the dawn? Both of them have, at different times, sketched that scene for me. I am resolved that Leila and I will go there one day. A pilgrimage, you might say.

Act IV began. In the final scene, the sibilant chanting of the priestesses of Isis as the renegade Radamès was condemned to entombment was hypnotic, and as I watched the tragic conclusion of the opera I had the impression that the old man beside me, having seen what he had come to see, had drifted off into sleep.

It was only when the curtain came down on a hurricane of applause, shouted bravos and huzzahs, and Donald still did not stir, that a wave of panic gripped me. I saw that his head had fallen forward onto his chest; on his other side, Aziz, ashen-faced, was standing over him, a finger on his wrist, his eyes full of tears.

The performers were now taking their curtain calls. All around people were on their feet, applauding wildly.

'Allah,' said Aziz softly. 'To God we belong, and to God we must return.'

I recall a wild cry from the back of the house, 'Long live the Khedive!' and the tubby little man in all his magnificence stepped to the front of his box as the audience surged forward to acclaim him. In that moment Sami was able to get through to us, accompanied, I was relieved to see, by the ever-watchful Draneht, the Director, determined that his master's moment of triumph should not be diminished.

While the audience cheered itself hoarse, a closed carriage was brought to the side door. My father was a big man, but the soldiers of the Pharaoh's stage army were even bigger and several were summoned to carry Osman Effendi discreetly out. Sami and Aziz, the eldest and the youngest of Donald's sons, went with him in the carriage Draneht had summoned.

It had been my mother's hope that Donald would one day return to the faith of his fathers, and had she lived she would have wished him to receive Christian burial. There were many *renegados* in

Egypt who had 'taken the turban', professed the Moslem faith, simply for reasons of commercial convenience. But Donald Macleod was certainly not one of them. Though his earlier conversion may have been forced, he had long, I knew, been a True Believer. His pilgrimage to Mecca with Mr Burckhardt had been a revelation to him, and that strong, simple faith remained an ever-present support through the vicissitudes of his long life. It was his ardent desire – never to be fulfilled – to convince my mother that Tom Paine's vision of the Equality of Man, which she had expounded to him in Scotland, was realised in Islam – as indeed it had once been in the Highland clans where their roots lay.

In the event, the people of the Suk el-Zalat claimed their brother Osman; that he had once attended kirk in the island of Skye was of no consequence to them whatsoever.

I was glad that Donald's eldest son, Sami, was there to do what had to be done, to summon the washer of the dead, to purchase the grave-cloths of muslin, cotton and silk, to engage the *yemeniya*, the blind men to walk behind the corpse, two by two, lugubriously intoning the profession of faith.

Every few paces, as the funeral procession made its way towards the great Moslem burial ground in the desert beyond the Bab el-Nasr, it would halt to enable old friends and neighbours to take their turn in carrying Osman's bier. I was proud my father was loved by so many – and thankful that the distance to the grave was not great.

It was Aziz who found the Last Will and Testament in the bottom right-hand drawer of Burckhardt's old ink-stained desk. The Will had clearly been made when Mother was still alive, for it bequeathed to her 'the small leather-bound volume of the poems of Alexander Macdonald', which was placed over the Will so that there could be no misunderstandings. For some time, I turned over the small book's yellowing pages, reading the passages underlined in pencil, poignant messages of love. The poet, I believe, was known as 'the Jacobite Nightingale', and the volume was left behind by my mother when her family emigrated to North Carolina, in the hope that it would fall into Donald's hands. I felt that both of them would wish me to keep the book, to be passed on to Leila in due time.

As for the rest of the Will, I was not surprised to find that of Osman's four houses in the old Turkish quarter he had bequeathed one to each surviving wife, to Elena, to Om Aziz, and to his Bedou wife, Nura. It seemed unlikely that any of these ladies would do anything with these bequests except sell them. But at least Donald had had the satisfaction of having obeyed the Koranic instruction that all wives should be treated equally. The fourth house, the original house left by Mr Burckhardt to Osman, went to Aziz.

The rest of his wordly goods, including his shares in the Compagnie Universelle du Canal Maritime de Suez, went to his 'Scottish daughter, Flora Macdonald', with a reminder – a dig at my husband George from beyond the grave – that under Islamic law a woman's property remained her own absolutely, even after marriage.

There was a more recent codicil bequeathing to his 'beloved granddaughter Leila Girgis', his 'Edinburgh Cabinet Library', as mentioned in the book by Kinglake, in the hope that with its aid she could one day enter into her 'true heritage'.

Fortunately, the Edinburgh Library was still in place, where it had always been, although its shelves were now supplemented by two of later date, filled with volumes often inscribed to Osman Effendi by their authors: Thomas Legh's *Narrative of a Journey in Egypt*, Dr Robert Richardson's *Travels along the Mediterranean and Parts Adjacent in the Company of the Earl of Belmore*, Dr William Yates's *The Modern History and Condition of Egypt*, to name only a few. I noticed they generally fell open at the pages on which my father's accomplishments were mentioned. Search as I might, though, I could not find a copy of *Eothen*, although it was Mr Alexander Kinglake who first made my father famous.

Aziz had told me that during the months that followed the opening of the Suez Canal, Donald had spent much time up in Burckhardt's old study, writing away, even late at night. When Aziz had inquired what was so urgent, he had just laughed and said: 'Time to set the record straight, boy.' I remembered then what my mother had told me, that on that first perilous transit of the Canal they had made together, following the grand procession of the ships of the crowned heads of Europe, my father had been constantly scribbling notes for his 'Log' as he called it.

Where was all this material?

It was Aziz who found it at last, a great pile of close-written sheets, and several notebooks with pencilled jottings, headed by places along the Canal and dates.

I read it, entranced. Here was a personal record over many years of events, small and great, in which the writer had been not only an eye-witness but often a participant. Clearly, it would be of great value to historians. It must be given to the world. But by whom? To let it pass into the hands of a stranger seemed a sort of desecration. But how to organise, how to arrange, such a diverse mass of paper, so wide-ranging a record of an extra-ordinary life?

It was a daunting task, and I passed many weeks pondering my plan. More than most, Donald Macleod's story was a bracing counterpoint of Past and Present, so I finally decided to begin using one of the 'logs', with the Grand Opening of the Canal Between Seas, which might be considered the high point of my father's life, his crowning achievement. From then his 'log' of the four-day transit, many perils confronted and averted, could punctuate his autobiography, culminating in the triumphant emergence of the ships into the Red Sea.

I trust readers will approve of my plan. In addition, I have added to the work a dedication that, as his daughter, I am sure Donald would have wished, had he lived long enough to publish his book himself.

The Facts of the Matter:
The Quest for Osman the Scotsman

Four houses of Osman Effendi in the Soog e' Zallut are also let
furnished, and one floor, or set of floors may be had at from
five to eight piastres a day, or by the month about 150
piastres ... the *hosh*, or entrance court below being common
to all who live in the house –

> – Murray's *Handbook to Egypt* (1847)

Alexander Kinglake, later historian of the Crimean War, but in
1834 an aspiring writer of twenty-five, lodged with 'Osman'
in Cairo during the terrible plague of that year and tells us that
he 'inspected' his harem 'after his wives had been bundled out'.
Subtitled *Traces of Travel Brought Home from the East*, *Eothen*
came out in 1844 after ten years' 'polishing'. Kinglake tells of the
ex-drummer-boy's being sold into slavery in Egypt following
the British military disaster at Rosetta in 1807, and of his conversion to Islam: 'Death or the Koran – he did not choose death'.
He notes, 'despite the Arab robes', Osman's 'inextinguishable
Scottishness, evinced in his pride and joy', his 'Edinburgh Cabinet
Library'.

But if Kinglake might claim to have made Donald Macleod
briefly famous, the enslaved Scot had been 'discovered' more
than twenty years earlier by Thomas Legh, scion of Lyme Park,
Cheshire, a twenty-year-old Member of Parliament making the
Grand Tour. In his *Narrative of a Journey in Egypt* (1816) we read
of young Legh's astonishment at encountering the lost Highland
soldier, splendidly turbaned, serving in the camp of a Mameluke
bey at Minya, 153 miles up the Nile from Cairo, and now 'in
every respect a complete Mussalman'. Thomas Legh was keen to

ransom 'Donald Donald' and carry him home in triumph. But Donald was by no means so keen to *be* ransomed, and after considering a few ransom bids 'the Bey married him off to a woman of his harem'. In any case, 'Osman had never shown much anxiety about obtaining his liberty'. A larger-than-life oil-painting of Thomas Legh, done on his return to England in 1813, stands over the main staircase in Lyme Park today, and on the library mantelpiece there are small *ushabti* figures brought back from Egypt.

Not very long after that, we have another 'sighting' of Osman, recorded in the *Autobiography* of the traveller-journalist-merchant James Silk Buckingham:

> Although his dress, air, and manner were completely those of the Turk, he preserved all his northern peculiarities, a light complexion, sandy hair and mustaches, freckled face, light blue eyes, and yellowish hair and eyebrows.

Buckingham, who had plenty of time to observe Osman, contributes one further important item of information: though his conversion had been forced, Donald Macleod had become a sincere practising Moslem. In November 1814, Osman attended a bizarre dinner-party which Buckingham had arranged on a British ship lying in Jeddah harbour. Present were Buckingham himself, the ship's master, Captain Bloag, 'Sheikh Ibrahim', otherwise known as Jean-Louis Burckhardt, the Swiss-born explorer, then planning a trip to Mecca, and Osman himself. The party of exiles went well and there was a 'a feast of reason and a flow of soul', but though wine was served 'Othman', abiding by the precepts of the Koran, refused to take a drop until rallied by his co-religionist, who drank a glass without a qualm. After much pressing, Othman too drank a glass, and was later sick, which he seriously attributed to 'divine wrath'.

In his own works Burckhardt mentions Osman only once, but Burckhardt's biographer, Katherine Sim, believes that the Scots lad was the 'companion' he took with him on his pilgrimage to Mecca around this time, when the war against the Wahabi 'rebels' was still raging. As a devout Moslem and still, theoretically at least, a slave, Osman would certainly have been an excellent choice for this perilous trip to Mecca many years before Burton.

The two volumes of J. J. Hall's *Life and Correspondence of Henry Salt* (London, 1834), fill in Osman's later background. Salt was British Consul in Egypt from 1816, hieroglyph scholar, employer of both Osman and Belzoni, and himself an energetic collector – and salesman – of Pharaonic antiquities. His letters shed some light on the curious old house which Burckhardt and Osman shared in the Turkish quarter. It was Salt who obtained from Mohammed Ali the certificate of emancipation which opened up a new life for Osman. And at Burckhardt's deathbed, Henry Salt took down to his dictation his Will leaving his house, two young house-slaves, and the residue of his cash 'to my friend, Osman'.

Later travellers up and down the Nile pay tribute to Osman Effendi's dedication to his role of man-about-Cairo and dragoman to milords. In *Egypt and Mohammed Ali* (1834), James Augustus St John tells us how Osman translated for him the songs of an *alma*, 'comparing them to the ballads of his native Scottish Highlands'. Osman took St John, as he did many others, to Burckhardt's grave in the Moslem cemetery outside Cairo's walls; he had taken it upon himself to keep it clean and tidy.

Then Dr Robert Richardson, author of the two-volume *Travels along the Mediterranean and Parts Adjacent in Company of Earl of Belmore* (1820), relates how he and 'my friend Osman' would often sit down on the edge of a bazaar and refresh themselves by buying 'bread and caraway seeds and water'; and even that great Orientalist Edward Lane, in his classic *The Manners and Customs of the Modern Egyptians* (1835), is to be found enlisting 'my neighbour Osman's' help in locating a certain magician.

But perhaps the most handsome testimonial to Osman Effendi is to be found in the unpublished journal of Henry Westcar, a Surrey squire whom Osman kitted out in the usual Turkish costume to brave the Cairo streets:

This man is a friend to all Englishmen . . . with him there is no fear of injury. As he goes along all salute him by the name of Hadji Osman, and, if they are disputing, they will always submit to his advice. He is, with all this, a gentleman in manners and behaviour, especially to officers coming to and from India and travellers . . .

But if Osman sometimes fairly leaps out of the page, the sharp focus quickly fades. Typically, the only portrait we have of Osman Effendi is a faint pencil sketch by Joseph Bonomi, like Osman an employee of the wealthy Pharaonic enthusiast Robert Hay. It shows the back of a turbaned figure, riding off between two other horsemen, scimitar swinging from his saddle.

Even those writers who got to know Osman quite well do not seem able to agree on such simple matters as his place of birth and first name. Thomas Legh, for instance, calls him Donald Donald and says he comes from Inverness. Another traveller says he hails from the isle of Lewis; yet another from Perth; Squire Westcar asserts that his 'real name' was Thomson and that he 'came out with the medical department on that fateful expedition'. Perhaps Osman did not always tell the same story – and military records do not help much, since in Highland regiments hundreds bear the identical name.

For my own part, I have preferred the witness of the Scot who, in the old clan tradition, personally recruited the tall fifteen-year-old Highland boy into the Ross-shire Buffs, then a new battalion of the Seaforth Highlanders being raised against Bonaparte. In his *Sketches of the Highland Regiments*, Captain – later General – David Stewart of Garth runs to a footnote to tell us that the enslaved drummer 'in the name of Macleod . . . being a smart lad, made himself useful to the [battalion] surgeon and [later] with this knowledge began to prescribe for his Master's family, thence extending his practice'. Taking a lead from that, I located him in the island of Skye, and, since blood will out, I have made his mother a member of the Beaton clan, which provided the hereditary physicians to Macleod of Macleod, Macdonald of Sleat, and other clan chiefs.

Clearly there is much that we shall now never know about Osman the Scotsman, and his hardly less remarkable mate in the Ross-shire Buffs, Thomas Keith, runaway gunsmith's apprentice of Leith, who shared the ordeal of Rosetta and the humiliations of Cairo, and, later the *renegado*'s lot, and, as Ibrahim Aga, became commander of Prince Tousson's cavalry in Mohammed Ali's long war against the Wahabi 'rebels' in Arabia. For a short time, the Scot was Deputy Governor of Medina, the second holiest city of Islam, until killed in an ambush in 1815.

Because of the unbridgeable gaps in their extraordinary stories, it is no longer possible to give either of these remarkable Scotsmen the 'definitive' biographies, buttressed by scholarly footnotes, they deserve. Should Osman Effendi, 'Osman the Scotsman', therefore be allowed to sink into oblivion? Perish the thought!

Though fragmentary, the testimony of witnesses and research both on the ground and into the surrounding circumstances make it possible to resurrect him and put flesh on the bones; as for the gaps, has it not been said that 'fiction is History's Fourth dimension?' In fact History – with the capital H – played a very large part in shaping the strange and dramatic career both of Drummer-boy Donald Macleod and of Osman Effendi. Donald was born in the bitter aftermath of the Highland Clearances which, willy-nilly, led to the Highlands falling into the grip of 'Emigration Fever'.

The great Highland Diaspora had a critical part in the shaping of Donald Macleod. He was a boy of seven when Britain's war against Bonaparte began. It was not to end until eighteen years later. Abercromby's expulsion of Bonaparte's army from Egypt in 1801 led to the anarchy in which Drummer Macleod and his comrades of the Ross-shire Buffs were sold into slavery and in which the Albanian adventurer Mohammed Ali seized Cairo's Citadel and founded the bizarre dynasty whose unpredictable whims and eccentricities plagued the life both of Osman the slave and of Osman Effendi, man about Cairo. He had to endure, too, the continuing hostilities of the English and French, whether among the tombs of the Pharaohs or over the construction of the Suez Canal. He lived through Egypt's headlong progression from the antique, barbaric splendours of the Mamelukes to the dizzy aspirations of the 'Khedive' Ismail's 'Paris-on-the-Nile'.

In the end I decided to let Osman the Scotsman tell his own story, 'ghosted', if you like, by myself. To qualify for this impudent role I spent much time in researching the often recondite circumstances of Donald/Osman's highly varied life, from the bloody clan feuding of his boyhood in the starving Highlands to his enlistment in the Ross-shire Buffs, from the Highland Diaspora to the 'Promised Land' of Gaelic-speaking North Carolina, to the bizarre costume and sexual proclivities of the Mamelukes; from the life of the harem and its guardian eunuchs to the titanic figure of Mohammed Ali, who held the slave Osman's life in his hands, and the dangerous eccentricities of his successors. Since Osman Effendi became a sincere practising Moslem, it was likewise necessary to make as thorough a study as I could of the tenets and way of life of Islam, which, though so closely linked with Christianity has been systematically maligned in the West ever since the Crusades.

I travelled the drove roads of Scotland from the island of Skye down to the 'Falkirk Tryst' in the hope of getting something of the feel of Donald's life as a drover of the 'black cattle' on which the Highlands depended. I followed the new recruits of his 'battalion of boys' from their barracks at Fort George on the Moray Firth to Shornecliffe camp above Folkestone, where they confronted Bonaparte's 'Army of England', and to Rosetta at the mouth of the Nile (where in a small museum a Redcoat is shown being bayoneted by a Turk to celebrate the Mackenzie Fraser expedition of 1807).

Though the British army does not trumpet its disasters, the shambles of Rosetta and el-Hamed were reported in detail in some newspapers, and in regimental and personal accounts. Military histories (like Fortescue's) authenticate the catalogue of horrors, the head-impalings, the parading of the prisoners, the long imprisonment, the selling into slavery, the long-drawn negotiations, the random ransoming.

Egypt during these years was a magnet that drew many remarkable characters, who inevitably crossed Osman Effendi's path.

All such 'real life' characters are historically authentic in detail and chronology. Quite often they simplified research by their own writings. Belzoni, for instance, wrote graphically about his own encounters with entombed Pharaohs; Tom Waghorn produced revealing pamphlets such as *Egypt as It is in 1834*; Edwin de Leon, the American consul, was also a memorialist – his *Thirty Years of My Life* has an 'I was there' account of the sensational murder of Abbas. More substantially, Burckhardt, the friend and liberator of the enslaved Donald Macleod, wrote a number of books about his explorations and pilgrimage to Mecca. The letters of Henry Salt, the British Consul and of Sam Shepheard the hotelier have been collected and published and de Lesseps published his extensive Journal. Admiral Charles Napier's *Life and Correspondence* was published in 1862.

We know that the services Osman Effendi performed for his distinguished clients were many and varied. Thanks to the researches of the Revd Selwyn Tillett (*Egypt Itself*, 1984) in the

Hay Archive in the British Library, we know that Osman obtained for that enthusiastic Egyptologist, Robert Hay, a new silk tassel for his tarbush and a young Greek girl – a prisoner of war – purchased in the Alexandria slave-market. The tassel was rejected as of inferior quality ('not fit for a corporal') but there were no complaints about the girl.

Readers who wish to trace the circuitous frontier between 'History' and 'Fiction' may like to know that the following characters are 'historical' and authentic in chronology and detail:

IN SCOTLAND:
Macleod of Macleod
Macdonald of Sleat
Macdonald of Keppoch
as named and the named members of their clans

Major Stewart of Garth
Colonel Patrick Macleod of Genies
Mr Munro, surgeon, and named officers and soldiers of the Ross-shire Buffs (2nd battalion Seaforth Highlanders)

John Cameron of Corriehoille

IN AMERICA
John Ross, Cherokee Chief
John Macdonald, Indian trader
William McIntosh, Creek Chief
General Andrew Jackson

IN EGYPT AND ARABIA

'Renegados'

Sheikh Ibrahim el-Shami (J.-L. Burckhardt)
Suleiman Pasha (Colonel Sèves)
Mohammed (Giovanni Finati)
Ibrahim Aga (Thomas Keith)
Osman Effendi (Donald Macleod)

Egyptologists/Collectors

Giovanni Battista Belzoni
Henry Salt

Bernardino Drovetti
John William Bankes
Robert Hay
Auguste Mariette

Ruling House and Followers

Mohammed Ali, Abbas, Mohammed Said,
Ismail, Ibrahim Pasha
Amine Hanem, Mohammed Ali's first wife
Ahmed Aga Bonaparte
Nubar Pasha

Travellers
Thomas Legh
Earl of Belmore and party
Dr Richardson
A.W. Kinglake

Consular etc.

Major Edward Missett
Henry Salt
Colonel Patrick Campbell
Colonel Murray
Edwin de Leon
Admiral Charles Napier
Lieut.-Col. George Fitzclarence

Entrepreneurs, engineers, doctors, artists

Dr Henry Abbott ('Old Abbott')
Arthur Anderson, P & O director
Samuel Briggs, merchant banker
Dr Antoine Clôt (Clôt Bey)
Joseph Bonomi, artist
Linant de Bellefonds
Draneht Bey
Galloway Bey
Alexis Jumel
Ferdinand de Lesseps
John Hill, hotelier
Samuel Shepheard, hotelier

David Roberts, artist
Robert Stephenson
Thomas Waghorn
David Wilkie, artist

Although no one could be more 'real' than Donald Macleod and his *alter ego*, Osman Effendi, the large gaps in his documentation have to be filled by 'fiction' or, shall we say, guess-work. Thus, we know that Donald became at one stage a Mameluke, but we do not know that he escaped from the infamous mass slaughter of that Order in the Citadel. Whether he was there or not, this gory event was a turning point in Egypt's history, and is itself amply documented.

Donald's families, both in Scotland and in Egypt, and his hand-fasted 'bride' Jeannie Macdonald, whose desertion to North Carolina drove him in desperation to take the King's shilling (as we know he did), are likewise authorial creations, although shaped by the contemporary historical circumstances.

All the detail and dramas both of the Grand Opening of the Suez Canal and its first transit which frame Donald's memoirs are historically authentic, as is the account of the struggle to get the Canal built in the face of the bitter hostility of England. Equally, the trials and tribulations of producing the first grand opera of Ancient Egypt to celebrate the Canal's opening are fully documented by Hans Busch in the *Aida Correspondence* (1978).

Finally, according to A.W. Kinglake in *Eothen*, 'poor Osman' died a few weeks after he lodged with him in Cairo during the great plague of 1834–5. However, the Macleods were a long-lived lot. According to the *Caledonian Mercury*, Osman's admired namesake walked from Inverness to London and back at the age of 103. So, despite two lines in *The Times*, I have decided that his death was – as Mark Twain put it – 'exaggerated'. It would have been a pity to deny him the opportunity to witness the triumph of his friend Tom Waghorn's much-derided vision of 'Steam Intercourse' in the completion and successful transit of the 'Canal Between Seas'. And after all, in his book on Egypt published in 1842, Dr William Yates is still writing about 'my friend Osman Effendi' as if he had just left him.

– *Harry Hopkins*

Glossary of Arabic & Ottoman Turkish Words

† = the words is/are Ottoman Turkish, not Arabic

Abba papa
Abu Zeidi story-teller; pl. =
  Abu Zeidiya
alma learned woman
antika antique
arusa bride
askari Ottoman soldier

bab sirr secret door of the
  harem
el-Bahr 'the Sea' = the Nile
Bairam el-Fitr Islamic festival
baklava sweetmeat
bakshish tip, gift of money
baladi cheap cotton
banduke charm, adornment
† *bashi* principal, chief
bawwab servant, door-keeper
† *bazouk* wild
bersim clover
burko long veil
bukra tomorrow

cangia type of boat
cantar noun: measure
† *chibouk* long-stemmed pipe
† *courbash* hide whip

dahabiya Nile boat with sails
dallals sellers at auctions
darabukka musical instrument
destour permission
dhalul riding-camel
diwan council chamber/court
djerid javelin
† *dragoman* interpreter, guide
  for foreigners
dulab tool for cleaning cotton
durra millet

ekta vb: cut

fantasia elaborate party
fas trowel-like tool
fatwa decree
feddan measure of land
fingan small coffee cup
firman official document
ful mudames broad beans
  cooked in oil
fustan white, pleated skirt
  worn by Albanian soldiers

galabiya long, cotton, dress
gamoose buffalo

gellab slave-trader
ghafir watchman
ghaziya female singer-dancer
giaour derogatory term for a non-Arab/infidel
gubli foreigner, outsider

habara long, woman's silk dress
Hadith the Traditions of the Prophet
hadj pilgrimage to Mecca
hadji man who's made the pilgrimage
hadz waalad khafifa three-year-old camel ridden for first time
hakim doctor
halan at once
halvah sweetmeat
hamdh salting bushes, for camels
hammam public bath
haram forbidden
haramlik women's quarters
hariya baiza white slave
hashash hashish-user
havinder treasurer to a Bey
hawi showman
hegab magic charm
heikal Coptic high altar
hirish male camel over thirty years old

ihram consecration
imam priest
inshallah if Allah wills it

jihad holy war

ka Pharaoh's alter ego
kamish house of idols, i.e. Coptic church
† *kara-gyuz* puppet show
kashif district governor, money collector
† *ken* dog
khadin effendi principal wife
khalig canal
khamsin wind that is not dust-laden
khasnadar treasurer to a Prince
khawah protection money, i.e. Bedou camel herds
khawal effeminate male dancer
khislar aga chief eunuch
koton, el press
kukucki tourist
kuttub Koranic school

Leilet el-Nukta the Night of the Drop
Leilet el-Ruya the Night of the Observation, before Ramadan
liban frankincense
liban shami resin

majlis assembly, council
malish never mind; doesn't matter
Mar Girga St George
marhaba welcome, greeting
masbud strong coffee
mashal torch, flare
mektub it is written
melaya head scarf or shawl
menat 'musical' bead necklace
mesamer Bedou love dance
mukhaeyt 'intact', sewn-up girl

mukhbar incense-burner

nabbut staff, Moroccan-style
naharak said may your day be
    happy
nai musical instrument
nargila oriental water pipe
niyyat part of ritual prayer
    during pilgrimage

okela slave market
omda village headman

rahla load-carrying camel
reis river-boat pilot
rekah one prayer

saadiya small coin
safra fawn-coloured camel
Said someone from Said
    province, upper Egypt; pl =
    Saidi
sakiya water-wheel
santon holy man
sebbah prayer beads
† *selamlik* men's quarters
shabash well done
shackala nigger-slave
shaduf pole with buckets
el-Shakba Coptic engagement-
    ring
sher story-teller
sibil fountain
sitt lady
stambouli European-style
    frock coat
suk market, bazaar

sura section of the Koran

tar tambourine
taun plague; lit. 'yellow wind'
tawaf circumambulation of
    Kaaba
tefaddal I beg you to enter
thaub red cotton that flies from
    Bedou woman's tent, for
    welcome
tumbak Persian tobacco

ud lute-like stringed
    instrument
udjat good luck charms

wadha white camel
wakala stopping place,
    caravanserai
wali official
wasm camel brand

Ya Sin in the Koran, read in
    the presence of the dying
yemeniya blind man,
    traditional follower of the
    corpse
Yom Gebr el-Bahr the Day of
    the Breaking Through of the
    Nile
Yunanni Greek
† *yuzbachi* army captain

zai sahetkum? are you well?
zaruk boat with a high-raking
    prow
zubb penis
zummara double-reed pipe

Glossary of Gaelic Words

NB: caps and rom/itals as in text

Bàn fair-haired
bean-shìdh fairy woman,
  banshee
bi sàmhach! shut up!
Blàr Milleadh Gàrraidh Battle
  of The Spoiled Dyke
Bliadhna nan Caorach Year of
  the Sheep
bodach old man
Bratach Sìdh fairy flag
breacan plaid
brochan porridge

cabar fèidh deer's antlers
cailin lassie
cailleach old woman
a choin! you rascal!
clachan beaga small stones
clèith luaidh waulking board
Còraichean nan Daoine The
  Rights of Man
critheann aspen
A cuid de Phàrras dhi May she
  have her share of paradise
Cuidich an Rìgh Assist the
  King

dearg red
deiseil sun-wise
dubh black-haired

Fear-riaghlaidh Ruler, Man of
  Government
Fèinn Fingalians – Finn
  MacCoal's followers
an fiabhras-critheach shaking
  fever; malaria
fual urine

garron small horse
ghràidh darling

hochmagandy fornication

lìonaraich type of sea-plant
luadh waulking

machair sandy land by the
  shore
magairlean testicles
màlair rent-payer pl =
  màlairean

màl dubh 'black rent' = blackmail
meallan round hills
meanbhchuileagan midges
Mhic an Diabhail Son of the Devil
mnathan-sìth fairy women
mo chridhe my heart
mòthan fairy flax, bog violet

nach ist thu won't you be quiet

obh onomatopoeic-interjection of complaint
Orain Arabhaig flyting song

painntear snare
pìobaireachd pibroch
poit-dhubh black pot, for illicit distilling

ruadh red-haired

saighdear soldier
sgealp slap
sgeulaiche story-teller
sgian-dubh knife carried in stocking
Sìol Tormoid Seed of Tormod
siubhal part of a pipe tune
spracks lively lads
stìom band of material

taibhsear person who has second sight
Tìr nan Òg Land of Eternal Youth

uisge-beatha literally 'water of life' = whisky